DANIELLE STEEL

Full Circle

WARNER BOOKS

A *Warner* Book

First published in Great Britain by Hodder & Stoughton 1984
Reprinted 1984 (three times), 1985 (three times), 1986, 1988 (twice),
1989, 1990, 1991, 1992, 1993
Reprinted by Warner Books 1994
Reprinted 1994, 1995, 1997, 1998, 1999

ISBN 0 7515 0544 7

Printed in England by Clays Ltd, St Ives plc

Warner Books
A Division of
Little, Brown and Company (UK)
Brettenham House
Lancaster Place
London WC2E 7EN

Danielle Steel is a descendant of the Löwenbräu beer barons. Her mother is Portuguese and her father is German. Their common language is French, although they all speak eight languages. Danielle's father's family, the prominent banking and brewing clan, has always lived in Munich and the family seat was a moated castle in Bavaria, Kaltenberg. Her mother's family were diplomats and her maternal grandfather was a Portuguese diplomat assigned to the United States for a number of years.

American-born, Danielle lived in Paris for most of her childhood. At the age of 20 she went to New York and started working for 'Supergirls', a before-its-time public relations firm run by women who organised parties for Wall Street brokerage houses and designed PR campaigns for major firms. When the recession hit, the firm went out of business and Danielle 'retired' to write her first book, *Going Home*.

Danielle has established herself as a writer of extraordinary scope. She has set her various novels all over the world, from China to New York to San Francisco, in time-frames spanning 1860 to the present. She has received critical acclaim for her elaborate plots and meticulous research, and has brought vividly to life a broad range of very different characters.

To Alex Haley,
my brother,
my friend,
with much, much love.

And with special love
and thanks
to Lou Blau.
                    D.S.

Part I

The Early Years

Chapter 1

On the afternoon of Thursday, December 11th, 1941, the country was still in a daze. The casualty list was complete, the names of those killed had already been released, and slowly, slowly, in the past few days, the monster of vengeance was raising its head. In almost every American breast pounded a pulse that had been unknown before. It had finally hit us at home, and it wasn't simply a matter of Congress declaring war. There was much more to it than that, much, much more. There was a nation of people filled with dread, with rage, and the sudden fear that it could happen here. Japanese fighter planes could appear overhead at any time of day or night and suddenly wreak destruction in cities like Chicago and Los Angeles, Omaha . . . Boston . . . New York . . . it was a terrifying thought. The war was no longer happening to a distant, remote "them", it was happening to *us*.

And as Andrew Roberts hurried east in the chill wind, his coat collar up, he wondered what Jean would say. He had already known for two days. When he had signed his name, there hadn't been any doubt in his mind, yet when he'd come home, he had looked into her face and the words had caught in his throat. But there was no choice now. He had to tell her tonight. Had to. He was leaving for San Diego in another three days.

The Third Avenue E1 roared overhead, as his feet pounded on the front steps of the narrow brownstone in which they lived. They had lived there for less than a year, and they hardly even noticed the train anymore. It had been awful at first, at night they had held each other tight and laughed as they lay in bed. Even the light fixtures shook as the elevated train careered by, but they were used to it now. And Andy had come to love the tiny flat. Jean kept it spotlessly clean, getting up sometimes at five o'clock to make him homemade blueberry muffins and leave everything immaculate before she left for work. She had turned out to be even more wonderful than he'd thought . . . and he smiled to himself as he turned the key in the lock. There was a chill wind whistling through the hall and two of the lights were burned out, but the moment he set foot inside, everything was cheery and bright. There were starched white organdy curtains, which Jean had made, a pretty little blue rug, slipcovers she had gone to a night class to learn how to make. And the furniture they'd bought secondhand shone like new beneath her hardworking hands. He looked around now, and suddenly felt the first shaft of grief he had felt since he signed up. It was an almost visceral ache as he thought of telling her that he was leaving New York in three days, and suddenly there were tears in his eyes as he realized that he didn't know when he'd be back . . . when . . . or even if . . . but hell, that wasn't the point, he told himself. If he didn't go to fight the Japs, then who the hell would? And if they didn't, then one of these days the bastards would be flying overhead and bombing the hell out of New York . . . and this house . . . and Jean.

He sat down in the armchair she had upholstered herself in a deep, cozy green, and was lost in his own thoughts . . . San Diego . . . Japan . . . Christmas . . . Jean . . . he didn't know how long he'd been sitting there when suddenly, startled, he looked up. He had just heard the key in the lock. She flung the door wide, her arms filled with brown bags from the A&P. She didn't see him at first, and then jumped as she turned on the light, and saw him smiling at her, his blond hair falling over one eye as it always did, the green eyes looking straight at her. He was still as handsome as he had been when they first met. He had been seventeen then, and she had been fifteen . . . six years . . . he was only twenty-three.

"Hi, sweetheart, what are you doing here?"

"I came home to see you." He walked toward her and easily grabbed the bags in his powerful arms, and she turned her big, dark brown eyes up to him with the same look of awe she always wore when she looked up at him. She was so impressed with him, always had been, he'd had two years of college, going at nights, had been on the track team in school, the football team for a few months till he hurt his knee, and had been a basket ball star when they met during his senior year. And he seemed no less heroic to her now. In fact, he seemed more so to her, and she was so proud of him. He had landed a good job. He sold Buicks in the biggest dealership in New York, and she knew that he'd be the manager eventually . . . one day . . . or maybe he'd go back to school. They had talked about that. But he brought home a nice paycheck for now, and combined with her own, they did all right. She knew how to stretch a dollar more than a mile. She'd been doing it for a long time. Both her parents had died in a car accident when she was just eighteen, and she'd been supporting herself since then. Fortunately, she had just finished secretarial school when they died, and she was a bright girl. She'd had a job in the same law firm now for almost three years. And Andy was proud of her too. She looked so cute when she went off to work in the well tailored suits that she made herself, and hats and gloves she always bought so carefully, checking the styles in the magazines, and then consulting with Andy to make sure they looked just right. He smiled at her again now, as she peeled off her gloves, and tossed her black felt fedora onto the big green chair. "How was your day, cutie pie?" He loved to tease her, pinch her, whisk her into his arms, nuzzle into her neck and threaten to ravish her as he walked in from work. It was certainly a far cry from her constantly proper demeanour at work. He dropped in to see her there once in a great while, and she looked so serious and sedate that she almost frightened him. But she had always been that kind of girl. And actually, she'd been a lot more fun since she'd been married to him. She was finally beginning to relax. He kissed her on the back of the neck now and she felt a shiver run up her spine.

"Wait till I put the groceries away. . . ." She smiled mysteriously and tried to wrest one of the bags from his hand, but he pulled it away from her and kissed her on the lips.

"Why wait?"

"Andy . . . come on. . . ." His hands were beginning to rove passionately over her, pulling off the heavy coat, unbuttoning the jet buttons on the suit jacket she wore underneath. The grocery bags had long since been cast aside, as they suddenly stood, their lips and bodies pressed tight against each other, until Jean finally pulled away for air. She was giggling when they stopped, but it didn't discourage his hands. "Andy . . . what's gotten into you . . . ?"

He grinned mischievously at her, afraid to make a remark that would shock her too much. "Don't ask." He silenced her with another kiss, and relieved her of coat, jacket, and blouse, all with one hand, and a moment later, her skirt dropped to the floor as well, revealing the white lace garter belt with matching pants, silk stockings with seams, and a pair of absolutely sensational legs. He ran his hands across her behind, and pressed hard against her again, and she didn't object as he pulled her down on the couch. Instead she pulled his clothes off as suddenly the elevated train roared by and they both started to laugh. "Damn that thing. . . ." he muttered under his breath as he unhooked her bra with one hand and she smiled.

"You know, I kind of like the sound of it by now. . . ." This time it was Jean who kissed him, and a moment later their bodies were enmeshed just as their mouths had been, and it seemed hours before either of them spoke in the silent room. The kitchen light was still on, near the front door, but there was no light in the living room where they lay, or the tiny bedroom beyond. But even in the darkness of the room, he could sense that Jean was looking at him. "Something funny's going on, isn't it?" There had been a small hard rock in the pit of her stomach all week. She knew her husband too well. "Andy. . . ?" He still didn't know what to say. It was no easier now than it would have been two days before. And it was going to be even worse by the end of the week. But he had to tell her sometime. He just wished it didn't have to be now. For the first time in three days, he suddenly wondered if he'd done the right thing.

"I don't quite know what to say."

But instinctively she knew. She felt her heart lurch as she looked up at him in the dark, her eyes wide, her face already sad, as it always was. She was very different from him. There was always laughter in his eyes, always a quick line on his tongue, a joke, a funny thought. He had happy eyes, an easy smile. Life had always been gentle with him. But it was not so with Jean. She had the tense nervousness of those who have had hard times from birth. Born to two alcoholic parents, with an epileptic sister who died in the bed next to Jean when she was thirteen and Jean nine, orphaned at eighteen, struggling almost since the day she was born, and yet in spite of it all, she had a certain kind of innate style, a joie de vivre which had never been allowed to bloom and which Andy knew would blossom in time, if nurtured enough. And he did nurture her, in every way he could. But he couldn't make it easier for her now, and the old sorrow he had seen when they first met suddenly stood out in her eyes again. "You're going, aren't you?"

He nodded his head, as tears filled the deep, dark eyes and she laid her head back on the couch where they'd just made love. "Don't look like that, baby, please. . . ." She made him feel like such a son-of-a-bitch, and suddenly unable to face her pain, he left her side and strode across the room to fish a pack of Camels out of his coat. He nervously tapped one out, lit it, and sat down in the green chair across from the couch. She was crying openly now, but when she looked at him, she didn't seem surprised.

"I knew you'd go."

"I have to, babe."

She nodded her head. She seemed to understand, but it didn't ease the pain. It seemed to take hours to get up the courage to ask the only thing she wanted to know, but at last she did. "When?"

Andy Roberts gulped hard. It was the hardest thing he'd ever said. "Three days."

She visibly winced and closed her eyes again, nodding her head as the tears slid down her cheeks.

And for the next three days, nothing was ever normal

13

again. She stayed home from work, and seemed to go into a frenzy, doing everything she possibly could for him, washing underwear, rolling socks, baking him cookies for the train. Her hands seemed to fly all day long, as though by keeping them as busy as she could, she would be able to keep a grip on herself, or perhaps even on him. But it was no use, by Saturday night, he forced her to put it all down, to stop packing the clothes he didn't need, the cookies he'd never eat, the socks he could have done without, he took her in his arms and she finally broke down again.

"Oh God, Andy . . . I can't . . . how will I live without you. . . ?" He felt as though he had a hole in his guts the size of a fist when he looked into her eyes and saw what he had done to her. But he had no choice . . . no choice . . . he was a man . . . he had to fight . . . his country was at war . . . and the worst of it was that when he didn't feel sick over what he'd done to her, he felt a strange, unfamiliar thrill of excitement about going to war, as though this was an opportunity he might never have again, something he had to do almost like a mystic rite, in order to become a man. And he felt guilty about that too. And by late Saturday night, it had gotten to him too. He was so torn between Jean's clinging little hands and what he knew he had to do that he wished it was already over with and he was on the train, heading west, but he would be soon enough. He had to report to Grand Central Station at five a.m. And when he finally got up in the tiny bedroom to get dressed, he turned and looked at her, she was quieter now, her tears were spent, her eyes swollen and red, but she looked a little bit more resigned than she had before. For Jean, in some terrible, desperate, frightening way, it was like losing her sister, or her parents, again. Andy was all she had left. And she would rather have died herself than lose him. And suddenly he was leaving her too.

"You'll be all right, won't you, babe?" He sat on the edge of the bed, looking at her, desperate for some reassurance from her now, and she smiled sadly and reached a hand out for his.

"I'll have to be, I guess, won't I?" And then she smiled

again, almost mysteriously. "You know what I wish?" They both knew that, that he weren't going to war. She read his thoughts, and kissed his fingertips. "Aside from that . . . I hope you got me pregnant this week. . . ." In the emotions of the past few days, they had thrown caution to the winds. He had been aware of it, but there had been so much else going on. He had just hoped that it wasn't her dangerous time. But he wondered now, as he looked at her. They had been so careful about that for the past year, they had agreed from the first that they didn't want babies for a while, at least not for the first few years until they both got better jobs, or maybe Andy went back to college for another two years. They were in no hurry, they were both young, but now . . . in the past week, their whole life had turned upside down.

"I kind of wondered what was happening this week. . . . Do you think you could have. . . ?" He looked worried. That hadn't been what he wanted at all. He didn't want her to be pregnant alone, with him God knows where, at war.

She shrugged. "I might. . . ." And then she smiled again and sat up. "I'll let you know."

"Great. That's all we need." He looked suddenly upset, and then glanced nervously at the bedside clock. It was ten after four. He had to go.

"Maybe it is." And then suddenly, as though she had to tell him before he left, "I meant what I said just now, Andy. I'd like that a lot."

"Now?" He looked shocked as she nodded her head, her voice a whisper in the tiny room.

"Yes."

Chapter 2

The elevated train roared past the windows of Jean Roberts' apartment, providing the only breeze she had felt in days as she sat motionless in front of the open windows. It felt as though the entire building had turned into an inferno, as the blazing August heat rose off the sidewalks, and seemed to bake right into the walls of the brownstone building. And sometimes at night, she had to leave her bed and sit on the stoop, just to get some air as the train hurtled by. Or she would sit in her bathroom, wrapped in a wet sheet. There seemed to be no way to cool down, and the baby made it worse. She felt as though her whole body were about to explode, and the hotter it got, the more the baby would kick her, as if it knew, as if it were stifling too. Jean smiled to herself at the thought. She could hardly wait to see the baby now . . . there were only four weeks left . . . four weeks until she held their baby . . . she hoped that it would look just like Andy. He was in the Pacific now, doing just what he had wanted to do, "fighting the Japs", as he said in his letters, although somehow the words always pained her. One of the girls in the law firm she had worked in was Japanese and she had been so nice to Jean when she found out she was pregnant. She even covered for her when Jean was almost too sick to move in the beginning. She would drag herself in to work, and stare into her typewriter, praying that she wouldn't throw up before she reached the bathroom. They had kept her for six months, which was decent of them, it was longer than most firms would have kept her, she knew, but they felt it was the patriotic thing to do, because of Andy, as she told him in one of her letters. She wrote to him almost every day, although she rarely heard from him more than once a month. Most of the time, he was too tired to write, and the letters took forever to reach her. It was a long way from selling Buicks in New York, as he said in one letter, making her laugh about the bad food, and his buddies. Somehow he always seemed to make her laugh with his letters. He made everything sound better than it was, and she was never as frightened after she heard from him. She had been terrified at first, particularly when she felt so ill. She had gone through agonies of conflict after she first found out she was pregnant. It had seemed like such a good idea at first, during those last few days before he left, but when she found out, she had panicked. It meant she had to give up her job, she'd be alone, and how would she support herself, and the baby? She had been desperately afraid of his reaction too, only when he finally wrote to her, he sounded so thrilled that it all seemed fine to her again, and by then, she was almost five months pregnant, and she wasn't as nervous.

And in the last few months she'd had plenty of time to turn their bedroom into a nursery for the baby. She had sewn everything herself in white eyelet with yellow ribbons, sewing and knitting, and making little hats and booties and sweaters. She had even painted pretty little murals on the baby's walls and clouds on the ceiling, although one of her neighbors had given her hell when he found out that she was doing the painting herself and standing on the ladder. But she had nothing else to do now that she wasn't working. She had saved every penny she could, and she wouldn't even go to a movie now, for fear of eating into those savings, and she was receiving part of Andy's paycheck from the army. She was going to need everything she had for the baby, and she was going to stay home for the first few months if she could, and after that she'd have to find a sitter and go back to work. She was hoping that elderly Mrs. Weissman on the fourth floor would baby-sit for her. She was a warm, grandmotherly woman who had lived in the building for years, and had been excited to hear about Jean's baby. She checked on her every day, and sometimes she would even come down late at night, unable to sleep herself in the heat, and tap on Jean's door, if she saw a light beneath it.

But tonight, Jean never turned on the lights. She just sat in the dark, feeling breathless and stifled in the killing heat, listening to train after train come by until they stopped and then started again just before the dawn. Jean even watched the sun come up. She wondered if she would ever be able to breathe normally again, or lie down without feeling as though she was being smothered. There were days when it was really very tiring and the heat and the train didn't help. It was almost eight o'clock in the morning when she heard the knock on her door, and assumed it was Mrs. Weissman. She put her pink bathrobe on, and with a tired sigh padded toward the front door in bare feet. Thank God she only had four weeks to go. She was beginning to think she couldn't take it for much longer.

"Hi. . . ." She pulled the door open with a weary smile, expecting to see her friend, and blushed to find herself looking into the face of a stranger, a stranger in a brown uniform with a cap and mustard colored braid, holding a yellow envelope toward her. She looked at him, uncomprehending, not wanting to understand because she knew only too well what that meant, and the man seemed to be leering at her. It was as though his face was distorted as she reeled from the shock and the heat, clutching the envelope and tearing it open without saying a word to him. And it was there, just as she had feared, and she looked at the messenger of death again, focusing on the words on his uniform as her mouth formed a scream, and she sank to his feet in a quiet heap on the floor, as he gaped at her in silent horror, and then suddenly called out for help. He was sixteen years old and he had never been that close to a pregnant woman before. Two doors opened across the hall, and a moment later, there was the sound of running feet on the stairs above, and Mrs. Weissman was putting damp cloths on Jean's head, as the boy backed slowly away and then hurried down the stairs. All he wanted to do was get out of the stifling little building. Jean was moaning by then, and Mrs. Weissman and two other ladies were leading her to the couch where she slept now. It was the same couch where the baby had been conceived, where she had lain and made love with Andy . . . Andy . . . Andy. . . . "We regret to inform

18

you . . . your husband died in the service of his country . . . killed in action at Guadalcanal . . . in action . . . in action . . ." Her head was reeling and she couldn't see the faces.

"Jean. . . ? Jean. . . ." They kept calling her name, and there was something cold on her face, as they looked at her and at each other. Helen Weissman had read the telegram, and had quickly shown it to the others. "Jean. . . ." She came around slowly, barely able to breathe, and they helped her to sit and forced her to drink a little water. She looked blankly at Mrs. Weissman, and then suddenly she remembered, and the sobs strangled her more than the heat, and she couldn't catch her breath anymore, all she could do was cry and cling to the old woman who held her . . . he was dead . . . just like the others . . . like Mommy and Daddy and Ruthie . . . gone . . . he was gone . . . she would never see him again . . . she whimpered almost like a small child, feeling a weight in her heart that she had never felt before, even for the others. "It's all right, dear, it's all right. . . ." But they all knew that it wasn't, and never would be again, not for poor Andy.

The others went back to their apartments a little while later, but Helen Weissman stayed. She didn't like the glazed look in the girl's eyes, the way she sat and stared and then suddenly began to sob, or the terribly endless crying she heard that night when she finally left Jean for a little while, and then returned to open the unlocked door and check on her again as she had all day. She had even called Jean's doctor before he left his office, and he had told Helen to tell Jean how sorry he was to hear the news, and warned Helen that Jean could go into labor from the shock, which was exactly what she was afraid of, and it was exactly what she suspected when she saw Jean press her fists into her back several times later that evening, and walk restlessly around the tiny apartment, as though it had grown too small for her in the past few hours. Her entire world had shattered around her, and there was nowhere left to go. There wasn't even a body to send home . . . just the memory of a tall, handsome blond boy . . . and the baby in her belly.

"Are you all right?" Helen Weissman's accent made Jean

smile. She had been in the country for forty years, but she still spoke with a heavy German accent. She was a wise, warm woman, and she was fond of Jean. She had lost her own husband thirty years before, and she had never remarried. She had three children in New York, who visited her from time to time, mostly to drop their respective children off so she could baby-sit, and a son who had a good job in Chicago. "You have pains?" Her eyes searched Jean's, and Jean started to shake her head. Her whole body ached after the day of crying, and yet inside she felt numb. She didn't know what she felt, just achy and hot and restless. She arched her back as though to stretch it.

"I'm all right. Why don't you get some sleep, Mrs. Weissman?" Her voice was hoarse after the long day. She glanced at the kitchen clock and registered the fact that it had been fifteen hours since she had gotten the telegram telling her about Andy ... fifteen hours, it felt like fifteen years ... a thousand years ... she walked around the room again as Helen Weissman watched her.

"You want to go for a walk outside?" The train whizzed past nearby and Jean shook her head. It was too hot to go for a walk, even at eleven o'clock at night. And suddenly Jean was even hotter than she'd been all day.

"I think I'll have something cold to drink." She fixed herself a glass of the lemonade she kept in a pitcher in the ice box, and it tasted good going down, but it came back up almost as quickly. She rushed to the bathroom, where she threw up and retched repeatedly and then emerged wanly a little while later.

"You should lie down." Meekly, she agreed. She was more uncomfortable when she did. It was easier to sit up than lie down, so she tried the comfortable old green chair again, but after a few minutes she found that she couldn't do that either. She had gnawing pains in her lower back and an unsettled feeling in her stomach, and Helen Weissman left her alone again at midnight, but only after insisting that Jean come and get her during the night if she had a problem. But Jean was sure she wouldn't have to. She turned off the lights, and sat alone in the silent apartment, thinking of her husband ... Andy ... of the big green eyes and straight blond hair ... track star ... football hero ... her first and only love ... the boy she had fallen head over heels in love with the first time she saw him, and as she thought of him, she felt a shaft of pain slice through her from her belly to her back, and then again, and again, and yet again, so that she couldn't catch her breath at all now. She stood up unsteadily, nausea overwhelming her, but determined to get to the bathroom, where she clung miserably to the toilet for almost an hour, the pains pounding her body, the retching tearing at her soul, until weakly at last, barely conscious, she began calling for Andy. It was there that Helen Weissman found her at one thirty in the morning. She had decided to check on her once more before going to bed. It was too hot for anyone to sleep that night, so she was awake unusually late. And she thanked God that she was, when she found her. She went back to her own apartment just long enough to call Jean's doctor and the police, who promised to send an ambulance at once. She climbed into a cotton housedress, grabbed her purse, kept the same sandals on her feet, and hurried back to Jean, to drape a bathrobe around her shoulders, and ten minutes later, they heard the sirens. Helen did, but Jean seemed to hear nothing at all as she retched and cried, and Helen Weissman tried to soothe. She was writhing with pain and calling Andy's name by the time they reached New York Hospital, and the baby didn't take long to come after that. The nurses whisked Jean away on a gurney, and they didn't have time to give her anything at all, before the wiry five pound four ounce little girl emerged with jet black hair, and tightly clenched fists, wailing loudly. Helen Weissman saw them both barely an hour later. Jean mercifully drugged at last, the baby dozing comfortably.

And she went back to the apartment house that night, thinking of the lonely years Jean Roberts had ahead, bringing up her baby girl alone, a widow at twenty-two. Helen brushed the tears from her cheek as the elevated train roared by at four thirty that morning. The older woman knew what kind of devotion it would take to bring the child up alone, a kind of religious zeal, a solitary passion to do all for this baby that would never know her father.

Jean gazed at her baby the next morning when they brought her to nurse for the first time; she looked down at the tiny face, the dark silky hair that the nurses said would fall out eventually, and she knew instinctively what she would have to do for her. It didn't frighten Jean at all. This was what she had wanted. Andy's baby. This was his last gift to her, and she would guard her with her life, do all she could, give her only the best. She would live and breathe and work and do, and give her very soul to this baby.

The tiny rosebud mouth worked as she nursed and Jean smiled at the unfamiliar feeling. She couldn't believe that it was twenty-four hours since she had learned of Andy's death, as a nurse came into the room to check on them both. They seemed to be doing fine, and the baby was a good size, considering that she'd been almost four weeks early.

"Looks like she has a good appetite." The woman in the starched white uniform and cap glanced at mother and child. "Has her daddy seen her yet?" They couldn't know . . . no one did . . . except Jean, and Helen Weissman. Her eyes filled with tears and she shook her head as the nurse patted her arm, not understanding. No, her daddy hadn't seen her yet, and he never would. "What are you going to name her?"

They had written back and forth to each other about that, and had finally agreed on a name for a girl, although they both thought they wanted a boy. Funny, how after the first moment of surprise and near disappointment a girl seemed so much better now, as though that had been their choice all along. Nature somehow managed things well. Had she been a boy, she would have been named after her father. But Jean had found a girl's name that she loved, and she tried it out on the nurse now as her eyes glowed with pride as she held her baby. "Her name is Tana Andrea Roberts. Tana. . . ." She loved the sound of it, and it seemed to suit her to perfection.

The nurse smiled as she lifted the tiny bundle from Jean's arms when she was finished nursing. She smoothed the covers expertly with one hand and looked at Jean. "Get some rest now, Mrs. Roberts. I'll bring Tana back to you when she's ready." The door closed, and Jean laid her head back against the pillow, with her eyes closed, trying not to think of Andy, but only of their baby . . . she didn't want to think of how he had died, what they had done to him . . . if he had screamed her name . . . a tiny sob broke from her as she turned in her bed, and lay on her stomach for the first time in months, her faced buried in the pillows . . . and she lay there and sobbed for what seemed like hours, until at last she fell asleep . . . and dreamt of the blond boy she had loved . . . and the baby he had left her . . . Tana . . . Tana. . . .

Chapter 3

The phone rang on Jean Roberts' desk only once before she answered it. She had a brisk, efficient way about her, which came from long years of managing a mammoth job. It had fallen into her lap twelve years before. She had been twenty-eight, Tana six, and Jean thought she would scream if she had to work one more day in another law firm. There had been three jobs in six years, in law firms that were one more boring than the other. But the pay was good, and she had Tana to think of now. Tana always came first, Tana upon whom the sun rose and set, in Jean's eyes.

"For God's sake, let the kid breathe . . .", one of her co-workers had told her once, and Jean had been cool to her after that. She knew exactly what she was doing, taking her to the theater and the ballet, museums, libraries, art galleries and concerts when she could afford to, helping her inhale every drop of culture. Almost every dime she made went to the education and support and entertainment of Tana. And she had saved every penny of the pension from Andy. And it wasn't that the child was spoiled, she wasn't. But Jean wanted her to have the good things in life, the things she herself had seldom had, and which she thought were so important. It was hard to remember objectively now if they would have had that kind of life with Andy. More likely he would have rented a boat and taken them sailing on Long Island Sound, taught Tana to swim at an early age, gone clam digging, or running in the park, riding a bike . . . he would have worshipped the pretty little blonde child who looked so exactly like him. Tall, lanky, blonde, green eyed, with the same dazzling smile as her father. And the nurses in the hospital had been right when she was born, the silky black hair had fallen out and had been replaced by pale golden peach fuzz, which as she got older, grew into straight wheat-like shafts of golden hair. She was a lovely looking little girl, and Jean had always been proud of her. She had even managed to get her out of public schools when she was nine and send her to Miss Lawson's. It meant a lot to Jean, and was a wonderful opportunity for Tana. Arthur Durning had helped her in, which he insisted was a small favor. He knew himself how important good schools were for children. He had two children of his own, although they went to the exclusive Cathedral and Williams Schools in Greenwich, and were respectively two and four years older than Tana.

The job came to Jean almost by accident when Arthur came to the law firm where she worked for a series of lengthy conferences with Martin Pope, the senior partner. She had worked for Pope, Madison and Watson for two years by then, and was bored to death, but the salary was more than she dared to hope for. She couldn't afford to run around looking for a "fun job", she always had Tana to think of. She thought of her night and day. Her whole life revolved around her daughter, as she explained to Arthur when he invited her to drinks after seeing her for almost two months during his meetings with Martin Pope.

Arthur and Marie were separated then, in fact, she had been in New England, at a "private institution". He seemed loath to discuss it and she didn't press him. She had her own problems and responsibilities. She didn't go around crying on other people's shoulders about the husband she had lost, the child she supported on her own, the responsibilities, the burdens, the fears. She knew what she wanted for Tana, the kind of life, the education, the friends. She was going to give her security, no matter what, the kind of life she herself had never had. And without Jean having to say too much, Arthur Durning had seemed to understand that. He was the head of one of the largest conglomerates in the country, in plastics, in glass, in food packaging, they even had enormous holdings in oil in the Middle East. He was an enormously wealthy man. But he had a quiet, unassuming way about him that she liked.

In fact, there had been a lot about Arthur Durning that

appealed to her, enough so that when he asked her out to dinner shortly after that first drink, she went. And then she went again, and somehow, within a month they were having an affair. He was the most exciting man Jean Roberts had ever met. There was a quiet aura of power about the man that one could almost touch, he was so strong, and yet he was vulnerable too, and she knew that he had suffered with his wife. Eventually he told her about that. Marie had become an alcoholic almost immediately after their second child was born, and Jean knew the pain of that only too well, having watched her parents attempt to drink themselves to death, and in the end, they killed themselves in their car, drunk on an icy road on New Year's Eve. Marie had also cracked up the car, driving a car pool full of little girls one night. Ann and her friends were ten years old, and one of the children had almost been killed. Marie Durning had agreed to put herself away after that, but Arthur didn't have much hope. She was thirty-five and she'd been a hopeless drunk for ten years, and Arthur was desperately tired of it. Enough so to be swept off his feet by Jean. At twenty-eight, there was something unusually dignified about her that he liked, and at the same time, there was something kind and gentle in her eyes. She looked as though she cared a great deal, about everything and in particular her daughter. Her basic warmth came through, and it was precisely what he had needed just then. He hadn't known what to do with her at first, or what to make of what he felt for her. He and Marie had been married for sixteen years, and he was forty-two years old. He didn't know what to do about the children, about his house . . . his life . . . about Marie. Everything seemed to be hanging so precariously that year, and it was an unusual way of life for him, and one that he didn't like. He didn't take Jean home at first, for fear of upsetting the children, but eventually he saw Jean almost every night, and she began to take care of things for him. She hired two new maids, a gardener he didn't have time to see, she orchestrated some of the small business dinners he liked to give, a party for the children at Christmas, helped him pick out a new car. She even took a few days off to take a couple of brief trips with him. Suddenly it seemed as though she were running his whole life and he couldn't function without her, and she began to ask herself more and more what it meant, except that deep in her heart she knew. She was in love with him, and he was in love with her, and as soon as Marie was well enough to be told, they'd get divorced, and he would marry Jean . . . .

Except that instead, after six months, he offered her a job. She wasn't sure what to do about that. She didn't really want to work for him. She was in love with him, and he was so wonderful to her, but the way he described it was like throwing open a window onto a vista she had longed for, for years. She could do exactly what she'd done for him in the past six months, just as a friend. Organize parties, hire help, make sure that the children had the right clothes, the right friends, the right nurses. He thought she had fabulous taste, and he had no idea that she made everything she and Tana wore herself. She had even upholstered the furniture in their tiny apartment. They still lived in the narrow brownstone, near where the Third Avenue E1 had been, and Helen Weissman still baby-sat for Tana, when Jean was at work. But with the job Arthur described, she could send Tana to a decent school, he'd even help her get in. She could move to a bigger place, there was even a building Arthur owned on the Upper East Side, it wasn't Park Avenue, he said with his slow smile, but it was far nicer than where they were. When he told her the salary he had in mind, she almost died. And the job would be so easy for her.

If she hadn't had Tana, she might have held out. It would have been easier not to be indebted to him, and yet it was such a wonderful chance to be side by side all the time . . . and when Marie was well. . . . He already had an executive secretary at Durning International, but there was a small secluded office just beyond the conference room which adjoined the handsome wood-panelled office he used. She would see him every day, be right nearby, she would be virtually essential to him, as she was rapidly becoming now. "It would just be more of the same", he explained, begging her to take the job, offering her even more benefits, an even higher salary. He was already dependent on her now, he needed her, and indirectly his children did too, although they hadn't met her yet. But she was the first person he had relied on in years. For almost two decades everyone else had relied on him, and suddenly here was someone he could turn to, who never seemed to let him down. He had given the matter a great deal of thought and he wanted her near him always, he said, in bed that night as he begged her again to take the job.

In the end, although she seemed to fight so hard, it was an easy choice to make, and her whole life seemed like a dream now as she went to work every day, sometimes after he had spent the night with her. His children were used to his spending a few nights in town. And the house in Greenwich was efficiently staffed now, Arthur was no longer as worried about them, although Ann and Billy had had a hard time at first when Marie left, but they seemed less anxious about it now. And once they met Jean, it was as though they had always been old friends. She took them to movies with Tana constantly, bought them toys, shopped for their clothes, drove their car pools, went to their schools, and their school plays when Arthur was out of town, and she took even better care of him. He was like a well-fed cat, polishing his paws by the fire as he smiled at her one night in the apartment he'd gotten her. It wasn't sumptuous but for Tana and Jean, it was more than enough, two bedrooms, a living room, dining room, handsome kitchen. The building was modern and well built and clean, and they had a view of the East River from the living-room windows. It was a far cry from the elevated train in Jean's old apartment.

"Do you know," she looked at him with a smile, "I've never been happier in my life."

"Neither have I."

But that was only days before Marie Durning tried to take her own life. Someone told her that Arthur was having an affair, although they didn't say with whom, and things were touch and go with her after that. Six months later, the doctors began talking of letting her go home, and by then Jean had worked for Arthur Durning for over a year. Tana was happy in her new school, new home, new life, as was Jean. And suddenly it was as though everything stopped. Arthur went to see Marie and came home looking grim.

"What did she say?" Jean looked at him with wide, terrified eyes. She was thirty years old now. She wanted security, stability, not a clandestine affair for the rest of her life. But she had never objected to their life because she knew how desperately ill Marie Durning was, and how it worried him. But only the week before he had been talking about marriage to Jean. He looked at her now with a bleak expression she had never seen before, as though he had no hope left, no dreams.

"She said that if she can't come home to us, she'll try to commit suicide again."

"But she can't do that to you. She can't keep threatening you for the rest of your life." Jean wanted to scream, and the bitch of it was that Marie could threaten, and did. She came home three months after that, with only a tenuous grip on her own sanity. She was back at the hospital by Christmas that year, home by spring, and this time she held out until fall, and began drinking heavily over bridge lunches with her friends. All in all it went on for more than seven years.

When she came out of the hospital the first time, Arthur was so upset that he actually asked Jean to help her out. "She's so helpless, you don't understand . . . she's nothing like you, sweetheart. She can't cope . . . she can barely think." And for love of Arthur, Jean found herself in the unenviable position of being the mistress caring for the wife. She spent two or three days a week, during the day, in Greenwich with her, trying to help her run the house. Marie was desperately afraid of the help; they all knew that she drank. And so did her kids. At first they seemed to view her with despair, and eventually with scorn. It was Ann who hated her most, Billy who cried when she got drunk. It was a nightmarish scene, and just like Arthur, within a few months, Jean was trapped. She couldn't let her down, let her go . . . it would have been like deserting her parents. It was as though this time she could make things happen right. Even though, in the end, Marie came to an almost identical end as Jean's parents. She was going to meet Arthur in town for a night at the ballet, and Jean swore that she was sober when she left, at least she thought she was, but she must have had a bottle with her. She spun out on an icy patch on the Merritt Parkway halfway to New York, and died instantly.

They were both still grateful that Marie never knew of their affair, and the agony of it all was that Jean had been fond of her. She had cried at the funeral more than the children had, and it had taken her weeks to be willing to spend a night with Arthur again. Their affair had gone on for eight years, and now he was afraid of what his children would say. "In any case, I've got to wait a year." She didn't disagree with that, and anyway he spent a great deal of time with her. He was thoughtful and attentive. She had never had any complaints. But it was important to her that Tana not suspect their long standing affair . . . but finally a year after Marie died, she turned and accused Jean.

"I'm not stupid, you know, Mom. I know what's going on." She was as long and lanky and beautiful as Andy had been, and she had the same mischievous light in her eyes, as though she were always about to laugh, but not this time. She had hurt for too long, and her eyes almost steamed as she glared at Jean. "He treats you like dirt and he has for years. Why doesn't he marry you instead of sneaking in and out of here in the middle of the night?" Jean had slapped her for that, but Tana didn't care. There had been too many Thanksgivings they spent alone, too many Christmases with expensive boxes from fabulous stores, but no one but the two of them there, while he went to the country club with his friends. Even the year that Ann and Billy were gone with their grandparents. "He's never here when it counts! Don't you see that, Mom?" Huge tears had rolled down her cheeks as she sobbed and Jean had had to turn away. Her voice was hoarse as she tried to answer for him.

"That's not true."

"Yes, it is. He always leaves you alone. And he treats you like the maid. You run his house, drive his kids around, and he gives you diamond watches and gold bracelets and briefcases and purses and perfume, and so what? Where is *he*? That's what counts, isn't it?" What could she say? Deny the truth to her own child? It broke her heart to realize how much Tana had seen.

"He's doing what he has to do."

"No, he's not. He's doing what he wants to do." She was very perceptive for a girl of fifteen. "He wants to be in Greenwich with all his friends, go to Bar Harbor in the summer, and Palm Beach in the winter, and when he goes to Dallas on business, he takes you. But does he ever take you to Palm Beach? Does he ever invite us? Does he ever let Ann and Billy see how much you mean to him? No. He just sneaks out of here so I won't know what's going on, well I do . . . dammit . . . I do. . . ." Her whole body shook with rage. She had seen the pain in Jean's eyes too often over the years, and she was frighteningly close to the truth, as Jean knew. The truth was that their arrangement was comfortable for him, and he wasn't strong enough to swim upstream against his children. He was terrified of what his own children would think of the affair with Jean. He was a dynamo in business, but he couldn't fight the same wars at home. He had never had the courage to call Marie's bluff and simply walk out, he had catered to her alcoholic whims right till the end. And now he was doing the same with his kids. But Jean had her own worries too. She didn't like what Tana had said to her, and she tried to talk to Arthur about it that night, but he brushed her off with a tired smile. He had had a hard day, and Ann was giving him some trouble.

"They all have their own ideas at that age. Hell, look at mine." Billy was seventeen, and had been picked up on drunk driving charges twice that year, and Ann had just gotten kicked out of her sophomore year at Wellesley, at nineteen. She wanted to go to Europe with her friends, while Arthur wanted her to spend some time at home. Jean had even tried to take her to lunch to reason with her, but she had brushed Jean off, and told her that she'd get what she wanted out of Daddy by the end of the year.

And true to her word, she did. She spent the following summer in the South of France, and picked up a thirty-seven-year-old French playboy, whom she married in Rome. She got pregnant, lost the child, and returned to New York with dark circles under her eyes and an enormous diamond ring. Not bad for a twenty-year-old girl. It had made the international press, of course, and Arthur had been sick about it when he met the "young man". It had cost him a fortune to buy him off, but he had, and he left Ann in Palm Beach to "recuperate" as he said to her, but she seemed to get into plenty of trouble there, carousing all night with boys her own age, or their fathers if she had the chance. She was a racy one, in ways of which Jean did not approve, but she was twenty-one now, and there was little Arthur could do. She had gotten an enormous trust from her mother's estate, and she had the funds she needed now to run wild. She was back in Europe, raising hell, before she was twenty-two. And the only thing that cheered Arthur a little bit was that Billy had managed to stay in Princeton that year in spite of several near fatal scrapes he'd been in.

"I must say, they don't give one much peace of mind, do they, love?" They had quiet evenings together in Greenwich now, but most nights she insisted on driving home, no matter how late she got in. His children were no longer there, but she still had Tana at home, and Jean wouldn't dream of staying out for the night unless Tana was at a friend's, or skiing for a weekend somewhere. There were certain standards she expected to maintain and it touched him about her. "You know, in the end they do what they want anyway, Jean. No matter how good an example you set." It was true in a way, but he didn't fight her very hard. He was used to spending his nights alone now, and it made it more of a treat when they awoke side by side. There was very little passion left in what they shared. But it was comfortable for them both, particularly for him. She didn't ask him for more than he was willing to give, and he knew how grateful she was for all that he had done for her over the years. He had given her a security she might never have had without him, a wonderful job, a good school for her child, and little extras whenever he could, trips, jewels, furs. They were minor extravagances to him, and though Jean Roberts

32

was still a wizard with a needle and thread, she no longer had to upholster her own furniture or make their own clothes, thanks to him. There was a cleaning woman who came twice a week, a comfortable roof over their heads, and Arthur knew that she loved him. He loved her too, but he was set in his ways, and neither of them had mentioned marriage in years. There was no reason to now. Their children were almost grown, he was fifty-four years old, his empire was doing well, and Jean was still attractive and fairly young, although there had been a matronly look to her now for the past several years. He liked her that way, though, and it seemed hard to believe that it had been twelve years. She had just turned forty that spring. And he had taken her to Paris for the week. It was almost like a dream. She brought back dozens of tiny treasures for Tana, and enchanted her with endless tales, including that of her birthday dinner at Maxim's. It was always sad coming home after trips like that, waking up in bed alone again, reaching out to him in the night and finding no one there, but she had lived that way for so long that it no longer bothered her, or at least she pretended that to herself, and after her outbreak three years before, Tana had never accused her again. She had been ashamed of herself afterwards. Her mother had always been so good to her. "I just want the best for you . . . that's all . . . I want you to be happy . . . not to be alone all the time. . . ."

"I'm not, sweetheart," tears had filled Jean's eyes, "I have you."

"That's not the same." She had clung to her mother then, and the forbidden subject had not come up again. But there was no warmth lost between Arthur and Tana when they met, which always upset Jean. Actually, it would have been harder on her if he'd insisted on marrying her after all, because of the way Tana felt about him. She felt that he had used her mother for the past dozen years, and given nothing in exchange.

"How can you say that? We owe him so much!" She remembered the apartment beneath the elevated train, which Tana did not, the meager checks, the nights she couldn't even afford to feed the child meat, or when she bought lamb chops or a little steak for her and ate macaroni herself for three or four days.

"What do we owe him? A deal on this apartment? So what? You work, you could get us an apartment like this, Mom. You could do a whole lot of things for us without him." But Jean was never as sure. She would have been frightened to leave him now, frightened not to work for Durning International, not to be at his right hand, not to have the apartment, the job, the security that she always knew was there . . . the car he replaced every two years so that she could go back and forth to Greenwich with ease. Originally, it had been a station wagon so that she could carpool his kids. The last two had been smaller though, pretty little Mercedes sedans he bought and replaced for her. And it wasn't as though she cared about the expensive gifts, there was more to it than that, much, much more. There was something about knowing that Arthur was there for her, if she needed him. It would have terrified her not to have that, and they had been together for so long now. No matter what Tana thought, she couldn't have given that up.

"And what happens when he dies?" Tana had been blunt with her once. "You're all alone with no job, nothing. If he loves you, why doesn't he marry you, Mom?"

"I suppose we're comfortable like this."

Tana's eyes were big and green and hard, as Andy's had been when he disagreed with her. "That's not good enough. He owes you more than that, Mom. It's so damn easy for him."

"It's easy for me too, Tan." She hadn't been able to argue with her that night. "I don't have to get used to anyone's quirks. I live the way I please. I make my own rules. And when I want, he takes me to Paris or London or LA. It's not such a bad life." They both knew it wasn't entirely true, but there was no changing it now. They were set in their ways, both of them. And as she tidied the papers on her desk, she suddenly sensed him in the room. Somehow, she always knew when he was there, as though years ago, someone had planted a radar in her heart, designed to locate him. He had walked silently into her office, not far from his own, and was looking at her, as she glanced up and saw him standing there.

"Hello," she smiled the smile that only they had been sharing for more than twelve years, and it felt like sunshine in his heart as he looked at her. "How was your day?"

"Better now." He hadn't seen her since noon, which was unusual for them. They seemed to touch base half a dozen times during the afternoons, met for coffee each morning, and often he took her to lunch with him. There had been gossip on and off over the years, particularly right after Marie Durning died, but eventually it had died down, and people just assumed they were friends, or if they were lovers, it was both discreet and dead-end, so no one bothered to talk about them anymore. He sat in his favorite comfortable chair across from her desk and lit his pipe. It was a smell she had come to love as part of him for more than a decade, and it pervaded all the rooms in which he lived, including her own bedroom with the East River view. "How about spending the day in Greenwich with me tomorrow, Jean? Why don't we both play hookey for a change?" It was rare for him to do that, but he'd been pushing very hard on a merger for the past seven weeks, and she thought the day off would do him good, and wished he would do things like that more frequently. But now she smiled at him regretfully.

"I wish I could. Tomorrow's our big day." He often forgot things like that. But she didn't really expect him to remember Tana's graduation day. He looked blankly at her and she smiled as she said the single word. "Tana."

"Oh, of course," he waved the pipe and frowned as he laughed at her, "how stupid of me. It's a good thing you haven't depended on me the way I have on you, or you'd be in trouble most of the time."

"I doubt that." She smiled lovingly at him, and something very comfortable passed between them again. It was almost as though they no longer needed words. And in spite of the things Tana had said over the years, Jean Roberts needed nothing more than she had. As she sat there with the man she had loved for so long, she felt totally fulfilled.

35

"Is she all excited about graduation day?" He smiled at Jean. She was a very attractive woman in her own way. Her hair was peppered with gray, and she had big, beautiful dark eyes, and there was something delicate and graceful about her. Tana was longer, taller, almost coltlike, with a beauty that would surely stop men in the street in the next few years. She was going to Green Hill College in the heart of the South, and had gotten in under her own steam. Arthur had thought it a damn odd choice for a girl from the North, since it was filled mostly with Southern belles, but they had one of the finest language programs in the States, excellent laboratories, and a strong fine arts program. Arthur had long since told Jean what he thought about that, "Ridiculous stuff for a girl to take", but Tana had made up her own mind, the full scholarship had come through, based on her grades, and she was all set to go. She had a job in New England at a summer camp, and she would be going to Green Hill in the fall. And tomorrow was going to be her big day – graduation.

"If the volume of her record player is any indication of how she feels," Jean smiled, "then she's been hysterical for the last month."

"Oh God, don't remind me of that . . . please . . . Billy and four of his friends are coming home next week. I forgot to tell you about that. They want to stay in the pool house, and they'll probably burn the damn thing down. He called last night. Thank God they'll only be here for two weeks before moving on." Billy Durning was twenty now, and wilder than ever, from the correspondence Jean saw from school. But she knew that he was probably still reacting to his mother's death. It had been hard on all of them. Billy most of all, he had been only sixteen when she died, a difficult age at best, and things were a little smoother now. "He's giving a party next week, by the way. Saturday night, apparently. I was 'informed', and he asked me to tell you."

She smiled. "I shall make due note. Any special requests?"

Arthur grinned. She knew them all well. "A band, and he said to be ready for two or three hundred guests. And by the way, tell Tana about that. She might enjoy it. He can have one of his friends pick her up here in town."

"I'll tell her. I'm sure she'll be pleased." But only Jean knew how big a lie that was. Tana had hated Billy Durning all her life, but Jean had forced her to be courteous whenever they met, and she would make the point to her again now. She owed it to Billy to be polite, and to go to his party if he invited her, after all his father had done for them. Jean never let her forget that.

". . . I will not." Tana looked stubbornly at Jean, as the stereo blared deafeningly from her room. Paul Anka was crooning "Put Your Head On My Shoulder" and she had already played it at least seven times.

"If he's nice enough to invite you, you could at least go for a while." It was an argument they had had before, but Jean was determined to win this time. She didn't want Tana to be rude.

"How can I go for a while? It takes at least an hour to drive out there, and another hour back . . . so what do I do, stay for ten minutes?" She tossed the long shaft of golden wheat-colored hair over her shoulder with a look of despair. She knew how insistent her mother always was about anything that emanated from the Durnings. "Come on, Mom, we're not little kids anymore. Why do I have to go if I don't want to? Why is it rude just to say no? Couldn't I have other plans? I'm leaving in two weeks anyway, and I want to see my friends. We'll never see each other again anyway. . . ." She looked forlorn and her mother smiled at her.

"We'll talk about it another time, Tana." But Tana knew just how those discussions went. She almost groaned. She knew how stubborn her mother was going to be about Billy Durning's party, and he was a creep, as far as she was concerned. There were no two ways about it, and Ann was even worse in Tana's eyes. She was snobby, stuck up, and she looked easy, no matter how polite she pretended to be to Jean. Tana knew she was probably a whore, she had seen her drink too much at some of Billy's other parties, and she treated Jean in a condescending manner that made Tana want to slap her face. But Tana also knew that any hint of her feelings to her mother would lead them into a major battle again. It had happened too often before, and she wasn't in the mood tonight.

"I just want you to understand how I feel now, Mother. I'm not going."

"It's still a week away. Why do you have to decide tonight?"

"I'm just telling you. . . ." The green eyes looked stormy and ominous and Jean knew better than to cross her when she looked like that.

"What did you defrost for dinner tonight?"

Tana knew the tactic of avoidance, her mother was good at that, but she decided to play the game for now, and followed her mother into the kitchen. "I took out a steak for you. I'm having dinner with some of my friends." She looked sheepish then. As much as she wanted her own life, she hated leaving Jean alone. She knew just how much her mother had given her, how much she had sacrificed. It was that which Tana understood all too well. She owed everything to her mother, not to Arthur Durning, or his selfish, spoiled, over-indulged children. "Do you mind, Mom? I don't have to go out." Her voice was gentle, and she looked older than her eighteen years as Jean turned to look at her. There was something very special between the two of them. They had been alone together for a very long time, and had shared bad times and good; her mother had never let her down, and Tana was a gentle, thoughtful child.

Jean smiled at her. "I want you to go out with your friends, sweetheart. Tomorrow is a very special day for you." They were going to dinner at "21" the following night. Jean never went there except with Arthur, but Tana's graduation day was occasion enough to warrant the extravagance, and Jean didn't need to be as careful now. She made an enormous salary from Durning International, at least compared to what she had made as a legal secretary twelve years before, but she was cautious by nature, and always a little worried. She had worried a lot over the past eighteen years since Andy had died, and sometimes she told Tana that was why things had turned out so well. She had worried all her life, in sharp contrast to Andy Roberts' easy ways, and Tana seemed to be a great deal like him. There was more joy in her than in her mother, more mischief, more laughter, more ease with life, but then again life had been easier for her with Jean to love and protect her, and Tana smiled now as Jean took out a pan to cook the steak.

"I'm looking forward to tomorrow night." She had been touched to learn that Jean was taking her to "21".

"So am I. Where are you all going tonight?"

"To the Village, for a pizza."

"Be careful." Jean frowned. She always worried about her, anywhere she went.

"I always am."

"Will there be boys along to protect you?" She smiled. Sometimes it was hard to know if they were protection or a threat, and sometimes they were both. Reading her mind, Tana laughed and nodded.

"Yes. Now will you worry more?"

"Yes. Of course."

"You're silly, but I love you anyway." She threw her arms around her neck, gave her a kiss, and disappeared into her room to turn the music up even louder, as Jean winced, and then found that she was singing along. She had certainly heard it all often enough, but by the time Tana finally turned it off and reappeared, wearing a white dress with big black polka dots and a wide black patent leather belt, with black and white spectator shoes, Jean was suddenly struck by how pleasant the silence sounded. And at the same moment she realized how quiet the apartment would be once Tana was gone, too much so. It would be tomblike when Tana was away.

"Have a good time."

"I will. I'll be home early."

"I won't count on it." Her mother smiled. At eighteen, she no longer had a curfew. Jean knew better than that, and Tana was reasonable most of the time. Jean heard her come in that night, around eleven thirty. She knocked softly on

Jean's door, whispered "I'm home", and went on to her own room, and Jean turned over and went to sleep.

The next day was one that Jean Roberts would long remember, with the long line of innocent looking young girls strung together with garlands of daisies, the boys coming in solemnly behind them, all of them singing in unison, their voices raised, so young, so strong, so powerful, and all of them so new and fresh, as though they were about to be born into the world, a world full of politics and ruses and lies and heartbreaks, and all of it out there, waiting to hurt them. Jean knew that life would never be as simple for them again, as the tears rolled slowly down her cheeks, and they filed slowly out of the auditorium, their voices raised together for a last time. She was embarrassed that a single sob escaped her, but she was not alone, and the fathers cried as hard as their wives, and suddenly all was pandemonium, and the graduates were shouting and cheering in the hallway, kissing and hugging, and making promises that couldn't possibly be fulfilled, to come back, to travel together, to never forget . . . to always . . . forever . . . next year . . . someday. . . . Quietly, Jean watched them, and most especially Tana, her face alight, her eyes almost an emerald green, and all of them so excited, so happy.

Tana was still bubbling over with excitement that night when they went to "21", where they ate a delicious dinner, and Jean surprised her by ordering champagne. Generally, she wasn't much in favor of Tana drinking. Her own experience with her parents, and Marie Durning, still frightened her, especially for someone as young as Tana, but graduation day was an exception. And after the champagne, she handed Tana the little box from Arthur. He had had Jean pick it out for him, like all the presents he gave, even those to his own children. Inside was a beautiful gold bangle which Tana slipped on her wrist with cautious pleasure.

"That was nice of him, Mom." But she didn't look overly excited. They both knew the reasons why, and Tana did not discuss it now. She didn't want to upset her mother. And by week's end, Tana had lost a major battle to her mother. She couldn't stand hearing about it anymore, and she had finally agreed to go to Billy Durning's party. "But this is the last time I'm going to one of their parties. Is that a deal?"

"Why do you have to be so rigid, Tana? It's nice of them to invite you."

"Why?" Tana's eyes flashed, and her tongue was too quick to control. "Because I'm an employee's daughter? Does that make it a special favor from the almighty Durnings? Like inviting the maid?" Tears quickly filled Jean's eyes, and Tana stalked into her room, furious with herself for losing her temper. But she couldn't stand the way her mother felt about the Durnings, not just Arthur, but Ann and Billy too. It was nauseating, as though every little word or gesture were some giant favor to be grateful for. And Tana knew all too well what Billy's parties were like. She had suffered through them before, with too much drinking, too much necking, everybody getting fresh, getting drunk. She hated going to his parties, and tonight was no different.

A friend of his who lived nearby picked her up in a red Corvette he had gotten from his father, and he drove to Greenwich driving eighty miles an hour to impress her, which it didn't, and she arrived feeling as annoyed as she had when she left her apartment. She was wearing a white silk dress, with flat white shoes, and her long slim legs looked particularly graceful as she climbed out of the low slung car, tossing her hair over her shoulder, glancing around, knowing that she would know no one at all. She had particularly hated coming to their parties when she was younger, and the children had pointedly ignored her, but it was easier now. Three boys in madras jackets made a beeline for her, and offered to get her a gin and tonic, or whatever else might be her pleasure. She was noticeably vague and managed to get lost in the crowd, anxious to ditch the boy who had driven her out there. She wandered in the garden for half an hour, wishing she hadn't come, and watching clumps of giggling girls, drinking beer or gin and tonics, the boys watching them. A little while later the music started, and couples began forming, and within half an hour the lights were dim, bodies were chafing happily, and Tana even noticed several couples strolling outside. It was only then that she finally saw Billy Durning. He had been nowhere when they arrived. He walked over to her, and seemed to be giving her a cool appraisal. They had met often enough before, but he always looked her over again, as though he might buy her. It made her angry at him every time she saw him, and tonight was no exception.

"Hello, Billy."

"Hi. Shit, you're tall." As a greeting it didn't excite her, and anyway he was considerably taller than she was, what was the point? But she noticed then that he was staring at the fullness of her breasts and for a minute she wanted to kick him, and then gritting her teeth, she decided to make one stab at good manners, for her mother's sake, if nothing else.

"Thank you for inviting me tonight." But her eyes said she didn't mean it.

"We can always use more girls." Like cattle. So many head . . . so many tits . . . legs . . . or better. . . .

"Thanks."

He laughed at her and shrugged. "Want to go outside?" She was about to turn him down, and then figured, why not? He was two years older than Tana, but he usually acted as though he were ten. Except ten years old with drinking. He grabbed her arm, and led her through the unfamiliar bodies until they reached the Durnings' elaborate garden which led, eventually, to the pool house, where Billy was camping with his friends. They had already burned a table and two chairs the night before, and Billy had told them to cool it or his old man would kill them. But unable to stand the torture of living in any kind of proximity with Billy, Arthur had wisely moved to the country club for the next week. "You should see the mess we're making." He grinned, waving at the pool house in the distance, and Tana felt annoyance sweep over her, knowing that it would be her mother's job to replace everything they damaged, to set it to rights again, and also to calm Arthur down when he saw the mess.

"Why don't you just try not to behave like animals?" She looked sweetly at him, and for a moment he was shocked, and then suddenly, something evil and angry glinted in his eyes as he glared back at her.

"That's a dumb thing to say, but I guess you were always dumb, weren't you? If my old man hadn't paid to keep you at that fancy school in New York, you'd probably have wound up in some public school whorehouse on the West Side, giving your teacher a blow job." She was so shocked that for a moment she was breathless as she stared at him, and then wordlessly, she turned and walked away, as behind her, she could hear him laugh. What an evil little bastard he was, she thought to herself, as she fought her way back into the house, noticing that the crowd had thickened considerably in the past half hour, and that most of the guests were several years older than she was, especially the girls.

She saw the boy who had driven her out from town, a little while later, his fly open, his eyes red, his shirttail out, and there was a girl frantically sliding her hands over his body as they shared a half full bottle of scotch. Tana looked at them in despair, and knew that she had just lost her ride to the city. There was no way she would have driven anywhere with anyone that drunk. Which left the option of the train, or finding someone sober, which did not, for the moment at least, appear likely.

"Wanna dance?" She turned, surprised to see Billy again, his eyes redder, his mouth leering at her, still gazing at her breasts, barely able to tear his eyes away, which he did at last, in time to see her shake her head.

"No, thanks."

"They're banging their asses off in the pool house. Wanna go watch?" Her stomach turned over at the prospect, and if he hadn't been so revolting she would have laughed. It was incredible how blind her mother could be to the Sacred Durnings.

"No, thanks."

"Whatsa matter? Still a virgin?" The look on his face made her sick, but she didn't want to let on that he was right. She'd rather he thought simply that he repulsed her, which was also correct. He did.

"I'm not into watching."

"Shit, why not? Best sport there is." She turned and tried to lose him in the crowd, but for some reason he was following her around tonight, and he was beginning to make her uncomfortable. She glanced around the room again, saw that he had disappeared, probably to the pool house to join his friends, and she figured that she had been there for long enough. All she had to do was call a cab, get to the train station, and go home. Not pleasant, but at least not difficult, and glancing over her shoulder to make sure that no one had followed her, she tiptoed up a small back staircase that she knew about, to a private phone. It was very simple, she called information, got the number, and called the cab. They promised to be out there within the next fifteen minutes, and she knew that she was in plenty of time for the last train. And for the first time all night, she felt relief, having gotten away from the drunks and creeps downstairs, and she wandered slowly down the thickly carpeted hall, glancing at the photographs of Arthur and Marie, Ann and Billy as children, and somehow it seemed as though the photographs should have included Jean. She had been so much a part of them, so much of their well being had been because of her, it didn't feel fair to leave her out, and then suddenly without thinking, Tana opened a door. She knew it was the family room her mother often used as a kind of office when she was there. The walls were covered with photographs too, but she didn't see them tonight. As the door opened slowly, she heard a nervous squeal, a "Shit!... Hey...!" She saw two white moons leap into the air, and heard a scuffle of embarrassment as she quickly closed the door again, and then jumped in horror as someone right behind her laughed.

"Ah!" She turned, and found Billy leering at her. "For heaven's sake...." She had thought he was downstairs.

"I thought you weren't into watching, Miss Lily Pure."

"I was just wandering around, and I stumbled across...." Her face flushed to the roots of her hair as he grinned at her.

"I'll bet ... what'd you come up here for, Tan?" He had

heard her mother call her that over the years, but it annoyed her hearing it from him. It was a private name and he had never been her friend.

"My mom usually works in that room."

"Nah." He shook his head, as though surprised at her mistake. "Not in there."

"Yes, she does." Tana was sure of it, as she glanced at her watch. She didn't want to miss her cab. But she hadn't heard him honk yet, anyway.

"I'll show you where she does work, if you want." He began to walk down the hall the other way, and Tana wasn't sure whether or not to follow. She didn't want to argue with him, but she knew that her mother used the family room where they stood. But it was his house after all, and she felt awkward standing there, particularly as groans began reaching her from the couple inside. She had five minutes until her cab and for lack of something better to do, she followed Billy down the hall. It was no big deal, and he swung open a door into another room. "That's it." Tana walked to the doorway and stepped in and looked around, realizing instantly that this wasn't where her mother worked. The most dominant thing in the entire room was an enormous bed, covered with gray velvet, trimmed in silk, there was both a gray opossum blanket and a chinchilla one draped across a matching chaise longue. The carpeting was gray too, and there were beautiful prints everywhere. Tana turned to him, looking annoyed.

"Very funny. That's your father's room, isn't it?"

"Yeah. And that's where your old lady works. Hell of a lot of work she does in here, old Jean." Suddenly Tana wanted to grab him by the hair and slap his face, but forcing herself not to say anything she started to walk out of the room, and instead he grabbed her arm, and yanked her back into it, kicking the door closed with his foot.

"Let go of me, you little shit!" Tana tried to pull her arm away, but was amazed to discover the strength he had. He grabbed her brutally by both arms and shoved her against the wall, knocking the air out of her.

"Want to show me what kind of work your mama does,

you little bitch?" She gasped, he was hurting her arms, and tears suddenly came to her eyes, more out of anger than fear of him.

"I'm getting out of here, right now." She attempted to pull herself away from him, but he slammed her hard against the wall, banging her head against it, and she looked into his eyes, and suddenly she was genuinely afraid of him. There was the look of a madman on his face, and he was laughing at her. "Don't be a jerk."

His eyes glinted evilly then, as he crushed her wrists in one powerful hand . . . she had never realized what strength he had . . . and with the other hand, he unzipped his fly and undid his pants, exposing himself, and then grabbing one of her hands in his own, pulling it down toward him. "Grab onto that, you little cunt." She was terrified of him now, her face deathly white, pulling away from him, as he pushed up against her, against the wall, and she pushed him away as hard as she could, getting nowhere, as he laughed at her. And suddenly, in horror, she realized what was happening, as she struggled against him . . . the limp penis he had exposed was getting hard and grinding against her . . . it felt like an evil ugly stump, as he smashed her back against the wall again and again, pulling at her dress suddenly, tearing it along the side, to expose the flesh he wanted to see, and suddenly his hands were all over her, her abdomen, her breasts, her thighs . . . he was pressing hard against her, crushing her, smearing her face with his tongue, breathing alcohol fumes in her face, touching her, holding her, grabbing her . . . he felt as though he were tearing at her, and suddenly his fingers plunged into her, between her legs, as she screamed, and bit him hard on the neck, but he didn't even move back. He just grabbed a hunk of her hair and twisted it around his hand . . . until she felt it would come out by the roots . . . and he bit her face viciously. She flailed at him . . . she attempted to fight him with her legs. She was breathless now, fighting for her life more than her virginity, and suddenly crying, sobbing, gasping for air, she felt him throw her down onto the thick gray carpeting . . . and tear her dress from collar to hem, revealing the last of her, tearing the white lace underpants off too, leaving her brown and bare and beautiful, and suddenly begging him, crying, gnashing her teeth, almost hysterical, as he pushed his pants down, and then kicked them off somewhere onto the carpeting, pressing his full weight on her, pinning her down, and only letting up to tear her flesh again, almost limb from limb, his fingers digging into her, ripping her flesh apart, tearing her, and then sucking at her flesh with his mouth as she cried and howled . . . and each time she attempted to move away from him he would smash her down again until at last she was barely conscious when he entered her, mounting her with all the force he had, plunging into her, as rivers of blood cascaded out onto the thick carpeting, until at last in final orgiastic glory, he exploded atop the barely whining, raggedly breathing girl, her eyes glazed, a trickle of blood coming from her mouth, another from her nose, as Billy Durning stood up and laughed at her, grabbing his own pants off the floor as she didn't move. She looked almost dead as she lay there and he looked down at her.

"Thanks."

And with that, the door opened, and one of Billy's friends walked in. "Christ, what did you do to her?" Tana still hadn't moved, although she could hear voices somewhere far, far away.

"No big deal." Billy shrugged. "Her old lady is my father's hired cunt."

The other boy laughed. "Looks like one of you had a good time at least." It was impossible not to see the sea of blood beneath her on the gray carpeting. "She got her period?"

"I guess." Billy seemed unconcerned as he zipped his pants and she still lay there with her legs spread like a rag doll's, while his friend looked down at her. Billy bent over and slapped her face. "Come on, Tan, get up." She didn't move, and he went into the bathroom, wet a towel and dropped it on her, as though she would know what to do with it, but it was another ten minutes before she slowly rolled over in her own mire and threw up. And he grabbed her by the hair again as the other boy watched, and yelled at her. "Shit, don't do that here, you little pig." He pulled her roughly to her feet and dragged her into the bathroom where she hung over the bowl, and then finally, reached over and slammed the door. It seemed hours before she could revive herself and there were jagged sobs in her throat. Her cab was long since gone and she had missed the last train, but more than that something hideous had happened to her that she knew she would never recover from. She had been raped. She was shaking from head to foot, trembling violently, her teeth were chattering, her mouth was dry, her head ached, and she couldn't begin to figure out how she was ever going to leave the house. Her dress was torn, her shoes were smeared with blood, and as she sat in the bathroom crouching on the floor, the door opened and Billy strode into the room and threw some things at her. She saw a moment later that it was a dress and a pair of shoes that were some of Ann's things. He looked at Tana tentatively now, and she could see how drunk he was. "Get dressed. I'll take you home."

"And then what?" She suddenly screamed at him. "How do you explain to your father about this?" She was hysterical and he glanced behind him into the room.

"About the rug?" He looked nervous now and she got totally hysterical.

"About *me!*"

"That's not my fault, you little tease." The horror of what he was saying to her made her even sicker than she was before, but suddenly all she wanted to do was get out of there, and she didn't care if she had to walk back to New York. She pushed past him, clutching the clothes to her, and dashed into the room where the rape had taken place. Her eyes were wild, her hair matted and tangled, her face streaked with tears, and she bolted naked from the room and smack into his friend, who laughed at her nervously.

"You and Billy had a good time, huh?" He laughed at her and wild eyed, she ran past him, and into a bathroom she knew was there. She pulled on the clothes he had given her, and she ran downstairs. It was too late to catch a train, no point to call a cab. She saw that the musicians were gone, and she ran down the driveway, leaving her torn dress and her handbag behind, but she didn't give a damn. She just wanted to get away from there. She could hitchhike if she had to, stop a police car ... anything ... the tears were caked on her face, and she was breathing hard as she began to run, and then suddenly bright headlights shone on her and she ran harder knowing instinctively that he was coming after her. She could hear his tires on the gravel road, and she began to dart in and out of the trees, crying softly, as the tears rolled into her hair, as he honked the horn and shouted at her.

"Come on, I'll take you home."

She didn't answer him. She just kept running as fast as she could, but he wouldn't go away. He just kept driving after her, zigzagging, following her course on the deserted road until finally she turned and screamed hysterically at him. "Leave me alone!" She stood bent over in the road, crying, sobbing, hugging her knees, and slowly he got out of the car and walked toward her. The night air was beginning to sober him, and he looked different than he had before, no longer crazed, but gray and grim, and he had brought his friend along, who was silently watching them from the passenger seat of Billy's long, sleek, dark green XKE.

"I'll drive you home." He stood in the road, legs spread, the car headlights behind him glaring eerily at them. "Come on, Tan."

"Don't call me that." She looked like a frightened little girl. He had never even been her friend, and now ... and now ... she wanted to scream each time she thought of it, but now she couldn't even scream anymore, and she no longer had the strength to run away from him. Her whole body ached, her head pounded, there was dried blood over her face and on her thighs, and now she stared blankly at him, stumbling along the road, as he reached out and tried to grab her arm, and she screamed at him and darted away again. He stood and stared at her for a moment, and then got back in the car and drove off. He had offered to take her home, if she didn't want to go, to hell with her, and she stumbled along the road, aching from head to foot. Not twenty minutes later he was back again. He screeched to a halt beside her, got out and grabbed her by the arm. She saw that the other boy was no longer in the car, and suddenly she wondered if he was going to rape her again. A wave of terror ran through her as he pulled her toward the car, and she pulled away, but this time he jerked her hard and shouted at her, and she could smell whiskey on his breath again.

"Goddammit, I told you I'd take you home. Now get in the fuckin' car!" He almost threw her onto the seat, and she realized that there was no arguing with him. She was alone with him, and he would do whatever he wanted with her. She had already learned that. She sat bleakly beside him in the XKE, and he roared off into the night, as she waited for him to take her somewhere else to torture her again, but he got on the highway, sank his foot to the floor, and the breeze whipping through the car seemed to sober both of them. He glanced over at her several times, and waved at the box of tissues on the floor. "You'd better clean yourself up before you go home."

"Why?" She looked straight ahead at the empty road. It was after two o'clock, and even her eyes felt numb. Only a few trucks went whizzing by, driving straight through the night.

"You can't go home like that." She didn't answer him, and she didn't turn to look at his face. She still half expected him to stop and try to rape her again, and this time she was expecting it. She would run as fast as she could, across the highway if she dared, and maybe one of the trucks would stop. She still couldn't believe what he had done to her, and she was wondering now if it had somehow been her fault, had she not fought him hard enough, had she done something to encourage him. . . ? They were hideous thoughts as she noticed the powerful sports car begin to weave. She turned and glanced at him, and noticed that he was falling asleep at the wheel. She jerked on his sleeve, and he started and looked at her. "Why the hell'd you do that? You could've caused an accident." She would have liked nothing better for him. She would have liked to see him lying dead by the side of the road.

"You were falling asleep. You're drunk."

"Yeah? So what?" He sounded more tired than surly now, and he seemed all right for a while, until she saw the car weave again, but this time before she had a chance to grab his arm or shake him awake, an enormous trailer truck sped by, and the sports car veered. There was a hideous, grinding shriek of brakes, as the truck jack-knifed and overturned, and miraculously the XKE whizzed just past the cab and came to rest with its nose crushed by a tree. Tana hit her head hard as they stopped, and she sat staring ahead for a long time, and then suddenly she was aware of a soft moaning beside her. His face was covered with blood and she didn't move. She just sat and stared, and then suddenly the door opened and there was a strong pair of hands on her arm, and then she began to scream. Suddenly the events of the endless night had caught up with her and she totally lost control, sobbing and hysterically trying to run from the car, as two passing trucks stopped, and the drivers tried to subdue her until the cops came, but her eyes were uncomprehending and wild. They had cold compresses on Billy's head, and he had a terrible gash over one eye. The police arrived a short time later, followed by an ambulance, and all three victims were taken to the New Rochelle Hospital Medical Center nearby. The truck driver was almost instantly released. His vehicle had suffered more damage than he had, miraculously. Billy was being stitched up. It was also noted that he had been driving under the influence of alcohol, and as his third offence, it would cost him his driver's license, which seemed to worry him more than the wounded eye. Tana's entire body seemed to be covered with blood, but oddly enough the staff noticed that most of it was dried. They couldn't seem to get her to explain what had happened to her, and she hyperventilated each time she tried. A pleasant young nurse gently wiped her off, while Tana just lay on the examining table and cried. They administered a sedative, and by the time her mother arrived at four o'clock she was half asleep.

"What happened. . . ? my God!" She was looking at the bandage on Billy's eye. "Billy, will you be all right?'

"I guess." He smiled sheepishly, and she noticed again what a handsome boy he was, although he had always looked less like his father and more like Marie. And suddenly the smile faded and he looked terrified. "Did you call Dad?"

Jean Roberts shook her head. "I didn't want to frighten him. They told me you were all right when they called, and I thought I'd take a good look at you both first myself."

"Thanks." He glanced over at Tana's dozing form and then shrugged almost nervously. "I'm sorry about . . . that I . . . we wrecked the car. . . ."

"The important thing is that neither of you were badly hurt." She frowned as she looked at Tana's matted blonde hair, but there was no longer any evidence of blood anywhere, and the nurse tried to explain how hysterical Tana had been.

"We gave her a sedative. She should sleep for a while."

Jean Roberts frowned. "Was she drunk?" She already knew that Billy was, but there would be hell to pay if Tana was too, but the young nurse shook her head.

"I don't think she was. Mostly frightened, I think. She got a nasty little bump on her head, but nothing more than that. We don't see any evidence of concussion or whiplash, but I'd keep an eye on her." And as she said the words, hearing them talking around her, Tana woke up, and she looked at her mother as though she had never seen her before, and then silently began to cry, as Jean took her in her arms and made gentle cooing sounds.

"It's all right, baby . . . it's all right. . . ."

She shook her head violently, taking great gulps of air, "No, it's not . . . it's not . . . he . . ." But Billy stood there staring at her, with an evil look in his eye, and she couldn't say the words. He looked as though he would hit her again, and she turned away, choking on her sobs, still feeling his eyes on her. She couldn't look at him again . . . couldn't see him . . . never wanted to see him again. . . .

She lay on the back seat of the Mercedes her mother had driven out, and they took Billy home. And Jean was inside with him for a long time. They threw the last people out, made half a dozen others get out of the pool, tossed two couples out of Ann's bed, and told the group in the pool house to settle down, and as Jean walked back to the car where Tana still was, she knew she had her week's work cut out for her. They had destroyed half the furniture, set fire to some of the plants, spoiled the upholstery, left spots on the rugs, and there was everything from plastic glasses to whole pineapples in the pool. She didn't want Arthur to even see the place until she had had it set to rights again. She got in to the car with a long tired sigh, and glanced at Tana's still form. Her daughter seemed strangely calm now. The sedative had taken effect.

"Thank God they didn't go into Arthur's room." She started the car, and Tana shook her head with a silent no, but she couldn't say the words. "Are you all right?" That was really all that mattered. They could have been killed. It was a miracle they hadn't been. It was all she could think of when the phone rang at three o'clock. She had already been worried sick for several hours, and instinctively, when she had heard the phone, she had known. And she had answered it on the first ring.

"How do you feel?" All she could do was stare at her mother and shake her head. "I want to go home." The tears slid down her cheeks again, and Jean wondered again if she was drunk. It had obviously been a wild night, and Tana had been part of it. She also noticed that she wasn't wearing the same dress she'd been wearing when she left.

"Did you go for a swim?" She sat up, her head reeling, and shook her head, as her mother glanced at her in the mirror and saw the strange look in Tana's eyes. "What happened to your dress?"

She spoke in a cold hard voice that didn't even sound like her to Jean's ears. "Billy tore it off."

"He did what?" She looked surprised, and then smiled. "Did he throw you in the pool?" It was the only image she had of him, and even if he had been a little drunk, he was harmless enough. It was just damn lucky he hadn't hit the truck. It was a good lesson for them both. "I hope you learned a lesson tonight, Tan." She began to sob again at the sound of the nickname Billy had used until finally Jean pulled off the road and stared at her. "What's happening to you? Are you drunk? Did you take drugs?" There was accusation in her voice, in her eyes, and none of that had been there when she drove Billy home. How unfair life was, Tana thought to herself. But her mother just didn't understand what Precious Little Billy Durning had done. She looked straight into her mother's eyes.

"Billy raped me in his father's room."

"*Tana!*" Jean Roberts looked horrified. "How can you say a thing like that? He would never do such a thing!" Her anger was at her own child, not at her lover's son. She couldn't believe a thing like that about Billy, and it was written all over her face as she glared at her only child. "That's a terrible thing to say." It was a terrible thing to do. But Jean only stared at her.

Two lonely tears rolled relentlessly down Tana's cheeks. "He did." Her face crumbled at the memory. "I . . . swear. . . ." She was getting hysterical again as Jean turned and started the car, and this time she did not glance into the back seat again.

"I don't ever want to hear you say a thing like that again, about anyone." Surely not someone they knew . . . a harmless boy they had known for half his life . . . she didn't even care to think about what would make Tana say a thing like that, jealousy perhaps of Billy himself, or Ann, or Arthur. . . . "I never want to hear you say that again. Is that clear?" But there was no answer from the back seat. Tana just sat there, looking glazed. She would never say it again. About anyone. Something inside her had just died.

Chapter 4

The summer sped past Tana easily after that. She spent two weeks in New York, recuperating, while her mother went to work every day. And Jean was concerned about her, but in an odd, uncomfortable way. There seemed to be nothing wrong with her, but she would sit and stare into space, listening to nothing, not seeing her friends. She wouldn't answer the phone when Jean, or anyone else, called. Jean even mentioned it to Arthur at the end of the first week. She almost had the house in Greenwich put to rights again, and Billy and his friends had moved on to Malibu. They had all but destroyed the house at the pool, but the worst damage of all was a section of the rug in Arthur's room which looked as though it had been cut out with a knife. And Arthur had had plenty to say to his son about that.

"What kind of savages are all of you? I ought to be sending you to West Point instead of Princeton for chrissake so they can teach you a thing or two about how to behave. My God, in my day, no one I'd ever known would behave like that. Did you see that carpeting? They tore the whole damn thing up." Billy had looked both subdued and chagrined.

"I'm sorry, Dad. Things got a little out of hand."

"A little? And it's a wonder you and the Roberts girl weren't killed." But on the whole he'd been all right. His eye was still bothering him a little when he left, but the stitches on the eyebrow had already been removed. And he still seemed to be out every night right up until they left for Malibu. "Damn wild kids . . ." Arthur had growled at her. "How's Tana now?" She had mentioned to Arthur several times how oddly Tana had behaved, and she really wondered if she hadn't had a worse blow on the head than they had first thought.

"You know she was almost delirious that first night . . . in fact she was. . . ." She still remembered the ridiculous tale about Billy that Tana had tried to tell. The girl really wasn't all there . . . and Arthur looked worried too.

"Have her looked at again." But when Jean tried to insist, Tana refused. Jean almost wondered if she was well enough to go to New England for her summer job, but on the night before she was due to leave, she quietly packed her bag, and the next morning she came to the breakfast table with a pale, wan, tired face, but for the first time in two weeks, when Jean handed her a glass of orange juice, she smiled, and Jean almost sat down and cried. The house had been like a tomb since the accident. There were no sounds, no music, no laughter, no giggles on the phone, no voices, only dead silence everywhere. And Tana's deadened eyes.

"I've missed you, Tan." At the sound of the familiar name, Tana's eyes filled with tears. She nodded her head, unable to say anything. There was nothing left for her to say. To anyone. She felt as if her life were over. She never again wanted to be touched by a man, and she knew she never would again. No one would ever do to her what Billy Durning had done, and the tragedy was that Jean couldn't face hearing it, or thinking of it. In her mind, it was impossible, so it didn't exist, it hadn't happened. But the worst of it was that it had. "Do you really think you're up to going to camp?"

Tana had wondered about that herself; she knew that the choice was an important one. She could spend the rest of her life hiding there, like a cripple, a victim, someone shrivelled and broken and gone, or she could begin to move out again, and she had decided to do that. "I'll be all right."

"Are you sure?" She seemed so quiet, so subdued, so suddenly grown up. It was as though the bump on her head in the car accident had stolen her youth from her. Perhaps the fear itself had done that. Jean had never seen such a dramatic change in such a short time. And Arthur kept insisting that Billy had been fine, remorseful, but almost his old self by the time he left for his summer holiday, which was certainly not the case here. "Look, sweetheart, if you don't feel up to it, just come home. You want to start college in the fall feeling strong."

"I'll be all right." It was almost all she said before she left, clinging to her single bag. She took the bus to Vermont as she had twice before. It was a summer job she had loved, but it was different this year, and the others noticed it too. She was quieter, kept to herself, and never seemed to laugh anymore. The only time she talked to anyone at all was with the campers themselves. It saddened the others who had known her before, "Something must be wrong at home. . . ." "Is she sick. . .?", "Wow, she's like a different girl. . . ." Everyone noticed, and no one knew. And at the end of the summer, she got on the bus and went home again. She had made no friends this year, except among the kids, but even with them, she wasn't as popular as she'd been before. She was even prettier than she'd been in previous years but all of the kids agreed this time, "Tana Roberts is weird". And she knew herself that she was.

She spent two days at home with Jean, avoided all her old friends, packed her bags for school, and boarded the train with a feeling of relief. Suddenly, she wanted to get far, far from home . . . from Arthur . . . from Jean . . . from Billy . . . from all of them . . . even the friends she'd had at school. She wasn't the same carefree girl who had graduated three months before. She was someone different now, someone haunted and hurt, with scars on her soul. And as she sat on the train and rolled through the south, she slowly began to feel human again. It was as though she had to get far, far from them, from their deceptions, their lies, the things they couldn't see, or refused to believe, the games they played . . . it was as though ever since Billy Durning had forced his way into her, no one could see her anymore. She didn't exist, because they couldn't acknowledge Billy's sin . . . but that was only Jean, she told herself. But who else was there? If her own mother didn't believe her . . . she didn't want to think about it anymore. Didn't want to think about any of it. She was going as far away as she could, and maybe she'd never go home, although she knew that too was a lie. Her mother's last words to her had been, "You'll come home for Thanksgiving, won't you, Tan?" It was as though her mother was afraid of her now, as though she had seen something in her daughter's eyes that she just couldn't face, a kind of bleeding, open, raw pain that she couldn't help and didn't want to be there. She didn't want to go home for Thanksgiving, didn't want to go home ever again. She had escaped their tiny, petty lives . . . the hypocrisy . . . Billy and his barbaric friends . . . Arthur and the years and years he had used Jean . . . the wife he had cheated on . . . and the lies Jean told herself . . . suddenly Tana couldn't stand it anymore, and she couldn't go far enough to get away from them. Maybe she'd never go back . . . never.

. . . She loved the sound of the train, and she was sorry when it stopped in Yolan. Green Hill College was two miles away and they had sent a lumbering old station wagon for her, with an old black driver with white hair. He greeted her with a warm smile, but she looked at him suspiciously as he helped her load her bags.

"You been on the train long, miss?"

"Thirteen hours." She barely spoke to him on the brief drive to the school, and had he ever seemed about to stop the car, she would have leapt out and begun to scream. But he sensed that about her, and he didn't push her by trying to get too friendly with her. He whistled part of the way, and when he got tired of that he sang, songs of the Deep South that Tana had never heard before, and in spite of herself, when they arrived, she smiled at him.

"Thanks for the ride."

"Anytime, miss. Just come on down to the office and ask for Sam, I'll give you a ride anywhere you want to go." And then he laughed the warm black laugh, smiling at her. "There ain't too many places to go around here." He had the accent of the Deep South, and ever since she had gotten off the train she had noticed how beautiful everything was. The tall majestic looking trees, the bright flowers everywhere, the lush grass, and the air still, heavy and warm. One had a sudden urge to just stroll off somewhere quietly, and when she saw the college itself for the first time, she just stood there and smiled. It was all she had wanted it to be. She had wanted to come here to visit the winter before, but she just hadn't had time. Instead, she had interviewed with their travelling representative up North, and gone on what she'd seen in the brochures. She knew that academically they were one of the best schools, but she had actually wanted something more – their reputation, and the legends she had heard about what a fine old school it was. It was old-fashioned, she knew, but in a way that appealed to her. And now as she looked at the handsome white buildings, perfectly kept, with tall columns, and beautiful French windows looking out on a small lake, she almost felt as though she had come home.

She checked in at the reception room, filled in some cards, wrote down her name on a long list, found out what building she'd be living in, and a little while later, Sam was helping her again, loading all of her luggage on an old country cart. It was almost like a trip back in time just being there, and for the first time in months, she felt peaceful again. She wouldn't have to face her mother here, wouldn't have to explain how she felt or didn't feel, wouldn't have to hear the hated Durning name, or see the unknowing pain Arthur inflicted on her mother's face . . . or hear about Billy again . . . just being in the same town with them had stifled her, and for the first month or two after the rape, all she had wanted to do was run away. It had taken all the courage she had to go on to camp that summer anyway, and each day there had been a battle too. She wanted to flinch each time someone came too close, especially the men, but even the boys frightened her now too. At least she didn't have to worry about that here. It was an all-women's school, and she didn't have to attend the dances or proms, or nearby football games. The social life had appealed to her when she had first applied, but she didn't care about that now. She didn't care about anything . . . or at least she hadn't in three months . . . but suddenly . . . suddenly . . . even the air here smelt good, and as Sam rolled the luggage cart along, she looked at him with a slow smile and he grinned at her.

"It's a long way from New York." His eyes seemed to dance, and the nubby white hair looked soft.

"It sure is. It really is beautiful here." She glanced out at the lake and then back at the buildings behind her, fanned out, with still smaller buildings ahead of them. It looked almost like a palatial estate, which was what it had once been, everything was so perfectly manicured, immaculately kept. She was almost sorry her mother couldn't see it now, but perhaps she would eventually.

"It used to be a plantation, you know." He told hundreds of girls that every year. He loved to tell the story to the girls. His grand daddy had been a slave right here, he always bragged, as they looked at him with wide eyes. They were so young and so fine, almost like his own daughter had been, except she was a grown woman now, with children of her own. And these girls would be married and have children soon too. He knew that every year, in the spring, girls came back from everywhere to get married in the beautiful church right there on the grounds, and after graduation ceremonies, there were always at least a dozen who got married in the ensuing days. He glanced at Tana as she loped along at his side, wondering how long this one would last. She was one of the prettiest girls he had ever seen, with long shapely legs, and that face, the shaft of golden hair, and those enormous green eyes. If he'd known her for a while he would have teased her and told her she looked like a movie star, but this one was more reserved than most. He had noticed all along that she was unusually shy. "You been here before?" She shook her head, looking up at the building where he had just stopped the cart. "This is one of the nicest houses we got. Jasmine House. I've already brought five girls here today. There should be about twenty-five or so here in all, and a housemother to keep an eye on all of you," he beamed, "though I'm sure none of you will be needing that." He laughed his deep, rich burst of laughter again, which sounded almost musical, and Tana smiled, helping him with some of the bags. She followed him inside, and found herself in a pleasantly decorated living room. The furniture was almost entirely antique, English and Early

American, the fabrics were flowery and bright, and there were big bouquets of flowers in large handsome crystal vases on several tables and a desk. There was a homey atmosphere as Tana stepped in and looked around, and one of the first things that struck her about the place was that it was ladylike. Everything looked proper and neat, and as though one ought to be wearing a hat and white gloves, and suddenly Tana looked down at her plaid skirt, her loafers and knee socks, and smiled at the woman coming across the room to her in a neat gray suit. She had white hair and blue eyes. She was their housemother, Tana soon learned. She had been housemother of Jasmine House for more than twenty years, she had a gentle Southern drawl, and when her jacket opened, Tana noticed a single strand of pearls. She looked like someone's aunt, and there were deep smile lines around her eyes.

"Welcome to Jasmine House, my dear." There were eleven other houses on campus much like this, "But we like to think that Jasmine is the very best." She beamed at Tana, and offered her a cup of tea as Sam took her bags upstairs. Tana accepted the flowered cup with the silver spoon, declined a plate of bland looking little cakes, and sat looking at the view of the lake, thinking of how strange life was. She felt as though she had landed in a different universe. Things were so different from New York . . . suddenly here she was, far from everyone she knew, drinking tea, eating cakes, talking to this woman with blue eyes and pearls . . . when only three months before she had been lying on Arthur Durning's bedroom floor being raped and beaten by his son. . . . ". . . don't you think, dear?" Tana stared blankly at the housemother, not sure of what she had just said, and demurely nodded her head, feeling suddenly tired. It was so much to take in all at once.

"Yes . . . yes . . . I do. . . ." She wasn't even sure what she was agreeing with, and suddenly all she wanted to do was escape to her room. At last, they finished their tea, set down their cups, and Tana had a sudden urge to laugh, wondering just how much tea the poor woman had had to drink that day, and then as though sensing Tana's impatience to settle in, she led the way to her room. It was up two handsomely curved flights of stairs, on a long hall, with flower prints and photographs of alumnae interspersed. Her room was at the very end of the hall. The walls were a pale pink, the curtains and bedspreads chintz. There were two narrow beds, two very old chests, two chairs, and a tiny corner sink. It was a funny old-fashioned room and the ceiling sloped directly over their beds. The housemother was watching her and seemed satisfied as Tana turned to her with a smile.

"This is very nice."

"Every room in Jasmine House is." She left the room shortly after that, and Tana sat staring at her trunks, not· quite sure what to do, and then she lay down on her bed, looking out at the trees. She wondered if she should wait for her roommate to arrive before simply taking over one of the chests or half of the hanging space, and she didn't feel like unpacking anyway. She was thinking of taking a walk around the lake when she heard a knock on the door and suddenly Old Sam appeared. She sat up quickly on the edge of the bed, and he walked into the room carrying two bags with a strange look on his face. He glanced over at where Tana sat, seemed to shrug, and just looked at her.

"I guess this is a first for us." What is? Tana looked confused as he shrugged again and disappeared, and Tana glanced over at the bags. But there seemed nothing remark-able there, two large navy blue and green plaid bags with railroad tags, a make-up case, and a round hat box, just like the ones filled with Tana's junk. She wandered slowly around the room, wondering when their owner would appear. She expected an endless wait as she imagined the tea ritual, but in the end she was surprised at how quickly the girl appeared. The housemother knocked first, stared into Tana's eyes portentously as she opened the door, and then stood aside, as Sharon Blake seemed to float into the room. She was one of the most striking girls Tana thought she had ever seen, with jet black hair pulled tightly back, brilliant onyx eyes, teeth whiter than ivory in a pale cocoa face that was so finely etched it barely seemed real. Her beauty was so unique, her movements so graceful, her style so marked that she literally took Tana's breath away. She was wearing a bright red coat, and a small hat, and she tossed both swiftly into one of the room's two chairs, to reveal a narrow tube of gray wool dress, the exact same color as her well-made gray shoes. She looked more like a fashion plate than a college girl, and Tana inwardly groaned at the things she had brought. They were all kilts and slacks, old wool skirts that she didn't really care about, a lot of plain shirts, V neck sweaters, and two dresses her mother had bought her at Saks just before she left.

"Tana," the housemother's voice said that she took the introduction *very* seriously, "this is Sharon Blake. She's from the North too. Although not as far north as you. She's from Washington, DC."

"Hello." Tana glanced shyly at her, as Sharon shot her a dazzling smile and extended a hand.

"How do you do."

"I'll leave you two girls alone." She seemed to look at Sharon almost with a look of pain, and Tana with immeasurable sympathy. It cut her to the core to do this to her, but someone had to sleep with the girl, and Tana was a scholarship student after all. It was only fair. She had to be grateful for whatever she got. And the others wouldn't have put up with it. She softly closed the door, and walked downstairs with a determined step. It was the first time this had ever happened at Jasmine House, at Green Hill for that matter, and Julia Jones was wishing that she could have had something a little stronger than tea that afternoon. She needed it. It was a terrible strain after all.

But upstairs Sharon only laughed as she threw herself into one of the room's uncomfortable chairs and looked at Tana's shining blonde hair. They were an interestingly contrasted pair. The one so fair, the other dark. They eyed each other curiously as Tana smiled, wondering what she was doing there. It would have been easier for her to go to a college in the North, than to come here. But she didn't know Sharon Blake yet. The girl was beautiful, there was no doubt about that, and she was expensively dressed. Tana noticed that again, too, as Sharon kicked off her shoes.

"Well," the delicate, dark face broke into a smile again, "what do you think of Jasmine House?"

"It's pretty, don't you think?" Tana still felt shy with her, but there was something appealing about the lovely girl. There was something raw and courageous and bold that stood out on the exquisite face.

"They gave us the worst room, you know." Tana was shocked at that.

"How do you know?"

"I looked as we walked down the hall." She sighed then and carefully took off her hat. "I expected that." And then she looked Tana over appraisingly. "And what sin did you commit to wind up rooming with me?" She smiled gently at Tana. She knew why she was there, she was the only token Negro to be accepted at Green Hill, and she was unusual, of course. Her father was an author of distinguished prose, winner of the National Book Award and the Pulitzer Prize, her mother was an attorney, currently in government, she would be different from most Negro girls. At least they expected her to be . . . although one could never be sure, of course . . . and Miriam Blake had given her oldest child a choice before sending her to Green Hill. She could have gone somewhere in the North, to Columbia in New York, her grades were good enough, or Georgetown closer to home . . . there was UCLA if she was serious about an acting career . . . or there was something important she could do, her mother said . . . "something that will mean something to other girls one day, Sharon." Sharon had stared at her, not sure what she meant. "You could go to Green Hill."

"In the South?" Sharon had been shocked. "They wouldn't even let me in."

Miriam had glared at her. "You don't understand yet, do you, babe? Your father is Freeman Blake. He's written books that people have read all around the world. Do you really think they'd dare to keep you out today?"

Sharon had grinned nervously. "Hell, yes. Mama, they'd tar and feather me before I even unpacked." The thought terrified her. She knew what had happened in Little Rock three years before. She read the news. It had taken tanks and the National Guard to keep black children in a white school. And this wasn't just any little old school they were talking about. This was Green Hill. The most exclusive woman's junior college in the South, where daughters of Congressmen and Senators, and the governors of Texas and South Carolina and Georgia sent their little girls, to get two years of smarts before settling down with boys of their own kind. "Mama, that's nuts!"

"If every black girl in this country thinks like that, Sharon Blake, then a hundred years from now we'll still be sleeping in black hotels, sitting at the back of the bus, and drinking out of water fountains that reek of white boys' piss." Her mother's eyes had blazed at her as Sharon winced. Miriam Blake thought that way, she always had. She had gone to Radcliffe on a scholarship, law school at UC, and ever since, she had fought hard for what she believed, for the underdog, the common man, and she was fighting for her people now. Even her husband admired her. She had more guts than anyone he'd ever known and she wasn't going to stop now. But it frightened Sharon sometimes. It frightened her a lot. As it had when she applied to Green Hill.

"What if I get in?" That scared her most of all and she told her father that. "I'm not like her, Daddy . . . I don't want to prove a point . . . to just get in . . . I want to have friends, to have a good time . . . what she wants me to do is too hard. . . ." Tears had filled her eyes and he understood. But he couldn't change either of them, Miriam and what she expected of them all, or the gentle, lovely girl, who was less fiery, and much more like him. She wanted to be an actress on the Broadway stage one day. And she wanted to go to UCLA.

"You can go there for your last two years, Shar," her mother said, "after you pay your dues."

"Why do I have to pay any dues at all?" she screamed. "Why do I owe anyone two years of my life?"

"Because you live here in your father's house, in a comfortable suburb of Washington, and you sleep in your nice, warm bed, thanks to us, and you've never known a life of pain."

"So beat me, then. Treat me like a slave, but let me do what I want to do!"

"Fine." Her mother's eyes had blazed black fire. "Do what you want. But you'll never walk proud, girl, not if all you think of is yourself. You think that's what they did in Little Rock? They walked every step of the way, with guns pointed at their heads, and the Klan itching for their necks every day. And you know who they did it for, girl? They did it for you. And who're you going to do it for, Sharon Blake?"

"Myself!" She had screamed before running up the stairs to her room and slamming the door. But the words had haunted her. Her mother's words always did. She wasn't an easy person to live with, or to know, or to love. She never made things comfortable for anyone. But in the long run, she made things good. For everyone.

Freeman Blake had tried to talk to his wife that night. He knew how Sharon felt, how badly she wanted to go to the western school. "Why don't you let her do what she wants for a change?"

"Because she has a responsibility. And so do I, and so do you."

"Don't you ever think of anything else? She's young. Give her a chance. Maybe she doesn't want to burn for a cause. Maybe you do enough of that for all of us." But they both knew that that wasn't entirely true. Sharon's brother Dick was only fifteen, but he was Miriam to the core, and he shared most of her ideas, except that his were angrier, more radical. No one was ever going to shove him down, and Freeman was proud of that, but he also recognized that Sharon was a different child. "Just let her be."

They had, and in the end, the guilt had won, as she told Tana later that night. "So here I am." They had been to dinner in the main dining hall, and were back in their room. Sharon in a pink nightgown that had been a going away present from her best friend at home, and Tana in a blue flannel nightgown, her hair in a long silky ponytail as she watched her new friend. "I guess I'll go to UCLA after I finish here." She sighed and looked at the pink polish she had just applied to her toes, and then looked up at Tana again. "She expects so damn much of me."

Tana smiled. "So does mine. She's devoted her whole damn life to doing the right thing for me, and all she wants me to do is come here for a year or two, and then marry some 'nice young man.'" She made a face which suggested she found it an unappealing idea, and Sharon laughed.

"Secretly that's what all mothers think, even mine, as long as I promise to crusade even after I marry him. What does your father say? Thank God for mine, he gets me off the hook whenever he can. He thinks all that stuff is a pain in the ass too."

"Mine died before I was born. That's why she gets so excited about everything. She's always scared to death that everything's going to go wrong, so she clutches whatever security we have, and she expects me to do the same." She looked strangely at Sharon then, "You know, actually your mother sounds more like my cup of tea." The two girls laughed and it was another two hours before they turned off the lights, and by the end of the first week at Green Hill, the two girls were fast friends. They shared much of the same schedule, met for lunch, went to the library, went for long walks around the lake, talking about life, about boys, about parents and friends. Tana told Sharon about her mother's relationship with Arthur Durning, even when he was married to Marie, and how she felt about him. The hypocrisy, the narrow views, the stereotyped life in Greenwich with children and friends and associates all of whom drank too much, in a house that was all for show, while her mother slaved for him night and day, lived for his calls, and had nothing to show for it after twelve years. "I mean, Christ, Shar, it really burns me up. And you know the worst thing about it?" Her eyes smoldered like fiery green rocks as she looked at her friend. "The worst thing is that she accepts all that shit from him. It's all right with her. She'd never walk out on him, and she'd never ask for more. She'll just sit there for the rest of her life, grateful for all the menial things she does for him, totally unaware that he does nothing for her, while she insists that she owes everything to him. What everything? She's worked like a dog all her life for whatever she has, and he treats her like a piece of furniture. . . ." . . . *a paid cunt* . . . Billy's words still rang in her ears and she forced them from her head for the ten thousandth time. "I don't know . . . she just sees things differently, but it makes me mad as hell. I can't go around kissing his ass for the rest of my life. I owe my mother a lot, but I don't owe Arthur Durning a damn thing, and neither does she, but she just doesn't see it that way. She's so damn scared all the time. . . I wonder if she was like that before my father died. . . ." Her mother often told her that she was a lot like him, and her face kind of lit up.

"I like my dad better than my mom." Sharon was always honest about what she felt, especially with Tana. They had told each other countless secrets by the end of the first month, although the one thing Tana had said nothing about was the rape. Somehow she could never quite bring the words to her mouth, and she told herself that it didn't matter anyway, but a few days before the first dance was scheduled on Halloween with a neighboring boys' school, Sharon rolled her eyes and lay back on her bed. "So much for that. What do I do? Go as a black cat, or in a white sheet as a member of the Klan?" The girls had all been careful not to get too close to her. They were polite to her, and none of them stared anymore, and all of the teachers treated her courteously, but it was almost as though they wanted to pretend that she wasn't there, as though by ignoring her, she would disappear. And the only friend she had was Tana, who went everywhere with her, and as a result, Sharon was Tana's only friend. Everyone stayed away from her. If she wanted to play with niggers, she was going to find herself playing alone. Sharon had shouted at her about it more than once. "Why the hell don't you go play with your own kind!" She had tried to sound harsh but Tana had always seen through the ruse.

"Go to hell."

"You're a damn fool."

"Good. That makes two of us. That's why we get along so well."

"Nah," Sharon would grin at her, "we get along because you dress like shit and if you didn't have my wardrobe and my expert advice at hand you'd go out looking like a total jerk."

"Yeah," Tana grinned delightedly, "you're right. But can you teach me to dance?" The girls would collapse on their beds, and you could hear their laughter out in the hall almost every night. Sharon had an energy and a spunk and a fire about her that brought Tana back to life again, and sometimes they just sat around and told jokes and laughed until the tears ran down their cheeks and they cried. Sharon also had a sense of style which Tana had never seen before, and the most beautiful clothes she had ever seen. They were both about the same size and after a while, they just began to shove everything into the same drawers, and wear whatever came to hand.

"So . . . what are you going to be for Halloween, Tan?" Sharon was doing her nails a bright orange this time, and it looked spectacular against her brown skin. She glanced at the wet polish and then over at her friend, but Tana looked noncommittal as she looked away.

"I don't know . . . I'll see. . . ."

"What does that mean?" She was quick to sense something different in Tana's voice, something she had never heard there before, except maybe once or twice when Sharon suspected that she had hit a nerve, but she wasn't yet sure what that nerve was, or precisely where it lay. "You're going, aren't you?"

Tana stood up and stretched, and then looked straight into Sharon's eyes. "No. I'm not."

"For heaven's sake, why not?" She looked stunned. Tana liked having a good time. She had a great sense of humor, she was a pretty girl, she was fun to be around, she was bright. "Don't you like Halloween?"

"It's all right . . . for kids. . . ." It was the first time Sharon had seen her behave like that and she was surprised.

"Don't be a party pooper, Tan. Come on, I'll put your costume together for you." She began digging into the closet they shared, pulling things out and throwing them on the bed, but Tana did not look amused, and that night when the lights were out, Sharon questioned her about it again. "How come you don't want to go to the Halloween Dance, Tan?" She knew that she hadn't had any dates yet, but so far none of them had. For Sharon it was a particularly lonely road, as the only black girl at the school, but she had resigned herself to that when she had agreed to come to Green Hill, and none of them really knew anyone yet. Only a few lucky girls had already won dates, but they were sure to meet a flock of young men at the dance, and Sharon was suddenly dying to get out. "Do you have a steady at home?" She hadn't mentioned it yet, but Sharon knew that it was possible she had held back. There were some things they still hadn't shared. They had avoided the subject of their virginity, or lack of it, which Sharon knew was unusual at Jasmine House. It seemed as though everyone else was anxious to discuss their status as far as that went, but Sharon had correctly sensed Tana's reticence, and she wasn't anxious to discuss the subject herself. But she propped herself up on one elbow now and looked at Tana in the moonlit room. "Tan. . .?"

"No, nothing like that. . . . I just don't like going out."

"Any particular reason why not? You're allergic to men? . . . get dizzy in heels? . . . turn into a vampire after twelve o'clock? . . . although actually," she grinned mischievously, "that might be kind of a neat trick on Halloween."

In the other bed, Tana laughed. "Don't be a jerk. I just don't want to go out, that's all. It's no big deal. You go. Go fall in love with some white guy and drive your parents nuts." They both laughed at the prospect of that.

"Christ, they'd probably kick me out of school. If old Mrs. Jones had her choice, they'd be fixing me up with Old Sam." The housemother had several times looked patronizingly at Sharon, and then glanced at Sam, as though there were some kind of kinship between them.

"Does she know who your father is?" Freeman Blake had just won another Pulitzer, and everyone in the country knew his name, whether they had read his books or not.

"I don't think she can read."

70

"Give her an autographed book when you come back from the holidays." Tana grinned and Sharon roared.

"She'd die. . . ." But it still didn't solve the problem of the Halloween Dance. In the end, Sharon went as an excruciatingly sexy black cat, in a black leotard, her warm cocoa face peeking out, her eyes huge, her legs seeming to stretch forever, and after an initial tense moment or two, someone asked her to dance, and she was on the floor all night long. She had a terrific time, although none of the girls talked to her, and Tana was tucked into bed and sound asleep when she got home just after one o'clock. "Tan? . . . Tana? . . . Tan. . . ? She stirred faintly, lifted her head, and opened one eye with a groan.

"D'ya have a good time?"

"It was great! I danced all night!" She was dying to tell her all about it but Tana had already turned over in bed.

"I'm glad . . . g'night. . . ." Sharon watched the other girl's back and wondered again why she hadn't gone, but nothing more was said, and when Sharon tried to bring it up again the next day, it was obvious that Tana didn't want to talk about it. The other girls began going out after that. The phone in the downstairs hall seemed to ring all the time, but only one boy called Sharon Blake. He asked her to a movie and she went, but when they arrived, the ticket taker wouldn't let them in. "This ain't Chicago, friends," he glared at them and the boy blushed a deep, anguished red, "you're in the South now." He addressed the young man, "Go home and find yourself a decent girl, son." Sharon was reassuring when they left.

"I didn't want to see it anyway. Honest, Tom, it's all right." But the silence was agonizing as he drove her back, and finally when they reached Jasmine House, she turned to him. Her voice was sultry and soft, her eyes kind, her hand like velvet as she touched his. "It really is all right, Tom. I understand. I'm used to this." She took a deep breath. "That's why I came to Green Hill." It seemed an odd thing to say and he looked questioningly at her. She was the first black girl he had ever asked out, and he thought her the most exotic creature he had ever seen.

71

"You came here to be insulted by some turd in a movie house in a one horse town?" He was still burning inside, he was angry for her even if she was not.

"No," she spoke softly, thinking of her mother's words, "I came here to change things, I guess. It starts like this, and it goes on for a long time, and eventually no one gives a damn, black girls and white guys go to movies, ride in cars, walk down streets, eat hamburgers anywhere they want. It happens in New York. Why shouldn't it happen here? People may look, but at least there they don't throw you out. And the only way to get to that point is to start small, like tonight." The boy looked at her, suddenly wondering if he'd been used but somehow he didn't think he had. Sharon Blake wasn't like that, and he had already heard who her father was. You had to be impressed by someone like that. And he admired her more after what she had just said. It confused him a little bit, but he knew that there was truth in it.

"I'm sorry we didn't get in. Why don't we try again next week?"

She laughed at that. "I didn't mean that we had to change it all at once." But she liked his spunk. He was getting the idea, and maybe her mother hadn't been so wrong.

"Why not? Sooner or later that guy'll get tired of kicking us out. Hell, we can go to the coffee shop . . . the restaurant across town. . . ." The possibilities were limitless and Sharon was laughing at him, as he helped her out of the car and walked her into Jasmine House. She offered him a cup of tea, and they were going to sit in the living room for a while, but the looks they got from the other couples sitting there were so ominous that eventually Sharon got up. She walked him slowly to the door, and for a moment she looked sad. It would have been so much easier at UCLA . . . anywhere in the North . . . anywhere but here. . . . Tom was quick to sense her mood, and he whispered as he stood in the open door, "Remember . . . it doesn't happen overnight." He touched her cheek then and was gone, as she watched him drive away . . . he was right of course . . . it didn't happen overnight.

And as she walked upstairs, she decided that it hadn't

been a totally wasted night. She liked Tom, and wondered if he would call her again. He was a good sport.

"Well? Did he propose?" Tana was grinning at her from the bed as Sharon walked in, and groaned.

"Yeah. Twice."

"That's nice. How was the movie?"

Sharon smiled. "Ask someone else."

"You didn't go?" She was surprised.

"They didn't let us in . . . you know . . . white boy . . . brown girl . . . 'Find yourself a *decent* girl, son. . . .'" She pretended to laugh but Tana could see the pain in her eyes, and she frowned.

"The shits. What did Tom say?"

"He was nice. We sat downstairs for a while when we got back, but that was even worse. There must be seven Snow Whites sitting downstairs with their Prince Charmings, and all of them had their eyes glued on us." She sighed and sat down, looking at her friend. "Shit . . . my mother and her bright ideas . . . for about a minute outside the movie house I felt very noble and brave and pure, and by the time we got back, I decided it was really a huge pain in the ass. Hell, we can't even go out for a hamburger. I could starve to death in this town."

"Not if you went out with me, I'll bet." They hadn't gone out to eat yet, they were too comfortable where they were, and the food was surprisingly good at school. They had both already gained three or four pounds, much to Sharon's chagrin.

"Don't be so sure, Tan. I'll bet they'd raise hell if I tried to go somewhere with you too. Black is black and white is white, no matter how you look at it."

"Why don't we try?" Tana looked intrigued, and the next night they did. They walked slowly into town, and stopped for a hamburger and the waitress gave them a long, slow, ugly look and then walked away without serving them, as Tana looked at her in shock. She signalled for her again, and the woman appeared not to see, until finally Tana walked over to her, and asked if they could order their dinner now, and the waitress looked at her with chagrin.

She spoke in a low voice so that Sharon wouldn't hear. "I'm sorry, honey. I can't serve your friend. I was hoping you two'd get the idea."

"Why not? She's from Washington," as though that would make a difference, ". . . her mother is an attorney and her father has won the Pulitzer twice. . . ."

"That don't make no difference here. This ain't Washington. It's Yolan." Yolan, South Carolina, home of Green Hill.

"Is there anywhere in town we can eat?"

The waitress looked nervously at the tall, green eyed blonde, there was a hardness in her voice that suddenly frightened her. "There's a place for her just down the street . . . and you could eat here."

"I mean together," Tana's eyes were as hard as green steel, and for the first time in her life she felt something tighten in her spine. She almost wanted to hit someone. It was a feeling she hadn't known before, an unreasoning, helpless rage. "Is there anyplace in this town where we can eat together, without taking the train to New York?" Tana glared at her, and slowly the waitress shook her head. But Tana wasn't moving an inch. "Okay, then I'll have two cheeseburgers, and two Cokes."

"No, you won't." A man appeared from the kitchen behind where they stood. "You'll go back to that damn fancy school you two come from." They were easily spotted in Yolan. Sharon's clothes alone were enough to draw attention anywhere. She was wearing a skirt and sweater her mother had bought her at Bonwit Tellers in New York. "And you can eat anything you damn well please there. I don't know what's gotten into them over there, but if they choose to let niggers into the school, then let them feed 'em over at Green Hill, we don't gotta feed 'em here." He looked pointedly at Tana, then at Sharon where she sat, and it was as though an enormous force had entered the room, and for a minute Tana thought he might physically throw them out. She hadn't been as frightened or as angry since she'd been raped.

And then, ever so quietly, and in her graceful, long-legged, ladylike way, Sharon stood up. "Come on, Tan." Her voice was a sexy purr, and for an instant, Tana saw the man's eyes almost paw at her and she wanted to slap his face. It reminded her of something she never wanted to think of again, and a moment later she followed Sharon out.

"Son-of-a-bitch. . . ." Tana was fuming as they walked slowly back to school, but Sharon was amazingly calm. It was the same feeling she had had the night before, with Tom, when they hadn't let them in to the movie house. For an instant, there had been a quiet surge of power, an understanding of why she was there, and then depression had set in. But tonight, the depression hadn't hit her yet.

"Life is strange, isn't it? If this were in New York or LA, or almost anywhere else, no one would give a damn. But down here, it's all important that I'm black, you're white. Maybe my mother is right. Maybe it is time for a crusade. I don't know, I always thought that as long as I was comfortable, it didn't matter if things like that were happening to someone else. But all of a sudden that someone else is me." Suddenly she knew why her mother had insisted on her coming here, and for the first time since she'd arrived, she wondered if she'd been right. Maybe she did belong here after all. Maybe she owed it to someone else for all the time that she had been comfortable. "I don't know what to think, Tan. . . ."

"Neither do I. . . ." They were walking along side by side. "I don't think I've ever felt so helpless or been so mad. . . ," And then suddenly Billy Durning's face came to mind, and she visibly winced, "Well . . . maybe once. . . ."

They suddenly felt closer than they ever had before. Tana almost wanted to put an arm around her to protect her from more hurt, as Sharon glanced over at her with a gentle smile. "When was that, Tan?"

"Oh a long time ago. . . ." She tried to smile, ". . . like five months. . . ."

"Oh yeah . . . a *real* long time ago. . . ." The two girls exchanged a smile and walked on as a car sped by, but no one bothered them, and Tana wasn't afraid. No one would ever do to her again what Billy Durning did. She would kill them first. And there was a strange ugly look in her eyes as Sharon glanced at her. "Must've been pretty bad."

"It was."

"Wanna talk about it?" Her voice was as soft as the charcoal gray night, and they walked along in silence for a time as Tana thought. She had never wanted to tell anyone about it before, not since she'd tried to tell her mom.

"I don't know."

Sharon nodded, as though she understood. Everyone had one of those. She had one herself. "It's okay, Tan." But as she said the words, Tana looked at her, and suddenly the words burst from her, almost of their own accord.

"Yeah, I do. . . ." And then, "I don't know . . . how do you talk about something like that?" She began to walk faster as though to run away, and Sharon followed her easily on her long, graceful legs; unconsciously Tana ran a hand through her hair nervously, looked away, and began to breathe harder than she had before. "There's nothing much to say. . . . I went to a party after I graduated in June . . . my mother's boss's house . . . he has this real little shit of a son . . . and I told my mother I didn't want to go. . . ." Her breath was coming in little short gasps and Sharon knew she wasn't aware of it as they hurried along. She knew that whatever it was, it was torturing the girl, and it would be better if she got it out. "Anyway, she said I had to go anyway . . . she always says that . . . that's the way she is, about Arthur Durning anyway, and his kids . . . she's blind to what they are, and . . ." the words stopped, and they walked on, hurrying, hurrying, as though she could still run away, and Sharon kept pace, watching her as she struggled with the memories and then began to speak again, ". . . anyway, this dumb boy picked me up and we got there . . . to the party, I mean . . . and everyone got drunk . . . and the dumb guy who brought me got drunk and disappeared and I was wandering around the house . . . and Billy . . . Arthur's son . . . asked me if I wanted to see the room where my mother worked, and I knew where it was. . . ." There were tears running down her cheeks now, but she didn't feel them in the wind, and Sharon didn't say anything to her, "and he

76

took me to Arthur's bedroom instead and everything was gray . . . gray velvet, gray satin . . . gray fur . . . even the rug on the floor was gray," it was all she could remember, the endless field of gray and her blood on the floor afterwards and Billy's face, and then the accident, she could barely breathe thinking of it, and she pulled at the neck of her shirt as she began to run, sobbing now, as Sharon followed her, keeping close, staying near. She wasn't alone anymore, there was a friend running through the nightmare with her and it was as though she sensed that as she went on, ". . . and Billy started to slap me and he pushed me down . . . and everything I did. . .", she remembered the helplessness again now, the desperation she felt, and then in the night air she screamed and then she stopped, burying her face in her hands, ". . . and I couldn't do anything to make him stop . . . I couldn't. . . ." Her whole body was shaking now as Sharon took her quietly in her arms and held her tight, ". . . and he raped me . . . and he left me there with blood all over me . . . my legs and my face . . . and then I threw up . . . and later he followed me all down the road and he made me get in his car and he almost hit this truck," the words just wouldn't stop now as she cried and Sharon began to cry with her, "and we hit a tree instead and he cut his head and there was blood all over him too and they took us to the hospital and then my mother came . . ." And suddenly she stopped again, and with her face ravaged by the memory she had tried to flee for five months, she looked up into Sharon's eyes, "and when I tried to tell her, she wouldn't believe anything I said . . . she said Billy Durning wouldn't do a thing like that." The sobs were deep and wracking now, but she looked better than she had before and Sharon dried her eyes.

"I believe you, Tan."

Tana nodded, looking like a bereft little girl. "I never want anyone to touch me again."

She knew exactly how Tana felt, but not for the same reasons as her friend. She hadn't been raped. She had gladly given it, to the boy she loved. "My mother never believed a single word I said. And she never will. The Durnings are gods to her."

"All that matters is that you're okay, Tan." They sat down on a tree stump, and Sharon offered her a cigarette, and for once Tana took a puff. "And you are okay, you know. A lot more so than you think." She smiled gently at her friend, deeply moved by her confidence, and she wiped the tears from her cheeks as Tana smiled at her.

"You don't think I'm awful because of that?"

"That's a dumb thing to ask. It's no reflection on you, Tan."

"I don't know . . . sometimes I think it is . . . as though I could have stopped him if I tried hard enough." It felt good just to say the words, just to get them out. They had haunted her for months.

"Do you really believe that, Tan? Do you really think you could have stopped him? Tell the truth."

She shook her head. "No."

"Then don't torture yourself. It happened. It was horrible. Worse than that. It was probably the worst thing that'll ever happen to you in your whole life, but no one will ever do that to you again. And it wasn't really you he touched. He couldn't touch the real you, no matter what, Tan. Just cut it off. Sump the memory. And move on."

"That's easy to say," Tana smiled tiredly, "but not so easily done. How do you forget something like that?"

"You make yourself. You don't let it destroy you, Tan. That's the only time a guy like that wins. He's sick. You're not. Don't make yourself sick over what he did. As awful as it was, put it out of your mind, and move on."

"Oh Sharon. . . ." She sighed and stood up, looking down at her friend. It was a beautiful night. "What makes you so smart, for a kid?"

Sharon smiled, but her eyes were serious tonight, almost sad, as Tana looked down at her. "I have my secrets too."

"Like what?" Tana felt calmer now than she ever had in her life, it was as though a raging animal had been released from her, as though Sharon had let it out of its cage and set it free, and Tana was finally at peace again. Her mother hadn't been able to do that for her five months before, but this girl had, and she knew that whatever else happened after that,

78

they would always be friends. "What happened to you?" Tana searched her eyes, knowing now that there was something there. And she was sure of it when Sharon looked up at her. She didn't mince any words. She had never told anyone, but she had thought about it a lot, and she and her father had talked about it one night before she left for Green Hill. He had told her the same thing she had just told Tana, that she couldn't let it destroy her life. It had happened. And now it was done. And she had to let it stay that way, and move on, but she wondered if she ever would.

"I had a baby this year."

For an instant Tana's breath caught and she looked at Sharon in shock. "You did?"

"Yeah. I've been going with the same boy at home since I was fifteen and when I was sixteen he gave me his senior ring . . . I don't know, Tan . . . it kind of seemed so cute . . . he looks like an African god, and he's smart as hell, and he dances . . ." she looked pretty and young as she thought of him. . . . "He's at Harvard now," her eyes grew sad, "but I haven't talked to him in almost a year. I got pregnant, I told him, and he panicked, I guess. He wanted me to have an abortion at this doctor's his cousin knew, and I refused . . . hell, I'd heard about girls who died. . . ." Her eyes filled with tears at the memory, and she forgot that Tana was standing there, looking down at her. "I was going to tell my mom, but . . . I just couldn't . . . I told my father instead . . . and then he told her . . . and everybody went nuts . . . and they called his parents, and everyone cried and screamed, my mother called him a nigger . . . and his father called me a slut . . . it was the worst night in my life, and when it was all over, my parents gave me a choice. I could have an abortion at a doctor's my mother had found out about, or I could have the baby and give it up. They said," she took a deep gulp of air as though this were the worst part, "that I couldn't keep it . . . that it would ruin my life. . .", her whole body shook, "to have a baby at seventeen . . . and I don't know why but I decided to have the baby, I think because I thought that Danny would change his mind . . . or my parents would . . . or a miracle would happen . . . but

79

nothing did. I lived in a home for five months and I kept up with all the work for my senior year, and the baby was born on April nineteenth . . . a little boy. . . ." She was trembling and Tana wordlessly reached out and took her hand, "I wasn't supposed to see him at all . . . but I did once . . . he was so little. . . . I was in labor for nineteen hours and it was horrible and he only weighed six pounds. . . ." Her eyes were a thousand miles away thinking of the little boy she would never see again, and she looked up at Tana now, "He's gone, Tan," she whimpered almost like a child and in many ways she still was a child. They both were. "I signed the final papers three weeks ago. My mother drew them up . . . some people adopted him in New York. . . ." She couldn't stop the sobs as she bent her head, "Oh God, Tan, I hope they're good to him . . . I never should have let him go . . . and all for what?" She looked angrily up at her friend, "For this? To come to this dumb school to prove a point, so that other colored girls can come here one day. So what?"

"That had nothing to do with this. They wanted you to have a fresh start, with a husband and a family at the right time."

"They were wrong, and so was I. You'll never know what it felt like . . . that emptiness when I went home . . . with nothing . . . with no one . . . nothing will ever replace that." She took a deep breath. "I haven't seen Danny since I went into the home in Maryland . . . and I'll never know where the baby is. . . . I graduated with my class . . . ," with a lead weight in her heart, ". . . and no one knew what I felt. . . ." Tana shook her head, watching her. They were both women now. It had been hard earned, hard won, and it was too soon to know if things would get better in time, but one thing they both knew as they walked slowly home, and that was that they each had a friend. Tana pulled Sharon off the stump, and they hugged each other tight, their tears fell on each other's cheeks, each feeling the other's pain, as much as they could.

"I love you, Shar." Tana looked at her with her gentle smile, and Sharon dried her eyes.

"Yeah . . . me too. . . ."

And they walked home arm in arm, in the silent night, went back to Jasmine House, got undressed and into their beds, each with her own thoughts.

"Tan?" It was Sharon's voice in the dark room.

"Yeah?"

"Thanks."

"For what? Listening. That's what friends are for . . . I need you too."

"My father was right, you know. You've got to move on in life."

"I guess." But how? "Did he have any suggestions about how to pull that off?"

Sharon laughed at that. "I'll have to ask him that." And then suddenly, she had an idea. "Why don't you ask him yourself? Why don't you come home for Thanksgiving with me?"

Tana mulled it over from her bed, with the beginnings of a smile. She liked the idea. "I don't know what my mother will say." But all of a sudden she wasn't sure she cared, and if she did, it wasn't as much as she would have cared six months before. Maybe it was time to try her wings and do what she wanted to do this time. "I'll call her tomorrow night."

"Good." Sharon smiled sleepily and turned over in her bed, with her back to her friend. "G'night, Tan. . . ." And a moment later, they were both asleep, more at ease than either of them had been in months, Tana's hands cast childlike above the blonde hair, and Sharon cuddled up into a little black purring ball. Even the long legs seemed to disappear and she looked like a kitten as she slept peacefully.

Chapter 5

Jean Roberts was disappointed when her daughter called to say that she had decided not to come home for Thanksgiving.

"Are you sure?" She didn't want to insist, but she would have preferred it if Tana were coming back. "You don't know this girl very well. . . ."

"Mother, I live with her. We share the same room. I know her better than I've known anyone in my life."

"Are you sure her parents won't mind?"

"Positive. She called them this afternoon. They have a room for me, and she said they were delighted that she was bringing someone home." Of course they were. From what Sharon had said, it proved Miriam's point that Sharon could be happy at Green Hill, even if she was the only black girl there, and now she was bringing one of "them" home, the ultimate proof of how well they had accepted her. They didn't know that Tana was her only friend, that there wasn't a single place in Yolan where she could be served, that she hadn't been able to go to a movie since she'd arrived, and even in the cafeteria at school, the girls avoided her. But, according to Sharon, even if they had known, Miriam would have felt it proved even more that Sharon was needed there. "They" had to accept Negroes one day, and the time was now. It was a good challenge for Sharon, particularly after last year, this would keep her from dwelling on herself, Miriam Blake thought, it would give her something else to think about, or so she had said. "Really, they said it was fine."

"All right, then be sure you invite her up sometime during the Christmas holidays." Jean smiled into the phone, "In fact, I have a little surprise for you. Arthur and I were going to tell you over Thanksgiving. . . ." Tana's heart stopped.

Was he finally marrying her? She was robbed of speech as her mother went on. "Arthur made it possible for you to have a little 'coming out' party of your own. There's a small cotillion here in town . . . well, not a cotillion really, but a deb party of sorts, and Arthur put up your name, I mean you did go to Miss Lawson's after all, dear, and . . . you're going to be a debutante, sweetheart. Isn't that wonderful?" For a moment, no words came to Tana's mind. It didn't seem particularly wonderful at all, and once again her mother would be kissing Arthur Durning's feet . . . marry her . . . what a joke. How could she have thought a thing like that . . . a "cotillion of sorts" . . . shit. . . . "Why don't you invite your new friend to come up then?" Tana almost choked. *Because my new friend is black, Mom.*

"I'll ask, but I think she's going away over the holidays." Shit. A debutante. And who would her escort be? Billy Durning? The son-of-a-bitch.

"You don't sound very excited, sweetheart." There was disappointment in Jean Roberts' voice, both because Tana wouldn't be coming home, and because she didn't sound very excited about the party Arthur had arranged. He knew how much it meant to Jean. Ann had come out at the International Ball four years before, of course, not at a small deb party like this, but nonetheless it would be a wonderful experience for Tana to have, or at least Jean thought it would.

"I'm sorry, Mom. I guess I'm just surprised."

"It is a beautiful surprise, isn't it?" No. She didn't really care. Things like that didn't matter to her. They never had. All the social nonsense of the Durnings' world seemed irrelevant to her, but it meant so much to Jean. It always had, ever since she had fallen in love with him. "You'll have to think of an escort for the dance. I was hoping Billy could," Tana felt her heart pound and her chest get tight, "but he's going skiing in Europe with friends. In Saint Moritz, the lucky boy," . . . lucky boy . . . *he raped me, Mom.* . . . "You'll just have to think of someone else. Someone suitable, of course." Of course. *How many other rapists do we know?*

83

"It's too bad I can't go alone." Tana's voice sounded dead at her end of the phone.

"That's a ridiculous thing to say." Jean sounded annoyed. "Well, anyway, don't forget to invite your friend . . . the one you're going home for Thanksgiving with."

"Sure." Tana smiled. If she only knew. Jean Roberts would have died if Tana had invited a black friend to the little "coming out" party Arthur had arranged. It almost amused Tana to think of it, but she would never have taken advantage of Sharon like that. They were all a bunch of rude pricks. She knew that even her mother wasn't ready for that. "What'll you do for Thanksgiving, Mom? Will you be all right?"

"I'll be fine. Arthur had already invited us to Greenwich for the day."

"Maybe now that I won't be there, you can spend the night." There was a dead silence on the phone, and Tana regretted the words. "I didn't mean it like that."

"Yes, you did."

"Well, what difference does it make? I'm eighteen years old now. It's not a secret. . . ." Tana felt sick as she thought of the endless gray room where . . . "I'm sorry, Mom."

"Take care of yourself." She drew herself up. She would miss seeing her, but she had a lot to do now, and Tan would be home in a month anyway. "And don't forget to thank your friend for having you there." Tana smiled to herself, it was like being seven years old again. Maybe it always would be.

"I will. Have a good Thanksgiving, Mom."

"I shall. And I'll thank Arthur for you." Jean said the words pointedly and Tana looked blank at her end.

"What for?"

"The ball, Tana, the ball . . . I don't know if you realize it yet, but something like that is very important for a young girl, and it's not something that I could provide for you myself." Important . . . ? Important to whom . . . ? "You have no idea what something like this means." Tears stung Jean Roberts' eyes. In some ways, it was a dream come true. Andy and Jean Roberts' little girl, the baby Andy had never

84

seen, would be coming out in New York society, and even if it was on the fringe, it was an important event for both of them . . . for Tana . . . and especially for Jean . . . it would be the most important moment in her life. She remembered Ann's coming out ball. She had planned every exquisite detail and had never thought that one day Tana would be coming out too.

"I'm sorry, Mom."

"You'd better be. And I think you ought to write Arthur a nice note. Tell him what it means to you." She wanted to scream into the phone. What the hell does it mean? That she'd find a rich husband some day, that they could mark it on her pedigree? Who cared? What accomplishment was that, to curtsy at a dumb ball, being gaped at by a lot of drunks? She didn't even know who she was going to take with her, and she shuddered at the thought. She had gone out with half a dozen different boys during her last two years at school, but there had never been anyone serious, and after what had happened in Greenwich in June, there was no one she wanted to go out with at all.

"I have to go, Mom." She was suddenly desperate to get off the phone, and when she returned to her room, she looked depressed and Sharon looked up. She was doing her nails again. It was an eternal process with both of them. Recently they had both tried beige, "Show Hat" by Fabergé.

"She said no?"

"She said yes."

"So? You look like someone just burst your balloon."

"I think she did." Tana sat down on her bed with a thump. "Shit. She got her damn friend to sign me up for some dumb coming out ball. Jesus Christ, Shar, I feel like a complete fool."

Sharon looked up at her and started to laugh. "You mean you're going to be a debutante, Tan?"

"More or less." Tana looked embarrassed and groaned at her friend. "How could she do that to me?"

"It might be fun."

"For who? And what the hell's the point? It's like a big cattle drive. They shove you around in a white dress and

85

show you off to a lot of drunks, and you're supposed to find a husband somewhere in the bunch. Pretty cute, huh?" She looked sick, and Sharon put her nail polish away.

"Who're you going to take?"

"Don't ask. She wanted Billy Durning to be my escort, of course, but thank God he'll be out of town."

"Be grateful for that." Sharon looked pointedly at her.

"I am. But the whole thing sounds like a farce."

"So are a lot of things in life."

"Don't be so cynical, Shar."

"Don't be so chicken, Tan. It'll do you good.'

"Says who?"

"Says I." Sharon advanced toward her and tried to stare her down. "You live like a nun around here."

"So do you. So what?"

"I don't have any choice." Tom had never called her again, it was more than he could cope with, Sharon knew, and in truth she understood. She hadn't expected more of him. But it didn't make her life very interesting at Green Hill. "You do."

"Never mind."

"You've got to start going out."

"No, I don't." Tana looked her right in the eye. "I don't have to do a goddamn thing I don't want to do. I'm eighteen years old, and I'm free as a bird."

"A lame duck." Sharon stared her down. "Get out there again, Tan." But Tana said nothing at all. She walked into the bathroom they shared with the next room, locked the door, ran a bath, and didn't come out for an hour. "I meant what I said." Sharon's voice was husky in the darkened room, once they were both in their beds.

"About what?"

"You should start going out again."

"So should you."

"I will one of these days." Sharon sighed. "Maybe over the holidays when I'm home. There's no one for me to go out with here." And then she laughed. "Hell, Tan, I don't know what I'm complaining about. At least I've got you."

Tana smiled at her and they chatted for a few minutes and then drifted off to sleep.

The following week Tana went home to Washington with her. They were met at the train by Sharon's father, Freeman Blake, and Tana was instantly struck by how tall and handsome he was. He was a regal looking man, with a proud, beautifully carved, almost mahogany face, broad shoulders, and Sharon's same endlessly long legs. He had a warm smile, brilliantly white teeth, and he was quick to pull his daughter into his arms and hold her tight. He knew just how much she'd been through in the last year, and she'd come through it like a champ, just as he'd known she would, and he was desperately proud of her.

"Hi, baby, how's school?" She rolled her eyes, and turned quickly toward her friend.

"Tana, this is my dad, Freeman Blake. Daddy, this is Tana Roberts, my roommate at Green Hill." He gave Tana's hand a powerful shake and she was magnetized by his eyes and the sound of his voice on the way home. He was filling Sharon in on all the local news, her mother's appointment to an even more important post, her brother Dick's big new romance, the remodelling of the house, the neighbor's new child, his new book. It was a warm friendly patter that touched Tana's heart, and she felt envious of the life that Sharon obviously had. And she felt it even more at dinner that night in the handsome colonial dining room. They had a beautiful house with a huge lawn and back yard, three cars in the garage, one of which was a Cadillac Freeman drove, despite the rude things his friends said. But he admitted that he had always wanted a Cadillac convertible and he had one now after all these years. They were obviously all four closely knit, and Tana found Miriam more than a little formidable. She was so intelligent and so direct that it took one's breath away, and she seemed to constantly expect the ultimate of everyone. One was never safe from her questions, her demands, and her ever searching gaze.

"See what I mean?" Sharon said when they were alone upstairs. "It's like being on the witness stand, just having dinner with her." She had wanted to know everything

Sharon had done in the last two months, and she was interested in both the incident with Tom at the movie house, and the one at the coffee shop with Tana after that.

"It's just that she cares so much, Shar . . . about everything!"

"I know that. And it drives me nuts. Daddy is just as smart as she is for chrissake, and he's so much gentler about everything." He was that, he told exquisite tales, made everyone laugh, and he had a way of making everyone comfortable, of bringing them closer together and forming an irresistible bond. Tana had noticed it all night long and she thought him the most remarkable man she had ever met.

"He's the most incredible man, Shar."

"I know."

"I read one of his books last year. I'm going to go home now and read them all."

"I'll give them to you."

"Only if I can have an autographed set." They both laughed, and a moment later, Miriam knocked at the door, anxious to know that they were all right.

"Do you have everything you need?" Tana smiled almost shyly at her.

"I do. Thank you very much, Mrs. Blake."

"Not at all. We're so glad you could come." The smile was even more dazzling than Shar's, and the eyes were driving, omniscient, almost frightening they plunged so deep and so hard. "How do you like Green Hill?"

"I do. Very much. The professors are pretty interesting." But there was a lack of enthusiasm in her voice which Miriam picked up at once.

"But?"

Tana smiled. She was sharp. Very sharp. "The atmosphere isn't as warm as I thought it would be."

"Why is that?"

"I don't know. The girls seem to stay in cliques."

"And the two of you?"

"We're together most of the time." Sharon looked at Tana and smiled, and Miriam didn't seem displeased. She thought that Tana was a bright girl, and there was a lot of potential there. Far more than Tana herself knew. She was quick, she was bright, she was funny at times, but cautious, laced up. She would have to open up one day, and when she did, God only knew what would be there.

"Maybe that's your problem then, girls. Tana, how many other friends do you have at Green Hill?"

"Just Shar. We're in class together most of the time. We share the same room."

"And you're probably being punished for that. I'm sure you realize that. If your closest friend is the only Negro girl there they're going to penalize you, you know."

"What for?"

"Don't be naive."

"Don't be so cynical, Mom." Sharon sounded suddenly annoyed.

"Maybe it's time you both grew up."

"What the hell's that supposed to mean?" Sharon lashed out at her. "Hell, I've been home for nine hours and you're already on my back with your speeches and your crusades."

"I'm not making any speeches. I'm just telling you to face facts." She looked at them both then. "You can't hide from the truth, girls. It isn't easy being black today . . . or a black girl's friend . . . you're both going to have to realize that and be willing to pay the price if you expect the friendship to last."

"Can't you do anything without turning it into a political crusade, Mom?"

Miriam looked at her and then at her friend. "I want you to do something for me, both of you, before you go back to school on Sunday night. There's a man I know speaking this Sunday in Washington. He's one of the most extraordinary men I've ever known, Martin Luther King, and I want you to come listen to him with me."

"Why?" Sharon was still glaring at her.

"Because it's something neither of you will ever forget."

And as they rode back toward South Carolina late that night, Tana was still thinking of it. Miriam Blake had been right. He was the most visionary man Tana had ever listened to. He made everyone else seem stupid and blind, and it was hours before she could even talk about what she had heard. Simple words about being black and being a black man's friend, about civil rights and the equality of everyone, and afterwards they had sung a song, swaying together, arms crossed, holding hands. She looked at Sharon an hour after they left Washington.

"He was amazing, wasn't he?"

Sharon nodded, thinking of his words again. "You know, it feels dumb just going back to school. I feel as though I should be doing something." She leaned her head back against the seat and closed her eyes, and Tana stared out into the dark night as they rode into the South. It seemed to make his words even more important than they had been. This was where it was happening, where people were being hurt, and ignored, and abused. And as the thoughts wandered through her head, she thought of the debutante party her mother had set up, and it was as though the two thoughts were so diametrically opposed that they just wouldn't fit into her head at the same time. When Sharon opened her eyes again, Tana was looking at her.

"What are you going to do?" One had to do something after hearing him. There was no choice at all. Even Freeman Blake had agreed.

"I don't know yet." Sharon looked tired, but she had been thinking of it since they'd left Washington, of what she could do to help . . . in Yolan . . . in Green Hill . . . "What about you?"

"I don't know." Tana sighed. "Anything I can, I guess. But I'll tell you, after hearing Dr. King speak, I know one thing . . . that party my mother is forcing me into in New York is the dumbest thing I've ever done."

Sharon smiled. She couldn't really disagree now, but there was another side to it as well. A more small-scale, human one. "It'll do you good."

"I doubt that." The two girls exchanged a smile, and rode on into the South until they reached Yolan, and took one of the town's two cabs to Green Hill.

Chapter 6

The train roared into Pennsylvania Station on December 21st just after two o'clock in the afternoon and there was a light snow falling as Tana watched. It made everything look Christmasy and almost like a fairy tale, and yet as she gathered her things, fought her way through the station and went outside to hail a cab, she realized again how depressed she was about coming home. It made her feel instantly guilty toward Jean, and she knew that she wasn't being fair, but she would rather have been anywhere, than on her way home to her own coming out dance. And she knew how excited her mother was. For the past two weeks, she had called Tana almost every night, about the guests, the flowers, the table decor, her date, her dress. She had picked the dress out for Tana herself, an exquisite white silk with white satin trim and tiny little white beads embroidered in floral patterns around the hem. It had cost a fortune, and Arthur had told her to charge it to his account at Saks.

"He's so good to us, sweetheart. . . ." As she rode home to the apartment in the cab, Tana could close her eyes and imagine her mother's face as she said the words . . . why, why was she so everlastingly grateful to him? What on earth did he do for her, except let her work her fingers to the bone, and wait for him all those times he never came when Marie was still alive . . . and even now, everything else always seemed to come first with him. And if he loved Jean so much, why the hell didn't he marry her? It depressed Tana to think about that too. Everything was such a goddamn farce . . . her mother and Arthur, how "good" the Durnings were to them, yeah, like the way Billy had been good to her . . . and the party she would have to go to the following night. She had invited a boy she had known for years and never liked, but he was the right type for an event like that, Chandler

91

George III. She had gone to a couple of dances with him before, and he bored her to tears, but she knew her mother would be pleased. And she also knew that she'd have a miserable time but that couldn't be helped.

The apartment was dark when she got in, Jean was still at work as Tana looked around. Everything looked the same except smaller somehow, and drearier than she had remembered it. And as she had the thought, it seemed somehow unfair. She knew how hard her mother tried to keep a nice home for them both, and she always had. But Tana felt as though things were different now, as though imperceptibly she had changed and no longer fit in this comfortable scene. She found herself thinking of the comfortable Blake house in Washington, and how much she had enjoyed being there. It wasn't pretentious, like the Durnings' house, but it was warm and beautiful and real. And she missed the Blakes as well, especially Sharon. Tana had watched her get off the train, feeling as though she were losing her best friend, and Sharon had turned back once to give her a big smile and a wave, and then she was gone and the train moved north, and now she was here, feeling as though she wanted to cry as she set her bags down in her room.

"Is that my little girl?" The front door slammed and Jean's voice rang out as Tana turned with a frightened look. What if her mother could read her thoughts, could see how uncomfortable she was just being there? But Jean saw nothing of the sort, all she saw was the daughter she loved, and she held her tight for an instant before stepping back again. "Boy, you look good!" And so did Jean. Her cheeks were pink from the cold, there were kisses of frost on the tips of her hair, and her eyes looked big and dark. She was so excited that she didn't even wait to take off her coat before running into her own room and emerging again with Tana's dress. It was exquisite as it hung from the padded satin hanger they had delivered it with. It looked almost like a wedding dress, and Tana smiled.

"Where's the veil?"

Her mother smiled back. "You never know. That'll come next."

Tana laughed and shook her head at the thought. "Now let's not rush into that. I'm only eighteen."

"That doesn't mean anything, sweetheart. You might meet the man of your dreams tomorrow night, you know. And who knows after that?" Tana stared at her in disbelief. Something in Jean's eyes said she was serious.

"Do you mean that, Mom?"

Jean Roberts smiled again. It was wonderful to see Tana again, and now that she saw the dress next to her, she knew just how fabulous it was going to look. A victory all around. "You're a beautiful girl, Tana. And some man is going to be very lucky to have you as his wife."

"But wouldn't you be upset if I met him now?"

"Why?" She didn't seem to understand and Tana looked stunned.

"But I'm eighteen years old. Don't you want me to go on with college and make something of myself?"

"You're doing that now."

"But this is just the beginning, Mom. When I finish my two years at Green Hill, I want to go on and do something else."

Jean frowned. "There's nothing wrong with getting married and having kids."

"Is that what this is all about?" Suddenly Tana felt sick. "This coming out bullshit . . . it's kind of like a slave auction, isn't it?"

Jean Roberts looked shocked. "Tana, that's a terrible thing to say."

"Well, it's true, isn't it? All these young girls lined up, curtsying like fools, and a bunch of men checking them out." She squinted her eyes as though the girls were lined up in front of her, ". . . let's see, I'll take . . . that one over there." Her eyes opened wide again, and she looked upset. "Hell, there has to be more to life than that."

"You make it sound sick somehow, and it's not. It's a beautiful tradition that means a lot to everyone." No, it doesn't, Mom, at least not to me . . . just to you . . . but she couldn't bring herself to say those words. Jean looked at her unhappily. "Why are you being so difficult about this? Ann

93

Durning came out four years ago, and she had a wonderful time."

"Good for her. But I'm not Ann." She also hadn't run off with some twit in Italy who had to be bought off.

Jean sighed and sat down, looking up at Tana from the chair. She hadn't seen Tana in three months and she could already feel the tension mounting between them. "Why don't you just relax and enjoy yourself, Tana? You never know, you might meet someone you like."

"I don't want to meet someone I 'like'. I don't even want to go, Mom."

Tears filled Jean's eyes as she looked at her, and Tana couldn't stand the look on her face. "I just wanted you to . . . I wanted you to have. . . ." Tana knelt and hugged her close.

"I'm sorry, Mom. I'm sorry . . . I know it'll be beautiful."

Jean smiled through her tears and kissed Tana's cheek. "One thing's for sure, you will be beautiful, sweetheart."

"I'd have to be in that dress. You must have spent a fortune on it." She was touched but it seemed such a useless expense. She would rather have had clothes to wear at school. She was borrowing Sharon's all the time.

But Jean was smiling at her. "It's a gift from Arthur, sweetheart." Tana felt her stomach tie in a knot. Another reason to be "grateful" to him. She was so tired of Arthur and his gifts.

"He shouldn't have done that." Tana was visibly less than thrilled, and Jean couldn't understand why except that Tana had always been jealous of him.

"He wanted you to have a pretty dress." And indeed it was. As she stood in front of the mirror the following night, her hair teased and swept up, the way her mother had seen Jackie Kennedy's hair done in *Vogue*, with the beautiful silk dress, she looked like a fairy princess with her spun gold hair and big green eyes. It filled Jean's eyes with tears just to look at her. She looked exquisite. Moments later, Chandler George arrived to pick her up, and Jean left with them. Arthur had said that he would try to come by, but he wasn't sure. There was a dinner he had to attend that night, and he'd do his "best". Tana didn't say anything about it to Jean in the cab, but she had heard that line before, and knew that it meant nothing at all. It had applied to Christmas, Thanksgiving, Jean's birthdays over the years. And usually doing his "best" meant that he wouldn't arrive, but a bunch of flowers, or a telegram, or a note would instead. She always remembered her mother's crestfallen face at those times, but not tonight. Jean was too excited about her to worry about Arthur very much. She hovered like a mother hen, joining a group of the other mothers at one side of a long bar. The fathers had found each other, too, and there were clumps of well wishers and old family friends, but most of the room was filled with young people about Tana's own age, girls in pink dresses, or red satin, or bright green, and only a dozen in the white dresses their parents had bought them to come out in that night. For the most part, they were a motley adolescent herd, with faces that would take years to thin out, with waistlines to match. There was something singularly undistinguished about girls that age, and because of that, Tana especially stood out. She was tall and slim, and she held her head high.

Jean watched her proudly from across the room. When the big moment came, and the drum roll came halfway into the night, and each girl was led out on her father's arm to curtsy to the guests, there were unrestrained tears of pride on Jean's cheeks. She had hoped that Arthur Durning would be there by then, and had even dared to hope that he might lead her out. But he couldn't make it, of course. He had done enough for them, she couldn't expect him to do more. Tana came out looking nervous and flushed on the arm of Chandler George. She curtsied prettily, lowered her eyes, and disappeared into the rest of the group, and the music began again shortly after that. It had happened, it was done. Tana had officially come out. She looked around the room afterwards, feeling like a complete fool. There was no exhilaration, no thrill, no romantic tingle up and down her spine. She had done it because her mother wanted her to and it was over now. She was grateful for the hubbub that happened afterwards, which allowed her to get lost for a while.

Chandler looked as though he had fallen madly in love with a chubby redheaded girl with a sweet smile and an elaborate white velvet dress, and Tana had discreetly disappeared, allowing him to go in pursuit of his prize, as Tana wandered into an alcove and collapsed in a chair. She laid her head back, closed her eyes, and sighed, grateful to be away from it all, from the music, the people, Chandler, whom she couldn't stand, and the desperately lonely look of pride in her mother's eyes. Tana sighed again just thinking of it, and then jumped halfway off her seat as she heard a voice.

"It can't be as bad as all that." She opened her eyes to see a powerfully built, dark-haired young man with eyes as green as hers. There was something rakish about him, even in black tie, a casual air about the way he stood, looking down at her, holding a glass, and smiling cynically at her, as a piece of dark hair fell over one emerald eye. "Bored, lovely one?" He managed to look both sarcastic and amused and Tana nodded her head tentatively in embarrassment and began to laugh.

"You caught me." She looked into his eyes and smiled. She had the feeling that she'd seen him somewhere, but couldn't imagine where. "What can I say? It's a drag."

"It certainly is. The cattle show. I make the rounds every year." But he didn't look as though he'd been doing them for long. Despite the air of sophistication, he didn't look very old.

"How long have you been doing this?"

He grinned boyishly. "This is my second year. Actually, this should be my first, but they invited me to the cotillion by mistake last year. And all the rest of the coming out balls, so I went." He rolled his eyes with a grin, "What a pain in the ass." And then he looked appraisingly at her, and took a sip of his scotch. "And how did you find your way here?"

"By cab." She smiled sweetly at him and he grinned.

"Lovely date you had." The sarcasm dripped from his words again and she laughed. "Engaged to him yet?"

"No thanks."

"That shows at least minimal good judgment on your part." He spoke in a lazy laconic way, with the accent of the upper crust, and yet he seemed to be laughing at it all, and Tana was amused by him. There was something outrageous about the boy, as proper as he was, as well dressed. But at the same time there was a shocking irreverence which showed through and suited her mood perfectly. "Do you know Chandler, then?"

The young man smiled again. "We went to the same boarding school for two years. He plays a great game of squash, stinks at bridge, handles himself pretty well on the tennis court, flunked math, history, and biology, and has absolutely nothing between his ears."

Tana laughed in spite of herself. She didn't like him anyway, but it seemed an almost surgically accurate, albeit unkind, portrait of him. "That sounds about right. Not nice, but right."

"They don't pay me to be nice." He looked mischievous as he sipped his drink again, and made an obvious appraisal of her cleavage and small waist.

"Do they pay you to do anything?"

"Not yet actually." He smiled benevolently at her. "And with luck they never will."

"Where do you go to school?"

He frowned, as though he had just forgotten something somewhere, and then gazed blankly at her. "Do you know . . . I can't seem to remember." He smiled again as she wondered what that meant. Maybe he wasn't going to college at all, although he didn't look that type either. "What about you?"

"Green Hill."

The impish smile appeared again, with one eyebrow raised. "How ladylike. Majoring in what? Southern plantations, or pouring tea?"

"Both." She grinned and stood up. "At least I go to school."

"For two years anyway. Then what, princess? Or is that what tonight is all about? The Great Hunt for Husband Number One." He pretended to speak into a megaphone. "Will all candidates line up against the far wall. All healthy young white males with pedigrees . . . have your fathers'

D&B's in hand, we will also want to know your schools, blood type, whether or not you drive, how large your personal trust is and how soon you come into it . . ." He went on as she laughed at him, and he lowered his voice. "Seen any likely ones so far, or are you too madly in love with Chandler George?"

"Much." She began to walk slowly toward the main ballroom and he followed her, just in time to see her escort kissing the chubby redhead on the other side of the room.

The tall dark handsome young man turned to Tana somberly. "I've got bad news for you. I think you're about to be jilted, princess."

She shrugged and met the green eyes so like her own. "Them's the breaks, I guess." There was laughter in her eyes. She didn't give a damn about Chandler George.

"Would you like to dance?"

"Sure."

He whirled her around the floor expertly. There was something very dashing and worldly about this boy, which seemed to belie his youth. One had the feeling that he had been around, although Tana didn't know where, or even who he was, a circumstance he remedied at the end of the first dance.

"By the way, what's your name, princess?"

"Tana Roberts."

"My name's Harry." He looked at her with the boyish grin and she smiled, and then unexpectedly he swept her a low bow. "Harrison Winslow the fourth, actually. But Harry will do."

"Should I be impressed?" She was, but she wouldn't give him the satisfaction of letting him know.

"Only if you read the social columns regularly. Harrison Winslow the third usually makes an ass of himself, in cities that circle the globe . . . Paris and London most of the time, Rome when he has time . . . Gstaad, Saint Moritz . . . Munich, Berlin. And New York when he has absolutely no choice, and needs to fight with the trustees my grandmother left in charge of her estate. But he isn't very fond of the States, or of me, come to think of it." He spoke in a flat monotone as Tana watched, wondering what was going on inside of him, but there was no clue as yet. "My mother died when I was four. I don't remember her at all, except once in a while, something comes back in a wave . . . like a perfume . . . or a sound, her laughter on the stairs when they went out . . . a dress that reminds me of her, but that's probably impossible. She committed suicide. 'High unstable', as my grandmother used to say, 'but a pretty piece.' And poor Dad's been licking his wounds ever since . . . I forgot to mention Monaco and St. Jean Cap Ferrat. He licks his wounds there too. With helpmates, of course. There's a regular one he parks in London for most of the year, a very pretty one in Paris . . . one with whom he likes to ski . . . a Chinese girl in Hong Kong. He used to take me along when I wasn't in school, but eventually I got too disagreeable, so he stopped. That, and . . ." the eyes grew vague, ". . . other things. Anyway," his eyes came back into focus and he smiled cynically at Tana again, "that's who Harrison Winslow is, or at least one of them."

"And you?" Her voice was soft and his eyes were sad. He had told her more than he had intended to. But it was also his fourth scotch, and although it hadn't hurt his feet when they danced, it had loosened his tongue, not that he cared. Everyone in New York knew who Harry Winslow was, both father and son. "Are you like him?" She doubted it. For one thing, he hadn't had time to develop all those skills. He couldn't have been much older than she, after all.

He shrugged carelessly. "I'm working on it." And then he smiled again. "Beware, lovely one! Beware!" And with that, he swept her into his arms and onto the dance floor again, and she saw her mother watching them. She watched them for a long time, and then inquired of someone who he was, and she didn't look displeased.

"Do you see your father very much?" She was still thinking of what he had said as he whirled her around the floor. It sounded like a lonely life . . . boarding schools . . . his mother dead by suicide when he was four . . . the father halfway around the world most of the time, and obviously a libertine.

"Actually, no. He doesn't have time." For just a minute, he sounded like a very young boy, and she was sorry for him, but he was quick to turn the tables on her. "What about you? What's your story, Tana Roberts, other than the fact that you have deplorable taste in men?" He glanced in the direction of Chandler George, crushing the little red-head to him, and they both laughed.

"I'm single, eighteen years old, and I go to Green Hill."

"Jesus. How dull. What else. Any major loves?"

Her face slammed shut, and he noticed it. "No."

"Relax. I meant other than Chandler, of course." She relaxed a little again. "Although admittedly, he's hard to beat." Poor guy, they were both being rotten to him, but he was the dullest boy she had ever known, and he was an easy target for the scorn of his peers. "Let's see, what else? Parents? Illegitimate children? Dogs? Friends? Hobbies? Wait," he patted his pockets, as though he had misplaced something. "I should have a form here somewhere. . . ." They both laughed. "All of the above . . . ? none of the above . . . ?"

"One mother, no dogs, no illegitimate kids."

He looked sad. "I'm disappointed in you. I thought you would have done better than that." The music was winding down and Harry looked around. "What a bunch of bores. Want to go somewhere for a hamburger or a drink?"

She smiled. "I'd like that, but do we take Chandler along?" She laughed and Harry bowed.

"Leave that to me." He vanished and returned again with an outrageous grin.

"Oh God, what did you do?"

"I told him you were upset about the way he's behaved all night with that redheaded tart, and I'm dropping you off at your psychiatrist's. . . ."

"You didn't!"

"I did." She feigned innocence and then laughed. "Actually, I just told him that you'd seen the light and preferred me. He congratulated you on your good taste, and ran off with his chubby little friend." But whatever Harry had said, Chandler was waving happily at them and leaving with the redhead, so there was obviously no harm done.

"I have to say something to my mother before we go. Do you mind?"

"Not at all. Well, actually, I do, but I guess I don't have much choice." But he behaved himself when Tana introduced him to Jean, and he looked very proper, much to her delight, as they left the ball, and Jean went home alone, wishing Arthur had been there to see it all. It had been a beautiful evening, and it was obvious that Tana had had a wonderful time. And she was leaving now with Harry Winslow IV. Jean knew who he was, or at least she knew the name.

"What about your old man?" He stretched his legs out in the cab, after giving the driver the address of "21". It was the hangout of his choice when he was in town, and Tana had been impressed. It was certainly a lot more fun than going out with Chandler George. And it was so long since she'd been out on a date, she'd forgotten how it felt, and her dates had never been like this. Usually, they all went out for a pizza in a group on Second Avenue.

"My father died before I was born, in the war."

"That was considerate of him. It's less of a wrench that way, than if they stick around for a few years." It made Tana wonder why his mother had committed suicide, but she would never have dared to ask. "Did your mother remarry?"

"No," Tana shook her head hesitantly, and then, "She has a friend."

He raised the mischievous eyebrow again. "Married?"

She blushed beet red but he couldn't see. "What made you say that?"

"Just smart, I guess." He was so impossible, one would have wanted to slap his face if he weren't so boyish and so appealing all at once. And he was so openly impudent that it somehow made it all right. "Was I right?"

Normally, she wouldn't have admitted it to anyone, but she did now. "Yes, or at least he was for a long time. He's been a widower now for four years, and he still hasn't married her. He's a real selfish son-of-a-bitch." It was the strongest thing she had ever said about him publicly, even to Sharon at school.

But Harry didn't look perturbed. "Most men are. You should meet my old man. He leaves them bleeding by the side of the road at least four times a week, just to keep his hand in."

"Sounds nice."

"He's not." Harry's eyes were hard. "He's only interested in one thing. Himself. It's no wonder she killed herself." He had never forgiven his father for that, and Tana's heart suddenly ached for him, as the cab pulled up in front of "21", and Harry paid and they stepped out. And a moment later, they were swept up in the excitement of the exclusive restaurant. Tana had only been there once or twice, like on graduation night, and she loved the toys hanging over the bar, the well-dressed people crowded in, there were even two movie stars she recognized at once, and the head waiter pounced on Harry with glee, obviously ecstatic to see him again. It was clearly his favorite haunt and he went there all the time. They stayed at the bar for a while, and then went to their table, where Harry ordered steak tartare for himself, and Tana ordered eggs benedict; but as they sipped the Louis Roederer champagne he had ordered for them, Harry saw her face go taut. She was looking across the room at a table of people who seemed to be having a good time and there was an older man with his arm around a fairly young girl. Harry watched her face, and then her eyes and a moment later he patted her hand. "Let me guess . . . an old love?" He was surprised to see that she went for older men. She didn't look the type.

"Not mine, anyway." And then he instantly knew.

"Your mother's friend?"

"He told her he had a business dinner tonight."

"Maybe it is."

"It doesn't look like it to me." Her eyes were hard as she turned to Harry again. "What irritates me more than anything is that he can do no wrong in her eyes. She always makes excuses for him. She sits and she waits and she's so goddamn grateful to him."

102

"How long have they been together?"

"Twelve years."

He winced. "Jesus, that's a long time."

"Yeah." Tana glanced malevolently in Arthur's direction again. "And it doesn't seem to be cramping his style." Seeing him made her think of Billy again, and she turned her head as though to avoid the thought, but Harry saw the sudden look of pain in her eyes.

"Don't take it so hard, princess." His voice was gentle in her ears and she turned to look at him.

"It's her life, not mine."

"That's right. Don't forget that. You can make your own choices with your life." He smiled, "And that reminds me, you never answered all my rude questions before. What are you going to do after Green Hill?"

"God knows. Maybe Columbia. I'm not sure. I want to go on."

"Not get married and have four little kids?" They both laughed.

"Not for a while, thanks, although it's my mother's fondest dream." And then she turned to him with a curious look. "And what about you, where do you go to school?"

He sighed as he put down his champagne. "Harvard actually. Sounds obnoxious, doesn't it?" It was why he hadn't told her at first.

"Is it true?"

"Unfortunately, yes." He grinned. "But there's hope. I may flunk out before the end of the year. I'm working on it."

"You can't be that bad or you wouldn't have gotten in."

"A Winslow not get in? Don't be absurd, my dear. We *always* get in. We practically built the place."

"Oh . . ." She looked impressed. "I see. And you didn't want to go?"

"Not especially. I wanted to go out West somewhere. I thought Stanford or UC, but Dad had a fit, and it wasn't worth arguing about it . . . so there I am, being a pain in the ass, and making them sorry they let me in."

"You must be a real treat for them." Tana laughed, and

she noticed that Arthur Durning and his group had just left. He hadn't noticed her.

"I try to be, princess. You'll have to come up and see me sometime, maybe during spring break."

She laughed at that and shook her head. "I doubt that."

"Don't you trust me?" He looked amused and very debonair for a boy of eighteen.

"As a matter of fact, no." She took another sip of champagne and they both laughed. She was feeling giggly now and she was having a good time with him. He was the first boy she had liked in a long time, and she liked him as a friend. He was fun to laugh with and she could say things to him that she hadn't been able to say to anyone else recently, except Shar. And then she had an idea. "I might come up if I could bring a friend."

"What kind of friend?" he asked suspiciously.

"My roommate at Green Hill." She told him about Sharon Blake then and he looked intrigued.

"The daughter of Freeman Blake? That's something else. Is she as wonderful as you say?"

"Wonderfuler." She told him then about their being unable to get served at the coffee shop in Yolan, and the lecture given by Martin Luther King and he seemed interested in all of it.

"I'd like to meet her sometime. Do you really think you'd come up to Cambridge at spring break?"

"Maybe, I'll have to ask her."

"What are you two, joined at the hip?" He looked Tana over appraisingly. She was one of the prettiest girls he had ever seen, and it would be worth putting up with someone else, just to see her.

"More or less. I visited them at Thanksgiving, and I want to go back."

"Why don't you have her here?"

There was a long pause and then Tana looked at him. "My mother would have a fit if she knew Sharon was black. I've told her everything except that."

"Great." Harry smiled. "I did tell you that my maternal grandmother was black, didn't I?" For an instant he looked so honest that she almost believed what he said and then he started to laugh and she made a face.

"Pain in the ass . . . why don't I just tell my mother about you?"

"Be my guest."

And she did the next day when he called to take her to lunch in two days. They had Christmas to endure in between.

"Isn't that the boy you met last night?" It was Saturday morning and Jean was relaxing with a book. She hadn't heard from Arthur since the day before and she was dying to tell him about the ball, but she didn't want to bother him. She usually waited for him to call. It was a habit she had picked up when he was still married to Marie. And it was Christmas after all. He'd be busy with Billy and Ann.

"Yes, it is." Tana explained to her mother about Harry's call.

"He seems nice."

"He is." But not in any way Jean would approve of, as Tana knew only too well. He was irreverent and outrageous and he drank too much, and he was obviously spoiled, but he had behaved decently when he had brought her home. He had said goodnight and there was no wrestling match. She had been nervous about that, but she hadn't needed to be. And when he came to pick her up for lunch two days later he wore a blazer and a tie and gray slacks, but as soon as they got downstairs, he put on roller skates and a crazy hat, and proceeded to behave like a complete madman as they walked downtown and Tana laughed at him. "Harry Winslow, you are completely nuts, do you know that?!"

"Yes, ma'am." He smiled and crossed his eyes, and insisted on wearing his roller skates into the Oak Room for lunch. The maitre d' didn't look pleased but he knew who he was and he didn't dare throw him out. He ordered a bottle of Roederer champagne, and guzzled a glass as soon as it was uncorked, and then set down the empty glass and smiled at Tana. "I think I'm addicted to that stuff."

"You mean you're a drunk."

"Yup." He said it with pride, ordered lunch for them

both, and after lunch they walked through Central Park and stopped at Wollman Rink where they watched the ice skaters for more than an hour and talked about life, and he sensed that there was a strange reticence about her. She didn't offer herself, in a romantic sense, she was careful and closed, and yet at the same time she was intelligent and warm. She cared about people and causes and things. But there was no hand held out. He knew that he had made a new friend, and no more, and she saw to it that he understood, in so many words, and it aroused his curiosity. "Are you involved with someone near Green Hill?"

She shook her head, and her eyes met his. "No, nothing like that. I don't want to get involved with anyone right now." He was surprised at her honesty. And it was a challenge too, of course, one he couldn't completely resist.

"Why not? Afraid to get hurt the way your mother has been?" She had never thought of it that way. It was why he didn't want kids. He didn't want to hurt anyone as badly as he himself had been hurt. And she had just told him how Arthur had stood her mother up for Christmas again that year.

"I don't know. Maybe. That, and other things."

"What kind of 'other things'?"

"Nothing I want to talk about." She looked away, and he tried to imagine what had marked her that way. She kept a safe distance between them, and even when they laughed and played, she sent out messages that said "don't get too close to me." He hoped that there was nothing strange about the girl, about her sexual propensities, but he didn't think it was that. It was more that she seemed to be hiding in a protective shell, and he wasn't sure why. Someone had driven her into it and he wondered who it was.

"Was there someone important in your life before?"

"No." She looked him square in the eye. "I don't want to talk about that." The look on her face made him back off at once. It was anger and hurt and something he couldn't even define, but it was so powerful it took his breath away, and he didn't scare easily. But this time he got the point. A blind man would have.

"I'm sorry." They changed the subject then and went back to talking about easier things. He liked her a lot, and he saw her several times during that Christmas holiday. They went to dinner and lunch, went ice skating in the park, to a movie one night, and she even invited him to dinner one night with Jean. But that was a mistake, she recognized at once. Jean was grilling him as though he were a hot marriage candidate, asking about his future plans, his parents, his career goals, his grades. She could hardly wait for him to leave, and when he did, she screamed at Jean.

"Why did you do that to him? He just came here to eat, not to ask me to marry him."

"You're eighteen years old, you have to start thinking about things like that now."

"Why?" Tana was enraged. "All he is is a friend, for chrissake. Don't act like I have to get married by next week."

"Well, when do you want to get married, Tana?"

"Never, dammit! Why the hell do I have to get married at all?"

"What are you going to do for the rest of your life?" Her mother's eyes were hunting her, shoving her into corners and pushing her hard and she hated it.

"I don't know what I'm going to do. Do I have to figure that out now? Right now? Tonight? This week? Shit!"

"Don't talk to me like that!" Now her mother was angry too.

"Why not? What are you trying to do to me?"

"I want to see you have some security, Tana. Not to be in the same boat I'm in when you're forty years old. You deserve more than that!"

"So do you. Did you ever think of that? I hate seeing you like this, waiting around for Arthur all the time, like his slave. That's all you've been for all these years, Mother. Arthur Durning's concubine." She was tempted to tell her about seeing him with another girl at "21", but she couldn't do that to her mother. She didn't want to cause her that much pain and it would have for sure. Tana restrained herself but Jean was irate anyway.

"That's not fair and it's not true."

"Then why don't you want me to be like you?" Jean turned her back on her, so that she wouldn't see her tears, and then suddenly she turned on Tana, and twelve years of sorrow showed in her eyes, and a lifetime before that.

"I want you to have all the things I didn't have. Is that too much to ask?"

Tana's heart suddenly went out to her and she backed down. Her voice was gentler as she spoke again. "But maybe I don't want the same things you did."

"What is there not to want? A husband, security, a home, children – what's wrong with all that?" She looked shocked.

"Nothing. But I'm too young to think about all that. What if I want a career?"

Jean Roberts looked shocked. "What kind of career?"

"I don't know. I just meant theoretically."

"That's a lonely life, Tana." She looked worried about her. "You'd be better off if you just settled down." But to Tana that felt like giving up, and she thought about it as she rode south on the train and she and Sharon talked about it their first night back in Jasmine House, once the lights were off.

"Jesus, Tan, she sounds just like mine . . . in a different way, of course. But they all want for us what they wanted for themselves, no matter who we are, or how different we are from them, or what we think and feel and want. My dad understands, but my mom . . . all I hear about is law school, and sit-ins, and being 'responsible' about being black. I'm so goddamn tired of being 'responsible', I could scream. That's why I came here in the first place, to Green Hill. I wanted to go somewhere where there would be other blacks. Hell, here I can't even date, and she tells me that there's plenty of time for that. When? I want to go out now, I want to have a good time, I want to go to restaurants and movies and football games." She reminded Tana then, and the pretty blonde smiled in the dark.

"Want to go to Harvard with me at spring break?"

"How come?" Sharon propped herself up on one elbow in the dark with an excited look. And Tana told her about

Harry Winslow then. "He sounds neat. Did you fall for him?"

"No."

"Why not?"

There was a silence which they both understood. "You know why."

"You can't let that screw you up for the rest of your life, Tan."

"You sound like my mother now. She wants me engaged to anyone by next week, as long as he's willing to marry me, buy me a house, and give me kids."

"It beats the hell out of going to sit-ins and getting raw eggs in your hair. Doesn't that sound like fun?"

Tana smiled. "Not much."

"Your Harvard friend sounds nice."

"He is." Tana smiled to herself. "I like him a lot, as a friend. He's the most honest, straightforward person I've ever met." The call he made to her later that week underlined why she so enjoyed him. He called pretending to be the owner of a laboratory in Yolan, and they needed young ladies to perform experiments on, he explained.

"We're trying to find out if young ladies are as intelligent as young men," he said, disguising his voice. "We realize of course that they are not, however . . .", and just before she flew into a rage, she recognized his voice.

"You shit!"

"Hi, kiddo. How's life in the Deep South?"

"Not bad." She let him speak to Sharon eventually, and the two girls stood beside the phone, passing it back and forth, and eventually Sharon went upstairs and Tana talked to him for hours. There were no romantic overtones at all, he was more like a brother to her, and after two months of phone calls, aside from Sharon he was her closest friend. He was planning to see her at spring break, and she tried to get Sharon to come along, but to no avail. She decided to brave her mother, and invite Sharon to stay with them, but Miriam Blake had been on the phone to Sharon almost every night. There was an enormous black rally scheduled in Washington with a candlelight vigil for Civil Rights over

Easter weekend and she wanted Sharon to be there. She felt that it was an important part of their life, and this was no time for a vacation trip. Sharon was depressed about it when they both left Green Hill.

"All you had to do was say no, Shar." Tana looked at her and shook her head and for a moment something angry flashed in the pretty black girl's eyes.

"Just like you did about the coming out party, huh, Tan?"

There was a silence, and then slowly Tana nodded her head. Her friend wasn't far wrong. It was difficult to fight with them all the time. She shrugged, with a sheepish grin. "Okay, you win. I'm sorry. We'll miss you."

"I'll miss you too." She flashed her the dazzling smile, and they chatted and played cards on the train. Sharon got off in Washington, and Tana went on to New York. It was balmy and warm when she walked out of the station and hailed a cab, and the apartment looked the same as it always had, and somehow, for no reason she could explain, it was depressing to be back. There was a sameness to it all. Nothing grew, nothing changed. There were never fresh drapes, new plants, wonderful flowers, something exciting going on. There was the same thing, the same life, the same worn-out couch, the same dreary looking plants year after year. It hadn't seemed quite so bad when she was living there every day, but now that she came and went, it looked different to her. Everything was shabbier, and the whole apartment seemed to have shrunk. Her mother was at work, and she threw her bags down into her room, just as the phone rang. She went back to the living room to pick it up, glancing around again.

"Hello?"

"Winslow here. How's it going, kid?"

She grinned. It was like a burst of fresh air in the stale, musty room. "Hello."

"When'd you get in?"

"About four seconds ago. How about you?"

"I drove down last night with a couple of guys. And," he looked lazily around the apartment his father owned at the Pierre, "here I am. Same old dump, same old town." But he looked boyish when he smiled, Tana recalled, and she was excited at the prospect of seeing him again. They had learned so much about each other in the last four months on the phone, it was as though they were old friends now. "Want to come up for a drink?"

"Sure. Where are you?"

"At the Pierre." He sounded unimpressed by his own whereabouts and Tana grinned.

"That's nice."

"Not very. My father had the apartment redone by some decorator last year. It looks like a fag hangout now, but at least it's free when I'm in New York."

"Is your father there?" She was intrigued and Harry laughed derisively.

"Don't be ridiculous. I think he's in Munich this week. He likes spending Easter there. The Germans are so emotional about Christian events. That and the Oktoberfest." He was slightly over her head. "Never mind. Come on over, and we'll drive room service nuts. What do you want? I'll order something now, and it'll take two hours to show up."

She was impressed. "I don't know . . . a club sandwich and a Coke? Does that sound all right?" There was something very impressive about all this, but Harry was nonchalant about it all and when she arrived, he was lying on the couch in jeans and bare feet watching a soccer match on TV. He swept her off her feet, and gave her a huge bear hug, and it was obvious that he was genuinely pleased to see her, much more than she realized. His whole body tingled as he gave her a friendly peck on the cheek. And there was a moment of awkwardness, translating the intimacy they had developed on the phone into real life, but by the end of the afternoon, they were like old friends, and Tana hated to leave to go home.

"Then stay. I'll put some shoes on and we'll go to "21"."

"Like this?" She looked down at her plaid skirt and loafers and wool socks, but she shook her head. "I have to go home anyway. I haven't seen my mother in four months."

"I keep forgetting rituals like that." His voice was flat,

and he looked even handsomer than he had before, but nothing stirred in Tana's heart for him, only the friendship that had continued to grow since they first met, nothing more than that, and she was sure that he had nothing other than platonic feelings for her as well.

She turned to look at him now, as she picked her raincoat up off the chair. "Don't you ever see your father at all, Harry?" Her voice was soft and her eyes were sad for him. She knew how alone he was. He had spent the holidays alone, he said he always did, or with friends, or in empty houses or hotels, and he only mentioned his father in the context of bad jokes about his women and his friends and his gallivanting here and there.

"I see him once in a while. We run into each other about once or twice a year. Usually here, or in the South of France." It sounded very grand, but Tana easily sensed how lonely Harry was. It was why he had opened up so much to her. There was something inside him which was dying to reach out and be loved. And there was something like that in her too. A part of her which had only had Jean and had wanted more, a father, sisters and brothers, a family . . . something more than just a lonely woman who spent her life waiting for a man who didn't appreciate her. And Harry didn't even have that. Tana hated his father, just thinking about him.

"What's he like?"

Harry shrugged again. "Good looking, I guess. At least that's what the women say . . . smart . . . cold. . . ." He looked Tana square in the eye. "He killed my mother, what do you think he's like?" Something shrivelled up in her as she watched her friend's eyes, and she didn't know what to say. She was sorry that she had asked, but Harry put an arm around her shoulders as he walked her to the door. "Don't let it upset you, Tan. It happened a long time ago." But she was sad for him. There was something so lonely about him, and he was so funny and decent and nice, it wasn't fair . . . and he was also spoiled and self-indulgent and mischievous. He had put on a British accent for the first room service waiter who'd come up, and pretended to the second one that he was French, and afterwards he and Tana were convulsed. She wondered if he always behaved like that and suspected that he did. And as she took the bus back uptown, she suddenly didn't mind the depressing little apartment she shared with Jean. Better that than the lavish, chilly decor of the Winslow suite at the Hotel Pierre. The rooms were large, and everything was chrome and glass and white, predictably expensive, there were two huge fabulous white fur rugs on the floor and there were priceless paintings and objects everywhere, but that's all there was. There was no one there when he arrived from school, and there wouldn't be that night or the next. There was only Harry, with an ice box filled with booze and Cokes, a wardrobe filled with expensive clothes, and a TV.

"Hi . . . I'm home . . . !" She called out as she got in and Jean came running to her, and held her tight with a look of delight.

"Oh baby, you look so good!" It made her think of Harry again, and all that he didn't have, in spite of his trusts, and his houses, and his fancy name . . . he didn't have this. And somehow Tana wanted to make it up to him. Jean was looking at her now and there was such obvious pleasure in her eyes that it actually felt good to be home. "I saw your bags. Where did you go?"

"I went to see a friend downtown. I didn't think you'd be home for a while."

"I left early, in case you'd come in."

"I'm sorry, Mom."

"Who did you go to see?" Jean always liked to know what she did, who she saw. But Tana wasn't as used to the questions anymore, and she hesitated for just a moment before she smiled.

"I went to see Harry Winslow at the Pierre. I don't know if you remember him."

"Of course I do." Jean's eyes lit up. "Is he in town?"

"He has an apartment here." Tana's voice was quiet, and there were mixed reviews in Jean's eyes. It was good that he was mature enough, and solvent enough, to have his own place, but also dangerous at the same time.

"Were you alone with him?" Jean looked concerned.

This time Tana laughed. "Sure. We shared a club sandwich and watched TV. All perfectly harmless, Mom."

"Still . . . I don't think you should." She watched Tana's eyes, as the pretty blonde's face began to tense.

"He's my friend, Mom."

"He's still a young man, and you never know what could happen in a situation like that."

"Yes, I do." Her eyes were instantly hard. She knew only too well. Only it had happened at precious Billy Durning's house, in his own father's bedroom, with a hundred kids right downstairs. "I know who I can trust."

"You're too young to be able to judge things like that, Tan."

"No, I'm not." Tan's face was like a rock. Billy Durning's raping her had changed her whole life. She knew everything about things like that, and if she sensed any threat from Harry at all, she would never have gone to his hotel, or stayed. But she knew instinctively that he was her friend and she would come to no harm at his hands, unlike her mother's lover's son. "Harry and I are just friends."

"You're being naive. There's no such thing between boys and girls, Tan. Men and women can't be friends."

Tana's eyes opened wide. She couldn't believe her mother was saying those words. "How can you say a thing like that, Mom?"

"Because it's true. And if he's inviting you to his hotel, he has something else in mind, whether you recognize it or not. Maybe he's just biding his time." And then she smiled. "Do you think he could be serious about you, Tan?"

"Serious?" Tana looked as though she were about to explode. "*Serious*? I just told you, all we are is friends."

"And I told you I didn't believe that." There was something almost insinuating about her smile. "You know, Tan, he would be quite a catch."

But it was too much for Tana to stand. She jumped to her feet, and looked down at her mother with scorn. "You make him sound like a fish, for chrissake. I don't want a 'catch.' I don't want to get married. I don't want to get laid. All I want is to have some friends and go to school. Can you understand that?" There were tears in her eyes, mirrored by those in Jean's.

"Why do you have to get so violent about everything? You never used to be like that, Tan." Jean's voice sounded so sad that it tore at Tana's heart, but she couldn't help how she felt or what she said anymore.

"You never used to push me all the time."

"When do I push?" She looked shocked. "I don't even see you anymore. I've seen you twice in six months. That's pushing?"

"That coming out party was pushing, and what you just said about Harry is pushing, and talking about catches, and settling down, and getting married is pushing. For chrissake, Mom, I'm eighteen years old!"

"And you're almost nineteen. And then wha ? When *are* you going to think about it, Tan?"

"I don't know, Mom. Maybe never, how's that? Maybe I'll never get married. So what? If I'm happy, who cares?"

"I care. I want to see you married to a nice man with nice children in a nice house. . . ." Jean was crying openly now, it was what she had always wanted for herself . . . yet, she was alone . . . with a couple of nights a week with a man she loved, and a daughter who was almost gone. . . . She bent her head and sobbed, as Tana came to her and hugged her close.

"Come on, Mom, stop . . . I know you want the best for me . . . but just let me work things out for myself."

Her mother looked at her with big, sad, dark eyes. "Do you realize who Harry Winslow is?"

Tana's voice was soft. "Yes. He's my friend."

"His father is one of the richest men in the United States. He even makes Arthur Durning look poor." Arthur Durning. The measuring stick for everything in Jean's life.

"So what?"

"Do you realize what kind of life you could have with him?"

Tana looked sad for her, and she suddenly felt sad for herself. Her mother was missing the point, and probably had all her life. But by the same token, Jean had given her so much. And Tana felt as though she owed her a lot now. But in spite of that, she hardly saw Jean during the entire two weeks she was in New York. She ran around with Harry almost every day, although she didn't admit it to Jean. She was still furious at what her mother had said. *Do you realize who he is?* As though that made a difference to her. She wondered how many people felt that way about him. It seemed a hideous thought, to be evaluated because of his last name.

Cautiously, she even asked Harry about it one day, when they were having a picnic in Central Park. "Doesn't that bug you, Harry? I mean people wanting to get to know you because of who you are?" The thought still horrified her, but he only shrugged and munched his apple as he lay on the grass.

"That's just the way people are, I guess. It gives them some kind of a thrill. I used to see people do that to my father all the time."

"Doesn't it get to him?"

"I don't really think he cares." Harry smiled at her. "He's so insensitive, I don't think he actually feels anything at all." Tana watched Harry's eyes.

"Is he really that bad?"

"Worse."

"Then how come you're so nice?"

He laughed. "Just lucky, I guess. Or maybe it's my mother's genes."

"Do you still remember her?" It was the first time she had asked him that, and he looked away from her.

"Sometimes . . . a little bit . . . I don't know, Tan." He looked back at her again. "Sometimes, when I was a kid, I'd pretend to my friends that she was alive, that she was out shopping or whatever when they came over to play. I didn't want to be different from the rest of them. But they always found out. Their mothers would tell them or something when they went home, and then they'd think I was weird, but I didn't give a damn. It felt nice to be normal just for a few hours. I'd just talk about her like she was out . . . or upstairs . . ." Tan saw tears stand out in his eyes, and then he looked at her almost viciously. "Pretty dumb, huh, to be hung up on a mother you never even knew?"

Tana reached out to him with her heart and her words, and the gentleness of her voice. "What else do you have? I'd do the same thing in your shoes."

He shrugged and looked away, and a while later they went for a walk and talked about other things, Freeman Blake, Sharon, Tana's classes at Green Hill, and then suddenly out of the blue, Harry took her hand. "Thanks for what you said before." She knew instantly what he meant. They had that kind of rapport, had from the moment they first met.

"It's okay." She squeezed his hand, and they walked on, and she was amazed at how comfortable she was with him. He didn't push her at all, didn't ask her anymore why she didn't go out with anyone. He seemed to accept her as she was, and she was grateful to him for that. She was grateful to him for a lot of things, for the way he saw life, for the fun they had, the sense of humor that always made her laugh. It felt wonderful to have someone to share her thoughts with.

He was almost like a sounding board for everything she had in her head, and she was particularly grateful for that when she went back to Green Hill. When she saw Sharon again, it was as though her family had sent someone else instead, and all of her moderate political ideas had disappeared. She had attended a series of rallies and sit-ins with her mother and her friends, and suddenly she was as rabid as Miriam Blake was. Tana couldn't believe the change that had taken place, and finally, after listening to her for two days, Tana turned to her and screamed.

"For chrissake, Shar, what's happened to you? This room has been like a political rally ever since we got back. Get off your soap box, girl. What the hell has happened to you?" Sharon just sat there and stared and suddenly the tears flooded her eyes and she bowed her head, the sobs choked her and her shoulders shook and it was almost half an hour before she could speak, as Tana watched her in astonishment. Something terrible had happened to the girl, but it was impossible to say what it was. She held her and rocked her, and at last Sharon spoke, as Tana's heart went out to her.

"They killed Dick on Easter Eve, Tan . . . they killed him . . . he was fifteen years old . . . and he was hanged . . ." Tana felt instantly sick. That couldn't be. That didn't happen to people one knew . . . to blacks . . . to anyone . . . but she could see on Sharon's face that it was true, and when she called Harry that night, she cried when she told him the news.

"Oh, my God . . . I heard something about it in school, that the son of an important black had been killed, but it didn't click . . . shit. . . ."

"Yeah." Tana's heart felt like lead. And when her mother called her later that week, she still sounded depressed.

"What's the matter, sweetheart? Did you and Harry have a fight?" She was trying a new tack, she was going to pretend to herself and Tana that it was a romance and maybe the idea would take, but Tana didn't have any patience with her and she was instantly blunt.

"My roommate's brother died."

"Oh, how terrible . . ." Jean sounded horrified. "In an accident?"

There was a long pause as Tana weighed her words . . . No, Mom, he was hanged, you see he's black . . . "Sort of." Wasn't death always an accident? Who expected it?

"Tell her how sorry I am. Those are the people you spent Thanksgiving with, aren't they?"

"Yes." Tana's voice sounded flat and dead.

"That's just terrible."

Tana couldn't stand talking to her anymore. "I've got to go, Mom."

"Call me in a few days."

"I'll try." She cut her off and hung up. She didn't want to talk to anyone, but she and Sharon were talking again late into the night. Suddenly everything in Sharon's life had changed. She had even contacted the local black church, and she was helping to organize sit-ins on weekends for the remainder of the spring. "Do you think you should, Shar?" Sharon looked angrily at her. "Is there a choice anymore?

I don't think there is." There was anger in her soul now, an anger that nothing would help, a fire that no love could quench. They had killed the little boy she had grown up with. ". . . and he was always such a pain in the ass . . ." She laughed through her tears one night as they talked in the dark, ". . . he was so much like Mom, and now . . . and now . . ." She gulped her sobs down, and Tana went to sit on her bed. It went on like that every night, either talking about marches elsewhere in the South, or sit-ins in town, or Dr. Martin Luther King, it was as though she wasn't really there anymore, and by mid terms she was panicking. She hadn't done any studying at all. She was a bright girl, but she was desperately afraid now that she was going to flunk. Tana helped her as much as she could, sharing notes, underlining her books for her, but she didn't have much hope, and Sharon's mind was on the sit-in she had organized in Yolan for the following week. The townspeople had already complained about her twice to the Dean of Green Hill, but because of who her father was, they had only called her in and talked to her. They understood what a strain she was under, after her brother's, er . . . unfortunate accident, but she had to behave herself nonetheless, and they didn't want her causing trouble in town anymore.

"You better lay off, Shar. They're going to kick you out of school if you don't stop." Tana had warned her more than once, but it was something she couldn't change now. She had no choice. It was something she had to do, and the night before the big sit-in in Yolan she turned to Tana just before they turned off the lights and there was something so intense in her eyes that it almost frightened Tana as she looked at her. "Is something wrong?"

"I want to ask you a favor, and I won't be mad if you say no. I promise, so do whatever you want. Is that a deal?"

"Okay. What's up?" Tana just prayed that she didn't want her to cheat on a test.

"Reverend Clarke and I were talking today, at the church, and I think it would make a big difference if there were whites involved in the sit-in tomorrow in town. We're going to walk into the white church."

"Holy shit." Tana looked shocked, and Sharon grinned.

"That's about right." The two girls exchanged a smile. "Dr. Clarke is going to see who he can get, and I . . . I don't know . . . maybe it's wrong, but I wanted to ask you. But if you don't want to, Tan, don't."

"Why would they get upset if I walk into their church? I'm white."

"Not if you walk in with us, you're not. That makes you white trash, or worse. If you walk in holding my hand, standing between me and Reverend Clarke or another black . . . that's different, Tan."

"Yeah," she felt a twinge of fear in her gut, but she also wanted to help her friend, "I guess I can see that."

"What do you think?" Sharon looked her square in the eye and Tana did the same.

"Honestly? I'm scared."

"So am I. I always am." And then very gently, "So was Dick. But he went. And I'm going too. I'm going to go every time I can for the rest of my life now, until things change. But it's my fight, Tana, not yours. If you come, you come as my friend. And if you don't come, I love you anyway."

"Thanks. Can I think about it tonight?" She knew that it could have repercussions if it got back to the school, and she didn't want to jeopardize her scholarship for the following year. She called Harry late that night, but he was out, and she woke up the next morning at dawn, thinking about going to church when she was a little girl, and things her mother had said about all people being the same in God's eyes, the rich, the poor, the white, the black, everyone, and then she thought about Sharon's brother Dick, a fifteen-year-old child, hanged until he died, and when Sharon turned over in bed as the sun came up, Tana was waiting for her.

"Sleep okay?"

"More or less." She sat up on the edge of the bed and stretched.

"You getting up?" There was a question in Sharon's eyes, and Tana smiled.

"Yeah. We're going to church today, aren't we?" And

with that Sharon grinned broadly at her friend. She hopped out of bed, and gave her a hug and a kiss and a victorious smile.

"I'm so glad, Tan."

"I don't know if I am, but I think it's the right thing to do."

"I know it is." It was going to be a long bloody fight, but Sharon would be there, and Tana, just this once. She put on a simple blue cotton shirtdress, the color of the sky, brushed her long blonde hair into a sleek pontytail, put her loafers on, and they walked into town side by side.

"Going to church, girls?" The housemother had smilingly asked and both had answered yes. They both knew that she had meant different ones, but Tana went to the black church with Sharon where they met Dr. Clarke and a small crowd of ninety-five blacks and eleven whites. They were told to stay calm, to smile if it seemed appropriate, but not if it would provoke anyone, and to remain silent no matter what anyone said to them. They were to hold hands and to enter the church solemnly and respectfully, in groups of five. Sharon and Tana were to remain together. There was another white girl with them, and two black men, both burly and tall, and they told Tana on the way to the other church that they worked at the mill. They were about Tana's own age, both were married, one had three children, the other four, and they didn't seem to question her being there. They called her Sister, and just before they walked into the church, the five companions exchanged a nervous smile. And then quietly, they stepped inside. It was a small Presbyterian church on the residential side of town, heavily attended every Sunday, with a Sunday School that was well filled, and as the black faces began to file in, every man and woman in the church turned around. There was a look of complete shock on everyone, the organ stopped, one woman fainted, another began to scream, and within a matter of moments all hell broke loose, the minister began to shout, someone ran to call the police, and only Dr. Clarke's volunteers remained calm, standing solidly along the back wall, causing no trouble at all, as people turned and jeered, hurled insults at them, even though they were in church. Within moments the town's tiny squad of riot police had arrived. They had been recently trained for the sit-ins that had begun to occur and were mostly composed of highway patrolmen, but they began to push and shove and drag the uncooperating black bodies out, as they made themselves limp, and allowed themselves to be dragged away . . . and suddenly Tana realized what was happening to them. She was next . . . this was not happening to a remote "them", it was happening to "us" . . . and suddenly two enormous policemen hovered over her and grabbed her roughly by both arms, waving their sticks in her face.

"You should be ashamed of yourself . . . white trash!" Her eyes were huge as they dragged her off, and with every ounce of her being she wanted to hit and bite and kick, thinking of Richard Blake and how he had been killed, but she didn't dare. They threw her into the back of the truck, with much of Dr. Clarke's group, and half an hour later she was being fingerprinted and she was in jail. She sat in a jail cell for the rest of the day, with fifteen other girls, all of them black, and she could see Sharon across the way. They had each been allowed one phone call, the whites at least, the blacks were still being "processed" according to the cops, and Sharon shouted to her to call her mom, which Tana did. She arrived in Yolan at midnight, and released Sharon and Tana simultaneously, congratulating them both. Tana could see that she looked harder and more drawn than she had six months before, but she seemed pleased with what the girls had done. She wasn't even upset when Sharon told her the news the next day. She was being kicked out of Green Hill, effective immediately. Her things had already been packed by the housemother of Jasmine House, and she was being asked to leave the campus before noon. Tana was in shock when she heard, and she knew what she could expect for herself when she was ushered into the Dean's office. It was just as she had thought. She was being asked to leave. There would be no scholarship the following year. In fact, there would be no following year at all. Like Sharon, it was all over for her. The only difference was that if she was willing to stay on in a probationary state, she could do so until the end of the year, which would at least mean that she could take her final exams and apply to another school. But where? She sat in her room in shock after Sharon had left. Sharon was going back to Washington with her mother, and there had already been talk of her spending a little time as a volunteer for Dr. King.

"I know Daddy'll be mad because he wants me to go to school, but you know, truthfully, Tan, I've had it up to here with school." She looked sorrowfully at Tana then. "But what about you?" She was devastated about the price of the sit-in for her friend. She had never gotten arrested before, although they had been warned before the church sit-in that it was a real possibility, yet she really hadn't expected it.

"Maybe it's all for the best." Tana tried to cheer her up, and she was still in shock when Sharon left, and she sat alone in her room until dark. Her probation meant that she had to eat alone at Jasmine House, keep to her room at night, and avoid all social activities including the freshman prom. She was a pariah of sorts, but she also knew that school would be over in three weeks.

The worst of it was that, as they had warned Tana they would, they informed Jean. She called, hysterical, that night, sobbing into the phone. "Why didn't you tell me that little bitch was black?"

"What difference does it make what color she is? She's my best friend." But tears filled Tana's eyes and the emotions of the past few days overwhelmed her suddenly. Everyone at school was looking at her as though she had killed someone, and Sharon was gone. She didn't know where she would go to school next year, and her mother was screaming at her . . . it was like being five years old and being told you had been very, very bad, but not being sure why.

"You call that a friend?" Her mother laughed through her tears. "She cost you your scholarship, and got you kicked out of school. And do you think you'll get accepted anywhere else after this?"

"Of course you will, you jerk." Harry reassured her

through her sobs the next day. "Shit, there are zillions of radicals at Boston University."

"I'm not a radical." She cried some more.

"I know that. All you did was go to a sit-in, for chrissake. It's your own goddamn fault for going to that prissy redneck school. I mean shit, you aren't even in the civilized world down there. Why the hell don't you come up here to school?"

"You really think I might be able to get in?"

"With your grades, are you kidding? They'd let you run the place."

"You're just trying to make me feel better." She started to cry again.

"You're giving me a mamoth pain in the ass, Tan. Why don't you just let me get you an application and see what happens?" And what happened was that she got in, much to her own astonishment and her mother's chagrin.

"Boston University? What kind of school is that?"

"One of the best in the country, and they even gave me a scholarship." Harry had taken the application over himself, put in a good word for her, which seemed like a crazy thing to do and touched her to the core, and by July 1st, it was settled. She was going to Boston University in the fall.

She was still numb from the events of two months before, and her mother still wanted to wrestle about it with her.

"I think you should get a job for a while, Tan. You can't hang around in school for the rest of your life."

Tana looked horrified. "How about for another three years, like until I get a degree?"

"And then what? What are you going to do then, Tana, that you couldn't do now?"

"Get a decent job."

"You could go to work for Durning International right now. I spoke to Arthur last week. . . ."

Tana seemed to be screaming at her all the time now, but she never understood. "For chrissake, don't condemn me to that for the rest of my life."

"Condemn you! *Condemn* you! How dare you say such a thing? You get arrested, kicked out of school, and you think

124

you have a right to the world. You're lucky a man like Arthur Durning would even consider hiring you."

"He's lucky I didn't bring charges against his son last year!" The words flew out of Tana's mouth before she could stop them and Jean Roberts stared at her.

"How dare you say a thing like that?"

Her voice was quiet and sad, "It's true, Mom."

She turned her back to Tana, as though shielding herself from the look on Tana's face, not wanting to hear. "I don't want to hear you tell lies like that." Tana walked quietly out of the room, and a few days later she was gone.

She went to stay with Harry at his father's place in Cape Cod, and they played tennis and sailed, swam, and visited his friends, and she never felt threatened by him at all. The relationship was entirely platonic as far as she was concerned and therefore comfortable for her. Harry's feelings were something else but he kept them carefully veiled. She wrote to Sharon several times, but the answers she got back were brief, scrambled, and obviously in haste. She'd never been so busy, or so happy, in her life. Her mother had been right, and she had a wonderful job working as a volunteer for Dr. Martin Luther King. It was amazing how their lives had changed in one short year.

And when Tana started school at Boston University, she was astonished at how different it was from Green Hill, how open, how interesting, how avant garde. She liked being in class with boys as well. Interesting issues were constantly raised and she did well in every class she took.

And secretly Jean was proud of her, although her rapport with Tana was no longer as good as it had once been. She told herself it was a passing phase. She had other things on her mind anyway. By the end of Tana's first year at Boston University, Ann Durning was getting married again. There was going to be an enormous wedding at Christ Episcopal Church in Greenwich, Connecticut, and a reception, organized by Jean, at the house. At the office, her desk was littered with lists, photographs, caterers' lists and Ann called her at least fourteen times a day. It was almost as though her own daughter was getting married, and after fourteen years as Arthur Durning's mistress and right arm, she felt possessive about the children anyway. And she was especially pleased at how well Ann had chosen this time. He was a lovely man of thirty-two, also previously married, and he was a partner at Sherman and Sterling, the law firm in New York, and from everything that Jean Roberts had heard, he was a very promising attorney, and he had plenty of money of his own. Arthur was also pleased about the match, and he gave Jean a beautiful gold bracelet from Cartier to thank her for all the work she did to make Ann's wedding a success.

"You're really a wonderful woman, you know." He sat in her living room, drinking a scotch, looking at her, wondering why he had never married her. Once in a while he felt like that, although most of the time he was comfortable now by himself. He was used to it.

"Thank you, Arthur." She handed him a small plate of the hors d'oeuvres he liked best, Nova Scotia salmon on little thin slices of Norwegian pumpernickel, little balls of steak tartare on white toast, the macadamia nuts she always kept in the house, in case he came by, along with his favorite scotch, favorite cookies ... soap ... eau de cologne ... everything he liked. It was easier to be always ready for him now, with Tana gone. In some ways, that had helped their relationship, and in others, it had not. She was freer now, more available, always ready for him to come by at the drop of a hat, but at the same time, she was much lonelier with Tana gone, more anxious for his company. It made her hungrier, and lonelier, and less understanding when two weeks slid by without his spending a night in her bed. She realized that she should be grateful to him that he came to her at all, and he made so many things in her life easier, but she wanted so much more of him, she always had, ever since they first met.

"Tana's coming to the wedding, isn't she?" He ate another mouthful of steak tartare, and she tried to look vague. She had called Tana about it only a few days before. She hadn't responded to the invitation Ann had sent, and she had chided her for it, telling her it wasn't polite, and her

126

Boston University manners didn't apply here, which of course had done nothing to warm Tana's heart.

"I'll answer as soon as I get around to it, Mom. I have exams right now. It only came last week."

"It only takes a minute to respond."

Her tone annoyed Tana as it always did now, and she was curt when she replied. "Fine. Then tell her no."

"I'll do nothing of the sort. You answer that invitation yourself. And I think you should go."

"Well, that comes as no surprise. Another command performance from the Durning clan. When do we get to say no to them?" She still cringed every time she imagined Billy's face. "I think I'm busy anyway."

"You could make the effort for my sake at least."

"Tell them that you have no control over me. That I'm impossible, that I'm climbing Mount Everest. Tell them whatever the hell you want!"

"You're really not going then?" Jean sounded shocked, as though that weren't possible.

"I hadn't thought about it till now, but now that you mention it, I guess I'm not."

"You knew it all along."

"Oh, for chrissake . . . look, I don't like Ann or Billy. Scratch that. I don't like Ann, and I hate Billy's guts. Arthur is your affair, if you'll pardon the pun. Why do you have to drag me into this? I'm grown up now, so are they, we've never been friends."

"It's her wedding, and she wants you there."

"Bullshit. She's probably inviting everyone she knows, and she's inviting me as a favor to you."

"That's not true." But they both knew it was. And Tana was getting stronger and stronger as time went on. In some ways, it was Harry's influence over her. He had definite ideas about almost everything, and it brought something similar out in her in order to respond to him. He made her think about how she felt and what she thought about everything, and they were as close as they had ever been. And he'd been right about BU too. Moving to Boston had been good for her, much more so than going to Green Hill.

And in an odd way, she had grown up more in the last year than ever before. She was almost twenty years old.

"Tana, I just can't understand why you behave this way." It was back to the wedding again, and her mother was driving her nuts.

"Mom, can we talk about something else? How are *you*?"

"I'm fine, but I'd like to think that you'll at least think about this. . . ."

"All right!" She screamed into the phone at her end. "I'll think about it. Can I bring a date?" Maybe it would be more bearable if Harry came along.

"I was expecting that. Why don't you and the Winslow boy take a lesson from Ann and John and get engaged?"

"Because we're not in love. That's the best reason why not."

"I find that hard to believe after all this time."

"Fact is stranger than fiction, Mom." Talking to her mother always drove her nuts, and she tried to explain it to Harry the next day. "It's as though she spends the whole day planning what to say to me so that it will irritate me the most possible, and she never fails. She hits the nail right on the head every time."

"My father has the same knack. It's a pre-requisite."

"For what?"

"For parenthood. You have to pass a test. If you're not irritating enough, they make you try again until you get it right. Then after the kid is born, they have to renew it every few years, so that after fifteen or twenty years, you've really got it down." Tana laughed at the idea as she looked at him. He was even more handsome than he had been when they first met, and the girls went crazy for him. There were always about half a dozen he was juggling at once, but he always made time for her. She came first, she was his friend, in fact she was much more than that to him, but Tana had never understood that. "You're going to be around for a long time, Tan. They'll be gone by next week." He never took any of them seriously, no matter how desperately they wanted him. He didn't fool anyone, he was careful that no

128

one got hurt, he was sensible about birth control. "No casualties, thanks to me, Tan. Life is too short for that, and there's enough hurt out there without making more for your friends." But there was no pretense offered either. Harry Winslow wanted to have fun, and nothing more than that. No I love you's, no wedding rings, no starry eyes, just some laughs, a lot of beer, and a good time, if possible in bed. His heart was otherwise engaged, albeit secretly, but other interesting parts of him were not.

"Don't they want more than that?"

"Sure they do. They've got mothers just like you. Only most of them listen to their mothers more than you do. They all want to get married and drop out of school as soon as possible. But I tell them not to count on me to help them out. And if they don't believe me, they figure it out soon enough." He grinned boyishly and Tana laughed at him. She knew that the girls dropped like flies every time he looked at them. She and Harry had been inseparable for the past year and she was the envy of all her friends. They found it impossible to believe that nothing was going on between them, they were as puzzled as her own mother was, but the relationship stayed chaste. Harry had come to understand her by now, and he wouldn't have dared to scale the walls she had put up around her sexuality. Once or twice he tried to fix her up with one of his friends, just as a friendly double date, but she wanted nothing to do with it. His roommate had even asked him if she was a lesbian, but he was sure that it wasn't that. He had a strong feeling that something had traumatized her, but she never wanted to talk about it, even with him, and he let it be. She went out with Harry, or her friends from BU, or by herself, but there were no men in her life, not in a romantic sense.

"It's a hell of a waste, you know, kid." He tried to talk to her about it teasingly, but she brushed him off as she always did.

"You do enough of that for both of us."

"That doesn't do you much good."

She laughed. "I'm saving it for my wedding night."

"A noble cause." He swept her a low bow and they both

laughed. People at Harvard and BU were used to seeing them, raising hell, cavorting, playing pranks on each other and their friends. Harry bought a bicycle for two at a garage sale one weekend, and they rode around Cambridge on it, with Harry in a huge raccoon hat in the winter months, and a straw boater when the weather got warm.

"Want to go to Ann Durning's wedding with me?" They were wandering across the Harvard Quad, the day after her mother had harassed her about it on the phone.

"Not particularly. Is it liable to be fun?"

"Not a chance." Tana smiled angelically. "My mother thinks I should go."

"I'm sure you expected that."

"She also thinks we should get engaged."

"I'll second that."

"Good. Then let's make it a double ceremony. Seriously, do you want to go?"

"Why?" There was something nervous in her eyes and he was trying to figure out what it was. He knew her well, but every now and then she hid from him, albeit not too successfully.

"I don't want to go alone. I don't like any of them. Ann's a real spoiled brat, and she's already been married once, but her daddy seems to be making a big fuss about this. I guess she did it right this time."

"What does that mean?"

"What do you think? It means the guy she's marrying has bucks."

"How sensitive." Harry smiled angelically and Tana laughed.

"It's nice to know where people's values are, isn't it? Anyway, the wedding's right after we get out of school, in Connecticut."

"I was going to the South of France that week, Tan, but I could put it off for a few days, if it'll help you out."

"That wouldn't be too big a pain in the ass for you?"

"It would." He smiled at her honestly. "But for you, anything." He bowed low, and she laughed, and he slapped her behind and they got back on the bicycle built for two, and he dropped her off at her dorm at BU. He had a big date that night. He had already invested four dinners in the girl, and he expected her to come through for him tonight.

"How can you talk like that!" Tana laughed and scolded him as they stood outside her dorm.

"I can't feed her forever, for chrissake, without getting something for it. Besides, she eats those huge steaks with the lobster tails. My income is suffering from this broad, but . . ." he smiled, thinking of her mammaries, ". . . I'll let you know how it works out."

"I don't think I want to know."

"That's right . . . virgin ears . . . oh well. . . ." He waved as he rode off on their bicycle.

That night, she wrote a letter to Sharon, washed her hair, and had brunch with Harry the next day. He had gotten nowhere with the girl, "The Eater" as he called her now. She had devoured not only her own steak, but most of his as well, her lobster as well as his once more, and then told him that she didn't feel well and had to go home and study for exams. He got nothing whatsoever for his pains except a large check at the restaurant and a night of good, restful sleep, alone in his bed. "That's the end of her. Christ, the trouble you have to go to, to get laid these days." But she knew from all she heard that he did fine most of the time, and she teased him about it all the way to New York in June. He dropped her off at her apartment and went on to the Pierre. When he picked her up the next day to go to the wedding, she had to admit that he looked spectacular. He was wearing white flannel slacks, a blue cashmere blazer, a creamy silk shirt his father had made for him in London the year before, and a navy and red Hermes tie.

"Shit, Harry, if the bride had any sense, she'd ditch this guy and run off with you."

"That headache I don't need. And you don't look bad yourself, Tan." She was wearing a green silk dress almost the exact same color as her eyes, her hair hung long and straight down her back, and she had brushed it until it shone, just like her eyes, which sparkled as she looked at him.

"Thanks for coming with me. I know it's going to be a bore, but I appreciate it."

"Don't be silly. I didn't have anything else to do anyway. I'm not leaving for Nice until tomorrow night." And from there he was driving to Monaco, where his father was picking him up on a friend's yacht. Harry was going to spend two weeks with him, and then his father was dropping him off and going on with friends, leaving Harry alone in the house on Cap Ferrat. "I can think of worse fates, Tan." He was hinting at the hell he would raise, chasing girls in the South of France, and living in the house alone, but it sounded lonely to her. He would have no one to talk to most of the time, no one who really cared about him. On the other hand, she was going to spend the summer being smothered by Jean. In a moment of weakness, feeling guilty for the independence that had been so hard won, she had agreed to take a summer job, working for Durning International. And her mother was thrilled.

"I could kill myself every time I think about it." She groaned to Harry every time the subject came up. "I was nuts. But I feel so sorry for her sometimes. She's so alone now that I'm gone. And I thought it would be a nice thing to do for her, but Christ, Harry . . . what have I done?"

"It won't be that bad, Tan."

"Want to make a bet?" Her scholarship had come through for the following year, and she wanted to make some pocket money to spend. At least this would help. But it depressed her beyond words to think of spending the whole summer in New York, living with Jean, and watching her kiss Arthur's feet at work every day. The very thought made her sick.

"We'll go to the Cape for a week when I come back."

"Thank God for that." They exchanged a smile as he drove her to Connecticut, and a little while later, they were standing in Christ Episcopal Church with the rest of the guests, painfully hot in the stifling June air, and then mercifully they were released and they drove to the Durning house, passing through the enormous gates, as Harry watched her face. It was the first time she had been back since the nightmare night two years before. Exactly two years in fact.

"You really don't like it here, do you, Tan?"

"Not much." She glanced out the window and looked vague as he watched the back of her head. But he could sense something inside her go tense, and it was worse once they parked the car and got out. They wandered down the receiving line saying the appropriate things. Tana introduced Harry to Arthur and the bride and groom, and then as she ordered a drink, she saw Billy staring at her. He was watching her intently, and Harry was watching him, as he wandered away, and Tana seemed to be in a stupor after that. She danced with Harry several times, with several people she didn't know, chatted with her mother once or twice, and then suddenly in a lull, she found herself face to face with Billy.

"Hello there. I wondered if you'd come." She had an overwhelming urge to slap his face, but instead she turned away. She couldn't breathe just looking at him. She hadn't seen him since that night, and he looked as malevolent as he had then, as weak and evil and spoiled. She could remember his hitting her, and then. . . .

"Get away from me." She spoke in a barely audible voice.

"Don't be so uptight. Hell, this is my sister's wedding day. It's a romantic event." She could see that he was more than slightly drunk. She knew that he had graduated from Princeton a few days before and he had probably been drinking non-stop since then. He was going into the family firm, so he could screw around and chase secretaries. She wanted to ask him who he'd raped recently, but instead she just started to walk away and he grabbed her arm. "That was a pretty rude thing to do."

She turned back to him, her teeth clenched, her eyes wild. "Get your hand off of me or I'm going to throw this drink in your face." She hissed like a snake, and suddenly Harry materialized at her side, watching her, seeing something he had never seen before, and also noting the look in Billy Durning's eyes.

Billy Durning whispered one word, "Whore," with a

vicious look in his eyes, and with a single gesture Harry grabbed his arm and twisted it back painfully until Billy groaned and tried to fight back, but he didn't want to make a scene and Harry whispered in his ear.

"Got the picture, pal? Good, then why don't you just take yourself off right now?" Billy wrenched his arm free, and without saying a word, he walked away as Harry looked at Tana. She was shaking from head to foot. "You all right?" She nodded, but he wasn't convinced. She was deathly pale, and her teeth were chattering despite the heat. "What was that all about? An old friend?"

"Mr. Durning's adorable son."

"I take it you two have met before."

She nodded. "Not very pleasantly." They stayed for a little while after that, but it was obvious that Tana was anxious to leave so Harry suggested it first. He didn't say anything for a while as they drove back to town, and he could see her visibly unwind as they put some distance between them and the Durning house. He had to ask her then. Something so powerful had been in the air, it frightened him for her.

"What was that all about, Tan?"

"Nothing much. An old hatred, that's all."

"Based on what?"

"He's a complete prick, that's what." They were strong words for her and Harry was surprised, and there was no humor in her voice. "A rotten little son-of-a-bitch."

"I figured you two weren't the best of friends." Harry smiled but she didn't respond. "What did he do to you, to make you hate him so much, Tan?"

"It's not important now."

"Yes, it is."

"No, it's not!" She was shouting at him, and there were suddenly tears rolling down her cheeks. None of it had healed in the past two years, because she hadn't allowed the air to get to it. She hadn't told anyone except Sharon, hadn't fallen in love, hadn't gone on any dates. "It doesn't matter anymore."

He waited for her words to die down. "Are you trying to

convince me or yourself?" He handed her his pocket hand-kerchief and she blew her nose.

"I'm sorry, Harry."

"Don't be. Remember me? I'm your friend." She smiled through her tears and patted his cheek.

"You're the best friend I've got."

"I want you to tell me what happened with him."

"Why?"

He smiled. "So I can go back and kill him if you want."

"Okay. Go ahead." She laughed for the first time in hours.

"Seriously, I think you need to get it off your chest."

"No, I don't." That frightened her more than living with it. She didn't even want to talk about it now.

"He made a pass at you, didn't he?"

"More or less." She was looking out the window again.

"Tana . . . talk to me. . . ."

She turned to him with a wintry smile. "Why?"

"Because I give a darnn." He pulled the car off the road, turned off the ignition and looked at her. He knew suddenly that he was about to open a door that had been sealed tight, but he knew that for her sake he had to open it. "Tell me what he did to you."

She stared into Harry's eyes and spoke expressionlessly. "He raped me two years ago. Two years ago tomorrow night, in fact. Happy Anniversary." Harry felt sick.

"What do you mean he raped you? Did you go out with him?"

She shook her head. "No. My mother insisted that I go to a party here in Greenwich, at the house. His party. I went with one of his friends, who got drunk and disappeared, and Billy found me wandering around the house. He asked me if I wanted to see the room where my mother worked. And like a complete fool, I said yes, and the next thing I knew he dragged me into his father's bedroom, threw me down on the floor and beat me up. He raped me and beat me for a few hours, and then he took me home and cracked up the car." She slowly began to sob, choking on her own words, feeling them rush out, almost physically. "I had hysterics at the hospital . . . after the police came . . . my mother came out . . . and she wouldn't believe me, she thought I was drunk . . . and little Billy could do no wrong in her eyes . . . I tried to tell her another time. . . ." She buried her face in her hands, and Harry pulled her into his arms, and cooed to her the way no one had ever done to him, but listening to her almost broke his heart. It was why she had never gone out with anyone since they'd met, nor with him.

"Poor baby . . . poor Tan. . . ." He drove her back to the city then, took her to dinner at a quiet place, and then they went back and talked for hours at the Pierre. She knew her mother would be staying in Greenwich again that night. She had been staying there all week, to make sure that everything went all right. And after Harry dropped her off, he wondered if things would change for Tana now, or even if possibly things might change between them. She was the most remarkable girl he had ever met, and if he had let herself, he would have fallen head over heels in love with her. But he had known better for the past two years, and he reminded himself of that now. He didn't want to spoil what they had, for what? A piece of ass? He had plenty of that, and she meant more than that to him. It was still going to take her a long time to heal, if she ever did, and he could help her more as her friend, than trying to meet his own needs by jumping into bed and playing therapist with her.

He called her the next day before he left for the South of France, and he had flowers sent to her the day after that, with a note that read, "Screw the past. You're okay now. Love, H." And he called her from Europe whenever he thought of it and had the time. His summer was a lot more interesting than hers, and they compared notes when he came back a week before Labor Day, and she finished her job and drove to Cape Cod with him. She was relieved to be out of Durning International at last. It had been a mistake, but she had lived up to her end.

"Any big romances while I was gone?"

"Nope. Remember me? I'm saving it for my wedding night." But they both knew why now. She was still traumatized by the rape, and they both also knew that she had to get over that. And after talking to him before he left, it seemed a little less painful now. It was finally beginning to heal.

"There won't be a wedding night if you never go out, you jerk."

"You sound like my mother again." She smiled. It was so good to see him again.

"How is your mother, by the way?"

"The same. Arthur Durning's devoted slave. It makes me sick. I never want to be like that with anyone."

He snapped his fingers with a look of despair. "Shit . . . and I was hoping that. . . ." They both laughed, and the week sped by as it always did when they had a good time, and there was something magical about being together on Cape Cod. But in spite of Harry's hidden feelings for her, they kept the relationship as it had been. And they both went back to their respective schools for their junior year, which seemed to fly by. The following summer Tana stayed in Boston to work, and Harry went to Europe again, and when he came back they went back to Cape Cod, and the easy days were almost over with. They had only one year left before real life set in. And each in their own way, they were trying to keep reality at bay.

"What are you going to do?" she asked him somberly one night. She had finally agreed to date one of his friends, but things were going very slowly and Tana wasn't really interested in him. Secretly, Harry was glad. But he thought that a few superficial dates would do her good.

"He's just not my type."

"How the hell do you know? You haven't gone out with anyone in three years."

"From what I can see, that's no loss."

"Bitch." He grinned.

"I'm serious. What the hell are we going to do next year? Have you thought about graduate school?"

"God, no! That's all I need. I've had enough of this place to last me the rest of my life. I'm getting the hell out."

"And doing what?" She had been tormenting herself for the past two months.

"I don't know. I guess I'll stay in the house in London for a while. My father seems to be in South Africa all the time these days so it wouldn't bother him. Maybe Paris ... Rome, then I'll come back here. I just want to play, Tan." And he was running away from something he wanted and knew he couldn't have. Not yet.

"Don't you want to work?" She looked shocked and he roared.

"Why?"

"That's disgusting!"

"What's disgusting about it? The men in my family haven't worked in years."

"How can you admit that?"

"Because it's true. They're a bunch of rich, lazy bums. Just like my old man." But there was more to them than that, especially him. Much, much more.

"Is that what you want your children to say about you?" She looked horrified.

"Sure, if I'm dumb enough to have any, which I doubt."

"You sound like me now."

"God forbid." They both smiled.

"Seriously, aren't you at least going to pretend to work?"

"Why?"

"Stop saying that."

"Who cares if I work, Tan? You? Me? My old man? The columnists?"

"Then why did you go to school?"

"I had nothing else to do with myself, and Harvard was fun."

"Bullshit. You studied your ass off for exams." She tossed the gold mane over her shoulder with an earnest look. "You were a good student. What for?"

"Myself. What about you? What were you doing it for?'

"Same thing. But now I don't know what the hell to do."

But two weeks before Christmas, the choice was made for her. Sharon Blake called, and asked her if she would be willing to go on a march with Dr. King. Tana thought about it for a night, and called Sharon back the next day, with a tired smile. "You got me again, kid."

"Hurray! I knew you would!" She filled Tana in on the details. It was to take place three days before Christmas in Alabama and it was relatively low risk. It all sounded fine to her, and the two girls chatted like old times. Sharon had never gone back to school, much to her father's chagrin, and she was in love with a young black attorney now. They were talking about getting married in the spring. Tana was excited for her when she hung up, and she told Harry about the march the following afternoon.

"Your mother's going to have a fit."

"I don't have to tell her about it, for chrissake. She doesn't have to know everything I do."

"She will when you get arrested again."

"I'll call you and you can come bail me out." She was serious and he shook his head.

"I can't. I'll be in Gstaad."

"Shit."

"I don't think you should go."

"I didn't ask you."

But when the time came, she was in bed with a fever of 102 degrees and a virulent flu. She tried to get up and pack the night before, but she was just too sick, and she called Sharon at the Blakes' home in Washington, and Freeman Blake answered the phone.

"You've heard the news then . . . ?" His voice sounded as though it came from the bottom of a well, and it was filled with gloom.

"What news?"

He couldn't even say the words. He just sat there and cried, and without knowing why, Tana began to cry too. "She's dead . . . they killed her last night . . . they shot her . . . my baby . . . my little girl. . . ." He was totally unglued and Tana was sobbing along with him, feeling frightened and hysterical, until Miriam Blake came to the phone. She sounded distraught but she was calmer than her husband had been. She told Tana when the funeral was. And Tana flew to Washington, fever and all, on the morning of

Christmas Eve. It had taken that long to get the body home, and Martin Luther King had made arrangements to come and speak about her.

There was national news coverage, press pushing their way into the church, flashbulbs going off in everyone's face, and Freeman Blake was completely undone. He had lost both of his children now, to the same cause, and afterwards Tana spent a little quiet time with them, with close friends, at their home.

"Do something useful with your life, child." Freeman Blake looked bleakly at her. "Get married, have kids. Don't do what Sharon did." He began to cry again, and eventually Dr. King and another friend led him upstairs and it was Miriam who came to sit beside Tana then. Everyone had been crying all day, and for days before, and Tana felt wrung out both from the emotions and the flu.

"I'm so sorry, Mrs. Blake."

"So am I. . . ." Her eyes looked like rivers of pain. She had seen it all, but she was still on her feet and always would be. She was that kind of woman, and in some ways Tana admired her. "What are you going to do now, Tana?"

She wasn't sure what Miriam meant. "Go home, I guess." She was going to catch a late flight that night to spend Christmas with Jean. As usual, Arthur had gone away with friends, and Jean was going to be alone.

"I mean when you finish school."

"I don't know."

"Have you ever thought about going into government? That's what this country needs." Tana smiled, she could almost hear Sharon speaking to her. Here, her daughter had just died, and she was already back at her crusades. It was frightening in some ways, and yet admirable too. "You could go into law. You could change things, Tana. You're that kind of girl."

"I'm not sure I am."

"You are. You've got guts. Sharon did too, but she didn't have your kind of mind. In some ways, you're like me." It was a frightening thought because Tana had always found her cold, and she didn't want to be like that.

"I am?" She looked a little stunned.

"You know what you want, and you go for it."

Tana smiled. "Sometimes."

"You didn't even skip a beat when you got kicked out of Green Hill."

"That was just luck, a friend, and Harry Winslow suggested BU."

"If he hadn't, you'd have landed on your feet anyway." She stood up with a small sigh. "Anyway, think about it. There aren't enough lawyers like you, Tan. You're what this country needs." It was a heady thing to say to a twenty-one-year-old girl, and on the plane home the words echoed in her head, but more than that, she kept seeing Freeman's face, hearing him cry . . . hearing things Sharon had said to her at Green Hill . . . the times they had walked into Yolan . . . the memories flooded her, and she dried her eyes again and again to no avail, and she found herself thinking constantly of the baby Sharon had given up four years before, wondering where he was, what had happened to him. And she wondered if Freeman had been thinking of him too. They had no one left now.

And at the same time, she kept thinking of Miriam's words. This country needs you . . . she tried the thought on her mother before she went back to school, and Jean Roberts looked horrified.

"Law School? Haven't you been in school for long enough? Are you going to stay there for the rest of your life?"

"Only if it does me some good."

"Why don't you get a job? You might meet someone that way."

"Oh, for chrissake, never mind . . ." It was all she thought about . . . meet someone . . . settle down . . . get married . . . have kids. . . . But Harry wasn't much warmer to the idea when she tried it out on him the following week.

"Jesus Christ, why?'"

"Why not? It might be interesting, and I might be good at it." She was getting more excited about it every day, and suddenly it seemed like the right thing to do. It made some sense, gave some purpose to her life. "I'm going to apply to Boalt, at UC Berkeley." She had already made up her mind. There were two other schools she was going to apply to also, but Boalt was her first choice.

Harry stared at her. "You're serious?"

"Yes."

"I think you're nuts."

"Want to come?"

"Hell, no!" He grinned. "I told you. I'm going to play . . . just kick up my heels."

"That's a waste of time."

"I can hardly wait."

And neither could she. In May she got the word. She'd been accepted at Boalt. They would give her a partial scholarship, and she had already saved the rest.

"I'm on my way." She grinned at Harry as they sat on the lawn outside her dorm.

"Tan, are you sure?"

"Never more so in my whole life." The two exchanged a long smile. The road would part for them soon. She went to his graduation at Harvard in June, and cried copiously for him, for herself, for Sharon Blake who was no more, for John F. Kennedy who had been killed seven months before, for the people they had met, and never would. An era had come to an end, for them both. And she cried at her own graduation, too. As Jean Roberts did, and Arthur Durning came along. And Harry sat in the back row, pretending to make conquests among the freshman girls.

But it was Tana his eyes were rivetted to, his heart leapt with pride for her and then sank as he thought of their going separate ways. He knew that inevitably their paths would cross again. He would see to that. But for her, it was still too soon. And with all his heart, he wished her godspeed, that she would be safe and well in California. It made him nervous to think of her so far from him. But he had to let her go for now . . . for now . . . tears filled his eyes as he watched her come down the steps with her diploma in hand. She looked so fresh and young, the big green eyes, the bright shining hair . . . and the lips he so desperately longed to kiss and had for almost four years . . . the same lips brushed his cheeks as he congratulated her again, and for an instant, just an instant, he felt her hold him close, and it almost took his breath away.

"Thanks, Harry." There were tears in her eyes.

"What for?" He had to fight back tears in his own.

"For everything." And then the others pressed in on them and the moment was gone. Their separate lives had begun.

Part II

Life Begins

Chapter 7

The ride to the airport seemed endless this time. Tana took a cab, and Jean insisted on coming with her. There were endless silences, pauses, staccato bursts of words, like machine-gun fire at the enemy as it disappeared into the brush, and then finally they were there. Jean insisted on paying for the cab, as though it were her last chance to do something for her little girl, the only chance she'd ever have, and it was easy to see she was fighting back tears as they checked Tana's bags in.

"That's all you had, dear?" She turned to Tana nervously, as Tana nodded and smiled. It had been a difficult morning for her, too. There was no pretending anymore. She wouldn't be coming home again, not for a long, long time. For a few days, a week, a brief trip. But if she managed to hang in at Boalt, she would probably never live at home again. She hadn't had to face that before when she went to Green Hill, or BU, and she was ready to go now. But it was easy to see the panic on Jean's face. It was the same expression she had worn twenty-three years before when Andy Roberts had gone to war. That look that comes of knowing that nothing will ever be the same again. "You won't forget to call me tonight, will you, dear?"

"No, Mother. I won't. But I can't promise after this." Tana smiled. "If everything I hear is true, I won't come up for air for the next six months." And she had already warned her that she wouldn't be coming home for Christmas that year. The trip was too expensive anyway. And Jean had resigned herself to that. She was hoping that Arthur might give her a ticket out, but then there would be no hope of spending Christmas with him. Life wasn't easy sometimes. For some, it never was.

They both had a cup of tea, and watched the planes take

off as Tana waited for her plane to be called, and she saw her mother staring at her more than once. Twenty-two years of caring for her was officially coming to an end, and it was difficult for both of them. And then suddenly Jean took her hand and looked into her eyes. "Is this what you really want, Tan?"

Tana answered her quietly. "Yes, Mom, it is."

"You're sure?"

Tana smiled. "I am. I know it seems strange to you, but it really is what I want. I've never been so sure of anything, no matter how hard it is."

Jean frowned and slowly shook her head before looking at Tana again. It was a strange time to be talking about it, just before she took off, and a strange place, with thousands of people all around, but this was where they were and what was in Jean's heart as she looked into her daughter's eyes again. "It seems more like a career for a man. I just never thought. . . ."

"I know." Tana looked sad. "You wanted me to be like Ann." She was living in Greenwich, near her dad, and had just had her first child. Her husband was a full partner of Sherman and Sterling now. He drove a Porsche, and she a Mercedes sedan. It was every mother's dream. "That just isn't me. It never was, Mom."

"But why not?" She didn't understand. Maybe she had gone wrong.

"Maybe I need more than that. Maybe I need it to be my accomplishment, instead of my husband's. I don't know, but I don't think I could be happy like that."

"I think Harry Winslow is in love with you, Tan." Her voice was gentle, but Tana didn't want to hear the words.

"You're wrong, Mom." It was back to that again. "We love each other dearly, as friends, but he's not in love with me, and I'm not in love with him." That wasn't what she wanted. She wanted him as her brother, her friend. Jean nodded and said nothing as they called Tana's plane. It was as though she were making a last attempt to change Tana's mind, but there was nothing to change it with, no lifestyle, no man, no overwhelming gift, and nothing would have

148

changed it anyway. She looked into her mother's eyes, and then held her close in a long hug as she whispered in her ear. "Mom, this is what I want. I'm sure. I swear it to you." It was like leaving for Africa as she said goodbye. As though she were leaving for a different world, a different life, and in a way she was. Her mother looked so grief-stricken that it broke her heart, and Jean's tears flowed unchecked down her cheeks as she waved goodbye and Tana boarded the plane, shouting back, "I'll call you tonight!"

"But it'll never be the same again," Jean whispered to herself, as she watched the doors close, the gangway pull back, and the giant bird head down the runway at last, and finally take off. And then at long, long last, it was only a speck in the sky, and feeling very small and very alone, she went outside, hailed a cab, and went back to the office where Arthur Durning needed her. At least someone still did, but she dreaded going home that night.

Chapter 8

Tana had taken a plane which landed at Oakland airport, and it seemed a small and friendly place when she arrived. Smaller than both Boston and New York, and much, much larger than Yolan, which didn't have an airport at all. She took a cab to the Berkeley campus with her conglomeration of things, checked into the room that had been rented for her as part of her scholarship, unpacked her bags, and looked around. Everything felt different and strange and new. It was a beautiful, warm, sunny day, and people looked relaxed in everything from blue jeans to cords to flowing robes. There was more than one caftan in sight, lots of shorts and T shirts, sandals, sneakers, loafers, bare feet. Unlike Boston University, the Jewish princesses from New York were not in evidence here, wearing expensive wools and cashmeres from Bendel's. This was strictly "come as you are", and it was anything but neat. But there was an excitement about it, too, and she felt exhilarated as she looked around. It was an exhilaration which stayed with her once classes began, and into the next month, as she ran from one class to the other every day, and then dashed home to study all afternoon and all night. The only other place she ever saw was the library, and whenever possible she ate in her room or on the run. She had lost six pounds which she didn't need to lose by the end of the first month. And the only good thing about the schedule she kept was that she didn't miss Harry quite as much as she feared she would. For three years, they had been almost joined at the hip, even though they attended different schools, and now suddenly he wasn't there, although he would call at off-hours. And on October 5th, she was in her room, when someone knocked on her door and told her that there was a call on the pay phone for her. She figured it was her mother again, and she really didn't want to go downstairs. She had a quiz the next day on contract law, and she had a paper due in another course.

"Find out who it is. Can I call back?"

"Okay, just a sec." And then she came back again. "It's from New York."

"Shit." Her mother again. "I'll call back."

"He says you can't." He? Harry? Tana smiled. For him, she would even interrupt her work.

"I'll be right out." She grabbed a pair of rumpled jeans off the back of a chair, and pulled them on as she ran to the phone. "Hello?"

"What the hell are you doing? Making it with some guy on the fourteenth floor? I've been sitting here for an hour, Tan." He sounded annoyed and he also sounded drunk, to her practised ear. She knew him well.

"I'm sorry, I was in my room, studying, and I thought it was my mom."

"No such luck." He sounded strangely serious.

"Are you in New York?" She was smiling, happy to hear him again.

"Yeah."

"I thought you weren't coming back till next month."

"I wasn't. I came back to see my uncle. Apparently, he thinks he needs my help."

"What uncle?" Tana looked confused. Harry had never mentioned an uncle before.

"My Uncle Sam. Remember him, the guy on the posters in the ridiculous red and blue suit with the long white beard." He was definitely drunk and she started to laugh, but the laughter faded on her lips. He was serious. Oh my God. . . .

"What the hell do you mean?"

"I got drafted, Tan."

"Oh shit." She closed her eyes. That was all they heard about. Vietnam . . . Vietnam . . . Vietnam . . . everyone had something to say about it . . . kick the shit out of them . . . stay out of it . . . remember what happened to the French . . . go to it . . . stay home . . . police action . . . war . . . it was impossible to know what was going on, but whatever it was, it wasn't good. "Why the hell did you come back? Why didn't you stay over there?"

"I didn't want to do that. My father even offered to buy me out if he could, which I doubt. There are some things which even his Winslow money won't buy. But that's not my style, Tan. I don't know, maybe secretly I've wanted to go over there and make myself useful for a while."

"You're nuts. My God. . . . You're worse than that. You could be killed. Don't you realize that? Harry go back to France." She was shouting at him now, standing in an open corridor, shouting at Harry in New York. "Why the hell don't you go to Canada, or shoot yourself in the foot . . . do something, resist the draft. This is 1964, not 1941. Don't be so noble, there's nothing to be noble about, asshole. Go back." There were suddenly tears in her eyes and she was afraid to ask what she wanted to know. But she had to. She had to know. "Where are they sending you?"

"San Francisco." Her heart soared. "First. For about five hours. Want to meet me at the airport, Tan? We could have lunch or something. I have to get to some place called Fort Ord by ten o'clock that night, and I arrive at three. And somebody told me it was about a two hour drive from San Francisco. . . ." His voice trailed off, they were both thinking the same thing.

"And then what?" Her voice was suddenly hoarse.

"Vietnam, I guess. Cute, huh?"

She suddenly sounded pissed. "No, not cute, you dumb son-of-a-bitch. You should have come to law school with me. Instead, you wanted to play and get yourself laid in every whorehouse in France, and now look at you, you're going to Vietnam to get your balls shot off. . . ." There were tears rolling down her face, and no one dared walk past her in the hall.

"You make it sound intriguing anyway."

"You're a jerk."

"So what else is new? You fallen in love yet?"

"Who has time, all I do is read. What time does your plane come in?"

"Three o'clock tomorrow."

"I'll be there."

"Thanks." He sounded so young again, on the last word, and when she saw him the next day, she thought he looked pale and tired. He didn't look as well as when she had seen him in June, and their brief visit was nervous and strained. She didn't know what to do with him. Five hours wasn't very long. She took him to her Berkeley room, and then they drove into town for lunch in Chinatown, wandered around, and Harry kept looking at his watch. He had a bus to catch. He had decided not to rent a car to get to Fort Ord after all, but that shortened the time he had with her. They didn't laugh as much as usual, and they were both upset all afternoon.

"Harry, why are you doing this? You could have bought your way out."

"That's not my style, Tan. You must know that by now. And maybe, secretly, I think I'm doing the right thing. There's a patriotic part of me I didn't know I had."

Tana felt her heart sink. "That's not patriotism, for chrissake. It isn't our war." It horrified her that he had an out he wouldn't use. It was a side of him she had never seen. Easygoing Harry had grown up, and she saw a man in him she had never known before. He was stubborn and strong, and although what he was doing frightened him, it was clearly what he wanted to do.

"I think it will be soon, Tan."

"But why you?" They sat silently for a long time and the day went too fast. She held him tight when they said goodbye, and she made him promise to call whenever he could. But that wasn't for another six weeks, and by then basic training was over. He had been planning to come back to San Francisco to see her, but instead of going north, he was being sent south. "I leave for San Diego tonight." It was Saturday. "And Honolulu, the beginning of the week." And she had mid-term exams, so she couldn't just run down to San Diego for a day or two.

"Shit. Will you stay in Honolulu for a while?"

"Apparently not." She sensed instantly that he wasn't telling her what she wanted to know.

"What does that mean?"

"It means I'm being sent to Saigon by the end of next week." His voice sounded cold and hard, almost like steel, and it didn't sound like Harry at all. She wondered how this had happened to him, and it was something he had wondered himself every day for six weeks. "Just lucky, I guess," he had said jokingly to his friends, but there was nothing to joke about, and you could have cut the air with a knife when they handed the assignments out. No one dared say anything to anyone, least of all those who had fared well, for fear that others had not. And Harry was one of the unlucky ones. "It's a bitch, Tan, but there it is."

"Does your father know?"

"I called last night. No one knows where he is. In Paris, they think he's in Rome. In Rome, they think he's in New York. I tried South Africa, and then I figured fuck the son-of-a-bitch. He'll find out sooner or later where I am." Why the hell didn't he have a father one could reach? Tana would even have called for him, but he had always sounded like the kind of man she didn't want to know anyway. "I wrote to him at the London address, and I left a message at the Pierre in New York. That's the best I can do."

"It's probably more than he deserves anyway. Harry, is there anything I can do?"

"Say a prayer." He sounded as though he were serious, and she was shocked. This wasn't possible. Harry was her best friend, her brother, practically her twin, and they were sending him to Vietnam. She had a sense of panic she had never known before and there was absolutely nothing she could do.

"Will you call me again before you leave . . . ? and from Honolulu . . . ?" There were tears in her eyes . . . what if something happened to him? But nothing would, she gritted her teeth, she wouldn't even let herself think like that. Harry Winslow was invincible, and he belonged to her. He owned a piece of her heart. But she felt lost for the next few days, waiting constantly for his calls. There were two from San Diego before he left, "Sorry I took so long, I was busy getting laid, probably got the clap, but what the hell." He was drunk most of the time, and even more so in Hawaii, and he called her twice from there, too, and after that he was gone, into the silence, the jungles and the abyss of Vietnam. She constantly imagined him in danger, and then began to get outrageous letters describing life in Saigon, the hookers, the drugs, the once lovely hotels, the exquisite girls, the constant use he had for his French, and she began to relax. Good old Harry, nothing ever changed, from Cambridge to Saigon, he was the same. She managed to get through her exams, Thanksgiving, and the first two days of the Christmas holiday, which she was spending in her room with a two-foot tall stack of books, when someone came and pounded on her door at seven o'clock one night.

"Call for you." Her mother had been calling her a lot, but Tana knew why, although neither of them ever admitted it. The holidays were difficult for Jean. Arthur never spent much time with her, and somehow she always hoped that he would. There were excuses and reasons and parties where he just couldn't take her along, and Tana suspected that there were probably other women too, and now there was Ann and her husband and her baby, and maybe Billy was there too, and Jean just wasn't family, no matter how many years she'd been around.

"I'll be right there," Tana called out, pulled on her bathrobe, and went to the phone. The hall was cold, and she knew it was foggy outside. It was rare for the fog to come this far east, but sometimes it did on particularly bad nights. "Hello?" She expected her mother's voice and was shocked when she heard Harry's instead. He sounded hoarse and very tired, as though he'd been up all night, which was understandable, if he was in town. His voice sounded exquisitely close. "Harry . . . ?" Tears instantly filled her eyes, "Harry! Is that you?"

"Hell, yes, Tan." He almost growled at her, and she could almost feel the beard stubble on his face.

"Where are you?"

There was only a fraction of a pause. "Here. San Francisco."

"When did you arrive? Christ, I'd have picked you up if I'd known."

"I just got in." It was a lie, but it was easier to tell her that than to explain why it had taken so long to call.

"You sure didn't stay long, thank God." She was so grateful to hear his voice that she couldn't stop the tears. She was smiling and crying all at once, and at his end, so was he. He had never thought he would hear her voice again, and he loved her more than he ever had before. He wasn't even sure that he could hide it now. But he would have to, for her sake, and his own. "Why'd they let you come back so soon?"

"I guess I gave them a bad time. The food stank, the girls had lice. Shit, I caught crabs twice, and the worst case of the clap I ever had. . . ." He tried to laugh but it hurt too much.

"You creep. Don't you ever behave yourself?"

"Not if I have a choice."

"So where are you now?"

There was that pause again. "They're cleaning me up at Letterman."

"Hospital?"

"Yeah."

"For the clap?" She said it so loud that two girls turned halfway down the hall and she started to laugh. "You know, you're impossible. You're the worst person I know, Harry Winslow the fourth, or whoever the hell you are. Can I come and visit you or will I get it too?" She was still laughing, and he still sounded tired and hoarse.

"Just don't use my toilet seat."

"Don't worry, I won't. I may not shake your hand either unless I see it boiled. God only knows where it's been." He smiled. It was so goddamn good to hear her voice. She looked at her watch. "Can I come over now?"

"Don't you have anything better to do on a Saturday night?"

"I was planning to make love to a stack of law books."

"You're about as amusing as you used to be, I see."

"Yeah, but I'm a lot smarter than you are, asshole, and nobody sent me to Vietnam." There was a strange silent pause, and Harry wasn't smiling when he answered her.

"Thank God, Tan." She felt strange as she heard his voice, and an odd feeling crept over her, that sent chills up her spine. "Do you really want to come over tonight?"

"Hell, yes, do you think I wouldn't come? I just don't want to catch the clap, that's all."

He smiled. "I'll behave myself." But he had to say something to her ... before she came ... it wasn't fair. "Tan. . . ." His voice caught on the words. He hadn't said anything to anyone yet. He hadn't even talked to his father yet. They hadn't been able to locate him anywhere although Harry knew he'd be in Gstaad by the end of the week. He always spent Christmas there, whether Harry was there or not. Switzerland meant Christmas to him. "Tan . . . I've got a little more than the clap. . . ." An odd chill raced up her spine and she closed her eyes.

"Yeah, asshole? Like what?" She wanted to fight back the words, to make him laugh, to make him all right in case he was not, but it was too late . . . to stop either the truth or the words. . . .

"I got a little bit shot up. . . ." She heard his voice crack, and felt a sudden pain in her chest as she fought back a sob.

"Oh yeah? Why'd you go do a thing like that?" She was fighting back tears and so was he.

"Nothing better to do, I guess. The girls were really all dogs. . . ." His voice grew sad and soft, ". . . compared to you, Tan."

"Jesus, they must have shot you in the brain." They both laughed a little bit, and she stood in her bare feet feeling as though her whole body had turned to ice. "Letterman. Right?"

"Yeah."

"I'll be there in half an hour."

"Take your time. I'm not going anywhere." And he wouldn't be for quite a while. But Tana didn't know any of that as she pulled on her jeans, shoved her feet into shoes, she didn't even know which ones, pulled a black turtleneck over her head, dragged a comb through her hair, and yanked her pea jacket off the foot of her bed. She had to get to him now, had to see what had happened to him. . . . *I got a little bit shot up.* . . . It was all she could hear again and again in her head as she took the bus into town, and then found a cab to take her to Letterman Hospital in the Presidio. It took twice as long as she had said it would be, but she had run like hell, and fifty-five minutes after she hung up, she walked into the hospital and asked for Harry's room. The woman at the reception desk asked Tana what department he was in, and she had a strong urge to say "The department for the clap", but she wasn't feeling funny now, and she felt even less so as she ran down the halls labelled Neurosurgery, praying that he was all right. Her face was so pale it was almost gray, but so was his when she walked into the room. There was a respirator standing by, and he was lying flat on a bed with a mirror overhead. There were racks and tubes, and a nurse watching over him. She thought he was paralyzed at first. Absolutely nothing moved, and then she saw him move a hand and tears filled her eyes, but she had been half right anyway. He was paralyzed from the waist down. He had been shot in the spine as he explained to her that night, as tears filled his eyes. He could finally talk to her, cry with her, tell her how he felt. He felt like shit. He wanted to die. He had wanted to die ever since they brought him back.

"So this is it. . . ." He could hardly speak, and the tears ran down the sides of his face, down his neck, onto the sheets. "I'll be in a wheelchair from now on. . . ." He was sobbing openly. He had thought he would never see her again, and suddenly there she was, so beautiful and so good and so blonde . . . just as she had always been. Everything was the same as it always had been. No one knew about Vietnam here. About Saigon or Da Nang or the Viet Cong, whom you never even saw. They just shot you in the ass from their hiding place in a tree, and maybe they were only nine years old, or just looked that way. But no one gave a damn about that here.

Tana was watching him, trying not to cry. She was grateful he was alive. From the story he had told, of lying face down in the mud, in the driving rains, in the jungle for five days, it was obviously a miracle that he was alive at all.

So what if he could never walk again? He was alive, wasn't he? And the thing Miriam Blake had seen in her so long before began to surface now. "That's what you get for screwing cheap whores, ya jerk. Now, you can lie there if you want to, for a while, but I want you to know right now that I'm not going to put up with much of this. Got that?" She stood up, and they were both unable to stop their tears, but she took his hand and she held it fast. "You're going to get off your ass and do something with yourself. Is that clear?" He stared at her in disbelief, and the crazy thing was that she was serious. "Is that clear?"

"You know you're a crazy girl. Do you know that, Tan?"

"And you're a lazy son-of-a-bitch, so don't get too excited about this lie-on-your-ass life of yours, because it's not going to last long. Got that, asshole?"

"Yes, ma'am." He saluted her, and a few minutes later, a nurse came in and gave him a shot for the pain, and Tana watched him drift off to sleep, holding his hand, as the tears rolled down her face and she cried, silently whispering her prayers and her thanks. She watched him for hours, just holding his hand, and at last she kissed his cheek, and his eyes, and she left the hospital. It was after midnight by then, and all she could think of as she took a bus back to Berkeley that night was "Thank God". Thank God he was alive. Thank God he hadn't died in that godforsaken jungle, wherever the hell it was. Vietnam had a new meaning to her now. It was a place where people went to be killed. It wasn't just someplace one read about, something to talk about between classes, with professors or friends. It was real to her now. She knew exactly what it meant. It meant Harry Winslow would never walk again. And as she stepped off the bus in Berkeley that night, the tears still running down her cheeks, she jammed her hands in her pockets, and walked back to her rented room, knowing that neither of them would ever be the same again.

Chapter 9

Tana sat at his side for the next two days, and never moved, except to go home and get a few hours' sleep, bathe, change her clothes and come back again, to hold his hand, talk to him when he was awake, about the years when he was at Harvard and she was at BU, the tandem bicycle they had, the vacations on Cape Cod. They kept him pretty doped up most of the time, but there were times when he was so lucid it hurt to look at him, and to realize the thoughts going through his mind. He didn't want to spend the rest of his life paralyzed. He wanted to die, he told Tana again and again. And she screamed at him and called him a son-of-a-bitch. But she was also afraid to leave him at night, for fear he would do something about it himself. She warned the nurses about how he felt, but they were used to it and it didn't impress them much. They kept a close eye on him, and there were others who were worse off, like the boy down the hall who had lost both arms and his entire face.

On the morning of Christmas Eve, her mother called just before she left for the hospital. It was ten o'clock in New York, and she had gone into the office for a few hours, and she thought she'd call Tana to see how she was. She had hoped right up until the last minute that Tana would change her mind and come home to spend Christmas with her, but Tana had insisted for months that there was no chance of that. She had stacks and stacks of work to do. And she said there wasn't even any point in Jean coming out. But it seemed a depressing way to spend the Christmas holidays, almost as depressing as the way she was spending them herself. Arthur was having a family Christmas in Palm Beach with Ann and Billy and his son-in-law, and the baby Ann had just had, and he hadn't included Jean. She understood, of course, that it would have been awkward for him.

"So what are you up to, sweetheart?" Jean hadn't called her in two weeks. She was too depressed to call, and she didn't want Tana to hear it on the phone. At least when Arthur was in New York over the holidays, there was some hope that he might stop by for a few hours, but this year she didn't even have that held out to her, and Tana was gone . . . "Studying as hard as you thought?"

"Yes . . . I . . . no. . . ." She was still half asleep. She had stayed with Harry until four o'clock. His fever had suddenly shot up the night before and she was afraid to leave him again, but at four in the morning, the nurses had insisted she go home and get some sleep. It was going to be a long, hard climb for him, and if she burned herself out now, she wouldn't do him any good later on, when he needed her most. "I haven't been. At least not for the past three days." She almost groaned with fatigue, as she sat down in the straight-backed chair they left near the phone. "Harry got back from Vietnam." Her eyes glazed as she thought of it. This would be the first time she had told anyone, and the thought of what there was to say made her sick.

"You've been seeing him?" Jean sounded instantly annoyed. "I thought you had studying to do. If I'd thought you could take time off to play, Tana, I wouldn't be sitting here spending the Christmas holidays by myself . . . if you have time to play around with him, the least you could have. . . ."

"Stop it!" Tana suddenly shrieked in the empty hall. "*Stop it*! He's in Letterman. No one's playing around, for God's sake." There was silence at Jean's end. She had never heard Tana sound like that. There was a kind of hysterical desperation in her voice, and a frightening despair.

"What's Letterman?" She imagined it was a hotel, but something instantly told her she was wrong.

"The military hospital here. He was shot in the spine. . . ." She began to take in great gulps of air so she wouldn't cry, but it didn't work. Nothing worked. She cried all the time when she wasn't with him. She couldn't believe what had happened to him. And she nearly collapsed now on the chair, like a little child. "He's a paraplegic now, Mom

. . . he may not even live . . . he got this terrible fever last night. . . ." She just sat there, crying, shaking from head to foot and unable to stop, but she had to let it out, as Jean stared at her office wall in shock, thinking about the boy she had seen so many times. He was so confident, almost debonair, if one could say that about a boy his age, he laughed all the time, he was funny and bright and irreverent and he had annoyed her most of the time, and now she thanked God Tana hadn't married him . . . imagine the life that would have been for her.

"Oh sweetheart . . . I'm so sorry. . . ."

"So am I." She sounded exactly as she had as a child when her puppy died, and it broke Jean's heart to listen to her. "And there's nothing I can do, except sit there and watch."

"You shouldn't be there. It puts too much strain on you."

"I *have* to be there. Don't you understand?" Her voice was harsh. "I'm all he has."

"What about his family?"

"His father hasn't shown up yet, and he probably never will, the son-of-a-bitch, and Harry's just lying there, barely hanging on."

"Well, there's nothing you can do. And I don't think you should see something like that, Tan."

"Oh, no?" She was belligerent now. "What should I see, Mom? Dinner parties on the East Side, evenings in Greenwich with the Durning clan? That's the worst crock of shit I've ever heard. My best friend has just had his ass shot off in Vietnam, and you don't think I should do something like that. Just what do you think should happen to him, Mom? Should I cross him off my list because he can't dance anymore?"

"Don't be so cynical, Tana." Jean Roberts sounded firm.

"Why the hell not? What kind of world do we live in anyway? What's wrong with everyone? Why don't they see what we're getting into in Vietnam?"

"That's not in your hands or mine."

"Why doesn't anyone care what we think . . . ? what I think . . . what Harry thinks . . . Why didn't anybody ask him before he went?" She was sobbing again and she couldn't go on.

"Get hold of yourself." Jean waited for a moment, and then, "I think you should come home for the holidays, Tan, especially if you're going to spend them around the hospital with that boy."

"I can't come home now." Her voice was sharp and suddenly there were tears in Jean's eyes.

"Why not?" Now she sounded like the child.

"I don't want to leave Harry now."

"How can he mean that much to you . . . ? more than I do . . . ?"

"He just does. Aren't you spending Christmas with Arthur anyway, or at least part of it?" Tana blew her nose and wiped her eyes, but Jean shook her head at her end.

"Not this year, Tan. He's going to Palm Beach with the kids."

"And he didn't invite you?" Tana sounded shocked. He was really the consummate selfish son-of-a-bitch, second only to Harry's dad, perhaps.

"It would be awkward for him."

"Why? His wife's been dead for eight years, and you're no secret anymore. Why couldn't he invite you?"

"It doesn't matter. I have work to do here anyway."

"Yeah," it drove her nuts thinking about her mother's subservience and devotion to him, "work for him. Why don't you just tell him to jump in the lake one of these days, Mom? You're forty-five years old, you could still find someone else, and no one could treat you worse than Arthur does."

"Tana, that's not true!" She was instantly outraged.

"No? Then how come you're spending Christmas alone?"

Jean's tongue was quick and sharp. "Because my daughter won't come home."

Tana wanted to hang up in her face. "Don't lay that shit on me, Mom."

"Don't talk to me like that. And it's true, isn't it? You want him around so there isn't any responsibility on you.

Well, it doesn't always work like that. You may not choose to come home, but you can't pretend it's the right thing to do."

"I'm in law school, Mom. I'm twenty-two years old. I'm grown up. I can't be there for you all the time anymore."

"Well, neither can he. And his responsibilities are far more important than yours." She was crying softly now and Tana shook her head. Her voice was calm when she spoke again.

"He's the one you should be mad at, Mom, not me. I'm sorry I can't be there for you, but I just can't."

"I understand."

"No, you don't. And I'm sorry about that, too."

Jean sighed into the phone. "I guess there's nothing we can do about it now. And I suppose you are doing the right thing." She sniffed, "But please, sweetheart, don't spend all your time at the hospital. It's too depressing, and you can't do the boy any good. He'll pull out of it on his own." Her attitude made Tana sick, but she didn't say anything to her.

"Sure, Mom." They each had their own ideas, and neither of them was going to change anymore. It was hopeless now. They had gone their own ways, and Jean knew it too. She thought of how lucky Arthur was to still have his children around so much of the time. Ann always wanted his help, financially and otherwise, and her husband practically kissed Arthur's feet, and even Billy was living at home. It was wonderful for him, she thought as she hung up. It meant he never really had enough time for her. Between his business obligations, his old friends who had been too close to Marie to accept Jean, according to him anyway, and Billy and Ann, there was scarcely ever any time for her. And yet, there was still something so special between them, and she knew there always would be.

It was worth all the hours she spent alone, waiting for him. At least that was what she told herself, as she straightened her desk and went home to her apartment to stare into Tana's empty room. It looked so painfully neat, so empty and deserted now. So unlike the room she was living in, in Berkeley, where her things were spread all over the floor, as she rapidly gathered her things, desperate to get back to Harry again. She had called the hospital after she and her mother hung up, and they said his fever was up again. He was asleep, and he had just had a shot, but she wanted to get back to him before he woke up again. And as she pulled a comb through her hair, and climbed into her jeans, she thought of the things her mother had said. It was unfair of Jean to blame her loneliness on her. What right did she have to expect Tana to always be there for her? It was her mother's way of absolving Arthur of his responsibilities. For sixteen years she had made excuses for him, to Tana, to herself, to her friends, to the girls at work. How many excuses could one make for the man?

Tana grabbed her jacket off a hook and ran downstairs. It took her half an hour to cross the Bay Bridge on the bus, and another twenty minutes to get to Letterman, peacefully nestled in the Presidio. The traffic was worse than it had been in the past few days, but it was the morning of Christmas Eve, and she had expected it. She tried not to think of her mother as she got off the bus. She could take care of herself at least, better than Harry could right now. That was all she could think about as she went up to his room on the third floor and walked softly inside. He was still asleep, and the curtains were drawn. It was a brilliantly sunny winter day outside, but none of the bright light and cheer entered here. Everything was darkness and silence and gloom. She slipped quietly into a chair next to the bed, and watched his face. He was deep in a heavy, drugged sleep, and he didn't stir for the next two hours, and finally just to move around a little bit, she walked out into the hall, and wandered up and down, trying not to look into rooms, or see the hideous machinery everywhere, the stricken faces of parents coming to see their sons, or what was left of them, the bandages, the half faces, severed limbs. It was almost more than she could stand, and she reached the end of the hall, and took a deep breath, as suddenly she saw a man who literally took her breath away. He was the tallest, most handsome man she had ever seen. Tall, dark haired, with brilliant blue eyes, a deep tan, broad shoulders, long, almost endless legs, an impeccably cut dark blue suit, and a camel's hair coat tossed over his arm. His shirt was so perfect and creamy white that it looked like something in an ad. Everything about him was beautiful and immaculate and magnificently groomed. He wore a crest ring on his left hand, and a troubled look in his eyes, and he stood watching her for a fraction of an instant, just as she stood watching him.

"Do you know where the neurosurgical area is?" She nodded, feeling childlike and stupid at first, and then shyly smiled at him.

"Yes, it's down this hall." She pointed in the direction she had come, and he smiled, but only with his mouth, not with his eyes. There was something desperately sad about the man, as though he had just lost the one thing he cared about, and he had, or almost.

But Tana found herself wondering why he was there. He looked about fifty years old, although he seemed youthful for his age and he was certainly the most striking man she had ever seen. The dark hair peppered with gray made him look even more handsome as he walked swiftly past her and down the hall, and she followed slowly back the way she had come, and saw him turn left in the direction of the nurses' station that they were all so dependent on. Her thoughts turned back to Harry then, and she realized that she had better get back. She hadn't been gone long, but he might have woken up, and there were a lot of things she wanted to say to him, things she had thought about all night, ideas that she had about what they could do now. She had meant what she'd said, she wasn't going to just let him lie on his ass. He had his whole life ahead of him. Two of the nurses smiled at her as she walked past where they stood, and she walked on tiptoe into Harry's room. The room was still dim, and the sun was going down outside anyway, and she instantly saw that Harry was awake. He looked groggy, but he recognized her, and he didn't smile. Their eyes met and held, and she felt suddenly strange as she entered the room, as though something was wrong, something more than had been wrong before, as though that could even be. Her eyes swept the room as though searching for a clue, and she found him standing there, in a corner, looking grim, the handsome man with the gray hair, in the dark blue suit, and she almost jumped. It had never occurred to her ... and now suddenly she knew ... Harrison Winslow III ... Harry's father ... he had finally come.

"Hi, Tan." Harry looked unhappy and uncomfortable. It was easier before his father had come. Now he had to deal with him, and his grief too. Tana was so much easier to have around, she always understood how he felt. His father never had.

"How do you feel?" For an instant, they both ignored the older man, as though deriving strength from each other first. Tana didn't even know what to say to him.

"I'm okay." But he looked a lot less than that, and then he looked from her to the well-dressed man. "Father, this is Tana Roberts, my friend." The elder Winslow said very little, but he held out his hand. He almost looked at her as though she were an intrusion. He wanted the details of how Harry had gotten there. He had reached London from South Africa the day before, had gotten the telegrams that were waiting for him and had flown to San Francisco at once, but he hadn't realized until he arrived what the full implications were. He was still reeling from the shock. Harry had just told him that he would be confined to a wheelchair for life, before Tana walked into the room. He hadn't wasted much time in telling him, and he hadn't been gentle or kind. But he didn't have to be, as far as he was concerned. They were his legs, and if they weren't going to work anymore, that was his problem, no one else's, and he could talk about it any way he wanted to. And he wasn't mincing words just then. "Tan, this is my father, Harrison Winslow," a sarcastic tone came into his voice, "the third." Nothing between them had changed. Not even now. And his father looked chagrined.

"Would you like to be alone?" Tana's eyes went back and forth between the two men and it was easy to read that Harry would not, and his father would prefer that they were. "I'll go get a cup of tea." She glanced at his father with a cautious glance. "Would you like some, too?"

He hesitated, and then nodded his head. "Yes, thanks.

Very much." He smiled, and it was impossible not to notice how devastatingly handsome he was, even here, in a hospital, in his son's room, listening to bad news. There was an incredible depth to the blue eyes, a strength about the chiselled jaw line, something both gentle and decisive about his hands. It was difficult to see him as the villain Harry had described, but she had to take Harry's word for it. Yet sudden doubts began to come to mind, as she took her time going to the cafeteria to get their tea. She returned in slightly less than half an hour, wondering if she should leave and come back the following day, or later that night. She had all that studying to do anyway, but there was a dogged look in Harry's eyes when she returned, as though he wanted to be rescued from his father, and the nurse saw it too when she came in, and not knowing what was causing Harry's distress, or who, and in a little while she asked them both to leave. Tana bent to kiss Harry goodbye and he whispered in her ear.

"Come back tonight . . . if you can. . . ."

"Okay." She kissed his cheek, and made a mental note to call the nurses first. But it was Christmas Eve, after all, and she thought maybe he didn't want to be alone. She wondered, too, if he and his father had just had an argument. His father glanced back over his shoulder at him, sighed unhappily as they left the room, and walked down the hall. His head was bowed, as he stared at his highly polished shoes, and Tana was afraid to say anything. And she felt like a total slob in her scuffed loafers and jeans, but she hadn't expected to meet anyone there, least of all the legendary Harrison Winslow III. She was even more startled when he suddenly turned to her.

"How does he seem to you?"

Tana took a sharp breath. "I don't know yet . . . it's too soon . . . I think he's still in shock." Harrison Winslow nodded. So was he. He had spoken to the doctor before coming upstairs, and there was absolutely nothing they could do. Harry's spinal cord had been so badly damaged, the neurosurgeon had explained, that he would never walk again. They had made some repairs, and there would be more surgery in the next six months, and there were some things about which he was very pleased. They had told Harry as much, but it was too soon for it all to have set in. The best news of all was that he would be able to make love, with some instruction, as that part of his nervous system still functioned, to a degree, and although he wouldn't have complete feeling or total control, he still had a considerable amount of sensation there. "He could even have a family," the doctor told his father as he stared, but there were other things that he would never do, like walk or dance, or run or ski . . . tears filled the father's eyes as he thought of it, and then he remembered the girl walking along at his side. She was pretty, he had noticed her when he first saw her walking down the hall, and had been struck by the lovely face, the big green eyes, the graceful way she moved, and had been surprised to see her walk into Harry's room.

"I take it you and Harry are close friends?" It was odd, Harry had never mentioned the girl to him, but Harry never mentioned anything to him anyway.

"We are. We've been friends for four years."

He decided not to beat around the bush as they stood in the lobby of Letterman Hospital. But he wanted to know what he was up against, and maybe this was the time to find out. Just how involved was Harry with this girl, another casual affair, a hidden love, maybe a hidden wife? He had Harry's financial affairs to think of, too, even if the boy wasn't sophisticated enough yet to protect himself. "Are you in love with him?" His eyes bore into hers and she was momentarily stunned.

"I . . . no . . . I . . . that is," she wasn't sure why he had asked, "I love him very much . . . but we . . . I'm not 'involved with him' physically, if that's what you mean." She flushed to the roots of her hair to be explaining that to him and he smiled apologetically.

"I'm sorry to even ask you a thing like that, but if you know Harry well, you know how he is. I never know what the hell is going on and I assume that one of these days I'll arrive and find out that he has a wife and three kids." Tana laughed. It was unlikely but not impossible. More likely three mistresses. And she suddenly realized that she was finding it difficult to dislike him as much as Harry would want her to, in fact, she wasn't sure she disliked him at all.

He was obviously powerful, and not afraid to ask what he wanted to know. He looked her over now, glanced at his watch, and at the limousine waiting at the curb outside for him. "Would you come to have a cup of coffee with me somewhere? At my hotel perhaps? I'm staying at the Stanford Court, but I could have the driver take you back to wherever you like afterwards. Does that sound all right?" Actually, it sounded faintly traitorous to her, but she didn't know what to say to him. The poor man had been through a lot, too, and he had come an awfully long way.

"I . . . I really should get back . . . I have an awful lot of studying to do. . . ." She blushed and he looked hurt, and suddenly she was sorry for him. As elegant and dashing as he was, there was at the same time something vulnerable about him. "I'm sorry, I didn't mean to sound rude. It's just. . . ."

"I know." He looked at her with a rueful smile that melted her heart. "He's told you what a bastard I am. But it's Christmas Eve, you know. It might do us both good to go and talk for a while. I've had a hell of a shock, and you must have too." She nodded sadly and followed him to the car. The driver opened the door and she got in, and Harrison Winslow sat next to her on the gray velvet seat. He looked pensive as the city slid by and it seemed moments later when they reached Nob Hill, and drove down the east face of it, turning sharply into the courtyard of the Stanford Court. "Harry and I have had a rough time of it over the years. Somehow we never managed to hit it off. . . ." He almost seemed to be talking to himself as she watched his face. He didn't look as ruthless as Harry had described. In fact, he didn't look ruthless at all. He looked lonely and sad, and he seemed very much alone. Harrison looked pointedly at Tana then. "You're a beautiful girl . . . inside as well, I suspect. Harry is lucky to have you as a friend."

And the oddest thing about her was something Harry couldn't really have known. She looked so much like his mother at the same age. It was uncanny as Harrison watched her step lightly out of the car, and he followed her into the hotel. They went to the Potpourri restaurant and slid into a booth. He seemed to be constantly watching her, as though trying to understand who she was, and what she meant to his son. He found it difficult to believe that she was only his "friend", as she claimed, and yet she was insistent about that as they talked and she had no reason to lie to him.

Tana smiled as she watched his eyes. "My mother feels the same way about it that you do, Mr. Winslow. She keeps telling me that "boys and girls can't be friends," and I tell her she's wrong. That's exactly what Harry and I are . . . he's my best friend in the whole world . . . he's like a brother to me. . . ." Her eyes filled with tears and she looked away thinking of what had happened to him. ". . . I'll do anything I can to help make him all right again." She looked at Harrison Winslow defiantly, not angry at him, but at the fate which had crippled his son. "I will, you'll see . . . I won't just let him lie there on his ass," she blushed at the word, but went on, "I'm going to get him up and moving and giving a damn again." She looked at him strangely then. "I have an idea, but I have to talk to Harry about it first." He was intrigued. Maybe she had designs on the boy after all, but he didn't think that would be so bad now. Aside from being pretty, she was obviously bright and the girl had a hell of a lot of spunk. When she spoke, her eyes lit up like green fire, and he knew that she meant everything she said.

"What kind of idea?" He was intrigued by her, and if he hadn't been so worried about his son, he would have been amused.

She hesitated. He'd probably think she was nuts, particularly if he was as unambitious as Harry said. "I don't know . . . it probably sounds crazy to you, but I thought . . . I don't know. . . ." It was embarrassing, admitting it to him. "I thought that maybe I could get him to go to law school with me. Even if he never uses it, it would be good for him, especially now."

"Are you serious?" There were laugh lines coming to light beside Harrison Winslow's eyes. "Law school? My son?"

He patted her hand with a grin, she was an amazing child, a little ball of fire, but he wouldn't put anything past this girl, including that. "If you can talk him into that, especially now," his face sobered rapidly, "you really would be even more remarkable than I think you are."

"I'm going to give it a try when he's well enough to listen to me."

"That'll be a while, I'm afraid." They both nodded silently, and in the silence heard someone singing carols outside, and then suddenly Tana looked at him.

"Why do you see so little of him?" She had to ask, she had nothing to lose, and if he got angry with her, she could always leave. He couldn't do anything to her, but he didn't actually look upset as he gazed into her eyes.

"Honestly? Because Harry and I have been a lost cause until now. I tried for a long, long time, but I never got anywhere. He's hated me ever since he was a small boy, and it's only gotten worse over the years. There was no point inflicting new wounds after a while. It's a big world, I have a lot to do, he has his own life to lead," tears flooded his eyes and he looked away, ". . . or at least he did, until now. . . ."

She reached across the table and touched his hand. "He will again. I promise you . . . if he lives . . . oh God . . . if he lives . . . please God, don't let him die." Tears flooded her eyes, too, and she brushed them from her cheeks. "He's so wonderful, Mr. Winslow, he's the best friend I've ever had."

"I wish I could say the same." He looked sad. "We're almost strangers by now. I felt like an intruder in his room today."

"Maybe that's because I was there. I should have left you two alone."

"It wouldn't make any difference anymore. It's gone too far, for too long. We're strangers now."

"You don't have to be." She was talking to him as though she knew the man, and somehow he didn't seem so impressive anymore, no matter how worldly or debonair or handsome or sophisticated he was. He was only another human being, with a devastating problem on his hands, a very sick son. "You could make friends with him now."

Harrison Winslow shook his head, and after a moment he smiled at her. He thought Tana a remarkably beautiful girl, and he suddenly wondered again exactly what the story was between Harry and this girl. His son was too much of a libertine, in his own way, to let an opportunity like this pass him by, except if he cared about her even more than she knew ... maybe that was it ... maybe Harry was in love with her ... he had to be. It couldn't be what she said it was between them. It seemed impossible to him.

"It's too late, my friend. Much, much too late. And in his eyes, my sins are unforgivable." He sighed. "I suppose I'd feel the same way in his shoes." He looked unwaveringly at her now. "He thinks I killed his mother, you know. She committed suicide when he was four."

She almost choked on her words. "I know." And the look in his eyes was devastating, raw pain that still lived in his soul. His love for her had never died, nor had his love for their son. "She was dying of cancer and she didn't want anyone to know. In the end, it would have disfigured her, and she couldn't have tolerated that. She'd already had two operations before she died ... and ..." he almost stopped, but went on, ". . . it was terrible for her ... for all of us. . . . Harry knew she was sick then, but he doesn't remember it now. It doesn't matter anyway. She couldn't live with the operations, the pain, and I couldn't bear to watch her suffer. What she did was a terrible thing, but I always understood. She was so young, so beautiful. She was very much like you, in fact, and almost a child herself. . . ." He wasn't ashamed of the tears in his eyes, and Tana looked at him, horrified.

"Why doesn't Harry know?"

"She made me promise I'd never tell." He sat back against the banquette as though he'd been punched. The feeling of despair over her death never really went away. He had tried to run away from it for years, with Harry at first, with women, with girls, with anyone, and finally by himself. He was fifty-two years old and he had discovered that there was only so far he could run, and he couldn't run that far anymore. The memories were there, the sorrow, the loss . . . and now Harry might go too ... he couldn't bear the thought as he looked at this lovely young girl, so full of life, so filled with hope. It was almost impossible to explain it all to her, it was all so long ago. "People felt differently about cancer then ... it was almost as though one had to be ashamed of it. I didn't agree with her at the time, but she was adamant that Harry not know. She left me a very long letter at the time. She took an overdose of pills when I went to Boston overnight to see my great aunt. She wanted Harry to think her flighty and beautiful, and romantic, but not riddled with disease, and so she went ... she's a heroine to him." He smiled sadly at Tana, "And she was to me. It was a sad way to die, but the other way would have been so much worse. I never blamed her for what she did."

"And you let him think it was your fault." She was horrified, and her green eyes were huge in her face.

"I never realized he would, and by the time I understood, it was already too late. I ran around a great deal when he was a child, as though I could flee from the pain of losing her. But it doesn't really work that way. It follows you, like a mangy dog, always waiting outside your room when you wake up, pawing at the door, whining at your feet, no matter how dressed up and charming and busy you are, how many friends you surround yourself with, it's always there, nipping at your heels, gnawing at your cuffs ... and so it was ... but by the time Harry was eight or nine, he had come to his own conclusions about me, and he got so hateful for a while that I put him into boarding school, and he decided to stay, and then I had nothing at all, so I ran even harder than before ... and," he shrugged philosophically, "she died almost twenty years ago, and here we are ... she died in January. ..." His eyes looked vague for a moment and then focused on Tana again, but that didn't help. She looked too much like her anyway, it was like looking into the past, just seeing her. "And now Harry is in this awful mess ... life is so rotten and so strange, isn't it?" She nodded, there wasn't much she could say. He had given her a great deal to think about.

"I think you should say something to him."

"About what?"

"About how his mother died."

"I couldn't do that. I made a promise to her . . . to myself . . . it would be self-serving to tell him now. . . ."

"Then why tell me?" She was shocked at herself, at the anger in her voice, at what she felt, at the waste people allowed in their lives, lost moments in which they could have loved each other, like this man and his son. They had wasted so many years they could have shared. And Harry needed him now. He needed everyone.

Harrison looked apologetically at her. "I suppose I shouldn't have told you all that. But I needed to talk to someone . . . and you're . . . so close to him." He looked at her point blank. "I wanted you to know that I love my son." There was a lump in her throat the size of a fist and she wasn't sure if she wanted to slap him or kiss him, or perhaps both. She had never felt that way about any man before.

"Why the hell don't you tell him yourself?"

"It wouldn't do any good."

"It might. Maybe this is the time."

He looked at her pensively, and then down at his hands, and then finally into her green eyes again. "Perhaps it is. I don't know him, though . . . I wouldn't know where to begin. . . ."

"Just like that, Mr. Winslow. Just the way you said it to me."

He smiled at her, and he suddenly looked very tired. "What makes you so wise, little girl?"

She smiled at him, and she felt an incredible warmth emanating from him. He was a lot like Harry in some ways, and yet he was more, and she realized with a pang of embarrassment that she was attracted to him. It was as though all the senses that had been deadened for years, ever since the rape, had suddenly come alive again.

"What were you thinking then?"

She flushed pink and shook her head. "Something that had nothing to do with all this . . . I'm sorry . . . I'm tired . . . I haven't slept for a few days. . . ."

"I'll get you home, so you can get some rest." He signalled for the check, and when it came he looked at her with a

175

gentle smile, and she felt a longing for the father she had never had, or even known. This was the kind of man she would have wanted Andy Roberts to have been, not Arthur Durning who breezed in and out of her mother's life when it suited him. This man was a great deal less selfish than Harry had wanted her to believe, or insisted on believing himself. He had put a lot of energy into hating this man over the years and Tana knew instinctively now that he had been wrong, very wrong, and she wondered if Harrison was right, if it was too late. "Thank you for talking to me, Tana. Harry is lucky to have you as his friend."

"I've been lucky to have him."

He put a twenty dollar bill under the check and looked at her again. "Are you an only child?" He suspected that about her, and she nodded with a smile.

"Yes. And I never knew my father, he died before I was born, in the war." It was something she had said ten thousand times in her life, but it seemed to have new meaning now. Everything did, and she didn't understand what that meant or why. Something strange was happening to her as she sat with this man, and she wondered if it was just because she was so tired. She let him walk her back to his car, and he surprised her by getting in with her, rather than letting the driver take her home.

"I'll ride with you."

"You really don't need to do that."

"I have nothing else to do. I'm here to see Harry, and I think he's better off resting for the next few hours." She agreed with him and they chatted on the drive across the bridge. He mentioned that he had never been to San Francisco before. He found it an attractive place, but he seemed distracted as they drove along. She assumed he was thinking about his son, but he was actually thinking about her, and he shook her hand when they arrived. "I'll see you at the hospital again. If you need a ride, just call the hotel and I'll send the car for you." She had mentioned that she'd been taking the bus back and forth and that worried him. She was young after all and pretty and anything could have happened to her.

"Thank you for everything, Mr. Winslow."

"Harrison." He smiled at her, and he looked exactly like Harry when he smiled, not quite as mischievous, but there was a sparkle there too. "I'll see you soon. Get some rest now!" He waved, and the limousine drove off, as she slowly climbed the stairs, thinking of all he had said. How unfair life was at times. She fell asleep thinking of Harrison . . . and Harry . . . and Vietnam . . . and the woman who had killed herself, and in Tana's dream she had no face, and when she woke it was dark, and she sat up with a start and couldn't catch her breath in the tiny room. She glanced at the clock and it was nine o'clock, and she wondered how Harry was. She went to the pay phone and called and discovered that the fever was down, he had been awake for a while, and now he was dozing again, but he hadn't gone to bed for the night. They hadn't given him his sleeping medicine yet, and they probably wouldn't for a while, and suddenly, as Tana heard caroling outside, she realized that it was Christmas Eve, and Harry needed her. She showered quickly and decided to dress for him. She wore a pretty white knit dress, high heeled shoes, and put on a red coat and a scarf that she hadn't worn since the winter before in New York, and thought she would never wear here. But somehow it all looked and felt Christmasy, and she thought that might be important to him. She put on some perfume, brushed her hair, and rode back into town on the bus, thinking of his father again. It was ten thirty at night when she arrived at Letterman, and there was a sleepy holiday air about it all. Little trees with blinking lights, plastic Santa Clauses here and there. But no one seemed to be in a particularly holiday mood, there were too many desperately serious things going on, and when she reached his room, she knocked softly and tiptoed in, expecting him to be asleep, and instead, he was lying there, staring at the wall, with tears in his eyes. He started when he saw her, and he didn't even smile.

"I'm dying, aren't I?" She was shocked at his words, at his tone, at the lifeless look in his eyes, and she suddenly frowned and approached the bed.

"Not unless you want to die." She knew she had to be

blunt with him. "It's pretty much up to you." She stood very close to him, looking into his eyes, and he did not reach for her hand.

"That's a dumb thing to say. It wasn't my idea to get shot in the ass."

"Sure it was." She sounded nonchalant and for a moment he looked pissed.

"What the hell is that supposed to mean?"

"That you could have gone to school. And you decided to play instead. So you got the short end of the stick. You gambled and you lost."

"Yeah. Only I didn't lose ten bucks, I lost my legs. Not exactly small stakes."

"Looks like they're still there to me." She glanced down at the useless limbs and he almost snarled at her.

"Don't be an ass. What good are they now?"

"You've got them, and you're alive, and there's plenty you can still do. And according to the nurses, you can still get it up," she had never been so blunt with him and it was a hell of a speech for Christmas Eve, but she knew it was time to start pushing him, especially if he thought he was going to die. "Hell, look at the bright side, you might even get the clap again."

"You make me sick." He turned away, and without thinking she grabbed at his arm, and he turned to look at her again.

"Look, dammit, you make *me* sick. Half the boys in your platoon were killed, and you're alive, so don't lie there whining at what you don't have. Think of what you do. Your life isn't over, unless you want it to be, and I don't want it to be," tears stung her eyes, "I want you to get off that dead ass of yours, if I have to drag you by the hair for the next ten years to make you get up and live again. Is that clear?" The tears were pouring down her cheeks. "I'm not going to let go of you. Ever! Do you understand that?" And slowly, slowly . . . she saw a smile dawn in his eyes.

"You're a crazy broad, do you know that, Tan?"

"Yeah, well maybe I am, but you'll find out just how crazy I am until you start making life easier for both of us by

178

doing something with yourself." She wiped the tears from her cheeks and he grinned at her, and for the first time in days, he looked like the Harry she knew.

"You know what it is?"

"What?" She looked confused. It was the most emotional few days of her life and she had never felt so overwrought as she did now.

"It's all that sexual energy you've got pent up, that's what gives you all this oomph to put into everything else. It makes you a real pain in the ass sometimes."

"Thanks."

"Anytime." He grinned, and closed his eyes for a minute and then he opened them again. "What are you all dressed up for? Going someplace?"

"Yes. Here. To see you. It's Christmas Eve." Her eyes softened and she smiled at him. "Welcome back to the human race."

"I liked what you said before." He was still smiling and Tana could see that the tides had turned. If he hung on to the will to live, he'd be all right, relatively. That was what the neurosurgeon had said.

"What did I say . . . ? you mean about booting you in the ass making something of yourself . . . it's about time." She looked pleased.

"No, about getting it up, and getting the clap again."

"Shit." She looked at him with total contempt and one of the nurses walked in and they started to laugh, and suddenly, for just a minute it was just like old times, and then Harry's father walked into the room, and they both looked like nervous kids, and the laughter stopped, and Harrison Winslow smiled. He wanted so desperately to make friends with his son, and he already knew how much he liked the girl.

"Don't let me spoil your fun. What was that all about?"

Tana blushed. It was difficult talking to someone as cosmopolitan as he was, but she had talked to him all afternoon after all.

"Your son was being as rude as he usually is."

"That's nothing new." Harrison sat down in one of the

179

room's two chairs, and glanced at them both. "Although you'd think on Christmas Eve, he could make an effort to be a little more polite."

"Actually, he was talking about the nurses and. . . ." Harry blushed and began to object, Tana laughed, and suddenly Harry's father was laughing too. There was something very tenuous in the room, and none of them looked totally at ease, but they chatted for half an hour and then Harry began to look tired, and Tana stood up. "I just came to give you a Christmas kiss, I didn't even think you'd be awake."

"Neither did I." Harrison Winslow stood up too. "We'll come back tomorrow, son." He was watching Harry look at her, and he thought he understood. She was innocent of what Harry felt for her, and for some reason he was keeping it a secret from her, and Harrison couldn't understand why. There was a mystery here which made no sense to him. He looked at his son again. "Do you need anything before we leave?"

Harry looked sad for a long moment and then shook his head. He needed something, but it was nothing they had to give. The gift of his legs. And his father understood and gently touched his arm.

"See you tomorrow, son."

"Good night." Harry's greeting to his father wasn't warm, but his eyes lit up when he looked at the beautiful blonde. "Behave yourself, Tan."

"Why should I? You don't." She grinned and blew him a kiss, as she whispered, "Merry Christmas, asshole." He laughed and she followed his father out into the hall.

"I thought he looked better, didn't you?" They were becoming friends over the disaster that had befallen his son.

"I did. I think he's over the worst. Now it's just going to be a long, slow climb back uphill." Harrison nodded, and they took the elevator downstairs again. There was a familiarity to it now, as if they had done this dozens of times before, when actually it had only been once. But their talk that afternoon had brought them much closer, and Harrison held the door open for her now, as she saw that the same silver limousine was there.

"Would you like something to eat?"

She started to say no and then realized that she hadn't had dinner yet. She had been thinking about going to midnight mass, but she didn't really want to go alone. She looked at him, wondering if it would mean something to him, too, particularly now.

"I might. Could I interest you in midnight mass afterwards?"

He looked very serious as he nodded his head, and Tana was struck once again by how handsome he was. They went out for a quick hamburger, and chatted about Harry, and their Cambridge days. She told Harrison some of the more outrageous things they'd done and he laughed with her, still puzzled by the odd relationship they shared. Like Jean, he couldn't quite figure them out. And then they went off to midnight mass, and tears streamed down Tana's cheeks as they sang Silent Night. She was thinking of Sharon, her beloved friend, and Harry and how lucky he was to be alive, and when she glanced over at his father, standing tall and proud at her side, she saw that he was crying too. He discreetly blew his nose when they sat down, and as he took her back to Berkeley afterwards, she noticed how comfortable it was just being with him. She was almost dozing as he drove her home. She was desperately tired.

"What are you doing tomorrow?"

"Seeing Harry, I guess. And one of these days I've got a lot of studying to do." She had all but forgotten it in the past few days.

"Could I take you to lunch before you go to the hospital?" She was touched that he would ask, and she accepted, worrying instantly what she should wear as soon as she stepped out of the car, but she didn't even have time to think of it when she got back to her room. She was so exhausted that she peeled off her clothes, dropped them on the floor, climbed into bed, and was instantly dead to the world. Unlike her mother in New York, who had been awake, sitting lonely in a chair and crying all night. Tana had not called, nor had Arthur in Palm Beach, and she had spent the entire night wrestling with the darker side of her soul, contemplating something she would never have thought she would do.

She had gone to midnight mass, as she and Tana used to do, and at one thirty she came home, and watched a little late night TV.

By two o'clock the most desperate loneliness she had ever felt in her life had set in. She was riveted to her seat, unable to move, almost unable to breathe. And for the first time in her life, she began to think of committing suicide, and by three o'clock it was an almost impossible urge to resist. Half an hour later, she went into her bathroom and got out a bottle of sleeping pills she never used, and trembling, she forced herself to put them down. She wanted to take them more than she had ever wanted to do anything in her life, and at the same time she did not. She wanted someone to stop her, to tell her everything would be all right. But who could tell her that now? Tana was gone, and would probably never live at home again, and Arthur had his own life, he only included her when it suited him, and never when she needed him. Tana was right about that, but it hurt her too much to admit it to her. Instead she defended everything he did, and his miserable selfish kids, that bitch Ann, who was always so rude to her, and Billy, he had been so sweet as a boy, but now . . . he seemed to be drunk all the time, and Jean wondered if Tana was right, if he wasn't the kind of young man she had always thought he was, but if that was true . . . the memory of what Tana had said four years before came crashing down on her now. What if it were true . . . ? if he had . . . if she hadn't believed . . . it was almost more than she could bear . . . it was as if her whole life were crashing in on her tonight and she couldn't bear it, as she sat staring longingly at the pills she held in her hand. It seemed the only thing left to do, and she wondered what Tana would think when they called her in California to tell her the news. She wondered who would find her body . . . the superintendent maybe . . . one of her co-workers . . . if they waited for Arthur to find her it could take two weeks. It was even more depressing to realize that there wasn't even anyone left who would discover her soon. She thought of writing Tana a note, but that seemed so melodramatic and there was nothing left to say, except how much she had loved her child, how hard she had tried. She cried as she thought of Tana growing up, the tiny apartment they had shared, meeting Arthur, hoping that he would marry her . . . her whole life seemed to be flashing before her eyes as she clutched the vial of sleeping pills, and the night ground agonizingly by. She didn't even know what time it was when the phone finally rang. It was five a.m., and Jean was shocked when she saw the clock. She wondered if it was Tana, maybe her friend had died . . . with a shaking hand, she lifted the phone, and at first she didn't recognize the voice that identified itself as John.

"John?"

"John York. Ann's husband. We're in Palm Beach."

"Oh. Of course." But she was still stunned, and the emotions of the night had left her drained. She quietly set down the bottle of pills, she could tend to them afterwards. She couldn't understand why they would be calling her, but John York was quick to explain.

"It's Arthur. Ann thought I should call. He's had a heart attack."

"Oh, my God." She could feel her heart pound in her breast, and she was suddenly crying into the phone. "Is he all right? Is he . . . did. . . ."

"He's all right now. But it was pretty bad for a while. It happened a few hours ago, and it's still touch and go, which is why Ann thought I should call."

"Oh, my God . . . oh, my God . . ." Here she had been thinking of taking her own life, and Arthur had almost died. What if she had . . . she almost shuddered at the thought. "Where is he now?"

"At Mercy Israel Hospital. Ann thought you might want to come down."

"Of course." She jumped to her feet, still holding the phone, grabbed a pencil, a pad, knocking over the vial of pills, and as they fell to the floor, she stood looking at them.

She was herself again. It was incredible to think what she might have done, and he needed her now. Thank God she hadn't done it after all. "Give me the details, John. I'll catch the next plane." She scribbled the name and address of the hospital, jotted his room number down, asked if there was anything they would need, and a moment later set down the phone, closed her eyes, thinking of him, and when she opened them there were tears on her cheeks, thinking of Arthur, and what might have been.

Chapter 10

Harrison Winslow sent the car to Berkeley to pick Tana up at noon the next day, and they went to Trader Vic's for lunch. The atmosphere was festive and the food was good; he had been told at the hotel that it would be an appropriate place to go. And he enjoyed her company almost too much as they chatted again, about Harry, but other things as well. He was impressed by how bright she was, and she told him about Freeman Blake, and her friend who had died, and Miriam who had influenced her into going to law school. "I just hope I survive. It's even harder than I thought it would be." She smiled.

"And you really think Harry could do something like that?"

"He can do anything he wants to do. The trouble is he'd rather screw around," she blushed and he laughed. "I'm sorry ... I've been out here talking to students for too long."

"I agree with you. He does like to screw around. He thinks it's congenital. But actually, I was a lot more serious than he in my youth, and my father was a very scholarly man. He even wrote two books on philosophy." They chatted on for a while, and it was the most pleasant interlude Tana had spent in a long, long time. She looked guiltily at her watch eventually, and they hurried off to the hospital, bringing Harry a bag of fortune cookies. Tana had insisted on bringing him a drink. They brought him a huge Scorpion with a gardenia floating in it, and he took a long sip and grinned.

"Merry Christmas to you too." But she could see that he didn't look pleased that she and his father had made friends, and finally when his father left the room and went downstairs to make a call, he glared at her.

"What are you looking so pleased about?" It was good

185

for him to be mad, she didn't mind. It would help bring him back to life.

"You know how I feel about him, Tan. Don't let him do a snow job on you."

"He's not. He wouldn't be here if he didn't care about you. Don't be so goddamn stubborn and give him a chance."

"Oh, for chrissake." He'd have walked out of the room and slammed the door if he could. "What a crock of shit that is. Is that what he's been telling you?" She couldn't tell him all that Harrison had been telling her because she knew he wouldn't want her to, but she also knew by now how he felt about his son, and she was convinced of his sincerity. She was growing fonder of him by the hour, and she wished Harry would try to be more open to him.

"He's a decent man. Give him a chance."

"He's a son-of-a-bitch and I hate his guts." And with that, Harrison Winslow walked into the room, just in time to hear Harry's words, And Tana went pale. The three looked at each other, and Harrison was quick to reassure her.

"That's not the first time I've heard that. And I'm sure it won't be the last."

Harry turned in his bed to snarl at him. "Why the hell didn't you knock?"

"Does it bother you that I heard? So what? You've said it to me before, usually to my face. Are you getting more discreet now? Or less courageous?" There was an edge to the older man's voice and a fire in Harry's eyes.

"You know what I think of you. You were never there when I needed you. You were always somewhere goddamn else, with some girl, in some spa, or on some mountaintop, with your friends. . . ." He turned away. "I don't want to talk about it."

"Yes, you do." He pulled up a chair and sat down. "And so do I. You're right, I wasn't there, and neither were you. You were in the boarding schools you chose to be in, and you were a goddamn impossible little snot every time I laid eyes on you."

"Why shouldn't I have been?"

"That was a decision you made. And you never gave me a chance from the time your mother died. I knew by the time you were six that you hated me. I could accept it at the time. But you know, at your age, Harry, I would have thought that you would have gotten a little smarter by now, or at least more compassionate. I'm not really as bad as you like to think, you know." Tana tried to fade into the wall, it was embarrassing being there, but neither of them seemed to mind. And as she listened, she realized that she had forgotten to call her mother again. She made a mental note to do it as soon as she left the hospital, maybe even from one of the phones downstairs, but she couldn't leave the room now, with World War III going on.

Harry stared angrily at his father now. "Why the hell did you come here anyway?"

"Because you're my son. The only one I've got. Do you want me to leave?" Harrison Winslow quietly stood up and his voice was low when he spoke. "I'll leave anytime you like. I will not inflict myself on you, but I will also not allow you to continue to delude yourself that I don't give a damn about you. That's a very nice fairy tale, poor little rich boy and all that, but in the words of your friend here, it's a crock. I happen to love you very much," his voice cracked but he went on anyway, struggling with the emotions and the words and Tana's heart went out to him. "I love you very, very much, Harry. I always have and I always will." He walked over to him then, bent and kissed him gently on the top of his head, and then strode out of the room, as Harry looked away and closed his eyes, and when he opened them, he saw Tana standing there with tears running down her cheeks at what she had just heard.

"Get the hell out of here." She nodded, and quietly left, and as she closed the door softly behind her, she heard the sobs from the direction of Harry's bed.

Harrison was waiting outside for her, he looked more composed now, and relieved as he smiled at her. "Is he all right?"

"He will be now. He needed to hear the things you said to him."

"I needed to say them to him. I feel better now too." And with that, he took her arm, and they walked downstairs arm in arm. It felt as though they had always been friends. And he looked at her with a broad smile. "Where are you going now, young lady?"

"Home, I guess. I still have all that work to do."

"That's a crock." He imitated her, and they both laughed. "How about playing hookey and going to the movies with an old man? My son has just thrown me out of his room, and I don't know a soul in this town, and it's Christmas for God's sake. How about it, Tan?" He had picked the name up from his son and she smiled, wanting to tell him that she had to go home, but she couldn't do it somehow; she wanted to be with him.

"I really should go home." But she didn't convince either of them, and he was in a festive mood as they climbed into the limousine.

"Good. Now that you've gotten that out of the way, where shall we really go?" She giggled like a little girl, and he told the limousine driver to drive them around. Eventually, they bought a newspaper, picked out a movie they both liked, ate as much popcorn as they could stand, and went to L'Etoile afterwards, for a small supper and drinks at the bar. She was getting spoiled just being with him. And she was trying to remind herself of what a cad Harry said he was, but she didn't believe that anymore, and she had never been as happy in her life, as when he drove her home to Berkeley again, and took her in his arms, and kissed her as naturally as if they had both been waiting for that all their lives. He looked at her afterwards, touching her lips with his fingertips, wondering if he should regret what he'd done, but he felt younger and happier than he had in years. "Tana, I've never met anyone like you before, my love." He held her tight and she felt a warmth and safety she had never even dreamed of before, and then he kissed her again. He wanted to make her his for the rest of time, but he also wondered if he was half mad. This was Harry's friend . . . his girl . . . but they both insisted that they were just friends, and yet he sensed something different than that, on Harry's part anyway. He looked deep into her eyes. "Tell me the truth about something, Tan. Are you in love with my son?"

Slowly, she shook her head. The driver of the limousine seemed to have disappeared. Actually, he had gone outside for a discreet walk. They were parked outside Tana's house. "No. I've never been in love with anyone .. until now. . . ." They were brave words for her, and she decided to tell him the truth all at once. He had been honest with her since they'd met. "I was raped four and a half years ago. It kind of stopped everything for me. As though my emotional clock no longer ran, and it hasn't run since. I didn't go out at all for the first couple of years I was in college, and then finally Harry forced me into double dating with him a few times. But it was no big deal, and I don't go out with anyone here. All I do is work." She smiled tenderly at him. She was falling head over heels in love with the father of her best friend.

"Does Harry know?"

"That I was raped?" He nodded. "Yes. I told him eventually. He thought I was weird, and eventually I told him why. Actually, we saw the guy at a party we went to, and he guessed."

"Was it someone you knew?" Harrison looked shocked.

"The son of my mother's boss. Lover and boss, actually. It was awful . . . no," she shook her head, "it was much, much worse than that." He pulled her into his arms again, and he understood things better now. He wondered if that was why Harry had never allowed himself to be more than friends with her. He instinctively sensed that the desire was there, even if she was innocent of what was in his mind. And he also knew what he felt for the girl. He hadn't been so taken with anyone since he met his wife twenty-six years before, and then he began to think of the age difference between them, wondering if it would bother her. He was exactly thirty years older than Tana, and there were those who would be shocked. But more importantly, would she? "So what?" She answered him. "Who cares about them?" She kissed him this time and she felt something come alive in herself that she had never felt before, a passion and desire which only he could fulfill, and she tossed and turned all night thinking about him, just as he did about her. She called him at seven o'clock the next day, and he was already awake, and surprised by her call. But he would have been even more surprised had he known what she felt for him.

"What are you doing up at this hour, little one?"

"Thinking about you." He was flattered and touched and enchanted and infatuated and a thousand other things. But there was much more to it than that. Tana trusted this man as she had trusted no other man before, not even his son, and he represented a great many things to her, even the father she had never known. He was all men in one, and had Harrison known, he might have been frightened that she expected too much of him. They visited Harry, they met for lunch, they had dinner together that night, and he had an overwhelming urge to take her to bed, but something told him that he could not, that it was dangerous, that he would form a lasting bond and that was wrong. For the next two weeks, they met and they walked and they kissed and they touched and the feelings and needs they had for each other grew. They visited Harry separately, for fear that he would find out, and finally Harrison sat down beside his son one day. The matter had to be broached, it was getting serious for both of them, and he didn't want to hurt the girl. But more than that, he wanted to offer her something he hadn't offered anyone in years, his heart, and his life. He wanted to marry her, and he had to know how Harry felt, now, before it was too late, before everyone got hurt, especially the one person he cared about most, his son. He would have sacrificed anything for Harry, especially now, even the girl he loved, and he had to know now.

"I want to ask you something. Honestly. And I want you to answer me." There had been a tenuous peace between the two men in the past two weeks, thanks to efforts on Tana's part, and Harrison had been enjoying the fruits of it.

"What's this all about?" Harry looked suspiciously at him.

"What's between you and that enchanting child?" He fought hard to keep his face blank, his eyes calm, and prayed that his son wouldn't see anything there, particularly not how much he loved the girl, though he couldn't imagine how Harry could not see. He felt as though he was wearing a neon sign.

"Tana?" Harry shrugged.

"I told you, I want you to answer me." His whole life depended on it now, as did hers.

"Why? What's it to you?" Harry was restless and his neck had hurt all day. "I told you, she's my friend."

"I know you better than that, whether you like it or not."

"So what? That's all it is. I've never slept with her." But he already knew that, though he didn't tell Harry that.

"That doesn't mean a damn thing. That could have to do with her and not you." There was no joking in his eyes or words. This was no joking matter to him, but Harry laughed and conceded the point.

"That's true, it could." And then suddenly he lay back against his pillows and looked up at the ceiling, feeling an odd closeness to his father he had never felt before. "I don't know, Dad . . . I was crazy about her when we first met, but she was so locked up as a stone . . . she still is." He told him about the rape then, and Harrison pretended to hear it for the first time. "I've never known anyone like her before. I guess I've always known that I'm in love with her, but I've been afraid to fuck it up by telling her that. This way, she won't run away. The other way, she might." His eyes filled with sudden tears. "I couldn't stand losing her. I need her too much." Harrison felt his heart sink like a rock, but he had to think for his son now. That was all he really cared about, all he would let himself care about now. He had finally found him and he wasn't willing to lose him again. Not even for Tana, whom he loved so desperately. But Harry's words burned through him like fire. "I need her so much. . . ." The funny thing was the elder Winslow needed her too, but not as Harry did, and he couldn't take her from him, not now. . . .

"One of these days, maybe you should be brave enough to tell her some of this. Maybe she needs you too." Harrison knew now how lonely and isolated Tana had been, but even Harry hadn't fully realized those depths.

"And what if I lose?"

"You can't live like that, son. Afraid to lose, afraid to live, afraid to die. You'll never win like that. She knows that better than anyone. It's the one lesson you can learn from her." And there were so many others he had learned from her too. Lessons he would have to abandon now.

"She's got more guts than anyone I know ... except about men." Harry shook his head. "She scares me to death as far as that goes."

"Give her time. Lots of time." He fought to keep his voice strong. He couldn't let Harry know. "And lots of love."

Harry was silent for a long time, searching his father's eyes. In the past two and a half weeks they had begun to discover each other as they never had before. "Do you think she could ever be in love with me?"

"Possibly." Harrison felt his heart tear again. "You have plenty of other things to think about right now. But once you're up again," he avoided saying "on your feet", "and out of here, you can think about things like that." They both knew that he wasn't totally impaired sexually, and the doctor had told them both that with a little "creativity" Harry would have a near-normal sex life again one day, he could even impregnate his wife, if he chose, which didn't turn Harry on much, at least not for now, but Harrison knew it would mean a great deal to him one day. He would have loved to have Tana's child. The very thought brought him near to tears.

They chatted on for a little while, and eventually Harrison left. He was supposed to have dinner with Tana that night, and instead he called it off. He explained over the phone that he had a stack of cables that had arrived, and he had to compose answers to all of them. They met for lunch the next day instead, and Harrison was honest with her. It was the worst day in his life, since his wife had died. His eyes looked sad and his face was grim, and she knew the moment she met him at the restaurant that he didn't have good news, and she felt her heart stop for an instant as he began to speak once they sat down. She knew instantly that he was going to say something she didn't want to hear.

"I spoke to Harry yesterday." He fought the emotions that were rising up in him. "I had to, for both our sakes."

"About us?" She looked stunned. It was so soon. Nothing had even happened yet. It was an innocent romance . . . but Harrison shook his head.

"About him, and what he feels for you. I had to know, before we went any further with this." He took her hand and looked into her eyes, and she felt her heart melt again. "Tana, I want you to know right now, that I'm in love with you. I've only loved one woman in my life as I think I love you, and that was my wife. But I also love my son, and I wouldn't hurt him for anything in this world, no matter what kind of son-of-a-bitch he thinks I am, and I've been one at times. I would have married you . . . but not until I knew where Harry stood." He didn't pull any punches with her. "He's in love with you, Tan."

"What?" She was shocked. "He is not!"

"He is. He's just scared to death to scare you off. He told me about the rape, about how you felt about going out with men. He's been biding his time for years, but I don't have any doubt. He has been in love with you for years. He admitted it himself." Harrison's eyes looked sad.

"Oh, my God." She looked shocked. "But I'm not . . . I don't . . . I don't think I ever could. . . ."

"I suspected that too. But that's between you and him. If he ever does get up the guts to declare himself, you'll have to deal with that yourself. What I wanted to know was how he felt. I know how you feel now. I knew it before I talked to him." There were tears spilling in her eyes, and suddenly in his, too, as he reached for her hand. "Darling, I love you more than life itself, but if I walked off with you now, if you'd even be willing to do that with me, it would kill my son. It would break his heart, and maybe destroy something he needs very much right now. I can't do that to him. Nor can you. I really don't think you could." She was crying openly, and he pulled her into his arms as tears rolled down his cheeks. They had nothing to hide here, or anywhere, only in front of his son. But it was the cruelest trick life had played on her so far, the first man she had loved couldn't love her because of his son ... who was her best friend, whom she loved, but not like that. She didn't want to do anything that would hurt Harry either, but she was so much in love with Harrison ... it was a ghastly day filled with tears and regrets. She wanted to sleep with him anyway, but he wouldn't let her do that to herself. "The first time that happens to you, after that awful experience you had, should be with the right man." He was gentle, and loving, and he held her while she cried, and once he almost cried himself. And the next week was the most painful in her life, as at last he left for London again, and Tana felt as though she had been left on the beach. She was alone, with her studies, with Harry again. She went to the hospital every day, took her books with her, and she looked tired and pale and grim.

"Boy, you're a pleasure to see. What the hell's wrong with you? Are you sick?" She almost was, over Harrison, but she knew he had been right, no matter how painful it was. They had both done the right thing for someone they loved. And now she was merciless with him, forcing Harry to do what the nurses asked, urging him on, insulting him, cajoling him, encouraging him when he needed it. She was tireless, and devoted beyond anything imaginable, and when Harrison called from halfway around the world, sometimes she would talk to him and she would feel her heart leap again, but he hadn't gone back on his resolve. It was a sacrifice he had made for his son, and Tana had to go along with it. He had given her no choice. Or himself, although he knew that he would never recover from what he felt for her. He only hoped she would.

Chapter 11

The sun streamed into the room as Harry lay on his bed, trying to read a book. He had already had an hour in the pool and two hours of therapy, and he was sick to death of his schedule. There was a sameness about it all, a tediousness he couldn't stand anymore. He glanced at his watch, knowing Tana would be there soon. He had been at Letterman for more than four months, and she came to see him every day, bringing her stacks of papers and notes, and mountains of books. And almost as soon as he thought of her, the door opened and she walked in. She had lost weight in the past few months. She was working too hard at school, and running herself ragged going back and forth between Berkeley and the hospital. His father had offered to buy her a car, but she had absolutely refused to even consider it.

"Hi kid, what's up, or is that rude?" She grinned at him and he laughed.

"You're disgusting, Tan." But at least he wasn't as sensitive about that anymore. Five weeks before, he had actually made love to a student nurse, a little "creativity" as he had said to his therapist, but with a little imagination here and there, things had gone fairly well for both of them, and he didn't give a damn that she was engaged. True love hadn't been on his mind, and he had no intention of trying beginner's luck on Tan. She meant much, much too much to him, as he had told his dad, and she had enough problems of her own. "What'd you do today?"

She sighed and sat down with a rueful smile. "What do I ever do? Study all night, turn in papers, take exams. Christ, I may not live through another two years of this."

"Sure you will." He smiled. She was the light of his life, and he would have been lost without her visits every day.

"What makes you so sure?" Sometimes she doubted it

herself, but somehow she always went on. Always. She wouldn't let herself stop. She couldn't let Harry down and she couldn't flunk out of school.

"You've got more guts than anyone I know. You'll make it, Tan." It was something they gave each other now — courage, faith. When he'd get depressed, she'd stand there and shout at him until he wanted to cry, but she made him try all the things he was supposed to do, and when she thought she couldn't make it through another day of Boalt, he quizzed her for exams, woke her up after she got a little sleep, underlined some of the textbooks for her. And now suddenly he grinned at her. "Besides, law school's not that hard. I've been reading some of that stuff you left here."

She smiled. That was what she had had in mind. But she looked nonchalant as she turned to him. "Oh yeah, then why don't you give it a try?"

"Why should I bust my hump?"

"What else have you got to do? Except sit on your can, and pinch nurses' aides. And how long will that last? They're going to kick you out of here in June."

"That's not sure yet." He looked nervous at the thought. He wasn't sure he was ready to go home. And home where? His father moved around so much, and he couldn't keep up with him now, even if he wanted to. He could go to a hotel, of course, there was the apartment at the Pierre in New York, but that sounded terribly lonely to him.

"You sure don't look excited about going home." Tana was watching him. She had talked to Harrison in Geneva several days before, and they had discussed the same thing. He called her at least once a week to see how Harry was, and she knew that he still felt the same about her as he had before, and she did for him as well, but they had taken their resolve and there was no turning back anymore. Harrison Winslow would not betray his son. And Tana understood.

"I don't have a home to go to, Tan." She had thought of it before, but not with any great seriousness, yet she had an idea. Maybe it was time to broach it to him.

"What about moving in with me?"

"In that dismal room of yours?" He laughed and looked

horrified at the same time. "Being confined to a wheelchair is bad enough. I might kill myself. Besides, where would I sleep? On the floor?"

"No, you ass." She was laughing at him as he made a hideous face. "We could get a place of our own, as long as it's reasonable so I could pay my share too."

"Like where?" The idea hadn't quite sunk in yet, but it had a certain appeal.

"I don't know ... the Haight Ashbury maybe?" The hippie boom was just taking hold, and she had driven through the Haight only recently. But she was teasing him. Unless one wore flowing robes and were permanently stoned on LSD, it would have been impossible to tolerate living there. "Seriously, we could find something if we looked."

"It would have to be on the ground floor." He looked pensively at the wheelchair parked at the end of the bed.

"I know that. And I have another idea too." She decided to hit him with it all at once.

"Now what?" He lay back against his pillows and looked happily at her. As difficult as these months had been, it had given them something very special to share, and they were closer than either of them had ever thought two human beings could be. "You know, you never give me a moment's peace. You've always got some damn plot or plan. You exhaust me, Ian." But it wasn't a complaint and they both knew it.

"Horseshit. It's good for you."

"So, what's your thought?"

"How about applying to Boalt?" She held her breath and he looked shocked.

"Me? Are you *nuts*? What the hell would I do there?"

"Probably cheat, but failing that, you could study your ass off like I do every night. It would give you something to do other than pick your nose."

"What a charming image you have of me, my dear." He swept her a bow from the bed and she laughed. "Why in God's name would I torture myself with law school? I don't have to do a dumb thing like that."

"You'd be good at it." She looked at him earnestly and he wanted to argue with her, but the worst of it was that he liked the idea.

"You're trying to ruin my life."

"Yes." She grinned. "Will you apply?"

"I probably won't get in. My grades were never as good as yours."

"I already asked, you can apply as a veteran. They might even make an exception for you. . . ." She was cautious about the way she said it, but he looked annoyed anyway.

"Never mind that shit. If you got in, so can I." And the damnedest thing was that suddenly he wanted to. He almost wondered if he had wanted to for a long time. Maybe he felt left out with all that studying she did, while he had nothing at all to do except lie around and watch the nursing shifts change.

She brought him the application forms that afternoon, and they mulled them over endlessly, and finally sent them in, and by then Tana was looking at flats for them. It had to be exactly right, and something that would work for him.

She had just seen two she liked when her mother called on an afternoon in late May. It was unusual for her to be home, but she had some things to take care of at home, and she knew Harry was all right. One of the girls from down the hall came and knocked on her door. She assumed it was Harry, wanting to know how the apartments were. One of them was in Piedmont, and snob that he was, she knew he would like that one best, but she wanted to be sure she could afford it too. She didn't have the income he had, even though she had lined up a good job for herself that summer. Maybe after that. . . .

"Hello?" There was a long-distance whir and her heart stopped, wondering if it was Harrison calling her again. Harry had never realized what had passed between them, or, more important, what could have and what sacrifice they had made. "Hello?"

"Tana?" It was Jean.

"Oh. Hi, Mom."

"Is something wrong?" She had sounded strange at first.

"No. I thought it was someone else. Is something wrong?" It was an unusual hour for her to call. Maybe Arthur had had another heart attack. He had stayed in Palm Beach for three months, and Jean had stayed there with him. Ann and John and Billy had gone back to New York, and Jean had stayed to nurse him back to health even after he left the hospital. They had only been back in New York for two months, and she must have had her hands full, because Tana almost never heard from her now.

"I wasn't sure you'd be home at this hour." She sounded nervous, as though she wasn't sure what to say.

"Usually I'm at the hospital, but I had something to do here."

"How's your friend?"

"Better. He's getting out in about a month. I was just looking at some apartments for him." She hadn't told her yet that they were thinking of living together. It made perfect sense to her, but she knew that it wouldn't to Jean.

"Can he live alone?" She sounded surprised.

"Probably if he had to, but I don't think he will."

"That's wise." She had no idea what that meant, but she had other things on her mind. "I wanted to tell you something, sweetheart."

"What's that?"

She wasn't at all sure how Tana would react, but there was no way to beat around the bush any longer. "Arthur and I are getting married." She held her breath and at her end, Tana stared.

"You're *what*?"

"Getting married . . . I . . . he feels that we've gotten older . . . we've been foolish for long enough. . . ." She stumbled over some of the words he had said to her only days before, blushing furiously and at the same time terrified of what Tana would say. She knew that she hadn't liked Arthur for years, but maybe now. . . .

"You weren't the fool in all that, Mom. He was. He should have married you fifteen years ago, at least." She frowned for a moment, mulling over what Jean had said. "Is that what you really want to do, Mom? He's not young anymore, and he's sick . . . he's kind of saved the worst for you." It was blunt, but true, but until his heart attack he hadn't even wanted to marry her. He hadn't thought of it in years, not since his wife had come home from the hospital sixteen years before in fact. But suddenly, everything had changed, and he realized his own mortality. "Are you sure?"

"Yes, Tana, I am." Her mother sounded strangely calm suddenly. It was what she had waited almost twenty years for, and she wouldn't have given it up for anything, not even for her only child. Tana had her own life now, and she had nothing at all, without Arthur. She was grateful to him for finally marrying her. They would have a comfortable, easy life, and she could finally relax. All those years of loneliness and worrying; would he show up, would he come by, should she wash her hair, and then just in case . . . and he didn't come for two weeks, until the night when Tana had flu, or she herself had a bad cold . . . it was all over now, and real life was about to begin. At last. She had earned every minute of it, and she was going to enjoy every minute of it now. "I'm very sure."

"All right then." But Tana did not sound thrilled. "I guess I should say congratulations or something like that." But somehow she didn't feel like it. It seemed like such a boring bourgeois life, and after all Jean's years of sitting there waiting for him, she would have liked to see her tell him to go to hell. But that was youth thinking, and not Jean. "When are you getting married?"

"In July. You'll come, won't you sweetheart?" She sounded nervous again, and Tana nodded to herself. She had planned to go home for a month anyway. She had worked it out with her summer job. She was working at a law firm in town, and they understood, or so they said.

"I'll sure try." And then she had an idea. "Can Harry come?"

"In a wheelchair?" Her mother sounded horrified, and something hardened instantly in Tana's eyes.

"Obviously. It's not exactly as though he has a choice."

"Well, I don't know . . . I should think it would be

embarrassing for him . . . I mean, all those people, and . . . I'll have to ask Arthur what he thinks. . . ."

"Don't bother." Tana's nostrils flared and she wanted to strangle someone, primarily Jean. "I can't make it anyway."

Tears instantly sprang to Jean's eyes. She knew what she'd done, but why was Tana always so difficult? She was so stubborn about everything. "Tana, don't do that, please . . . it's just . . . why do you have to drag him along?"

"Because he's been lying in a hospital for six months and he hasn't seen anyone except me, and maybe it would be nice for him. Did that occur to you? Not to mention the fact that this did not happen in a car accident, it happened defending a stinking country we have no right to be in anyway, and the least people can do for him now is show him some gratitude and courtesy. . . ." She was in a blind rage and Jean was terrified.

"Of course . . . I understand . . . there's no reason why he can't come. . . ." And then suddenly, out of nowhere, "John and Ann are having another baby, you know."

"What the hell does that have to do with anything?" Tana looked blank. It was hopeless talking to her. They never saw eye to eye about anything.

"Well, you could be thinking of that one of these days. You're not getting any younger, dear. You're almost twenty-three."

"I'm in law school, Mom. Do you have any idea what that's like? How hard I work night and day? Do you have any idea how ridiculous it would be for me to be thinking of marriage and babies right now?"

"It always will be if you spend your time with him, you know." She was picking on Harry again and Tana saw red at the words.

"Not at all." Her eyes were fierce, but her mother couldn't see that. "He can still get it up, you know."

"Tana!" Jean was appalled by Tana's vulgarity. "That's a disgusting thing to say."

"But it's what you wanted to know, isn't it? Well, you can relax, it works. I hear he screwed a nurse a few days ago, and she said it was great." She was like a big dog refusing to release its prey, and her mother was hanging there, by the neck, and unable to escape. "Feel better now?"

"Tana Roberts, something has happened to you out there." In the flash of a moment, Tana thought of the grueling hours of studying she had put in, the love she had felt for Harrison, to no avail, the heartbreak of seeing Harry return crippled from Vietnam. . . .

"Yeah . . . I think I've grown up. That's not always real pretty, is it, Mom?"

"It doesn't have to be ugly or rude, except in California, I suppose. They must be savages out there at that school."

Tana laughed. They were worlds apart. "I guess we are. Anyway, congratulations, Mom." It suddenly dawned on her that she and Billy were going to be stepbrother and sister now, and the thought almost made her sick. He would be at the wedding, and it was almost more than she could stand. "I'll try to be home in time."

"All right." Jean sighed, it was exhausting talking to her. "And bring Harry, if you must."

"I'll see if he's up to it. I want to get him out of the hospital first, and we've got to move. . . ." She cringed at the slip, and there was a deafening silence at the other end. That really was too much.

"You're moving in with him?"

Tana took a breath. "I am. He can't live alone."

"Let his father hire a nurse. Or are they going to pay you a salary?" She could be as cutting as Tana when she tried, but Tana was undaunted by her.

"Not at all. I'm going to split the rent with him."

"You're out of your mind. The least he could do is marry you, but I'd put a stop to that."

"No, you wouldn't." Tana sounded strangely calm. "Not if I wanted to marry him, but I don't. So relax. Mom . . . I know this is hard for you, but I just have to live my life my own way. Do you think you can just try to accept that?" There was a long pause and Tana smiled. "I know, it's not easy." And then suddenly she heard Jean crying at the other end.

"Don't you see that you're ruining your life?"

"How? By helping a friend out? What harm is there in that?"

"Because you'll wake up next week and you'll be forty years old and it'll be all over, Tan. You'll have wasted your youth, just like I did, and at least mine wasn't a total waste, I had you."

"And maybe one day I'll have children of my own. But right now I'm not thinking of that. I'm going to law school so I can have a career and do something useful with my life. And after that, I'll think about all that other stuff. Like Ann." It was a dig, but a friendly one, and it went right over Jean's head.

"You can't have a husband and a career."

"Why not? Who said that?"

"It's just true, that's all."

"That's bullshit."

"No, it's not, and if you hang around with that Winslow boy long enough, you'll marry him. And he's a cripple now, you don't need a heartbreak like that. Find someone else, a normal boy."

"Why?" Tana's heart ached for him. "He's human, too. More so than most, in fact."

"You hardly know any boys. You never go out." Thanks to your darling stepson, Mom. But actually, lately, it was thanks to law school. Ever since Harrison, she had begun to feel differently about men, in some ways more trusting and open, and yet so far no one measured up to him. He had been so good to her. It would have been wonderful to find someone like him. But she never had time to go out with anyone now. Between going to the hospital every day and preparing for exams . . . everyone complained of it. Law school was enough to destroy an existing relationship, and starting a new one was almost impossible.

"Just wait a couple of years, Mom. And then I'll be a lawyer, and you'll be proud of me. At least I hope you will." But neither of them was too sure just then.

"I just want a normal life for you."

"What's normal? Was your life so normal, Mom?"

"It started out to be. It wasn't my fault that your father was killed and things changed after that."

"Maybe not, but it was your fault you waited almost twenty years for Arthur Durning to marry you." And the truth was that if he hadn't had his heart attack, he might never have married her. "You made that choice. I have a right to my choices, too."

"Maybe so, Tan." But she didn't really understand the girl, she didn't even pretend to anymore. Ann Durning seemed so much more normal to her. She wanted what every other girl wanted, a husband, a house, two kids, pretty clothes, and if she'd made a mistake early on, she'd been smart enough to do better the second time. He had just bought her the most beautiful sapphire ring at Cartier's, and that was what Jean wanted for her child, but Tana didn't give a good goddamn.

"I'll call you soon, Mom. And tell Arthur I said congratulations to him too. He's the lucky one in this deal, but I hope you'll be happy too."

"Of course I will." But she didn't sound it when she hung up. Tana had upset her terribly, and she told Arthur about it, as much as she could, but he just told her to relax. Life was too short to let one's children get the best of one. He never did. And they had other things to think about. Jean was going to redecorate the Greenwich house, and he wanted to buy a condo in Palm Beach, as well as a little apartment in town. They were giving up the apartment she had had for years. And Tana was shocked when she discovered that.

"Hell, I don't have a home anymore either." She was shocked when she told Harry that, but he looked unimpressed.

"I haven't had one in years."

"She said there'll always be a room for me wherever they live. Can you imagine my spending the night in the Greenwich house, after what happened there? I get nightmares thinking of it. So much for that." It depressed her more than she wanted to admit to him, and she knew that marrying

Arthur was what Jean wanted, but somehow it seemed so depressing to her. It was so ultimately middle class, so boring and bourgeois, she told herself, but what really bothered her was that Jean was still at Arthur's feet after all the shit she had taken from him over the years. But when she told Harry that, he got annoyed with her.

"You know you've been turning into a radical, and it bores the shit out of me, Tan."

"Have you ever considered the fact that you're more than a little right wing?" She started to look uptight.

"Maybe I am, but there's nothing wrong with that. There are certain things I believe in, Tan, and they aren't radical, and they aren't leftist, and they aren't revolutionary, but I think they're good."

"I think you're full of shit." There was an unusual vehemence about what she said, but they had already disagreed about VietNam several times. "How the hell can you defend what those assholes are doing over there?" She leapt to her feet and he stared at her, there was an odd silence in the room.

"Because I was one of them. That's why."

"You were not. You were a pawn. Don't you see that, you fucking jerk? They used you to fight a war we shouldn't be fighting in a place we shouldn't be in."

His voice was deathly quiet as he looked at her. "Maybe I think we should."

"How can you say a dumb thing like that? Look what happened to you over there!"

"That's the whole point." He leaned forward in his bed, and he looked as though he wanted to strangle her. "If I don't defend that . . . if I don't believe in why I was there, then what the hell good was it anyway?" Tears suddenly sprang to his eyes and he went on, "What does it all mean, goddamn it, Tana . . . what did I give them my legs for if I don't believe in them? Tell me that!" You could hear him shouting all the way down the hall. "I have to believe in them, don't I? Because if I don't, if I believe what you do, then it was all a farce. I might as well have gotten run over by a train in Des Moines. . . ." He turned his face away from her and started to cry openly and she felt terrible. And then he turned to her, still in a rage. "Now get the hell out of my room you insensitive radical bitch!"

She left, and she cried all the way back to school. She knew that he was right for him. He couldn't afford to feel about it as she did, and yet, ever since he had come back from Vietnam, something had begun to rage in her that had never been there before, a kind of anger that nothing could quench, and possibly never would. She had talked to Harrison about it on the phone one night and he had put it down to youth, but she knew it wasn't just that, it was something more. She was angry at everyone because Harry had been maimed, and if people were willing to take more chances politically, to stick their necks out . . . Hell, the President of the United States had been killed a year and a half before, how could people not see what was happening, what they had to do . . . but Tana didn't want to hurt Harry with all of it. She called him to apologize but he wouldn't talk to her. And for the first time in six and a half months since he'd gotten to Letterman, she didn't go to see him for three days. And when she finally did, she stuck an olive branch through the door of his room, and followed it in sheepishly.

"What do you want?" He glared at her, and she smiled tentatively.

"The rent, actually."

He tried to suppress a grin. He wasn't angry at her anymore. So she was turning into a crazy radical. So what? That's what Berkeley was all about. She'd grow out of it. And he was more intrigued by what she had just said. "You found a place?"

"I sure did." She grinned at him. "It's on Channing Way, a teeny little two-bedroom house with a living room and a kitchenette. It's all on one floor, so you'd have to behave yourself somewhat or at least tell your lady friends not to scream too loud," they both grinned and Harry looked ecstatic at the news, "you're going to love it!" She clapped her hands and described it in detail to him, and that weekend the doctor let her drive him over there. The last of the surgeries had been completed six weeks before; his therapy was going well. They had done all for him they were going to do. It was time to go home. Harry and Tana signed the lease as soon as he saw it. The landlord didn't seem to object to the fact that they had different last names, and neither of them offered to explain. Tana and Harry shook hands with a look of glee, and she drove him back to Letterman. Two weeks later, they moved in. He had to arrange for transportation for his therapy, but Tana promised to take him. And the week after her exams, he got the letter congratulating him on his acceptance to Boalt. He sat in his wheelchair waiting for her when she got home, with tears streaming down his cheeks.

"They took me, Tan . . . and it's all your fault. . . ." They hugged and kissed, and he had never loved her more. And Tana knew only that he was her very dearest friend as she cooked him dinner that night and he uncorked a bottle of Dom Perignon champagne.

"Where did you get that?" She looked impressed.

"I've been saving it."

"For what?" He had been saving it for something else, but he decided that enough good things had happened in one day to warrant drinking it.

"For you, you jerk." She was wonderfully obtuse about the way he felt. But he loved that about her too. She was so engrossed with her studies and her exams and her summer job and her political ideas that she had no idea what was going on right beneath her nose, at least not with regard to him, but he wasn't ready yet anyway. He was still biding his time, afraid to lose.

"It's good stuff." She took a big gulp of champagne and grinned at him, slightly drunk, happy and relaxed. They both loved their little house and it was working out perfectly, and then she remembered that she had to ask him something. She had meant to ask him before, but with the rush to move, and buy furniture, she had forgotten to ask. "Listen, by the way, I hate to ask you this . . . I know it's going to be a drag . . . but. . . ."

"Oh Jesus, now what? First she forces me to go to law school, and now God knows what other torture she has in

207

mind. . . ." He pretended to look terrified, but Tana looked sincerely grim.

"Worse than that. My mother's getting married in two weeks." She had long since told him that, but she hadn't asked him to go to the wedding with her. "Will you come with me?"

"To your mother's wedding?" He looked surprised as he set down his glass. "Is that appropriate?"

"I don't see why not." She hesitated, and then went on, her eyes huge in her face. "I need you there."

"I take it her charming stepson will be on hand."

"Presumably. And the whole thing is a little much for me. The happily married daughter with one child and another on the way, Arthur pretending that he and my mother fell in love only last week."

"Is that what he's saying?" Harry looked amused and Tana shrugged.

"Probably. I don't know. The whole thing is just hard for me. It's not my scene."

Harry thought it over, looking into his lap. He hadn't been out like that yet, and he had been thinking of going to Europe to meet his dad. He could stop on the way . . . he looked up at her. There was nothing he would have denied her, after all she had done for him. "Sure, Tan, no sweat."

"You don't mind too much?" She looked doggedly grateful to him and he laughed.

"Sure I do, but so do you. At least we can laugh together."

"I'm happy for her . . . I just . . . I just can't play those hypocritical games anymore."

"Just behave yourself while we're there. We can fly in and I'll go to Europe the day afterwards. I thought I'd meet Dad in the South of France, for a while." It was so good to hear him talking about things like that again. It was amazing to realize that only a year before he had been talking about playing for the rest of his life, and now, thank God, he was playing again, at least for a month or two, before he started law school in the fall. "I don't know how I let you talk me into that." But they were both glad she had. Everything was working out perfectly. They had divided the chores in the house. She did the things he was unable to do, but it was amazing how much he did. Everything from dishes to beds, although he had practically strangled himself vacuuming one week, and now that was her task to do. They were both comfortable. She was about to start her summer job. Both of them thought life pretty damn grand in the summer of '65, and Harry picked up two of the stewardesses on their flight to New York in July. And Tana sat back in her seat, laughing at him.

Chapter 12

The wedding was simple and well done. Jean wore a very pretty gray chiffon dress, and she had bought a pale blue one for Tana to wear, in case she herself didn't have time to shop. It certainly wasn't the kind of thing she would have bought herself, and she was horrified when she saw the price tag on it. Her mother had bought it at Bergdorf's, and it was a gift from Arthur, of course, so Tana couldn't say anything.

Only the family were present at the ceremony, but Tana had insisted on bringing Harry along, much to his chagrin, since they arrived from the city in the same limousine. Tana was staying with him at the Pierre. She insisted to her mother that she couldn't leave him alone. And she was relieved that her mother and Arthur were leaving the next day on a honeymoon so she didn't have to stay in New York for an extended period after all. She would have refused to stay in the Greenwich house, and she was going to fly out of New York when Harry did. He was going to Nice to meet Harrison in St. Jean Cap Ferrat, and she was flying back to San Francisco to her summer job. And Jean and Arthur were threatening to come out and see her in the fall. Her mother looked pointedly at Harry each time she spoke of it, as though she expected him to disappear by then, and eventually Tana had to laugh at it.

"It's really awful, isn't it?" But the worst of all was Billy, who managed to sidle up to her halfway through the afternoon, drunk as usual, and make some sly comment about her boyfriend not being able to get it up, and he'd be glad to help her out anytime, as he recalled she had been a fairly worthwhile piece of ass, but just as she contemplated putting her fist through his mouth, she saw a larger one come whizzing by, meet Billy's chin, and Billy reeled backwards before collapsing neatly on the lawn. Tana turned to see Harry smiling in his wheelchair just behind where she stood. He had reached up and put Billy out cold with one blow and he was immensely pleased with himself.

"You know, I wanted to do that a year ago." He smiled at her, but her mother was horrified at how they had behaved. And as early as possible Tana and Harry got back into the limousine and went back to New York. There was a tearful goodbye between Tana and Jean before that. Or, at least, Jean cried and Tana was tense. Arthur had kissed her on the cheek and announced that she was his daughter now, too, and there wouldn't have to be any more scholarships. But she insisted that she couldn't accept a gift like that, and she couldn't wait to get away from all of them, especially cloying, pregnant Ann, with her whiny voice, her showy gems, and her boring husband, making eyes at someone else's wife halfway through the afternoon.

"Jesus, how can they live like that?" She had fumed to Harry on the way home and he patted her knee.

"Now, now, one day the same thing will happen to you, little one."

"Oh, go fuck yourself." He laughed at her and they went back to the Pierre. They were both leaving the next day, and he took her to "21" that night. Everyone was happy to see him there, although chagrined to see that he was in a wheelchair now. And for old times' sake, they drank too much champagne, and were drunk when they got back to the hotel. Just drunk enough for Harry to do something he had promised himself he wouldn't do for another year or two. They were into their second bottle of Roederer, and actually they had been drinking all day, when he turned to her with a gentle look and touched her chin, and unexpectedly kissed her lips.

"Do you know that I've always been in love with you?" At first Tana looked shocked, and then suddenly she looked as though she might cry.

"You're kidding me."

"I'm not." Was her mother right? Was Harrison?

"But that's ridiculous. You're not in love with me. You never were." She focused on him tipsily.

"Oh yes I am. I always was." She stared at him, and he took her hand in his. "Will you marry me, Tan?"

"You're crazy." She pulled her hand away and stood up and suddenly there were tears in her eyes. She didn't want him to be in love with her. She wanted them to be friends forever, just friends, no more than that. And he was spoiling everything. "Why are you saying that?"

"Couldn't you love me, Tan?" Now he looked as though he were going to cry and she felt more sober than she had all night.

"I don't want to spoil what we have . . . it's too precious to me. I need you too much."

"I need you too. That's the whole point. If we get married then we'll always be there." But she couldn't marry him . . . she was still in love with Harrison . . . it was insane, the whole thing . . . all of it . . . she lay on her bed and sobbed that night, and Harry never went to bed at all. He was waiting for her when she came out of her room the next morning, looking pale and tired, with circles under her eyes. He wanted to retrieve what they'd had before, and it wasn't too late yet. That meant everything to him. He could live without being married to her, but he couldn't stand losing her. "I'm sorry about what happened last night, Tan."

"So am I." She sat down next to him in the room's spacious living room. "What happens now?"

"We put it down to one drunken night. It was a rough day for both of us . . . your mother getting married . . . my first time out socially in the chair . . . no big deal. We can put it behind us. I'm sure of it." He was praying that she would agree with him and slowly she shook her head, as his heart sank.

"What happened to us? Have you really been . . . in love with me for all that time?"

He looked at her honestly. "Some of it. Sometimes, I hate your guts." They both laughed and she felt some of what they had shared before, and she put her arms around his neck then.

"I'll always love you, Harry. Always."

"That's all I wanted to know." He could have cried if he'd

let himself, but instead they ordered room service, laughed, raised hell, teased, trying desperately to regain the ease of what they'd had before, and as she watched his plane take off that afternoon, there were tears in her eyes. It might never be quite the same again, but it would be close. They'd see to that. They both had too much invested in each other by now to let anything spoil it for them.

When Harry finally arrived at Cap Ferrat, brought there by the car and driver Harrison had sent for him, his father came running across the lawn to help his son from the car and into his chair, gripping his arm powerfully and looking at him.

"You all right, son?" There was something in Harry's eyes that worried him.

"More or less." He looked tired. It had been a long flight, a long couple of days, and this time he hadn't played games with the stewardesses. He had been thinking of Tana as he flew to France. She would always be his first great love, the woman who had brought him back to life again. Feelings like that couldn't be lost, and if she didn't want to marry him . . . he had no choice. He had to accept it. He could see in her eyes that it simply wasn't there for her. And as much as it hurt, he knew that he had to force himself to accept that now. But it wasn't going to be easy for him. He had waited for so long to tell her what he felt. And it was all over now. It was never going to happen between them. The thought of that reality brought tears to his eyes again and Harrison took his son's shoulders in his powerful hands.

"How's Tana?" Harrison was quick to ask, and for just an instant he saw Harry hesitate, and then instinctively he understood. Harry had tried and lost. His father's heart went out to him.

"Tana's fine . . ." he tried to smile ". . . but difficult." He smiled cryptically, and Harrison instantly understood. He knew that one day it would come to that.

"Ah yes . . ." He smiled, as a pretty girl walked across the lawn to him and caught Harry's eye, ". . . but difficult."

Chapter 13

When Harry returned from Europe in the fall he was deeply tanned and happy and rested. He had followed his father everywhere, to Monaco, to Italy, to Madrid for a few days, Paris, New York. It had been the whirlwind life again, the life he had felt so left out of as a boy, but suddenly there was a place reserved in it for him. Pretty women, lovely girls, galas, endless concerts and parties and social events. He was actually tired of it when he finally got on the plane in New York and flew west. Tana met him at the Oakland airport, and she looked reassuringly as she had before. She looked healthy and brown, her blonde mane flying in the wind, she had loved her summer job, gone to Malibu for a few days with some friends she'd made at work, and she was talking about going to Mexico over the holidays, and when law school began, they were constantly together, yet apart. She would drop him off at the library, but her classes were different than his. She seemed to be making new friends now. With Harry out of the hospital, she had more free time, and the survivors of the first year grind seemed to stick together now. It was a healthier arrangement than they'd had before, and by Christmas there always seemed to be three of them, including a pretty, petite blonde girl from Australia, named Averil. She seemed to be Harry's shadow. She was studying for a master's degree in art, but she seemed far more interested in following Harry around everywhere, and he didn't seem to object to it. Tana tried to be nonchalant the first time Averil emerged from his room on a Saturday morning and suddenly all three of them laughed nervously.

"Does this mean you guys are kicking me out?" Tana laughed nervously.

"Hell no, you jerk. There's room for all of us." And by the

end of Harry's first year, she was living with them. She was actually adorable, shared the chores, was cheerful, pleasant, helpful, she was so sweet she made Tana nervous sometimes, particularly when she had exams, but on the whole the arrangement worked out perfectly. She flew to Europe with Harry that summer to meet Harrison, and Tana worked in the same law firm again. She had promised her mother that she would come East, but she was looking for every possible excuse not to go, and was spared a lie when Arthur had another heart attack, a mild one this time, but her mother took him to Lake George to rest, and promised to come out to see Tana in the fall. But Tana knew what that meant by now. She and Arthur had flown out once the year before, and it was nightmarish. She was "revolted" by the house they shared, "shocked" that she and Harry were still living under one roof, and she would be even more so now when she discovered that they had added another girl. Tana laughed at the thought. She was obviously beyond hope, and the only consolation was that Ann had gotten divorced again, through no fault of hers, of course. John had actually had the nerve to walk out on her, and was having a flagrant affair with her best friend. So all was not entirely wholesome anywhere these days . . . poor Ann . . . Tana smiled at the thought.

Tana actually enjoyed her summer alone that year. She loved Harry and Averil, too, but there was so much pressure on her with law school, that it was nice to be alone now and then. And she and Harry seemed to fight about politics all the time these days. He continued to support the war in Vietnam, and she became crazed when the subject came up at all, as Averil would try desperately to keep the peace. But Harry and Tana had known each other for too long. After six years, they no longer felt they had to be polite and the language they threw at each other made Averil cringe, although he would never have spoken in that way to her, nor she to him. Averil was a far gentler soul than Tana was. Tana had been on her own for a long time. And at twenty-four, she was powerful and unafraid, and sure of her own ideas. She had a long, strong stride, and eyes that did not shy from anything or anyone. She was curious about everything around her, definite about what she thought, and courageous enough to say it to anyone. It got her into trouble sometimes, but she didn't mind. She liked the discussions that arose like that. And when she registered for school that year, hallelujah her last, she thought to herself with a grin, she found herself in the midst of a lengthy conversation in the cafeteria. There were at least eight or nine people talking heatedly about Vietnam, as usual, and she was quick to leap into it, as she always did. It was the subject she felt strongest about, because of Harry of course, no matter how he chose to feel, she had her own ideas, and Harry wasn't there anyway. He was off somewhere with Averil, probably, copping a quick feel before class, as Tana teased him often enough. The two of them seemed to spend most of their life in bed, challenging his creativity, which seemed to pose no problem at all. But Tana was deep in the ideologies of Vietnam and not thinking of Harry specifically as she spoke that day, and was surprised to find herself sitting next to someone even more radical than she. He had a wild mane of tightly curled black hair that sprang from his head almost angrily, sandals, blue jeans, a turquoise T shirt, strangely electric blue eyes, and a smile that tore at something deep inside of her. When he stood up, every muscle seemed to ripple through his flesh, and everything about him seemed oddly sensual, and she had an almost irresistible urge to reach out and touch his arm, hanging so near to her.

"Do you live nearby?" She shook her head. "I didn't think I'd seen you here before."

"I usually hang out in the library. Third year law."

"Shit." He looked impressed. "That's tough."

"You?"

"The master's program in political science, what else?" They both laughed. He had chosen well anyway, and he followed her to the library where she left him regretfully. She liked his ideas and he was strikingly beautiful, and she knew instantly that Harry wouldn't approve of him. He had very square ideas these days, especially with Averil around. It was something Tana knew about them both and it didn't bother her. Harry could have grown ferns on his head and sprouted horns, and she would have loved him anyway. He was her brother by then, and Averil was a part of him, so she accepted that. Most of the time, she tried not to discuss politics with them. It made things easier.

And she was intrigued to see her new friend making a speech on campus a few days later, about the same issues they had discussed. It was an impassioned, brilliant confrontation of the mind and she told him as much when she saw him afterwards. She knew by then that his name was Yael McBee. It was a funny name, but he was not a funny man. He was brilliant and intense and his anger reached out almost like a lash to touch those he wished to reach. She admired his skill in addressing crowds, and she went to see him several more times that fall, before he finally asked her out to dinner one night. They each paid their share, and went back to his apartment to talk afterwards. There were at least a dozen people living there, some of them on mattresses, and it didn't have the neat, well-polished air of the cottage which Harry and Tana and Averil shared. She would, in fact, have been embarrassed to bring Yael there. It was too bourgeois, too sweet, almost too foreign to him. And she liked visiting him where he lived. She felt uncomfortable at home anyway these days. Averil and Harry were always making love or hiding out, going in his room and closing the door. She wondered how he got any studying done at all, and yet she knew he did from the look of his grades, which were surprisingly good. But it was more fun being with Yael and his friends, and when Harry flew to Switzerland at Christmastime, and Averil flew home, Tana finally invited Yael to come and see her. And it was odd to see him in the tidy little house, without his strident friends around. He had worn a deep green turtleneck and his well worn jeans. He had military combat boots, although he had served a year in jail for refusing to be drafted and go to Vietnam. They sent him to a prison in the south west, and paroled him after a year.

"That's incredible." She was awed by him, by his remarkable, almost Rasputin-like eyes, his courage in going against every current imaginable, there was something outstanding about the man, and she wasn't surprised that he had been fascinated by communism as a child. Everything about him was intriguing and unusual, and when he gently took her in his arms and made love to her on Christmas Eve, that seemed intriguing too. Only once did she have to force Harrison Winslow from her mind. And in a peculiar way he had readied her for this. Not that he had anything in common with Yael McBee. Yael managed to unleash her flesh in a way she had never dreamed could happen to her, reaching deep into her, into all she had wanted and denied herself for so long. He reached into her very soul, and pulled out a passion and desire she had never suspected in herself, and gave her something she had never dreamed a man could give, until she felt addicted to everything he gave to her. She was almost his slave by the time Harry and Averil came home, and more often than not, she slept at Yael's apartment now, on a mattress with him, curled up, cold, until he laid a hand on her, and then suddenly life was exotic and tropical, there were brilliant hues everywhere. She couldn't live without him now, and after dinner, they would sit around the living room with the others, talking politics and smoking dope, and Tana suddenly felt like a woman now, a woman in full bloom, living daringly at the feet of her man.

"Where the hell are you all the time, Tan? We never see you anymore." Harry questioned her.

"I have a lot of work to do at the library for exams." She had five months of law school left before finals came up, and then the bar to face, and in some ways it panicked her, but actually most of the time she was with Yael, and she had still said nothing about him to Harry or Averil. She didn't know what to say. They lived in such different worlds that it was impossible to conceive of them in the same place, same house, same school.

"You have a romance going on or something, Tan?" He was suspicious of her now, in addition to her absences. She was looking strange to him, numb almost, glazed, as though she had joined a Hindu cult, or smoked dope all the time, which he suspected too. But it wasn't until Easter that he saw her with Yael, and when he did he was horrified. He waited for her after class, and like an irate parent, he berated her. "What the hell are you doing with that creep? Do you know who he is?"

"Of course I do . . . I've known him all year. . . ." She had known he wouldn't understand and she told him as much.

"Do you know what kind of reputation he has? He is a violent radical, a Communist, a trouble maker of the worst sort. I watched him get arrested last year, and someone told me he's served time in prison before this . . . for chrissake, Tan, wake up!"

"You fucking jerk!" They were screaming at each other outside the main library, and now and then someone turned around but neither of them cared. "He served time for evading the draft, which I'm sure you think is worse than Murder One, but as it so happens, I don't."

"I'm well aware of that. But you better watch your goddamn fucking ass, or you won't have to worry about taking the bar in June. He'll get you arrested and kicked out of school so fast your head will spin."

"You don't know what you're talking about!" But the next week, over Easter holiday, he arranged a major demonstration outside the administration building, and two dozen students were carted off to jail.

"See what I mean?" Harry had been quick to rub it in and she had slammed out of the house again. Harry didn't understand anything. Mostly, he didn't understand what Yael meant to her. Fortunately, he had managed not to get arrested himself, and she stayed with him for the following week. Everything about him excited her. Every sense was aroused when he walked into the room, and things were pretty interesting at his place these days. Everyone seemed to be getting more wound up for demonstrations set up for the end of the school year, but she was so panicked about exams that she had to stay at her own house more than once just to get some studying done. And it was there that Harry tried to reason with her, gently this time, he was terrified that something would happen to her, and he'd do anything to stop it if he could, before it was too late. "Please, Tan, please . . . listen to me . . . you're going to get in trouble with him . . . are you in love with him?" He looked heartbroken at the thought, not because he was still in love with her himself, but because he considered it a hideous fate for her. He hated the guy, he was a rude, boorish, uncivilized, selfish creep, and Harry had heard plenty about him around the school in the last six months. The guy was violent and sooner or later there was going to be serious trouble involving him. Harry just didn't want him to pull Tana down with him when he went. And he thought there was a good chance he might. If she let him. And she looked as though she would. She had a blind passion for the man. Even his politics excited her, and the thought of that made Harry sick. She insisted that she wasn't in love with him, but he knew that it wasn't that simple for her, that this was the first man she had willingly given herself to, and she had been so chaste for so long that in some ways her judgment was impaired. He knew that if the right man, or the wrong one as it were, came along and aroused her in a way she'd never known before, she might fall prey to him, and in this instance she had. She was mesmerized by Yael, and his unorthodox life and friends. She was fascinated by something she had never seen before, and at the same time he played her body like a violin. It was a difficult combination to defeat. And then, just before her final exams, six months into their relationship, Yael took matters in his own hands, and put her to the test.

"I need you next week, Tan."

"What for?" She looked over her shoulder distractedly. She had two hundred pages more to read that night.

"Just a meeting, sort of. . . ." He was vague, smoking his fifth joint of the night. Usually, it didn't affect him visibly, but lately he was tired.

"What kind of meeting?"

"We want to make a point with the people who count." She smiled at him. "Who's that?"

"I think it's time we took things directly into government. We're going to the mayor's house."

"Christ, you'll get busted for sure." But it didn't seem to faze her much. She was used to that by now, not that she'd gotten arrested with him yet, although all the others had.

"So what?" He was unconcerned.

"If I'm with you, and I go, and no one bails me out, I'll miss my exams."

"Oh, for chrissake, Tan, so what? What are you going to be after all? Some two-bit lawyer to defend society as it exists? It sucks, get rid of it first, then go to work. You can wait a year to take your exams, Tan. This is more important." She looked at him, horrified at what she had just heard him say to her. He didn't understand her at all if he could say something like that. Who was this man?

"Do you know how hard I've worked for this, Yael?"

"Don't you realize how meaningless it is?"

It was the first fight they had ever had, and he pressured her for days, but in the end she did not go. She went back to her own house to study for exams, and when she watched the news that night, her eyes almost fell out of her head. The mayor's house had been bombed, and two of his children had almost been killed. As it turned out, they were going to be all right, but an entire side of the house had been destroyed, his wife was badly burned by a bomb that had exploded nearby. "And a radical student group at UC Berkeley had taken credit for it." Seven students had been arrested on charges of attempted murder, assault, assorted weaponry charges, and sundry other things, and among them Yael McBee . . . and if she had listened to him, she realized with trembling knees, her whole life would have been over . . . not just law school, but her freedom for many, many years. She was deathly pale as she sat watching them being loaded into police wagons on TV and Harry watched her face and said nothing at all. She stood up after a long moment and looked down at him, grateful that he hadn't said anything. In one second, everything she had felt for Yael exploded into nothingness, like one of his bombs.

"He wanted me to be there tonight, Harry. . . ." She started to cry. "You were right." She felt sick. He had almost destroyed her life, and she had been completely under his spell. And for what? A piece of ass? How sick was she? She felt sick thinking of it. She had never realized how deeply committed they were to their ideals, and it terrified her now to have known them at all. She was afraid that she might be taken in for questioning. And eventually she was, but nothing ever came of it. She was a student who had slept with Yael McBee. She wasn't the only one. She took her exams. She passed the bar. She was offered a job in the district attorney's office, as a prosecutor, and grown-up life began then and there. The radical days were past, along with student life, and living with Harry and Averil in their little house. She rented an apartment in San Francisco, and slowly packed up her things. Everything was suddenly painful to her, everything was over, finished, done.

"You look like a picture of cheer." Harry wheeled slowly into her room, as she threw another stack of law books into a box. "I guess I should call you Madam Prosecutor now." She smiled and looked at him. She was still shocked at what had happened to Yael McBee, and almost to her through him. And she was still depressed at the thought of what she had felt for him. Now it had all begun to seem unreal. They hadn't come to trial yet, but she knew that he and his friends would be sent away for a long, long time.

"I feel like I'm running away from home."

"You can always come back, you know, we'll still be here." And then he suddenly looked sheepishly at her. Tana laughed as she looked at him. They had known each other for too long to be able to get away with anything.

"Now what does that look like? What mischief are you up to now?"

"Me? Nothing."

"Harry . . ." She advanced on him menacingly and he wheeled away as he laughed.

"Honest, Tan . . . oh shit!" He ran smack into her desk and she carefully put her hands around his handsome throat. He looked more like his father every day, and she still missed him sometimes. It would have been a lot healthier having an affair with him than Yael McBee. "All right . . . all right . . . Ave and I are getting married." For a moment, Tana looked shocked. Ann Durning had just gotten married for the third time, to a big movie producer in

222

LA. He had given her a Rolls-Royce as a wedding present and a twenty carat diamond ring, which Tana had heard a lot about from Jean. But that was something people like Ann Durning did. Somehow she had never thought about Harry getting married.

"You are?"

He smiled. "I thought after all this time . . . she's a terrific girl, Tan. . . ."

"I know that, you dummy," Tana grinned. "I've been living with her too. That just seems like such a grown-up thing to do." They were all twenty-five years old, but she didn't feel old enough to get married yet, she wondered why they did. Maybe they had had more sex, she laughed to herself, and then she smiled at him and bent to kiss his cheek. "Congratulations. When?"

"Pretty soon." And then suddenly Tana saw something funny in his eye. It was, at the same time, both embarrassment and pride.

"Harry Winslow . . . do you mean to tell me that . . . you didn't. . . ." She was laughing now, and Harry was actually blushing for one of the few times in his life.

"I did. She's knocked up."

"Oh, for chrissake." And then her face sobered suddenly. "You don't have to get married, you know. Is she forcing you to?"

He laughed and Tana thought she'd never seen him look so happy in his life. "No, I forced her. I told her I'd kill her if she got rid of it. It's our kid, and I want it, and so does she."

"My God," Tana sat down hard on the bed, "marriage *and* a family. Jesus, you guys don't mess around."

"Nope." He looked about to burst with pride and his intended walked into the room with a shy smile.

"Is Harry telling you what I think he is?" Tana nodded, watching their eyes. There was something so peaceful and satisfied there. She wondered what it felt like to feel like that, and for a moment she almost envied them. "He has a big mouth." But she bent and kissed his lips and he patted her behind, and a little while later he wheeled out of the room. They were getting married in Australia, where Averil was from, and Tana was invited to the wedding, of course, and after that they would come back to the same little house, but Harry was starting to look for a nice place in Piedmont for them to live until he finished school, it was time for the Winslow funds to come into play a little bit. He wanted Averil living decently now. And he turned to Tana later that night.

"You know, if it weren't for you, Tan, I wouldn't be here at all." He had told that to Averil ten thousand times at least in the past year, and he believed it with all his heart.

"That's not true, Harry, you know that. You did it yourself."

But he grabbed her arm. "I couldn't have made it without you. Give yourself credit for that, Tan. The hospital, law school, all of it . . . I wouldn't even know Ave, if it weren't for you. . . ."

She was smiling gently at him and she was touched. "What about the baby, is that my doing too?"

"Oh, you jerk. . . ." He tugged at the long blonde hair and went back to his future wife, sound asleep in the bed where their baby had been conceived. His "creativity" had paid off, and Tana smiled to herself wistfully that night as she fell asleep. She was happy for him, for them both. But she suddenly felt so alone. She had lived with him for two years, with Averil for half of that, it would be strange living alone without them, and they would have their own life . . . it all seemed so strange . . . why did everyone want to get married . . . Harry . . . her mother . . . Ann . . . what was the magic about that? All Tana had wanted was to get through law school, and when she had finally had an affair with someone, he had turned out to be some wild nut, and had wound up in jail for the rest of his life . . . it was mystifying as she fell asleep . . . she didn't have any of the answers, not then or when she moved out.

She moved into a pleasant little flat in Pacific Heights, with a view of the bay, and it took her fifteen minutes to get to City Hall in the secondhand car she bought. She was trying to save everything she could to go to Harry and Averil's wedding, but Harry insisted on giving her the ticket as a gift. She went just before she started her new job, and she could only stay in Sydney with them for four days. Averil looked like a little doll in a white organza dress, and nothing showed yet at all. Her parents had no idea that there was a baby on the way, and Tana even forgot about it. She forgot everything when she saw Harrison Winslow walk toward her again.

"Hello, Tan." He kissed her gently on the cheek and she thought she would melt. And he was as he had always been, charming, and debonaire, sophisticated in every possible way, but the romance that had been stopped so long ago was not destined to be revived again. They talked for hours, and went for a long walk late one night. He found her different and more grown up, but in his mind, she would always be Harry's friend, and he knew that no matter what, in Harry's mind, Tana would always belong to him, and he still respected that.

He took her to the airport when she left. Harry and Averil had already left on their honeymoon, and he kissed her as he had so long ago, and every ounce of her soul reached out to him. There were tears rolling down her cheeks as she boarded the plane, and the stewardesses left her alone, wondering who the handsome man had been. They wondered if she was his girlfriend or his wife, and they watched her curiously. She was a tall, pretty blonde, in a simple beige linen suit, with an assurance about the way she moved, a proud way she held her head, and what they didn't know was that inside she felt frightened and alone. Everything she was going back to was going to be new all over again. New job, new home, and no one to share it with. She suddenly understood why people like Ann Durning and her mother got married. It was safer than being out there on your own, and yet, it was the only way Tana knew by now.

Part III

Real Life

Chapter 14

The apartment Tana had rented had a pretty view of the bay and a little garden in the back. There was a tiny bedroom, a living room, a kitchen with a brick wall and a little French window that looked out into the garden, where she sat sometimes, soaking up the sun. Unconsciously, she had looked for something on the ground floor, so that when Harry came to see her, he wouldn't have a problem with the chair. And she felt comfortable living there. She was surprised at how quickly she adapted to living alone. Harry and Averil came to see her frequently at first, they missed her, too, and Tana was surprised at how rapidly Averil lost her shape. She blew up into a pretty little balloon, and the whole thing seemed foreign to her. Her own life was involved in such a different world. The world of prosecution, of the DA, of murders and robberies and rapes. It was all she thought of all day, and the idea of having babies seemed light years away, although her mother had reported that Ann Durning was pregnant again, not that Tana gave a damn. All of that was too far behind her now. Hearing about the Durnings had no effect at all, even her mother knew that, she had all but given up. And it was the final blow when she heard that Harry had married that other girl. Poor Tana, all those years taking care of him, and he'd gone off with someone else.

"What a rotten thing to do." Tana had been stunned by her words at first and then she had begun to laugh. It seemed so funny to her. Her mother really never had believed that they were just friends.

"Of course it's not. They're perfect for each other."

"But don't you mind?" What was wrong with all of them? How did they think these days? And she was twenty-five years old, when was she ever going to settle down?"

"Of course I don't mind. I told you years ago, Mom,

Harry and I are just friends. The best of friends. And I'm thrilled for them." She waited a respectable interval to tell her about the child, when she called again.

"And what about you, Tan? When are you going to think about settling down?"

Tana sighed. What a thought. "Don't you ever give up, Mom?"

"Have you, at your age?" What a depressing thought.

"Of course not. I haven't even started to think about that." She was just out of her affair with Yael McBee, who was the last person one would have thought of settling down with, and she didn't even have time to think of romance at her new job. She was too busy learning to be an assistant DA. It was almost six months into the job before she even had time for her first date. A senior investigator asked her out, and she went because he was an interesting guy, but she had no real interest in him. She went out with two or three lawyers after that, but her mind was always on her work, and in February she had her first important case, covered by national press. She felt as though all eyes were on her, and she was anxious to do well. It was a fiercely ugly rape. The rape of a fifteen-year-old-girl, who had been lured into an abandoned house by her mother's lover. She had been raped nine or ten times, according to the testimony, badly disfigured and eventually killed, and Tana wanted to get the gas chamber for him. It was a case that struck a chord near her heart, although no one knew that, and she worked her ass off, preparing the case, and reviewing the testimony and the evidence every night. The defendant was an attractive man of about thirty-five, well educated, decently dressed, and the defense was trying to pull every trick in the book. She was up until two o'clock every night. It was almost like trying to pass the bar again.

"How's it going, Tan?" Harry called her late one night. She glanced at the clock, surprised that he was still up. It was almost three.

"Okay. Something wrong? Averil all right?"

"Sure she is." She could almost see him beam. "We just had a baby boy, Tan. Eight pounds one ounce, and she's the bravest girl in the whole world . . . I was there, and oh Tan, it was so beautiful . . . his little head just popped out, and there he was, looking at me. They handed him to me first. . . ." He was breathless and excited and he sounded as though he were laughing and crying at the same time. "Ave just went to sleep so I thought I'd give you a call. Were you up?"

"Of course I was. Oh Harry, I'm so happy for both of you!" There were tears in her eyes too, and she invited him up for a drink. He was there five minutes later, and he looked tired, but the happiest she'd ever seen. And it was the strangest feeling, watching him, listening to him tell it all, as though it had been the first baby that had ever been born, and Averil were miraculous. She almost envied them, and yet at the same time, she felt a terrible void deep in her soul, as though that part of her just wasn't there, almost as though it had been left out. It was like listening to someone speak a foreign tongue and admiring them tremendously, but having no understanding of the language at all. She felt completely in the dark, and yet she thought it was wonderful for them.

It was five o'clock in the morning before he left, and she slept for a little less than two hours before getting up to get ready for court, and she went back to her big case. It dragged on for more than three weeks, and the jury stayed out for nine days, after Tana argued before them heroically. And when they finally came in, she had won. The defendant was convicted of every charge and although the judge refused to impose capital punishment on him, he was sentenced to prison for life, and deep within her, Tana was glad. She wanted him to pay for what he had done, although his going to prison would never bring the girl back to life.

The newspapers said that she had argued the case brilliantly, and Harry teased her about it when she came to see the baby in Piedmont after that, calling her Madam Hotshot, and giving her a bad time.

"All right, all right, enough. Let me see this prodigy you've produced, instead of giving me a bad time." She was fully prepared to be acutely bored and was surprised to discover how sweet the baby was. Everything was tiny and perfect and she hesitated when Averil tried to hand him to her. "Oh God . . . I'm afraid to break him in two. . . ."

"Don't be silly." Harry grabbed the baby easily from his wife and plopped him into Tana's arms, and she sat staring down at him, utterly amazed at how lovely he was, and when she handed him back, she felt as though she had lost something and she looked at them both almost enviously, so much so that when she left, he told Averil victoriously, "I think we got to her, Ave", and indeed she thought about them a great deal that night, but by the following week, she had another big rape case on her hands, and two big murder cases after that. And the next thing she knew, Harry called her victoriously. He had not only passed the bar, but he'd been offered a job, and he could hardly wait to start.

"Who hired you?" She was happy for him. He had worked hard for it. And now he laughed.

"You won't believe this, Tan. I'm going to work for the PD."

"The public defender's office?" She laughed too. "You mean I have to try my cases against you?" They went out to lunch to celebrate and all they talked about was work. Marriage and babies were the last thing on her mind. And the next thing she knew, the rest of the year had flown by, and another one on its heels, trying murders and rapes and assaults and assorted other crimes. Only once or twice did she actually find herself working on the same case Harry was on, but they had lunch whenever they could, and he had been in the public defender's office for two years when he told her that Averil was pregnant again. "So soon?" Tana looked surprised. It seemed as though Harrison Winslow V had been born just moments before, but Harry smiled.

"He'll be two next month, Tan."

"Oh my God. Is that possible?" She didn't see him often enough, but even at that it seemed impossible. He was going to be two. It was incredible. And she herself was twenty-eight years old, which didn't seem so remarkable actually, except that everything had gone so fast. It seemed like only yesterday when she was going to Green Hill with Sharon

Blake, and taking long walks with her into Yolan. Only yesterday when Sharon was alive, and Harry could dance. . . .

Averil had a baby girl this time, with a tiny pink face, a perfect little mouth, and enormous almond shaped eyes. She looked incredibly like her grandfather, and Tana felt an odd tug at her heart when she looked at her, but again, it didn't feel like anything she could ever do herself. She said as much to Harry when they had lunch the following week.

"Why not for chrissake? You're only twenty-nine years old, or you will be in three months." He looked at her seriously then. "Don't miss out on it, Tan. It's the only thing I've ever done that really matters to me, the only thing I really give a damn about . . . my children and my wife." She was shocked to hear him say that. She thought his career was more important to him than that, and then she was even more startled to hear that he was thinking of giving up his job with the PD, and going into practice for himself.

"Are you serious? Why?"

"Because I don't like working for someone else, and I'm tired of defending those bums. They all did whatever it is they claim they didn't do, or at least most of them anyway, and I'm just sick of it. It's time for a change. I was thinking of going into partnership with another lawyer I know."

"Wouldn't it be dull for you? Ordinary civil law?" She made it sound like a disease and he laughed as he shook his head.

"No. I don't need as much excitement as you do, Tan. I couldn't run the crusades you do every day. I couldn't survive that day in, day out. I admire you for doing it, but I'll be perfectly happy with a small comfortable practice, and Averil and the kids." He had never set his sights high, and he was happy with things just as they were. She almost envied him that. There was something deeper and hungrier that burned within her. It was the thing that Miriam Blake had seen in her ten years before, and it was still there. It wanted tougher cases, across the board convictions, it wanted harder and more, and greater challenges all the time. She was particularly flattered when, the following year, she was

233

assigned to a panel of attorneys that met with the governor over a series of issues that affected the criminal processes all over the state. There were half a dozen lawyers involved, all of them male except for Tana, two of them from Los Angeles, two from San Francisco, one from Sacramento, and one from San Jose, and it was the most interesting week she thought she had ever spent. She was exhilarated day after day. The attorneys and the judges and politicians conferred long into the night, and by the time she got into bed every night, she was so excited about what they'd been talking about that she couldn't sleep for the next two hours. She lay awake running it all through her mind.

"Interesting, isn't it?" The attorney she sat next to on the second day leaned over and spoke to her in an undervoice as they listened to the governor discuss an issue she had been arguing about with someone the night before. He was taking exactly the position she had herself and she wanted to stand up and cheer.

"Yes, it is." She whispered back. He was one of the attorneys from Los Angeles. He was tall and attractive and had gray hair. They were seated next to each other at lunch the next day, and she was surprised to discover how liberal he was. He was an interesting man, from New York originally, he had gone to Harvard Law School, and had then moved to Los Angeles. "And actually, I've been living in Washington for the last few years, working with the government, but I just came back out West again, and I'm glad I did." He smiled. He had an easy way, a warm smile, and she liked his ideas when they talked again that night, and by the end of the week, all of them felt as though they had become friends. It had been a fascinating exchange of ideas for the past week.

He was staying at the Huntington. And he offered her a drink at L'Etoile before he left. Of all the people there, they had had the most thoughts in common, and Tana had found him a pleasant companion on the various panels they'd been on. He was hard-working and professional, and pleasant almost all the time.

"How do you like working in the DA's office?" He had

been intrigued by that. Generally, the women he knew didn't like it there. They went into family practices, or other aspects of the law, but female prosecutors were rare everywhere, for obvious reasons. It was a damn tough job, and no one made things easy for them.

"I love it." She smiled. "It doesn't leave me much time for myself, but that's all right." She smiled at him, and smoothed back her hair. She still wore it long, but she wore it in a knot when she worked. She was given to wearing suits and blouses when she went to court, but she still lived in jeans at home. And she was wearing a gray flannel suit now, with a pale gray silk shirt.

"Married?" He raised an eyebrow and glanced at her hand, and she smiled.

"No time for that either, I'm afraid." There had been a handful of men in her life in recent years, but they never lasted long. She ignored them for weeks on end, preparing trials, and just never had enough time for them. It wasn't a loss that had bothered her very much, although Harry kept insisting she'd be sorry one day. "I'll do something about it then." "When? When you're ninety-five?"

"What were you doing in government, Drew?" His name was Drew Lands and he had the bluest eyes she'd ever seen. She liked the way he smiled at her, and she found herself wondering how old he was, and correctly guessed that he was around forty-five.

"I had an appointment to the Department of Commerce for a while. Someone died, and I was filling in until they made a permanent change." He smiled at her, and she realized again that she liked the way he looked, more than she had anyone in a long time. "It was an interesting job for a time. There's something incredibly exhilarating about Washington. Everything centers around the government, the people involved with it. If you're not in government, you're absolutely no one there. And the sense of power is overwhelming. It's all that matters there, to anyone." He smiled at her, and it was easy to see that he had been part of that.

"That must be hard to give up." She was intrigued by

that, and she herself had wondered more than once if she would be interested in politics, but she didn't really think it would suit her as well as the law.

"It was time. I was happy to get back to Los Angeles." He smiled easily and put down his scotch again, looking at her. "It almost feels like home again. And you, Tana? What's home to you? Are you a San Francisco girl?"

She shook her head. "New York originally. But I've been here since I went to Boalt." It had been eight years since she arrived, and that in itself was incredible, since 1964. "I can't imagine living anywhere else now ... or doing anything else. ..." She loved the district attorney's office more than anything. There was always excitement for her there, and she had grown up a lot in her five years on the job. And that was another thing ... five years as an Assistant DA. That was as hard to believe as the rest ... where did the time run to, while one worked? Suddenly one woke up and ten years had drifted past ... ten years ... or five ... or one ... it all seemed the same after a while. Ten years felt like one felt like an eternity.

"You looked awfully serious just then." He was watching her, and they exchanged a smile.

She shrugged philosophically. "I was just thinking how quickly time rushes by. It's hard to believe I've been out here this long ... and in the DA's office for five years."

"That was how I felt about Washington. The three years felt more like three weeks, and suddenly it was time to go home."

"Think you'll go back one day?"

He smiled, and there was something there she couldn't quite read. "For a while anyway. My kids are still there. I didn't want to pull them out of school halfway through the year, and my wife and I haven't resolved yet where they're going to live. Probably half and half eventually. It's the only thing that's fair to us, although it might be difficult for them at first. But kids adjust." He smiled at her. He had obviously just gotten divorced.

"How old are they?"

"Thirteen and nine. Both girls. They're terrific kids, and

they're very close to Eileen, but they've stayed close to me too, and they're really happier in LA than they are in Washington. That's not really much of a life for kids back there, and she's awfully busy," he volunteered.

"What does she do?"

"She's assistant to the ambassador to the OAS, and actually she has her sights on an ambassadorial post herself. That'll make it pretty impossible to take the kids with her, so I'd have them then. Everything is still pretty much up in the air." He smiled again, but a little more hesitantly this time.

"How long have you two been divorced?"

"Actually, we're working it out right now. We took our time deciding while we were in Washington, and now it's definite. I'm going to file as soon as things settle down. I'm hardly unpacked yet."

She smiled at him, thinking of how difficult it had to be, children, a wife, traveling three thousand miles, Washington, Los Angeles. But it didn't seem to shake up his style. He had made incredible sense at the conference. Of the six attorneys involved, she had been most impressed with him. She had also been impressed with how reasonable he was about being liberal. Ever since her experiences with Yael McBee five years before, her liberalism had been curbed considerably. And five years in the DA's office was making her less liberal by the hour. She was suddenly for tougher laws, tighter controls, and all the liberal ideas she had believed in for so long no longer made as much sense to her, but somehow Drew Lands made them palatable again, and even if the actual positions no longer appealed to her, he didn't alienate anyone expressing his views. "I thought you handled it beautifully." He was touched and pleased, and they had another drink, before he dropped her off at her place with his cab, and went on to the airport to go back to Los Angeles.

"Could I call you sometime?" He asked hesitantly, as though he were afraid there might be someone important to her, but at the moment there was no one at all. There had been a creative director in an ad agency for a few months the year before, and actually no one at all since then. He had been too busy and too harassed and so had she, and the affair had ended as quietly as it had begun. She had taken to telling people that she was married to her work, and she was the DA's "other wife", which made her colleagues laugh. But it was almost true by now. Drew looked at her hopefully, and she nodded with a smile.

"Sure. I'd like that." God only knew when he'd be back in town again anyway. And she was trying a big Murder One case anyway for the next two months.

But he astounded her and called her the next day, as she sat in her office, drinking coffee and making notes, as she outlined her approach for the case. There was going to be a lot of press involved and she didn't want to make a fool of herself. She wasn't thinking of anything but the case when she grabbed the phone and barked into it. "Yes?"

"Miss Roberts, please." He was never surprised by the rudeness of people who worked for the DA.

"That's me." She sounded playful suddenly. She was so damn tired, she was slap happy. It was almost five o'clock, and she hadn't left her desk all day. Not even for lunch. She hadn't eaten anything since dining the night before, except for the gallons of coffee she'd consumed.

"It didn't sound like you." His voice was almost a caress, and she was startled at first, wondering if it was a crank call.

"Who's this?"

"Drew Lands."

"Christ . . . I'm sorry . . . I was so totally submerged in my work, I didn't recognize your voice at first. How are you?"

"Fine. I thought I'd give you a call and see how *you* were, more importantly."

"Preparing a big murder case I'm starting next week."

"That sounds like fun." He said it sarcastically and they both laughed. "And what do you do in your spare time?"

"Work."

"I figured as much. Don't you know that's bad for your health?"

"I'll have to worry about that when I take my retirement. Meanwhile, I don't have time."

"What about this weekend? Can you take a break?"

"I don't know . . . I. . . ." She usually worked weekends, especially right now. And the panel had cost her a whole week she should have spent preparing her case. "I really should. . . ."

"Come on, you can afford a few hours off. I thought I'd borrow a friend's yacht in Belvedere. You can even bring your work along, although it's a sacrilege." But it was late October then, and the weather would have been perfect for an afternoon on the bay, warm and sunny with bright blue skies. It was the best time of the year, and San Francisco was lyrical. She was almost tempted to accept, but she just didn't want to leave her work undone.

"I really should prepare. . . ."

"Dinner instead . . . ? lunch . . . ?" And then suddenly they both laughed. No one had been that persistent in a long time and it was flattering.

"I'd really like to, Drew."

"Then, do. And I promise, I won't take more time than I should. What's easiest for you?"

"That sail on the bay sounded awfully good. I might even play hookey for a day." The image of trying to juggle important papers in the breeze did not appeal to her, but an outing on the bay with Drew Lands did.

"I'll be there then. How does Sunday sound?"

"Ideal to me."

"I'll pick you up at nine. Dress warmly in case the wind comes up."

"Yes, sir." She smiled to herself, hung up and went back to work, and promptly at nine o'clock Sunday morning, Drew Lands arrived, in white jeans, sneakers, a bright red shirt, and a yellow parka under his arm. His face already looked tan, his hair shone like silver in the sun, and the blue eyes danced as she followed him out to the car. He was driving a silver Porsche he had driven up from LA on Friday night, he said, but true to his word, he hadn't bothered her. He drove her down to the Saint Francis Yacht Club where the boat was moored, and half an hour later they were out on the bay. He was an excellent sailor, and there was a skipper aboard, and she lay happily on the deck, soaking up the sun, trying not to think of her murder case, and suddenly glad she'd let him talk her into taking the day off.

"The sun feels good, doesn't it?" His voice was deep, and he was sitting on the deck next to her when she opened her eyes.

"It does. Somehow everything else seems so unimportant all of a sudden. All the things one scurries around about, all the details that seem so monumental, and then suddenly poof . . . they're gone." She smiled at him, wondering if he missed his kids a lot, and it was as though he read her mind.

"One of these days, I'd like you to meet my girls, Tana. They'd be crazy about you."

"I don't know about that." She sounded hesitant, and her smile was shy. "I don't know much about little girls, I'm afraid."

He looked at her appraisingly, but not accusingly. "Have you ever wanted children of your own?"

He was the kind of man one could be honest with and she shook her head. "No, I haven't. I've never had the desire, or the time," she smiled openly then, "or the right man in my life, not to mention the right circumstances."

He laughed. "That certainly takes care of pretty much everything, doesn't it?"

"Yup. What about you?" She was feeling breezy and carefree with him. "Do you want more?"

He shook his head, and she knew that that was the kind of man she would want one day. She was thirty years old and it was too late for children for her. She had nothing in common with them anyway. "I can't anyway, or not at least without going to an awful lot of trouble. Eileen and I decided when Julie was born that that was it for us. I had a vasectomy." He spoke of it so openly that it shocked her a little bit. But what was wrong with not wanting more kids? She didn't want any, and she didn't have any at all.

"That solves the problem anyway, doesn't it?"

"Yes," he smiled mischievously, "in more ways than one." She told him about Harry then, his two children, Averil . . . and when Harry came back from Vietnam, the incredible year of watching him fight for his life and go through surgery, and the courage he had had.

"It changed my life in a lot of ways. I don't think I was ever the same after that. . . ." She looked out over the water pensively, and he watched the sunlight dancing on her golden hair. ". . . it was as though things mattered so much after that. Everything did. You couldn't afford to take anything for granted after that." She sighed and looked at him. "I felt that way once before too."

"When was that?" His eyes were gentle as he looked at her and she wondered what it would be like to be kissed by him.

"When my college roommate died. We went to Green Hill together, in the South," she explained seriously and he smiled.

"I know where it is."

"Oh." She smiled back. "She was Sharon Blake . . . Freeman Blake's daughter, and she died on a march with Martin Luther King nine years ago . . . She and Harry changed my life more than anyone else I know."

"You're a serious girl, aren't you?"

"Very, I guess. Maybe 'intense' is the right word. I work too hard, I think too hard. I find it hard to turn all that off a lot of the time." He had noticed that, but he didn't mind that. His wife had been like that too, and it hadn't bothered him. He hadn't been the one who wanted out. She was. She was having an affair with her boss in Washington, and she wanted some "time off", she said, so he gave it to her and came home, but he didn't want to go into details about that.

"Have you ever lived with anyone? I mean, romantically, not your friend, the Vietnam vet." It was funny to hear Harry referred to that way, it was so impersonal.

"No. I've never had that kind of relationship."

"It would probably suit you very well. Closeness without being tied down."

"That sounds about right."

"It does to me too." He looked pensive again, and then he smiled at her almost boyishly. "Too bad we don't live in the same town." It was a funny thing to say so soon, but everything happened quickly with him. In the end, it turned out that he was just as intense as she said she was. He came back to see her for dinner twice that week, flying up from Los Angeles, and then flying back afterwards, and the following weekend he took her sailing again, even though she was totally immersed in her murder case and she was anxious for it to go well. But if anything he soothed her, and made things easier for her, and she was amazed at that. And after their second day on the bay in his friend's boat, he brought her home, and they made love in front of the fire in her living room. It was tender and romantic and sweet, and he made her dinner afterwards. He spent the night, and remarkably, he didn't crowd her at all. He got up at six o'clock, showered, dressed, brought her breakfast in bed, and left in a taxi for the airport at seven fifteen. He caught the eight o'clock plane to Los Angeles, and was in his office by nine twenty-five, looking neat as a pin. And within weeks, he had established a regular commuting schedule, almost without asking her, but it all happened so easily, and made her life so much happier that she suddenly felt as though her whole life had improved. He came to see her in court twice, and she won her case. He was there when the verdict came in and took her out to celebrate. He gave her a beautiful gold bracelet that day that he had bought her at Tiffany in Los Angeles, and that weekend she went down to Los Angeles to visit him. They had dinner at Morton's and Ma Maison, and spent the days shopping on Rodeo Drive or lounging around his swimming pool, and on Sunday night, after a quiet dinner he cooked her himself on his barbecue, she flew back to San Francisco alone. She found herself thinking about him all the way home, about how quickly she had gotten involved with him, and it was a little frightening to think about, but he seemed so definite, so anxious to establish a relationship with her. She was also aware of how lonely he was. The house he lived in was spectacular, modern, open, filled with expensive modern art, and with two empty rooms for his two girls. But there was no one else there, and he seemed to want to be with her all the time. By Thanksgiving she had grown used to his spending half the week in San Francisco with her, and after almost two months, it didn't even seem strange to her anymore. It was the week before the holiday when he suddenly turned to her.

"What are you doing next week, sweetheart?"

"For Thanksgiving?" She looked surprised. She really hadn't thought of it. She had three small cases in her files that she wanted to close out, if the defendants would agree to making a deal. It would certainly make life simpler for her, and none of them were really worth taking to trial. "I don't know. I haven't given it much thought." She hadn't gone home in years. Thanksgivings with Arthur and Jean were absolutely unbearable. Ann had gotten divorced again several years before, and she lived in Greenwich now, so she was on hand with her unruly kids. Billy came and went if he had nothing better to do. He hadn't gotten married. Arthur got more tiresome with age, her mother more nervous, and she seemed to whine a lot now, mostly about the fact that Tana had never married and probably wouldn't now. "A wasted life", was usually the headline of time spent with her, to which Tana could only answer, "Thanks, Mom." The alternative was Thanksgiving with Averil and Harry, but as much as she loved them, their friends in Piedmont were so painfully dull, with their little children and large station wagons. Tana always felt totally out of place with them, and infinitely glad she was. She marveled at how Harry could tolerate it. She and his father had laughed about it together one year. He couldn't stand it any better than Tana could, and he rarely appeared. He knew that Harry was happy, well cared for, and didn't need him, so he kept to the life he enjoyed.

"Want to go to New York with me?" Drew looked at her hopefully.

"Are you serious? Why?" She looked surprised. What was in New York for him? Both of his parents were dead, he had said, and his daughters were in Washington.

"Well," he had already thought it all out ahead of time, "you could see your family, I could stop off in Washington first to see the girls, and then meet you in New York and we

243

could play a little bit. Maybe I could even bring them up with me. How does that sound?"

She thought about it and slowly nodded her head, her hair falling around her like a fan. "Possible." She smiled up at him. "Maybe even very possible, if you leave out the part about my family. Holidays with them are what drive people to suicide."

He laughed. "Don't be so cynical, you witch." He gently tugged a lock of hair and kissed her lips. He was so deliciously affectionate, she had never known a man like him before, and parts of her were opening up to him that had never opened up to anyone. She was surprised at how much she trusted him. "Seriously, could you get away?"

"Actually, right now I could." And that was unusual for her too.

"Well?" Stars danced in his eyes and she threw herself into his arms.

"You win. I'll even offer a visit to my mother up as a sacrifice."

"You'll go to heaven for that for sure. I'll take care of everything. We can both fly East next Wednesday night. You spend Thursday in Connecticut, and I'll meet you in New York on Thursday night with the girls at . . . let's see. . . ." He looked pensive and she grinned. "The Hotel Pierre?" She fully intended offering to pay her share, but he shook his head.

"The Carlyle. I always try to stay there if I can, especially with the girls, it's nice for them up there." It was also where he had gone with Eileen for the last nineteen years, but he didn't tell Tana that. He arranged everything, and Wednesday night found them on separate planes, heading East, she wondering for a moment at how easily she had let him make her plans for her. It was sort of a novelty for her, no one had ever done that before, and he seemed to do it so well and so easily. He was used to it. And when she arrived in New York, she suddenly realized that she was actually there. It was bitter cold, and traces of the first snow were already on the ground as she rode in the cab to Connecticut from John F. Kennedy Airport. She was thinking of Harry as they rode along, and the time he had punched Billy in the face. She was sorry he wasn't there now. She was really not looking forward to Thanksgiving with them. She would have preferred to go to Washington with Drew, but she didn't want to intrude on his private Thanksgiving with his girls after not seeing them for two months. Harry had invited her to join them in Piedmont, as he did every year, but she explained that she was going to New York this year.

"My God, you must be sick," he laughed.

"Not yet. But I will be by the time I leave. I can already hear my mother now . . . 'a wasted life. . . .'"

"Speaking of which, I wanted to introduce you to my associate, finally." He had started his own law firm after all, and Tana had never gotten around to meeting the other half. She just never had time, and they were actually surprisingly busy. Things were going well for them on a small but pleasant scale. It was exactly what they had both wanted, and Harry was ecstatic about it whenever he talked to her.

"Maybe when I get back."

"That's what you always say. Shit, you're never going to meet him, Tan, and he's such a nice guy."

"Oh oh. I smell a blind date. Am I right? A hungry one even . . . oh no!" She was laughing now, the way they used to in the old days and Harry laughed too.

"You suspicious bitch. What do you think, everyone wants to get into your pants?"

"Not at all. I just know you. If he's under ninety-five and has no objection to getting married, you want to fix him up with me. Don't you know I'm a hardened case, Winslow? Give up, for chrissake. Never mind, I'll have my mother call you from New York."

"Don't bother, you jerk. But you don't know what you're missing this time. He's *wonderful*, Averil thinks so too."

"I'm sure he is. Fix him up with someone else."

"Why? Are you getting married?"

"Maybe." She was teasing him, but his ears instantly perked up and she regretted saying it.

"Yeah? To who?"

"Frankenstein. For chrissake, get off my back."

"The hell I will. You're seeing someone, aren't you?"

"No . . . yes! . . . I mean no. Shit. Yes, but not seriously. Okay? Will that suffice?"

"Shit, no. Who is he, Tan? Is it serious?"

"No. He's just a guy I'm seeing like all of the others. That's all. Nice guy. Nice date. No big deal."

"Where's he from?"

"LA."

"What's he do?"

"He's a rapist. I met him in court."

"Not cute. Try again." It was like being a hunted animal and she was getting annoyed at him.

"He's an attorney, now lay off, dammit. It's no big deal."

"Something tells me that it is." He knew her well. Drew was different from the others, but she didn't want to admit that yet, least of all to herself.

"Then you have your head up your ass, as usual. Now, give Averil my love, and I'll see you both when I get back from New York."

"What are you doing for Christmas this year?" He was half inviting and half prying, and she felt like hanging up on him.

"I'm going to Sugar Bowl, is that all right with you?"

"Alone?"

"Harry!" Of course not. She was going with Drew. They had already decided that. Eileen was taking the girls to Vermont with her, so he would be alone, and the holidays were going to be difficult for him. They both expected it. But Tana wasn't going to tell Harry any of it. "Goodbye. See you soon."

"Wait . . . I wanted to tell you more about. . . ."

"No!" She had finally hung up on him, and as she approached Greenwich in the cab, she smiled to herself, wondering what he'd think of Drew. She suspected that they'd like each other, even though Harry would give him the third degree, which was why she wanted to wait a while. It was rare that she introduced any of her men to him. Only after she decided she didn't give a damn about them. But this time was different. . . .

Her mother and Arthur were waiting for her when she arrived, and it shocked her to see how much he had aged. Her mother was only fifty-three years old, which was still young, but Arthur was sixty-seven now and he wasn't aging gracefully. The years of stress with his alcoholic wife had taken their toll, running Durning International, and it all showed now. He had had several heart attacks and a small stroke, and he looked terribly old and frail, and Jean was very nervous, watching him. She seemed to cling to Tana like a life raft in a troubled sea, and when Arthur went to bed that night, her mother came to her room and sat at the foot of the bed. It was the first time Tana had actually stayed at the house, and she had the newly decorated bedroom her mother had promised her. It was just too much trouble to stay in town, or at a hotel, and Tana knew her mother would have been terribly hurt. They saw too little of her as it was. Arthur only went to Palm Beach, to their condominium there, and her mother didn't like to leave him to fly out to San Francisco, so they only saw Tana when she came East, which was more and more infrequently.

"Is everything all right, sweetheart?"

"Fine." It was better than that, but she didn't want to say anything about it to Jean.

"I'm glad." She usually waited a day to start complaining about Tana's "wasted life", but this time she didn't have much time so she would have to move fast, Tana knew. "Your job's all right?"

"It's wonderful." She smiled and Jean looked sad. It always depressed her that Tana liked her job as much as she did. It meant she wouldn't be giving it up soon. She still secretly thought that one day Tana would drop everything for the right man, it was hard for Jean to imagine that she wouldn't do that. But she didn't know her daughter very well. She never really had, and she knew her even less now.

"Any new men?" It was the same conversation they always had, and Tana usually said no, but this time she decided to throw her mother a small bone.

"One."

Jean's eyebrows shot up. "Anything serious?"

"Not yet." Tana laughed. It was almost cruel to tease her that way. "And don't get excited, I don't think it ever will be. He's a nice man, and it's very comfortable, but I don't think it's more than that." But the sparkle in her eyes said that she lied and Jean saw that too.

"How long have you been seeing him?"

"Two months."

"Why didn't you bring him East?"

Tana took a deep breath and hugged her knees on the single guest bed, her eyes fixed on Jean's. "As a matter of fact, he's visiting his little girls in Washington." She didn't tell her that she was meeting him in New York the following night. She had let Jean think she was flying back out West. It gave her brownie points for coming home just for a day, and gave her the freedom to float around New York at will with Drew. She didn't want to drag him out to meet her family, especially not with Arthur and his offspring around.

"How long has he been divorced, Tana?" Her mother sounded somewhat vague as she glanced away.

"A while." She lied, and suddenly her mother's eyes dug into her.

"How long?"

"Relax, Mom. He's actually working on it right now. They just filed."

"How long ago?"

"A few months. For heaven's sake . . . relax!"

"That's exactly what you shouldn't do." She got off the foot of Tana's bed and suddenly paced the room nervously, and then stood glaring at Tana again. "And the other thing you shouldn't do is go out with him."

"What a ridiculous thing to say. You don't even know the man."

"I don't have to, Tana." She spoke almost bitterly. "I know the syndrome. The man doesn't even matter sometimes. Unless he's already divorced, with his papers in his hand, steer clear of him."

"That's the dumbest thing I ever heard. You don't trust anyone, do you, Mom?"

"I'm just a whole lot older than you are, Tan. And as

sophisticated as you think you are, I know better than you. Even if he thinks he's going to get divorced, even if he's absolutely sure of it, he may not. He may be so totally wound up in his kids, for all you know, that he just can't divorce his wife. Six months from now, he could go back to her, and you'll be left standing there, in love with him by then, with no way out, and you'll talk yourself into sticking around for two years . . . five years . . . ten . . . and the next thing you know, you'll be forty-five years old, and if you're lucky," her eyes were damp, "he'll have his first heart attack and need you by then . . . but his wife may still be alive, and then you'll never have a chance at him. There are some things you can't fight. And most of the time, that's one of them. It's a bond that no one else can break for him. If he breaks it himself, or already has, then more power to you both, but before you get badly hurt, sweetheart, I'd like to see you stay out of it." Her voice was so compassionate and so sad that Tana felt sorry for her. Her life hadn't been much fun since she and Arthur had gotten married, but she had won him at last, after long, hard, desperately lonely years. "I don't want that for you, sweetheart. You deserve better than that. Why don't you stay out of it for a while, and see what happens to him?"

"Life is too short for that, Mom. I don't have much time to play games with anyone. I have too much else to do. And what difference does it make? I don't want to get married anyway."

Jean sighed and sat down again. "I don't understand why. What do you have against marriage, Tan?"

"Nothing. It makes sense if you want kids, I guess, or have no career of your own. But I do, I have too much else in my life to be dependent on anyone, and I'm too old for children, now. I'm thirty years old, and I'm set in my ways. I could never turn my life upside down for anyone." She thought of Harry and Averil's house which looked as though a demolition squad stopped to visit them every day. "It's just not for me." Jean couldn't help wondering if it was something she had done, but it was a combination of everything, knowing that Arthur had cheated on Marie, seeing how badly her mother had been hurt for so long, and not wanting that for herself, she wanted her career, her independence, her own life. She didn't want a husband and kids, she was sure of it. She had been for years.

"You're missing out on so much." Jean looked sad. What hadn't she given this child to make her feel like that?

"I just can't see that, Mom." She searched her mother's eyes for something she saw but didn't understand.

"You're the only thing that matters to me, Tan." She found that hard to believe and yet for years her mother had sacrificed everything for her, even putting up with Arthur's gifts of charity, just so she would have something more for her child. It tore at Tana's heart to remember that, and it reminded her of how grateful she should be. She hugged her mother tight, remembering the past.

"I love you, Mom. I'm grateful for everything you did for me."

"I don't want gratitude. I want to see you happy, sweetheart. And if this man is good for you, then wonderful, but if he's lying to you or himself, he'll break your heart. I don't want that for you . . . ever. . . ."

"It's not like what happened to you." Tana was sure of it, but Jean was not.

"How can you know? How can you be sure of that?"

"I just can. I know him by now."

"After two months? Don't be a fool. You don't know anything, anymore than I did twenty-four years ago. Arthur wasn't lying to me then, he was lying to himself. Is that what you want, seventeen years of lonely nights, Tan? Don't do that to yourself."

"I won't. I've got my work."

"It's no substitute." But in her case it was, she substituted it for everything. "Promise me you'll think about what I said."

"I promise." She smiled and the two women hugged each other goodnight again. Tana was touched by her mother's concern, but she knew for certain that she was wrong about Drew. She went to sleep with a smile on her face, thinking of him and his little girls. She wondered what he was doing with them. She had the name of his hotel in Washington, but she didn't want to intrude on them.

The Thanksgiving dinner at the Durning home the next day was predictably dull for everyone, but Jean was grateful that Tana was there. Arthur was somewhat vague, and fell asleep twice in his chair, the maid gave him a gentle nudge, and eventually Jean helped him upstairs. Ann arrived with her three brats, who were even worse than they had been several years before. She was talking about marrying a Greek shipping magnate and Tana tried not to listen to her, but it was impossible. The only blessing of the day was that Billy had gone to Florida with friends instead of being there.

And by five o'clock Tana was checking her watch regularly. She had promised Drew she would be at the Carlyle by nine, and they hadn't called each other all day. She was suddenly dying to see him again, to look into his eyes, touch his face, feel his hands, peel away his clothes as she dropped her own. She had an almost veiled smile as she went upstairs to pack her bags, and her mother came into the room as she did. Their eyes met in the large mirror over the chest of drawers, and Jean spoke to her first.

"You're going to meet him, aren't you?"

She could have lied to her, but she was thirty years old, what was the point? "Yes." She turned to face her mother across the room. "I am."

"You frighten me."

"You worry about things too much. This isn't a replay of your life, mother, it's mine. There is a difference."

"Not always as much as we'd like to think, I'm afraid."

"You're wrong this time."

"I hope for your sake that I am." But she looked grief-stricken when Tana finally called a cab, and rode into New York at eight o'clock. She couldn't get her mother's words out of her mind, and by the time she arrived at the hotel, she was angry with her. Why did she burden her with her own bad experiences, her disappointments, her pain? What right did she have to do that? It was like a blanket of cement one had to wear everywhere to prove that one had been loved, well, she didn't want to be loved that much. She didn't need it anymore. She wanted to be left alone to lead her own life now.

The Carlyle was a beautiful, exquisite hotel, the thickly carpeted steps down to the lobby's marble floor, the Persian rugs, the antique clocks, the gentlemen at the desk in morning coats. It was all from another world, and Tana smiled to herself. This was not her mother's life, it was her own. She was sure of that now. She gave Drew's name, and went upstairs to the room. He had not yet arrived, but they obviously knew him well. The room was as sumptuous as the lobby had promised it would be, a sweeping view of Central Park, the skyline shimmering like jewels, more antiques, this time upholstered in a deep rose silk, heavy satin drapes, and a magnum of champagne waiting in a bucket of ice, a gift from the management. "Enjoy your stay" were the bellboy's final words, and Tana sat down on the handsome couch, wondering if she should run a bath for herself, or wait. She still wasn't sure if he was bringing the girls, but she thought he was. She didn't want to shock them by being undressed when they came. But an hour later, they had not yet arrived, and it was after ten o'clock when he finally called.

"Tana?"

"No, Sophia Loren."

He laughed. "I'm disappointed. I like Tana Roberts better than her."

"Now I know you're nuts."

"I am. About you."

"Where are you?"

There was the briefest pause. "In Washington. Julie has an awful cold, and we thought that Elizabeth might be coming down with the flu. I thought maybe I ought to wait here, and I might not bring them up at all. I'll come up tomorrow, Tan. Is that all right?"

"Sure." She understood, but she had also noticed the "we" that had snuck in. "We thought that Elizabeth. . . ." And she wasn't too crazy about that. "The room is fabulous."

"Aren't they wonderful? Were they nice to you?"

252

"They sure were." She looked around the room, "But it's no fun without you, Mr. Lands. Keep that in mind."

"I'll be there tomorrow. I swear."

"What time?"

He thought for a minute. "I'll have breakfast with the girls . . . see how they feel . . . that should make it ten o'clock. I could catch a noon plane . . . I'll be at the hotel by two without fail." That meant half the day was shot, and she wanted to say something about that, but thought wiser of it.

"All right." But she didn't sound pleased, and when she hung up the phone she had to push her mother's words out of her head again. She took a hot bath, watched television, ordered a cup of hot chocolate from room service, and wondered what he was doing in Washington, and then suddenly she felt guilty for what she hadn't said to him. It wasn't his fault the kids were sick. It was certainly a pain in the ass for them, but it was no one's fault. She picked up the phone and asked for the hotel where he was staying in Washington, but he wasn't there. She left a message that she had called, watched the late show, and fell asleep with the television still on. She woke at nine o'clock the next day, and went out to discover that it was an absolutely gorgeous day. She went for a long walk down Fifth Avenue, and over to Bloomingdale's where she puttered for a while and bought a few things for herself, a handsome blue cashmere sweater for him, and gifts for the girls, a doll for Julie and a pretty blouse for Elizabeth, and then she went back to the Carlyle to wait for him, but there was a message this time. Both the girls were deathly ill, "will arrive Friday night", which he did not. Julie had a fever of one hundred and five, and Tana spent another night at the Carlyle alone. On Saturday she went to the Metropolitan, and on Saturday afternoon at five o'clock, he arrived finally, in time to make love to her, order room service, apologize to her all night, and take the plane back to San Francisco with her the next day. It had been a great weekend for them in New York.

"Remind me to do that again with you sometime," she said half sarcastically as they finished dinner on the plane.

"Are you furious with me, Tan?" He had looked miserable ever since he'd arrived in New York, consumed with guilt toward her, worried about the girls, he talked too much, too fast, and he wasn't himself for days.

"No, disappointed more than furious. How was your ex-wife by the way?"

"Fine." He didn't seem anxious to talk about her and was surprised Tana had asked. It didn't seem an appropriate subject for them, but she was haunted by her mother's words. "What made you ask that?"

"Just curious." She took a mouthful of the dessert on the tray, looking strangely cool as she glanced at him. "Are you still in love with her?

"Of course not. That's ridiculous. I haven't been in love with her for years." He looked downright annoyed and Tana was pleased. Her mother was wrong. As usual. "You may not be aware of it, Tan," he hesitated, looking pale, "but I happen to be in love with you." He looked at her for a long time, and she watched his face searchingly. And then at last she smiled, but she said nothing at all. She kissed his lips, put down her fork, and eventually closed her eyes for a nap. There was nothing she wanted to say to him, and he was oddly uncomfortable. It had been a difficult weekend for both of them.

Chapter 15

December flew by, with a series of small cases on Tana's desk, and a number of parties she went to with Drew. He seemed to think nothing of flying up for the night, and sometimes he came just to have dinner with her. They shared delicious tender moments, quiet nights at home, and a kind of intimacy that Tana had never known before. She realized now how lonely she had been for so long. There had been her mad affair with Yael years before, and since then only casual relationships that came and went, without meaning much to her. But everything about Drew Lands was different. He was so sensitive, so intense, so thoughtful in small ways that meant a great deal to her. She felt surrounded and protected and alive, and they laughed most of the time. By the time the holidays came, he was excited about seeing his two little girls again. They were coming out from Washington to spend Christmas with him. He had cancelled his skiing trip to Sugar Bowl with her.

"Will you come down and spend some time with us, Tan?"

She smiled at him; she knew how crazy he was about his kids. "I'll try." She had a big case coming up, but she was pretty sure it wouldn't actually go to trial for a while. "I think I can."

"Do your best. You could come down on the twenty-sixth, and we could spend a few days in Malibu." He was renting a little weekend place there, but she was not surprised by that so much as by the date he had said . . . the twenty-sixth . . . she realized then he wanted to be alone with the girls for the holidays. "Will you, Tan?" He sounded like a little kid and she hugged him tight and laughed at him.

"Okay, okay, I'll come down. What do you think the girls would like?"

"You." They exchanged a smile and he kissed her again.

He spent the week before getting everything ready for them in LA. Tana was trying to clean up the work on her desk so she could take a few days off from the district attorney's office, and she had lots of shopping to do. She bought Drew a suede shirt, and a very expensive briefcase that he'd seen and loved, and eau de cologne that he wore, and a wild tie she knew he'd love. And she bought each of the girls a beautiful doll at F.A.O. Schwarz, some stationery, some barrettes, an adorable sweat suit for Elizabeth that looked just like one Tana had, and a rabbit made of real fur for the little one. She wrapped all the gifts, and put them in a suitcase to take to LA with her. She hadn't bothered with a tree this year; she didn't really have time and there was no one to see it anyway. She spent Christmas Eve with Harry and Averil and their kids, and it was relaxing just being with them. Harry had never looked better, and Averil looked contented as little Harrison ran around waiting for Santa Claus. They sliced carrots for the reindeer, put chocolate chip cookies out, a big glass of milk, and finally got him into bed. His sister was already asleep, and when he finally fell asleep too, Averil tiptoed into their rooms to look at them with a quiet smile, as Harry watched her go, and Tana watched him. It made her feel good just to see him like that, contented and alive. His life had turned out well, although it certainly wasn't what he had expected to do with his life. He glanced at Tana with a smile, and it was as though they both understood.

"Funny, isn't it, Tan, how life works out. . . ."

"Yeah, it is." She smiled at him. They had known each other for twelve years, almost half their lives. It was incredible.

"I figured you'd be married in two years when I met you that first time."

"And I thought you'd die a hopeless degenerate . . . no . . .", she looked pensive and amused, ". . . a playboy drunk. . . ."

He laughed at the idea. "You've got me mixed up with my old man."

"Hardly." She still had a soft spot for Harrison, but Harry had never been quite sure of that. He had suspected it once, but he had never been sure, and his father had never let on to anything. Nor had Tan.

Harry looked at her oddly then. He hadn't expected to be spending Christmas with her this year, not after the hints she had dropped about Drew once or twice. He had the strangest feeling that it was serious for her, more so even than she would let on to him. "Where's your friend, Tan? I thought you were going to Sugar Bowl." She looked blank at first, but she knew instantly who he meant and he grinned. "Come on, don't pull that 'who do you mean' shit on me. I know you better than that."

She laughed at him. "All right, all right. He's in LA with his kids. We cancelled Sugar Bowl because his kids were coming out. I'm going down on the twenty-sixth." Harry thought that strange but he didn't say anything to her.

"He means a lot to you, doesn't he?"

She nodded cautiously, but she didn't meet his eyes. "He does . . . for whatever that's worth."

"What is it worth, Tan?"

She sighed and leaned back in her chair. "God only knows."

Harry kept wondering something and he finally had to ask. "How come you're not down there today?"

"I didn't want to intrude." But that wasn't true. He hadn't invited her.

"I'm sure you're not an intrusion to him. Have you met his kids yet?" She shook her head.

"Day after tomorrow will be the first time."

Harry smiled at her. "Scared?"

She laughed nervously. "Hell, yes. Wouldn't you be? They're the most important thing in his life."

"I hope you are too."

"I think I am."

And then Harry frowned. "He's not married, is he, Tan?"

"I told you before, he's in the process of getting a divorce."

"Then why didn't he spend Christmas with you?"

"How the hell do I know?" She was annoyed at the persistent questions and she was beginning to wonder where Averil was.

"Didn't you ask?"

"No. I was perfectly comfortable like this," she glowered at him, "until now."

"That's the trouble with you, Tan, you're so used to being alone that it doesn't even occur to you to do things differently. You should be spending Christmas with him. Unless. . . ."

"Unless what?" She was angry at him now. It was none of his business whether or not she spent Christmas with Drew, and she respected his need to be alone with his kids.

But Harry wasn't content to leave it alone. "Unless he's spending Christmas with his wife."

"Oh, for chrissake . . . what an assinine thing to say. You are the most cynical, suspicious son-of-a-bitch I know . . . and I thought I was bad. . . ." She looked furious, but there was something else lurking in her eyes, as though he had hit a nerve. But that was ridiculous.

"Maybe you're not bad enough."

"Shit." She stood up and looked for her bag, and when Averil finally came back, she found them both tense, but she didn't think anything of it. They were like that sometimes. She was used to them by now, they had their own special relationship and sometimes they fought like cats and dogs but they didn't mean any harm.

"What have you two been up to out here? Beating each other up again?" she smiled.

"I'm considering it." Tana glared irritatedly at her.

"It might do him good." All three of them laughed then.

"Harry's been making an ass of himself, as usual."

He suddenly grinned at her. "You make it sound as though I've been exposing myself."

Averil laughed. "Did you do that again, sweetheart?" And then finally Tana warmed up again.

"You know, you're the biggest pain in the ass in the world. World cup goes to you."

He bowed politely from his chair, and Tana went to get her coat. "You don't have to leave, Tan." He was always sorry to see her go, even when they disagreed. They still had a special bond between them. It was almost like being twins.

"I should go home and get organized. I brought home a ton of work."

"To do on Christmas Day?" He looked horrified, and she smiled.

"I have to do it sometime."

"Why don't you come here instead?" They were having friends over, his partner and another dozen or so, but she shook her head. She didn't mind being home alone, or at least so she said.

"You're weird, Tan." But he kissed her cheek and his eyes were filled with the love he felt for her.

"Have a good time in LA." He wheeled beside her to the door and looked at her pensively. "And Tan . . . take care of yourself . . . Maybe I was wrong . . . but it doesn't hurt to be careful about things. . . ."

"I know." Her voice was soft again, and she kissed them both as she left. But driving home in the car, she found herself thinking about what he had said. She knew he couldn't be right. Drew was *not* spending Christmas with his wife . . . but nonetheless she *should* have been spending it with him. She had tried to tell herself that it didn't matter, but it did. And suddenly it reminded her of all the lonely years she had felt so sorry for Jean . . . waiting for Arthur, sitting by the phone, hoping he would call . . . they were never able to spend their major holidays together when Marie was alive, and even afterwards there was always an excuse . . . his in-laws, his children, his club, his friends . . . and there was poor Jean, with tears in her eyes, holding her breath . . . waiting for him . . . Tana fought back the thoughts. It was *not* like that with Drew. It was *not*. She wouldn't let it be. But the next afternoon, as she worked, the questions kept coming to her. Drew called her once, but it had been a very brief call, and he sounded rushed. "I have to go back to the girls," he had said hastily and then hung up on her.

And when she landed in Los Angeles the next day, he was waiting for her at the airport, and he swept her into his arms, and held her so tight she could barely breathe.

"My God . . . wait . . . ! stop . . . !" But he crushed her to him, and they were laughing and kissing all the way to the parking lot as he juggled her bags and packages, and she was ecstatic to see him. It had been a lonely holiday without him after all. And she had secretly wanted it to be different and exciting this year. She hadn't even admitted that to herself, but suddenly she knew it was true. And it was, it was wonderful driving into town with him. He had left the girls at the house with a baby-sitter he knew, just so he could pick her up alone, and spend a few quiet minutes with her.

". . . before they drive us both nuts." He looked at her and beamed.

"How are the girls?"

"Wonderful. I swear they've doubled in size in the last four weeks. Wait till you meet them, Tan." And she was enchanted with them when she did. Elizabeth was lovely and grown up and looked strikingly like Drew, and Julie was a cuddly little ball who almost instantly climbed onto Tana's lap. They loved the presents she had brought, and they seemed to have no resistance to her, although Tana saw Elizabeth looking her over more than once. But Drew handled it remarkably well. He cut out all the necking and the cuddly stuff. It was as though they were just friends, spending a cozy afternoon. It was obvious that he knew Tana well, but it would have been impossible to guess the relationship they shared from the way he behaved to her. And Tana wondered if he always acted that way around the girls.

"What do you do?" Elizabeth was looking her over again, and Julie was watching them both, as Tana smiled, shaking back her mane of pale blonde hair. Elizabeth had envied that since they first met.

"I'm an attorney like your dad. In fact, that's how we met."

"So's my mom." Elizabeth was quick to add. "She's assistant to the ambassador of the OAS in Washington, and they might give her her own ambassadorship next year."

"Ambassadorial post." Drew corrected her and glanced at the three "girls".

"I don't want her to do that." Julie pouted. "I want her to come back here to live. With Daddy." She stuck her lower lip out defiantly, and Elizabeth was quick to add, "He could come with us wherever Mom's sent. It depends on where it is." Tana felt an odd feeling in her gut, and she looked at him, but he was doing something else, and Elizabeth went on. "Mom may even want to come back here herself, if they don't offer her the right job. That's what she said, anyway."

"That's very interesting." Tana noticed that her mouth felt dry, and she wished that Drew would regain control of the conversation again, but he didn't say anything. "Do you like living in Washington?"

"Very much." Elizabeth was painfully polite and Julie hopped into Tana's lap again, and smiled up into Tana's eyes.

"You're pretty. Almost as pretty as our mom."

"Thank you!" It was definitely not easy talking to them, and other than with Harry's children, it was rare for Tana to be in a spot like this, but she had to make the effort for Drew. "What'll we do this afternoon?" Tana felt almost breathless as she asked, desperate to divert them from the topic of his almost ex-wife.

"Mommy's going shopping on Rodeo Drive." Julie smiled up at her, and Tana almost gasped.

"Oh?" Her eyes turned toward Drew in astonishment and then back to them. "That's nice. Let's see, how about a movie? Have you seen *Sounder*?" She felt as though she were running up a mountain as fast as she could and she wasn't getting anywhere . . . Rodeo Drive . . . that meant she had come to Los Angeles with the girls . . . and why hadn't he wanted Tana to come down yesterday? Had he spent Christmas with her after all? The next hour seemed to trickle by as Tana chatted with the girls, and finally they ran outside to play, and Tana finally turned to him. Her eyes spoke volumes before her mouth said a word. "I take it your wife is in Los Angeles." She looked rigid and inside something had gone numb.

"Don't look at me like that." His voice was soft while his eyes avoided her.

"Why not?" She stood up and walked toward him. "Did you spend the holiday with her, Drew?" He couldn't avoid her now, she was standing directly in front of him. And she already assumed he had. And when he lifted his eyes to face her, she knew instantly that she was right and the girls had given him away. "Why did you lie to me?"

"I didn't lie to you. I didn't think ... oh, for chrissake...." He looked at her almost viciously. She had cornered him. "I didn't plan it that way, but the girls have never had a Christmas with us separated before, Tan ... it's just too damn hard on them...."

"Is it now?" Her eyes and voice were hard, concealing the pain she felt inside ... the pain he had inflicted on her by lying to her.... "And just exactly when do you plan to let them get used to it?"

"*Goddammit*, do you think I like seeing my children hurt by this?"

"They look fine to me."

"Of course they do. That's because Eileen and I are civilized. That's the least we can give them now. It's not their fault things didn't work out for us." He looked at Tana sorrowfully and she had to fight the urge to sit down and cry, not for him or the girls, but for herself.

"Are you sure it's not too late to salvage it with Eileen?"

"Don't be ridiculous."

"Where did she sleep?" He looked as though he had received an electric shock.

"That's an inappropriate thing to ask, and you know it damn well."

"Oh, my God...." She sat down again, unable to believe how transparent he was. "You slept with her."

"I did *not* sleep with her."

"You did, didn't you?" She was shouting now and he

262

strode around the room like a nervous cat as he turned to face her again.

"I slept on the couch."

"You're lying to me. Aren't you?"

"Goddammit, Tana! Don't accuse me of that! It isn't as easy as you think. We've been married for almost twenty years, Goddammit . . . I can't just walk out on everything from one day to the next, and not when the girls are involved," he looked at her mournfully and then walked slowly to where she sat. "Please . . ." There were tears in his eyes. "I love you, Tan . . . I just need a little time to work this out. . . ." She turned away from him and walked across the room, keeping her back to him.

"I've heard that before." She wheeled to face him then, and there were tears in her eyes, too. "My mother spent seventeen years listening to bullshit like that, Drew."

"I'm not giving you bullshit, Tan. I just need time. This is very difficult for all of us."

"Fine." She picked up her bag and coat from a chair. "Then call me when you've recovered from it. I think I'd enjoy you more then." But before she reached the door, he grabbed her arm.

"Don't do this to me. Please . . ."

"Why not? Eileen is in town. Just give her a call. She'll keep you company tonight." Tana smiled at him sardonically to hide the hurt. "You can sleep on the couch . . . together, if you like." She yanked open the door and he looked as though he were going to cry.

"I love you, Tan." But as she heard the words, she wanted to sit down and cry. And suddenly she turned to him and her energy seemed to drain as she looked at him.

"Don't do this to me, Drew. It's not fair. You're not free . . . you have no right to. . . ." But she had opened the door to her heart just wide enough for him to slip into it again. Wordlessly, he pulled her into his arms, and kissed her hard, and she felt everything inside her melt. And when he pulled away from her, she looked at him. "That doesn't solve anything."

"No." He sounded calmer now. "But time will. Just give

263

me a chance. I swear to you, you won't regret it." And then he said the words that frightened her most. "I want to marry you one day, Tan." She wanted to tell him to stop, to move the film back to before he had said those words, but it didn't matter anyway, the girls came running in, laughing and shouting and ready to play with him and he looked over their heads at her and whispered two words to her, "please stay." She hesitated. She knew she should go back, and she wanted to. She didn't belong here with them. He had just spent the night with the woman he was married to, and they had had Christmas with their two girls. Where did Tana belong in all this? And yet when she looked at him, she didn't want to leave. She wanted to be part of it, to be his, to belong to him and the girls, even if he never married her. She didn't really want that anyway. She just wanted to be with him, the way they had been since they first met, and slowly she put down her bag and coat and looked at him, and he smiled at her, and her insides turned to mush, and Julie hugged her around the waist while Elizabeth grinned at her.

"Where were you going, Tan?" Elizabeth was curious, she seemed fascinated by everything that Tana did and said.

"Nowhere." She smiled at the pretty adolescent child. "Now, what would you girls like to do?" The two girls laughed and teased and Drew chased them around the room. She had never seen him as happy as this, and later that afternoon they went to the movies, and ate buckets of popcorn, then he took them to the La Brea Tar Pits, and to Perino's for dinner that night, and when they finally came home all four of them were ready to fall into bed. Julie fell asleep in Drew's arms, and Elizabeth made it into bed before falling asleep, too, and Tana and Drew sat in front of a fire in the living room, whispering, as he gently touched the golden hair he loved.

"I'm glad you stayed, sweetheart . . . I didn't want you to go. . . ."

"I'm glad I stayed too." She smiled at him, feeling vulnerable and young, which didn't make sense for a woman her age, at least not to her. She imagined that she should be more mature than that by now, less sensitive. But she was more sensitive to him than she had ever been to any man. "Promise it won't happen again. . . ." Her voice drifted off and he looked at her with a tender smile.

"Baby, I promise you."

Chapter 16

The spring Tana and Drew shared was so idyllic it was almost like a fairy tale. Drew flew up roughly three times a week, she went to LA every weekend. They went to parties, sailed on the bay, met each other's friends. She even introduced him to Harry and Ave, and the two men had gotten along splendidly. And Harry gave her the okay when he took her out to celebrate the following week.

"You know, kid, I think you finally did good for yourself." She made a face and he laughed. "I mean it. I mean, look at the guys you used to drag around. Remember Yael McBee?"

"Harry!" She threw her napkin at him in the restaurant and they both laughed. "How can you compare Drew to him? Besides, I was twenty-five years old. I'm almost thirty-one now."

"That's no excuse. You're no smarter than you used to be."

"The hell I'm not. You just said yourself. . . ."

"Never mind what I said, you jerk. Now, are you going to give me some peace of mind and marry the guy?"

"No." She laughed, and she said it too fast, and Harry, looking at her, saw something he had never seen before. He had been looking for it for years, and suddenly there it was. He saw it as clearly as he saw the big green eyes, a kind of vulnerable, sheepish look she had never worn before for anyone.

"Holy shit, it's serious, isn't it, Tan? You're going to marry him, aren't you?"

"He hasn't asked." She sounded so demure that he roared.

"My God, you will! Wait till I tell Ave!"

"Harry, calm down." She patted his arm. "He isn't even divorced yet." But it didn't worry her. She knew how hard he was working on it. He told her every week about his meetings with his lawyer, his conversations with Eileen to speed things up, and he was going East to see the girls for Easter week, and hopefully she'd sign the settlement papers then, if they were drawn up in time.

"He's working on it, isn't he?" Harry looked momentarily concerned, but he had to admit, he liked the guy. It was almost impossible not to like Drew Lands. He was easygoing, intelligent, and it was easy to see he was crazy about Tan.

"Of course he is."

"Then relax, you'll be married six months from now, and nine months after that, you'll have a baby in your arms. Count on it." He looked thrilled and Tana sat back and laughed at him.

"Boy, do you have a wild imagination, Winslow. In the first place, he hasn't asked me to marry him yet, at least not seriously. And in the second, he's had a vasectomy."

"So he'll have it reversed. Big deal. I know plenty of guys who've done that." But it made him a little nervous thinking about it.

"Is that all you think about? Getting people pregnant?"

"No," he smiled innocently, "just my wife."

She laughed and they finished the meal, and they both went back to their offices. She had an enormous case coming up, probably the biggest of her career. There were three murder defendants involved in the most gruesome series of murders committed in the state in recent years, and there were three defense attorneys and two prosecutors and she was in charge of the case for the DA. There was going to be a lot of press involved and she had to really know her stuff, which was why she wasn't going East with Drew when he went to see the girls over the Easter holiday. It was probably just as well she didn't anyway. Drew would be a nervous wreck getting the papers signed, and she had the case on her mind. It made more sense to stay home and do her work than to sit around in hotel rooms waiting for him.

He came up to San Francisco to spend the weekend with her before he left, and they lay on the rug in front of the fire for hours on his last night, talking, thinking aloud, saying almost anything that came to mind, and she realized again how deeply she was falling in love with him.

"Would you ever consider marriage, Tan?" He looked pensively at her and she smiled in the firelight. She looked exquisite in the soft glow, her delicate features seeming to be carved in a pale peach marble, her eyes dancing like emeralds.

"I never have before." She touched his lips with her fingertips and he kissed her hands and then her mouth.

"Do you think you could be happy with me, Tan?"

"Is that a proposal, sir?" He seemed to be beating around the bush and she smiled at him. "You don't have to marry me, you know, I'm happy like this."

"You are, aren't you?" He looked at her strangely and she nodded her head.

"Aren't you?"

"Not entirely." His hair looked even more silvery, his eyes a bright topaz blue, and she never again wanted to love any man but him. "I want more than this, Tan . . . I want you all the time. . . ."

"So do I. . . ." She whispered the words to him, and he took her in his arms and made love to her ever so gently in front of the fire, and afterwards he lay for a long, long time and looked at her, and then finally he spoke, his mouth nestled in her hair, his hands still stroking the body he loved so much.

"Will you marry me when I'm free?"

"Yes." She said the word almost breathlessly. She had never said it to anyone, but she meant it now, and suddenly she understood what people felt when they promised . . . for better or worse . . . until death do us part. She never wanted to be without him again, and when she took him to the airport the next day, she was still a little overwhelmed by what she felt, and she looked at him searchingly. "Did you mean what you said last night, Drew?"

"How can you ask me something like that?" He looked

horrified, and instantly crushed her against his chest as they stood in the terminal. "Of course I did."

She grinned at him, looking more like his thirteen-year-old child than the Assistant DA. "I guess that means we're engaged then, huh?" And suddenly he laughed, and he felt as happy as a boy as he looked at her.

"It sure does. I'll have to see what kind of ring I can find in Washington."

"Never mind that. Just come back safe and sound." It was going to be an endless ten days of waiting for him. And the only thing that would help was her enormous case.

He called her two and three times a day for the first few days, and told her everything he did from morning till night, but when things began to get rough with Eileen, he called once a day and she could hear how uptight he was, but they had started jury selection by then, and she was totally engrossed in that, and by the time he got back to Los Angeles, she realized that they hadn't spoken to each other in more than two days. He had stayed longer than he had expected to, but it was for a "worthy cause" he said, and she agreed with him, and she could barely think straight anymore by then. She was too worried about the jury that was being picked, and the tack they were going to take, the evidence that had just turned up, the judge to whom they had been assigned. She had plenty on her mind, and one of Drew's rare litigation situations had occurred. Almost everything he did settled before it went to court, and this was a rare exception for him, and it kept him away from her for almost another week, and when they both finally met, they almost felt like strangers again. He teased her about it, asked if she had fallen in love with anyone else, and made passionate love to her all night long.

"I want you to be so bleary eyed all day in court that everyone wonders what the hell went on last night." And he got his wish. She was half asleep and she couldn't get him out of her mind she was so hungry for him. She never seemed to get enough of him anymore, and all through her trial, she was lonely for him, but it was too important to screw up and she kept her nose to the grindstone constantly.

It went on till late May, and finally, in the first week in June, the verdict came in. It went just the way she had wanted it to, and the press gave her high praise as usual. Over the years, she had earned a reputation for being rigid, tough, conservative, merciless in court, and brilliant at the cases she tried. They were nice reviews to have, and it often made Harry smile when he read about her.

"I'd never recognize the liberal I knew and loved in this, Tan." He grinned broadly at her.

"We all have to grow up sometime, don't we? I'm thirty-one this year."

"That's no excuse to be as tough as you are."

"I'm not tough, Harry, I'm good." And she was right, but he knew it too. "Those people killed nine women and a child. You can't let people get away with shit like that. Our whole society will fall apart. Someone has to do what I do."

"I'm glad it's you and not me, Tan." He patted her hand. "I'd lie awake at night, worrying that they'd get me eventually." He hated even saying it, and he worried about it sometimes for her, but it didn't seem to bother her at all. "By the way, how's Drew?"

"Fine. He's going to New York on business next week, and he's bringing the girls back with him."

"When are you getting married?"

"Relax." She smiled. "We haven't even talked about it since I started this case. In fact, I've hardly talked to him." And when she told him about her success before it hit the press, he sounded strange.

"That's nice."

"Well, don't get too excited. It might be bad for your heart."

He laughed at her. "All right, all right, I'm sorry. I had something else on my mind."

"What?"

"Nothing important." But he was that way until he left, and he sounded worse from the East, and when he got back to Los Angeles, he didn't call her at all. She almost wondered if something was wrong, or if she should fly down to surprise him and get everything on the right track again.

All they needed was a little time alone to sort things out, they'd both been working too hard, and she knew all the signs. She looked at her watch late one night, trying to decide if she should catch the last plane down, and decided to call him instead. She could always go down the next day, and they had a lot of catching up to do after her two months of grueling work. She dialed the phone number she knew by heart, heard it ring three times and smiled when it was picked up, but not for long. A woman's voice answered it.

"Hello?" Tana felt her heart stop, and she sat there endlessly staring into the night, and then hurriedly she put down the phone.

Her heart was pounding hideously, she felt dizzy, awkward, disoriented, strange. She couldn't believe what she had heard. She had to have dialed the wrong number, she told herself, but before she could compose herself to try again, the phone rang, and she heard Drew's voice, and suddenly she knew. He must have known she'd called and now he was panicking. She felt as though her whole life had just come to an end.

"Who was that?" She sounded half hysterical, and he sounded nervous too.

"What?"

"The woman who answered your phone." She fought for composure but her voice was totally out of control.

"I don't know what you mean."

"Drew . . . ! answer me . . . ! please . . ." She was half crying, half shouting at him.

"We have to talk."

"Oh my God . . . Goddammit, what have you done to me?"

"Don't be so melodramatic, for chrissake. . . ." She cut him off with a shriek.

"Melodramatic? I call you at eleven o'clock at night and a woman answers your phone, and you tell me I'm being melodramatic? How would you like to have a man answer you when you call me here?"

"Stop it, Tan. It was Eileen."

"Obviously." Instinctively, she had known.

"And where are the girls?" She didn't even know why she had asked.

"In Malibu."

"In Malibu? You mean you're alone with her?"

"We had to talk." His voice sounded dead suddenly.

"Alone? At this hour? What the hell does that mean? Did she sign?"

"Yes, no . . . look, I have to talk to you. . . ."

"Oh, now you have to talk to me. . . ." She was being cruel to him and now they were both beginning to sound hysterical. "What the fuck is going on down there?" There was an endless silence which he couldn't fill. Tana hung up and cried all night, and he arrived in San Francisco the next day. It was Saturday and he found her at home, as he knew he would. He used his key and let himself in, and he found her sitting mournfully on her deck looking out over the bay. She didn't even turn when she heard him come in, but spoke to him with her back turned. "Why did you bother to come up?"

He knelt beside her and touched her neck with his fingertips. "Because I love you, Tan."

"No, you don't." She shook her head. "You love her. You always did."

"That's not true. . . ." But they both knew it was, in fact, all three of them did. "The truth is that I love both of you. That's an awful thing to say, but it's the truth. I don't know how to stop loving her, and at the same time I'm in love with you."

"That's sick." She continued to stare out at the bay, passing judgment on him, and he yanked her hair to make her look at him, and when she did, he saw tears on her face and it broke his heart.

"I can't help what I feel. And I don't know what to do about what's happening. Elizabeth almost flunked out of school, she's so upset about us, Eileen and me. Julie is having nightmares. Eileen quit her job at the OAS, she turned down the ambassadorial post they tried to tempt her with, and she came home, with the girls. . . ."

"They're living with you?" Tana looked as though he had

just driven a stake into her heart, and he nodded. He didn't want to lie to her anymore. "When did all this happen?"

"We talked about it a lot in Washington on Easter week . . . but I didn't want to upset you when you were working so hard, Tan. . . ." She wanted to kick him for what he'd said. How could he not tell her something like that? "And nothing was sure. She did it all without consulting me, and just showed up last week. And now what do you expect me to do? Throw them out?"

"Yes. You should never have let them in again."

"She's my wife, and they're my kids." He looked as though he were on the verge of tears but Tana stood up then.

"I guess that solves it then, doesn't it?" She walked slowly to the door and looked at him. "Goodbye, Drew."

"I'm not leaving here like this. I'm in love with you."

"Then get rid of your wife. It's as simple as that."

"No it's *not*, goddammit!" He was shouting now. She refused to understand what he was going through. "You don't know what it's like . . . what I feel . . . the guilt . . . the agony. . . ." He started to cry and she felt sick as she looked at him. She turned away and had to fight to speak above the tears in her own voice.

"Please go. . . ."

"I won't." He pulled her into his arms, and she tried to push him away, but he wouldn't let her do that, and suddenly, without wanting to, she succumbed, and they made love again, crying, begging, shouting, railing at each other and the Fates, and when it was all over, they lay spent in each other's arms and she looked at him.

"What are we going to do?"

"I don't know. Just give me time."

She sighed painfully. "I swore I'd never do something like this. . . ." But she couldn't bear the thought of losing him, nor he the pain of giving her up. They cried and lay in each other's arms for the next two days, and when he flew back to Los Angeles, nothing was solved, except that they both knew it wasn't over yet. She had agreed to give him more time, and he had promised her he'd work it out, and for the next six months they drove each other mad with promises and threats, ultimatums and hysteria. Tana called and hung up on Eileen a thousand times. Drew begged her not to do anything rash. The children were even aware of what terrible shape he was in. And Tana began avoiding everyone, especially Harry and Averil. She couldn't bear the questions she saw in his eyes, the sweetness of his wife, the children which only reminded her of Drew's. It was an intolerable situation for all of them, and Eileen was even aware of it, but she said that she wasn't moving out again. She could wait for him to work it out, she wasn't going anywhere, and Tana felt as though she were going mad. She spent her birthday and the Fourth of July and Labor Day and Thanksgiving alone, predictably. . . .

"What do you expect of me, Tana? You want me to just walk out on them?"

"Maybe I do. Maybe that's exactly what I expect of you. Why should I be the one who's always alone? It matters to me too. . . ."

"But I've got the kids. . . ."

"Go fuck yourself." But she didn't say that for real, until she had spent Christmas alone. He had promised to come up, both then and on New Year's Eve, and she sat and waited for him all night and he never came. She sat in an evening dress until nine a.m. on New Year's Day, and then slowly, irrevocably, she took it off and threw it in the trash. She had bought the dress just for him. She had the locks changed the next day, and packed up all the things he'd left with her over the past year and a half and had them sent to him in an unmarked box. And after that she sent him a telegram which said it all. "Goodbye. Don't come back again." And she lay drowning in her tears. For all the bravery, the final straw had almost broken her back, and he came flying up as soon as he began to get the messages, the telegram, the package, he was terrified that she might mean it this time, and when he tried his key in her lock, he knew she did. He drove frantically to her office and insisted on seeing her, and when he did her eyes were cold and the greenest he had ever seen.

"I have nothing left to say to you, Drew." A part of her had died. He had killed it with the hopes that had never been fulfilled, the lies he'd told to both of them, and most of all himself. She wondered now how her mother had stood it for all those years without killing herself. It was the worst torture Tana had ever been through and she never wanted to go through it again, for anyone. And least of all for him.

"Tana, please. . . ."

"Goodbye." She walked out of her office and down the hall, disappearing into a conference room, and she left the building shortly after that, but she didn't go home for hours. And when she did, he was still waiting there, outside, in the driving rain. She slowed her car, as she saw him and drove off again. She spent the night in a motel on Lombard Street, and the next morning when she went back, he was sleeping in his car. When, instinctively, he heard her step, he woke and leapt out to talk to her. "If you don't leave me alone, I'll call the police." She sounded tough and threatening, looked furious to his eyes, but what he didn't see was how broken she felt inside, how long she sobbed once he was gone, how desperate she felt at the thought of never seeing him again. She actually thought of jumping off the Bridge, but something stopped her when she thought of it and she didn't even know what. And then, as though by miracle, Harry sensed something wrong when he called her repeatedly and no one answered the phone. She thought it was Drew, and she lay on the living room floor and sobbed, thinking of the time when they had made love there and he had proposed to her. And then suddenly there was a pounding on the door and she heard Harry's voice. She looked like a derelict when she opened it, standing there in her tear-stained face and bare feet, her skirt covered with lint from the rug, her sweater all askew.

"My God, what happened to you?" She looked as though she'd been drinking for a week, or had been beaten up, or as though something terrible had happened to her. Only the last was true. "Tana?" She dissolved in tears as he looked at her, and he held her close to him as she hovered akwardly over his chair, and then he sat her down on the couch and she told him her tale.

"It's all over now . . . I'll never see him again. . . ."

"You're better off." Harry looked grim. "You can't live like this. You've looked like shit for the past six months. It's just not fair to you."

"I know . . . but maybe if I'd waited . . . I think eventually. . . ." She felt weak and hysterical, and suddenly she had lost her resolve and Harry shouted at her.

"No! Stop that! He's never going to leave his wife if he hasn't by now. She came back to him seven months ago, damn it, Tan, and she's still there. If he wanted out, he'd have found the door by now. Don't kid yourself."

"I have been for a year and a half."

"That's how things go sometimes." He tried to sound philosophical, but he wanted to kill the son-of-a-bitch who had done this to her. "You just have to pick yourself up and go on."

"Oh yeah, sure. . . ." She started to cry again, forgetting who she was talking to, "That's easy for you to say."

He looked long and hard at her. "Do you remember when you dragged me back to life by the teeth, and then into law school the same way? Remember me? Well, don't give me that shit, Tan. If I made it, so can you. You'll live through it."

"I've never loved anyone like I loved him." She whimpered horribly and it broke his heart as she looked at him, with those huge green eyes. She didn't look more than twelve years old and he wanted to make everything all right for her, but he couldn't make Drew's wife disappear, although he would have liked to do that for her. Anything for Tan, his best and dearest friend.

"Someone else will come along. Better than him."

"I don't want someone else. I don't want anyone." And Harry feared that more than anything.

And in the next year she set out to prove just that. She refused to see anyone except her colleagues at work. She went nowhere, saw no one, and when Christmas came, she even refused to see Averil and Harry. She had turned thirty-two alone, had spent her nights alone, would have eaten Thanksgiving turkey alone, if she'd bothered to eat any at all, which she didn't. She worked overtime and double time and golden time and all the time, sitting at her desk until ten and eleven o'clock at night, taking on more cases than she ever had before, and for literally a year, she had no fun at all. She rarely laughed, called no one, had no dates with anyone, and took weeks to answer Harry's calls.

"Congratulations." He finally reached her in February. She had mourned Drew Lands for more than a year, and she had inadvertently learned through mutual friends that he and Eileen were still together and had just bought a beautiful new home in Beverly Hills. "Okay, asshole." Harry was tired of chasing her. "How come you don't return my calls anymore?"

"I've been busy for the last few weeks. Don't you read the papers? I'm waiting for a verdict to come in."

"I don't give a fuck about that, in case you're interested, and that doesn't account for the last thirteen months. You *never* call me anymore. I always call you. Is it my breath, my feet, or my IQ?" She laughed. Harry never changed.

"All of the above."

"Asshole. Are you going to go on feeling sorry for yourself for the rest of your life? The guy wasn't worth it, Tan. And a whole year is ridiculous."

"It had nothing to do with that." But they both knew that wasn't true. It had everything to do with Drew Lands, and his not leaving his wife.

"That's new too. You never used to lie to me."

"All right, all right. It's been easier not to see anybody."

"Why? You ought to celebrate! You could have done what your mother did and sat there for fifteen years. Instead, you were smart enough to get the hell out. So what did you lose, Tan? Your virginity? Eighteen months? So what? Other women lose ten years over married men . . . they lose their hearts, their sanity, their time, their lives. You got off lucky if you ask me."

"Yeah." Somewhere in her heart, she knew he was right,

but it still didn't feel good yet. Maybe it never would. She still alternated between missing him and being angry at him. It wasn't the indifference she would have liked to feel, and she finally admitted that to Harry when she let him take her to lunch.

"That takes time, Tan. And a little water over the dam. You have to go out with some other people. Fill your head with other stuff, not just him. You can't just work all the time." He smiled gently at her, he loved her so much, and he knew he always would. It wasn't like what he felt for his wife. She was more like a sister to him now. He remembered the tremendous crush he had had on her for years and he reminded her of that now. "And I survived."

"That wasn't the same thing. Shit, Drew had proposed marriage to me. He was the only man I'd ever even wanted to marry. Do you know that?"

"Yes, I do." He knew her better than anyone. "So, he's a jerk. We already know that. And you're a little slow. But you'll want to get married again. Someone else will come along."

"That's all I need." She looked revolted at the thought. "I'm going to be thirty-three years old this year. Teen romance is not my style anymore, thanks."

"Fine, then find some old fart who thinks you're cute, but don't sit around like this and waste your life."

"It isn't exactly wasted, Harry." She looked somberly at him. "I have my work."

"That's *not* enough. Christ, you're a pain in the ass." He looked at her and shook his head, and invited her to a party they were giving the following week, but she never showed up in the end. And he had to go on a campaign to drag her out of her shell. It was as though she had been raped again. And then, to make matters worse, she lost a major case and got depressed about that. "Okay, okay, so you're not infallible. Give yourself a break, for chrissake. Get off the cross. I know it's Easter week, but one's enough. Can't you find something else to do except torment yourself? Why don't you come spend a weekend in Tahoe with us?" They had just rented a house, and Harry loved going up there with the kids. "We can't go up for much longer anyway."

"Why not?" She glanced at him as he paid the check, and he smiled at her. She had given him a hard time for the past few months, but she was starting to come out of it.

"I can't take Averil up much longer. She's pregnant again, you know." For a minute, Tana actually looked shocked and he laughed at her, and then blushed. "It's happened before after all . . . I mean, it's not that remarkable. . . ." But they both knew it was. And suddenly Tana grinned at him. It was as if life had come back into focus again, and suddenly Drew Lands was gone and she wanted to shout and sing. It was like having had a toothache for over a year, and discovering miraculously that the tooth was gone.

"Well, I'll be damned. Don't you two ever stop?"

"Nope. And after this, we'll go for four. I want another girl this time, but Ave wants a boy." Tana was beaming at him, and she gave him a big hug as they left the restaurant.

"I'm going to be an aunt again."

"That's the easy way, if you ask me. Not fair, Tan."

"It suits me just fine." One thing she knew she didn't want was children, no matter what man wandered into her life. She didn't have time for that, and she was too old now anyway. She had made that decision long ago; her baby was the law. And she had Harry's children to spoil when she wanted someone little to sit on her lap. They were both adorable, and she was happy for them that a third one was coming along. Averil always had a pretty easy time, and Harry was always so proud of himself, and he could certainly afford as many as they chose to have. Only her mother disapproved when she talked to her.

"That seems awfully unreasonable to me." She was always opposed to everything these days; babies, trips, new jobs, new homes. It was as though she wanted to play out the rest of her life cautiously and thought everyone else should too. It was a sign of age which Tana recognized but her mother seemed too young for that. She had aged rapidly since she and Arthur had gotten married. Nothing had turned out quite right for her, and when she had gotten what she'd wanted for so long, it was not the same as it had once been. Arthur was sick and getting old.

But Tana was happy for Harry and Ave, and when the baby came on November 25th, Averil got her wish. It was a bouncing, squalling boy. They named him after his great grandfather, Andrew Harrison, and Tana smiled down at him in his mother's arms and felt tears come to her eyes. She hadn't had that reaction to the others before, but there was something so sweet and touching about the baby's innocence, his perfect pink flesh, the big round eyes, the tiny fingers so gently curled. Tana had never seen such perfection, and all of it so small. She and Harry looked at each other and exchanged a smile, thinking of how far they had come, and he looked so proud, one hand tightly holding his wife's, and the other gently touching his son.

Averil went home the day after Andrew was born, and made the Thanksgiving dinner herself, as she always did, practically refusing any help at all, as Tana stared at her, amazed at all she did, and did so well.

"It kind of makes you feel dumb, doesn't it?" She was nursing in the window seat looking out at the bay, and Tana looked at her as Harry grinned.

"Shit, Tan, you could do it too, if you wanted to."

"Don't count on it. I can barely boil myself an egg, let alone give birth, and cook a turkey two days later for my family, making it seem as though I had nothing to do all week. You'd better hang on to her, Harry, and don't get her knocked up again." She grinned at him, and she knew that they had never been happier. Averil just radiated happiness and so did he.

"I'll do my best. Will you come to the christening, by the way? Ave wants to do it on Christmas Day, if you're going to be here."

"Where else would I be?" She laughed at him.

"What do I know? You might go home to New York. I was thinking of taking the kids to Gstaad to see Dad, but now he says he's going to Tangiers with some friends, so that blows that."

"You're breaking my heart." She laughed at him. She

hadn't seen Harrison in years, but Harry said he was all right. He seemed the kind of man who would be handsome and healthy for all his life. It was a little startling to realize that he was in his early sixties now, sixty-three, to be exact, Harry reminded her, though he didn't look more than half of it, Harry had told her. It was odd to remember how much Harry had once hated him, but he didn't anymore. It was Tana who had changed all that, and Harry never forgot any of it. He wanted her to be godmother again, and she was touched by it.

"Don't you have any other friends? Your kids are going to be sick to death of me by the time they grow up."

"Too bad for them. Jack Hawthorne is Andrew's god-father. At least you two will finally meet. He thinks you've been avoiding him." In all the years of Harry's partnership with him, the two had never met. But Tana had no reason to meet him, although she was curious to now. And when they met at St. Mary the Virgin Church on Union Street on Christmas Day, he was almost as she had expected him to be. Tall, blond, handsome, he looked like an All-American football player in a college game, and yet he looked intelligent as well. He was tall and broad and had enormous hands, and he held the baby with a gentleness that startled her. He was talking to Harry outside afterwards and she smiled at him.

"You do that awfully well, Jack."

"Thanks. I'm a little rusty, but I can still manage in a pinch."

"Do you have children?" It was casual conversation outside the church. The only thing they could have talked about was law, or their mutual friend, but it was easier and more pleasant to talk about the new godchild that they shared.

"I have one. She's ten."

"That's seems incredible." Ten seemed so old somehow . . . of course Elizabeth had been thirteen, but Drew had been a lot older than this man. Or at least he looked that way. Tana knew Jack was about thirty-seven or eight, but he had a boyish air. And at the party at Averil and Harry's house later that day, he told funny stories and jokes, and had everyone laughing, including Tana, for most of the day. She smiled at Harry when she found him in the kitchen pouring someone another drink. "No wonder you like him so much. He's a nice guy."

"Jack?" Harry didn't look surprised. Other than Tana and Averil, Jack Hawthorne was his best friend, and they had worked well together for the past few years. They had established a comfortable practice, and they worked in the same way, not with Tana's burning drive, but with something a little more reasonable. And the two men were well matched. "He's smart as hell, but he's very relaxed about it."

"I noticed that." At first he seemed very casual, almost indifferent to what was going on, but Tana had noticed rapidly that he was a lot sharper than he looked.

Eventually, at the end of the day, he offered her a ride home, and she accepted gratefully. She had left her own car outside the church in town. "Well, I finally meet the famous Assistant DA. They certainly like to write about you, don't they?" She was embarrassed by what he said but he seemed unconcerned.

"Only when they have nothing else to do."

He smiled at her. He liked her modesty. He also liked the long shapely legs peeking out beneath the black velvet skirt she wore. It was a suit she had bought at I. Magnin just for her godchild's christening day. "Harry is very proud of you, you know. I feel as though I know you myself. He talks about you all the time."

"I'm just as bad. I don't have kids, so everyone has to listen to stories about Harry and when we went to school."

"You two must have been hell on wheels back then." He grinned at her and she laughed.

"More or less. We had a hell of a good time, at times. And some nasty run-ins now and then." She smiled at the memories and then smiled at Jack. "I must be getting old, all this nostalgia. . . ."

"It's that time of year."

"It is, isn't it? Christmas always does that to me."

"Me too." She wondered where his daughter was, if that was part of the nostalgia for him. "You're from New York, aren't you?" She nodded her head. That seemed light years away too.

"And you?"

"I'm from the Midwest. Detroit, to be exact. A lovely place." He smiled and they both laughed again. He was easy to be with, and it seemed harmless to her when he offered to take her out for drinks. But everything seemed so empty when they looked around and it was depressing to go to a bar on Christmas night, she wound up inviting him back to her place instead, and he was perfectly agreeable to her. So much so he was almost innocuous, and she didn't even recognize him at first when she ran into him at City Hall the next week. He was one of those tall, blond, handsome men who could have been almost anyone, from a college pal, to someone's husband or brother or boyfriend and then suddenly she realized who he was and blushed with embarrassment.

"I'm sorry, Jack . . . I was distracted. . . ."

"You have a right to be." He smiled at her, and she was amused at how impressed he was by her job. Harry must have been lying to him again. She knew he exaggerated a lot about her, about the rapists she fought off in holding cells, the judo holds she knew, the cases she cracked herself without investigators' help.

". . . Why do you lie like that?" She had challenged him more than once but he felt no remorse.

"Some of it's true anyway."

"The hell it is. I ran into one of your friends last week who thought I had been knifed by a coke dealer in the holding cell. For chrissake, Harry, knock it off."

She thought of it now and assumed he had been at it again as she smiled at Jack. "Actually, things are pretty quiet right now. How 'bout you?"

"Not bad. We have a few good cases. Harry and Ave went up to Tahoe for a few weeks, so I'm holding the fort on my own."

"He's such a hardworking type." They both laughed and

he looked at her hesitantly. He had been dying to call her for a week and he hadn't dared.

"You wouldn't have time for lunch, would you?" Oddly enough, for once she did. He was ecstatic when she said yes, and they went to the Bijou, a small French restaurant on Polk, which was more pretentious than good, but it was pleasant chatting with Harry's friend for an hour or so. She had heard about him for so many years, and between her heavy caseload and her turmoil over Drew Lands they'd never met.

"It's ridiculous, you know. Harry should have gotten us together years ago."

Jack smiled. "I think he tried." He didn't say anything that indicated that he knew about Drew, but Tana could talk about it now.

"I was being difficult for a while." She smiled.

"And now?" He looked at her with the same gentle look he had used on their godchild.

"I'm back to my old rotten self again."

"That's good."

"Actually, Harry saved my life this time."

"I know he was worried about you for a while."

She sighed. "I made an ass of myself . . . I guess we all have to sometime."

"I sure did." He smiled at her. "I got my kid sister's best friend pregnant in Detroit ten years ago when I went home over the holidays. I don't know what happened to me, except I must have gone nuts or something. She was this pretty little redhead . . . twenty-one years old . . . and bang, the next thing I knew I was getting married. She hated it out here, she cried all the time. Poor little Barb had colic for the first six months of her life, and a year later, Kate went back again and it was all over. I now have an ex-wife and a daughter in Detroit, and I don't know anything more about them than I did then. It was the craziest thing I ever did, and I'm not about to do it again!" He looked extremely determined as he said the words, and it was easy to see that he meant every bit of it. "I've never drunk straight rum either since then." He grinned ruefully and Tana laughed.

"At least you have something to show for it." It was more than she could say, not that she would have wanted Drew's child, even if he hadn't had the vasectomy. "Do you see your daughter sometimes?"

"She comes out once a year for a month," he sighed with a careful smile. "It's a little difficult to build a relationship based on that!" He had always thought it was unfair to her, but what else could he do? He couldn't ignore her now. "We're really strangers to each other. I'm the oddball who sends her birthday cards every year and takes her to baseball games when she's here. I don't know what else to do with her. Ave was pretty good about keeping an eye on her in the daytime last year. And they lent me the house in Tahoe for a week. She loved that," he smiled at Tana, "and so did I. It's awkward making friends with a ten-year-old child."

"I'll bet it is. The relationship . . . the man I was involved with had two of them, and it was odd for me. I don't have children of my own, and it wasn't like Harry's kids, suddenly here were these two big people staring at me. It felt awfully strange."

"Did you get attached to them?" He seemed intrigued by her and she was surprised at how easy it was to talk to him.

"Not really. There wasn't time. They lived in the East," she remembered the rest of it, "for a while."

He nodded, smiling at her. "You've certainly managed to keep your life simpler than the rest of us." He laughed softly then. "I guess you don't drink rum."

She laughed too. "Usually not, but I've managed to do a fair amount of damage to myself in other ways. I just don't have any kids to show for it."

"Are you sorry about that?"

"Nope." It had taken thirty-three and a half years to say it honestly. "There are some things in this life that aren't for me, and children are one of them. Godmother is more my style."

"I probably should have stuck to that myself, for Barb's sake, if no one else's. At least her mother is remarried now, so she has a real father figure to relate to for the eleven months I'm not around."

"Doesn't that bother you?" She wondered if he felt possessive about the child. Drew had been very much so about his, especially Elizabeth.

But Jack shook his head. "I hardly know the kid. That's an awful thing to say, but it's true. Every year I get to know her again, and she leaves and when she comes back she's grown up by a year and changed all over again. It's kind of a fruitless venture, but maybe it does something for her. I don't know. I owe her that much. And I suspect that in a few years she'll tell me to go to hell, she has a boyfriend in Detroit and she's not coming out this year."

"Maybe she'll bring him." They both laughed.

"God help me. That's all I need. I feel the way you do, there are some things in this life I never want inflicted on me . . . malaria . . . typhoid . . . marriage . . . kids. . . ." She laughed at his honesty, it was certainly not a popular view or one that one could admit to most of the time, but he felt he could with her, and she with him.

"I agree with you. I really think it's impossible to do what you do well and give enough to relationships like that."

"That sounds noble, my friend, but we both know that that has nothing to do with it. Honestly? I'm scared stiff, all I need is another Kate out from Detroit and crying all night because she has no friends out here . . . or some totally dependent woman with nothing to do all day except nag me at night, or decide after two years of marriage that half of the business Harry and I built is hers. He and I see too much of that as it is, and I just don't want any part of it." He smiled at her. "And what are you scared of, my dear? Chillblains, childbirth? Giving up your career? Competition from a man?" He was surprisingly astute and she smiled appreciatively at him.

"Touché. All the above. Maybe I'm afraid of jeopardizing what I've built, of getting hurt . . . I don't know. I think I had doubts about marriage years ago, although I didn't know it then. It's all my mother ever wanted for me, and I always wanted to say 'but wait . . . not yet . . . I've got all these other things to do first.' It's like volunteering to have your head cut off, there's never really a good time." He laughed, and she remembered Drew proposing to her in front of the fire one night, and then she forced it from her with a flash of pain. Most of the time the memories of him didn't hurt much now, but a few still did. And that one most of all, maybe because she felt he had made a fool of her. She had been willing to make an exception for him, she had accepted the proposal and then he had gone back to Eileen . . . Jack was watching her as she frowned.

"No one is worth looking that sad for, Tana."

She smiled at him. "Old, old memories."

"Forget them, then. They won't hurt you anymore."

There was something wonderfully easy and wise about the man, and she began going out with him almost without thinking of it. A movie, an early dinner, a walk on Union Street, a football game. He came and went, and became her friend, and it wasn't even remarkable when they finally went to bed with each other late that spring. They had known each other for five months by then, and it wasn't earth shattering, but it was comfortable. He was easy to be around, intelligent, and he had a wonderful understanding of what she did, a powerful respect for her job, they even shared a common best friend, and by summertime when his daughter came out, even that was comfortable. She was a sweet eleven-year-old child with big eyes and hands and feet and bright red hair, like an Irish Setter puppy. They took her to Stinson Beach a few times, went on picnics with her. Tana didn't have much time – she was trying a big case just then – but it was all very pleasant, and they went up to Harry's place where Harry eyed them carefully, curious as to whether it was serious with them. But Averil didn't think it was and she was usually right. There was no fire, no passion, no intensity, but also no pain. It was comfortable, intelligent, amusing at times, and extremely satisfying in bed. And at the end of a year of going out with him, Tana could well imagine herself going out with Jack for the rest of her life. It was one of these relationships one saw between two people who had never married, and never wanted to, much to the chagrin of all their friends who had been in and out of divorce courts for years; one saw people like that eating in restaurants on Saturday nights, going on holidays, attending Christmas parties and gala events, and enjoying each other's company, and sooner or later they'd wind up in bed, and the next day the other one would go home to his or her own place, to find the towels exactly the way they wanted them, the bed undisturbed, the coffee pot in perfect readiness for their needs. It was so perfect for both of them that way, but they drove Harry nuts and that amused them too.

"I mean, look at you both, you're so goddamn complacent I could cry." The three of them were having lunch, and neither Tana nor Jack looked concerned.

She looked up at Jack with a smile. "Hand him a handkerchief, sweetheart."

"Nah, let him use his sleeve. He always does."

"Don't you have any decency? What's wrong with you?"

They exchanged a bovine glance. "Just decadent, I guess."

"Don't you want kids?"

"Haven't you ever heard of birth control?" Jack looked at him and Harry looked as though he wanted to scream as Tana laughed.

"Give it up, kid. You aren't gonna win this one with us. We're happy like this."

"You've been dating for a year. What the hell does that mean to you both?"

"That we have a lot of stamina. I now know that he gets homicidal if anyone touches the sports section on Sundays and he hates classical music."

"And that's it? How can you be so insensitive?"

"It comes naturally." She smiled sweetly at her friend and Jack grinned at her.

"Face it, Harry, you're outnumbered, outclassed, outdone." But when Tana turned thirty-five six months later, they surprised Harry after all.

"You're getting *married*?" Harry barely dared to breathe the words to Jack when he told him they were looking for a house, but Jack laughed at him.

"Hell no, you don't know your friend Tan if you think there's even a chance of that. We're thinking about living together."

Harry spun his wheelchair around, glaring at Jack. "That's the most disgusting thing I've ever heard. I won't let you do that to her."

Jack roared. "It was her idea, and besides — you and Ave did it." His daughter had just gone home, and it had gotten very complicated going back and forth from his house to hers for a month. "Her place is too small for both of us, and so is mine. And I'd really like to live in Marin. Tana says she would too."

Harry looked miserable. He wanted a happy ending, rice, rose petals, babies, and neither of them was cooperating with him. "Do you realize how complicated it is to invest in real estate if you're not married?"

"Of course I do, and so does she. That's why we'll probably rent." And it was exactly what they did. They found the house they wanted with an overwhelming view, in Tiburon. It had four bedrooms, and was dirt cheap compared to what it might have cost, and it gave them each an office, a bedroom for them, and a bedroom for Barb when she came to town from Detroit, or if they had guests. It had a lovely sun deck, a porch, a hot tub, which looked out at the view, and neither of them had ever been happier. Harry and Averil came to check it out with the kids, and they had to admit that the setting was beautiful but it still wasn't what Harry had hoped for her, but she only laughed at him. And, worst of all, Jack shared all of her views. He had no intention of getting hooked into marriage again, by anyone. He was thirty-eight years old, and his little escapade in Detroit twelve years before had cost him dearly.

Jack and Tana did Christmas dinner that year, and it was beautiful, with the bay below, and the city shimmering in the distance. "It's like a dream, isn't it, sweetheart?" Jack whispered to her after everyone went home. They had exactly the life that suited them, and she had even finally given her own apartment up in town. She had hung onto it for a while to play it safe, but in the end, she had let it go. She was safe with him, and he took good care of her. When she had appendicitis that year, he took two weeks off from work to take care of her. When she turned thirty-six, he gave her a party in the Trafalgar Room at Trader Vic's for eighty-seven of her closest friends, and the following year, he surprised her with a cruise in Greece. She came home rested and brown, and happier than ever with their life. There was never any talk of marriage between the two, although once in a while they talked about buying the house in which they lived, but Tana wasn't even sure about that, and secretly Jack was wary of it too. Neither of them wanted to rock the boat that had sailed along so comfortably for so long. They had lived together for almost two years and it was perfect for them both. Until October after the cruise to Greece. Tana had a big case coming up, and she had stayed up almost all night going over her notes and the files, and she'd fallen asleep at her desk, looking out over the bay in Tiburon. The phone woke her before Jack did with a cup of tea, and she stared at him as she picked it up.

"Huh?" She looked blank and Jack grinned at her. She was a mess when she stayed up all night like that, and as though hearing his thoughts, she turned her eyes toward him, and then suddenly she saw them open wide and stare at him. "What? Are you crazy? I'm *not* . . . oh God. I'll be there in an hour." She put down the phone and stared at him as he set down the cup of tea with a worried frown.

"Something wrong?" It couldn't be anything back home if she'd promised to be there in an hour, it had to be work . . . and it wasn't for him. "What happened, Tan?" She was still staring at him.

"I don't know . . . I have to talk to Frye."

"The district attorney?"

"No. God. Who the hell do you think?"

"Well, what are you getting so excited about?" He still didn't understand. But neither did she. She had done a fantastic job. It just didn't make sense. She'd been there for years . . . there were tears in her eyes when she looked at Jack and stood up at her desk, spilling the tea across her files, but she didn't even care now.

"He said I'm being fired." She started to cry and sat down again as he stared at her.

"That can't be, Tan."

"That's what I said ... the DA's office is my whole life. ..." And the saddest thing of all was that they both knew it was true.

Chapter 17

Tana showered, dressed and drove into the city within the hour, her face set, eyes grim. It was obvious that it was an emergency. She looked as though someone had died. Jack offered to go with her, but she knew he had his own problems that day, and Harry had been out of the office a lot recently, so everything rested on him.

"Are you sure you don't want me to drive you in, Tan? I don't want you to have an accident." She kissed him vaguely on the lips and shook her head. It was so odd. They had lived together for so long, but they were almost more friends than anything else. He was someone to talk to at night, as she worked on her strategy. He understood her life, her quirks, he was content with the life they shared and he wanted relatively little from her, it seemed. Harry claimed it was unnatural, and it was certainly different from what he and Averil shared. But she felt Jack's concern now as she started her car and he watched her leave. He still couldn't understand what had happened to her, and neither could she. She walked into her office, feeling numb, half an hour later, and without even knocking walked into the office of the DA. She couldn't hold the tears back anymore, and they rolled down her face as she looked at him.

"What the hell did I do to deserve this?" She looked stricken and he felt instant remorse at what he'd done. He had just thought it would be fun to give her the news in a roundabout way, but he never realized she'd be so heartbroken. It made him all the sorrier to lose her now. But he had been sorry anyway.

"You're too good at your job, Tan. Stop crying and sit down." He smiled at her and she felt even more confused.

"So you're firing me?" She was still on her feet, staring at him.

"I didn't say that. I said you were out of a job." She sat down with a thump.

"Well, what the hell does that mean?" She reached into her handbag and pulled out a handkerchief and blew her nose. She was unashamed of how she felt. She loved her job, and she had from the first day. She'd been in the DA's office for twelve years. That was a lifetime to give up now, and she would have preferred to give up anything but that. Anything. The district attorney felt sorry for her then, and he came around his desk to put an arm around her.

"Come on, Tan, don't take it so hard. We're going to miss you, too, you know." A fresh burst of tears escaped from her and he smiled. It brought tears to his eyes too. She would be leaving soon, if she accepted it. And she had suffered long enough. He forced her to sit down, looked her square in the eye. "You're being offered a seat on the bench, sweetheart. Judge Roberts. How does that sound to you?"

"I am?" She stared at him, unable to absorb it all. "I am? I'm not being fired?" She started to cry all over again, and she blew her nose again, suddenly laughing at the same time. "I'm not . . . you're kidding me. . . ."

"I wish I were." But he looked delighted for her and she suddenly gave a small scream, realizing what he'd done to her.

"Oh, you son-of-a-bitch . . . I thought you were firing me!" He laughed.

"I apologize. I just thought I'd create a little excitement in your life."

"Shit." She looked at him in disbelief and blew her nose again but she was too stunned at what he was telling her to even be angry at him. "My God . . . how did that happen?"

"I've seen it coming for a long time, Tan. I knew it would happen eventually. I just didn't know when. And I'll lay you odds you're in Superior Court by this time next year. You're perfect for it after your track record here."

"Oh, Larry . . . my God . . . an appointment to the bench. . . ." The words were almost beyond her ken. "I just can't believe it." She looked up at him. "I'm thirty-seven years old, and I never even thought of that."

"Well, thank God someone did." He held out a hand and shook hers as she beamed. "Congratulations, Tan, you deserve every bit of it. They want to induct you in three weeks."

"So soon? What about my work . . . Christ, I have a case that goes to trial on the twenty-third. . . ." She knit her brows and he laughed at her and waved a hand magnanimously.

"Forget it, Tan. Why don't you take some time off, and get ready for the new job? Just dump it all on someone else's desk for a change. Use this week to wrap and then get yourself sorted out at home."

"What do I have to do?" She still looked stunned and he smiled at her. "Shop for robes?"

"No." He laughed. "But I think you may have some house hunting to do. Do you still live in Marin?" He knew she'd lived with someone for the past couple of years, but he wasn't sure if she'd kept her own place in town or not. She nodded at him. "You've got to have a place in town, Tan."

"How come?"

"It's a condition of being a San Francisco judge. You can keep the other place, but your main residence has to be here."

"Do I really have to stick to that?" She looked upset.

"Pretty much. During the week anyway."

"Christ." She stared into space for a minute, thinking of Jack. Suddenly her whole life had turned upside down. "I'll have to do something about that."

"You've got plenty to do in the next few weeks, and first of all you have to respond." He put on an official voice. "Tana Roberts, do you accept the seat on the bench that has been offered you, to serve as a municipal court judge in the city and county of San Francisco?"

She looked at him in awe. "I do."

He stood up and smiled at her, happy at the good fortune that had befallen her so deservedly. "Good luck, Tan. We'll miss you here." Tears sprang to her eyes again and she was still in shock when she went back to her own desk and sat down. There were a thousand things she had to do. Empty her desk, look over her caseload, brief someone else about the cases she was passing on, call Harry, tell Jack . . . Jack . . . . ! She suddenly looked at her watch and grabbed the phone. The secretary said he was in a meeting but Tana told her to get him anyway.

"Hi babe, you okay?"

"Yes." She sounded breathless on the phone. She didn't know where to start. "You won't believe what happened, Jack."

"I wondered what the hell was going on when they called you at home. What is it, Tan?"

She took a deep breath. "They just offered me a seat on the bench." There was total silence at the other end.

"At your age?"

"Isn't that incredible?" She was beaming now. "I mean, would you believe . . . I never thought. . . ."

"I'm happy for you, Tan." He sounded quiet, but pleased, and then she remembered what the DA had said. She had to find a place in town, but she didn't want to tell him that on the phone.

"Thank you, sweetheart. I'm still in shock. Is Harry there?"

"No, he's not in today."

"He's sure out a lot lately, isn't he? What's up?"

"I think he's in Tahoe with Ave and the kids for a long weekend. You can call him there."

"I'll wait till he gets back. I want to see his face." But the face she didn't want to see was Jack's when she told him she had to move out of Marin.

"I wondered about that after you called." He looked sad when she told him that night. He was obviously upset and so was she, but she was terribly excited too. She had even called her mother, and Jean had been stunned. "My daughter, a judge?" She had been thrilled for Tana. Maybe things did work out in the end, and she had met Jack once and he seemed nice to her. She hoped they would get married eventually, even if Tana was too old for children now. But as a judge, maybe that didn't matter as much. Even Arthur had been thrilled for her. Jean had explained it to him several times.

Tana looked at Jack now. "How do you feel about living in town during the week?"

"Not great." He was honest with her. "It's so damn comfortable for us here."

"I thought I'd look for something small that we don't have to worry about. An apartment, a condo, a studio, even. . . ." As though she could pretend it wasn't happening but he shook his head.

"We'd go nuts after all the room we're used to here." For two years they had lived like kings, with a huge master bedroom, offices for each of them, a living room, dining room, guest room for Barb, sweeping view of the bay. A studio would feel like a jail cell after that.

"Well, I've got to do something, Jack, and I only have three weeks." She looked faintly annoyed at him, he wasn't making it easier for her, and she wondered if the appointment bothered him. It would be natural that it would, at least at first, but she hardly had time to think of that in the next few weeks. She divided her caseload up, emptied her desk, and ran around looking at every condo available until the real estate agent called halfway into the second week. She had something "very special" she wanted Tana to see, in Pacific Heights.

"It's not exactly what you had in mind, but it's worth a look." And when she went, it was more than that. It was a dollhouse that took her breath away, a tiny ginger-bread jewel, painted beige with dollops of cinnamon and cream. It was absolutely impeccable, with inlaid floors, marble fire-places in just about every room, huge closets, perfect light-ing, double French doors, and a view of the bay. Tana would never have thought of looking for something like it, but now that she was here, there was no way she could resist.

"How much is the rent?" She knew it would be ferocious. The place looked like something out of a magazine.

"It's not for rent." The agent smiled at her. "It's for sale." She told her the price, and Tana was amazed at how reasonable it was. It wasn't cheap, but it wouldn't have destroyed her savings at one blow, and at the price that was being asked, it was actually a good investment for her. It was irresistible in every possible way, and it was perfect for her. One large bedroom on the second floor, a dressing room with mirrored walls, a tiny den with a brick fireplace, and downstairs, one large, beautiful living room, and a tiny country kitchen that gave out onto a patio framed with trees. She signed away her life, put the deposit down, and turned up in Jack's office, looking nervous about what she'd done. She knew it wasn't a mistake, but still . . . it was such an independent thing to do, so solitary, so grown up . . . and she hadn't asked him.

"Good lord, who died?" He stepped into the anteroom and saw her face, as she laughed nervously. "That's better." He kissed her neck. "You practicing to be a judge? You're going to scare people half to death running around with a face like that."

"I just did a crazy thing." The words tumbled out and he smiled. He had had a rough day, and it wasn't even two o'clock yet.

"So what else is new? Come on in and tell me about it." Tana saw that Harry's door was closed, and she didn't knock. She passed right into Jack's large, pleasant room in the Victorian they'd bought five years before. That had been a good investment for them, maybe it would help make him understand what she'd done. He smiled at her from across his desk. "So what'd you do?"

"I think I just bought a house." She looked like a frightened kid and he laughed at her.

"You *think* you did. I see. And what makes you think that?" He sounded as he always did, but his eyes were different now and she wondered why.

"Actually, I signed the papers . . . oh Jack . . . I hope I did the right thing!"

"Do you like it?"

"I'm in love with it." He looked surprised, neither of them had wanted to own a house before. They had talked about it several times. They had no need of permanence, and he hadn't changed his mind. But apparently she had and he wondered why. A lot seemed to have changed in the last ten days, mostly for her. Nothing had changed for him.

"Won't that be a lot of trouble for you, Tan? Keeping it up, worrying about a leaky roof, and all that stuff we talked about before and didn't want."

"I don't know . . . I guess. . . ." She looked nervously at him. It was time to ask. "You'll be there too, won't you?" Her voice was frightened and soft and he smiled at her. She was at once so vulnerable and soft, and yet so incredibly powerful as well. He loved that about her and knew he always would. It was what Harry loved in her too, that and her loyalty, her fierce heart, bright mind. She was such a lovely girl, judge or not. She looked like a teenager sitting there, watching him.

"Is there room in it for me?" His voice sounded tentative and she nodded vehemently, and her hair swung wild. She had cut it straight to her shoulders only weeks before she got the news, and it looked very elegant and sleek, hanging in a smooth blonde sheet from crown to nape.

"Of course there is." But he wasn't sure he agreed when he saw the place that night. He agreed that the place was beautiful, but it was awfully feminine to his eyes. "How can you say a thing like that? There's nothing here but walls and floors."

"I don't know. It just feels that way, maybe because I know it's your house." He turned to her and he looked sad all at once. "I'm sorry, Tan, it's beautiful . . . I don't mean to rain on your parade."

"It's all right. I'll make it comfortable for both of us. I promise you." He took her to dinner that night and they talked for hours, about her new job, the "judges' school" she would have to attend in Oakland for three weeks, holed up in a hotel with other recent appointees. Everything seemed suddenly exciting and new, and she hadn't felt that way in years.

"It's like starting life all over again, isn't it?" Her eyes danced as she looked at him and he smiled at her.

"I guess." They went home after that and made love, and

nothing seemed to have changed in important ways. She spent the next week shopping for furniture for her new house, closing the deal, and buying a new dress for her induction ceremony. She had even asked her mother to come out, but Arthur wasn't well enough and Jean didn't want to leave him alone. But Harry would be there, and Averil, and Jack, and all the friends and acquaintances she had collected over the years. In the end, there were two hundred people at the ceremony, and Harry gave her a reception afterwards at Trader Vic's. It was the most festive occasion she had ever been to, and she laughed as she kissed Jack halfway through the afternoon.

"It's kind of like getting married, isn't it?" He laughed back at her and they exchanged a look which said they both understood.

"Better than that, thank God." They laughed again and he danced with her, and they were both a little drunk when they went home that night, and the following week, she started "judges' school".

She stayed at the hotel, in the room they had given her, and she had planned to spend weekends in Tiburon with Jack, but there was always something to do at her new house, a painting she wanted to hang up, lights she had to fix, a couch that had arrived, a gardener she wanted to interview, and for the first two weeks she slept in town when she wasn't at "judges' school."

"Why don't you come sleep here with me?" There was a plaintive note in her voice and she sounded irritable. He hadn't seen her in days but that was par for the course these days. She had too much else to do.

"I've got too much work to do." He sounded curt.

"You can bring it here, sweetheart. I'll make some soup and a salad, you can use my den." He noticed the possessive term, and like everything else these days, it rankled him, but he had a lot on his mind just then.

"Do you know what it's like to drag all your work over to someone else's house?"

"I'm not someone else. I'm me. And you live here too."

"Since when?" She was hurt by his tone and she backed

off, and even Thanksgiving was strained, spent with Harry and Averil and the kids.

"How's the new house, Tan?" Harry was happy about everything that had happened to her, but she noticed that he looked tired and drawn, and Averil looked strained too. It was a difficult day for everyone and even the children whined more than usual, and Jack and Tana's godchild cried most of the day. She sighed as they drove back to town at last, and Jack visibly unwound in the silence in the car.

"Doesn't it make you glad you don't have kids?" He looked at her as he spoke and she smiled at him.

"Days like this do, but when they're all dressed up and cute, or sound asleep, and you watch Harry look at Ave . . . sometimes I think it would be sweet to be like that. . . ." She sighed then and glanced at him. "I don't think I could stand it though."

"You'd look cute on the bench, with a string of kids." He said it sarcastically and she laughed. He had been sharp with her a lot recently and she noticed that he was driving her into town and not to Tiburon, and she looked at him, surprised.

"Aren't we going home, sweetheart?"

"Sure . . . I thought you wanted to go back to your place. . . ."

"I don't mind . . . I. . . ." She took a deep breath. It had to be said eventually. "You're mad at me for buying the house, aren't you?"

He shrugged and drove on, keeping his eyes on the other cars. "I guess it was something you had to do. I just didn't think you'd do something like that."

"All I did was buy a little house because I had to have a place in town."

"I just didn't think you wanted to *own* something, Tan."

"What difference does it make if I own or rent? It's a good investment this way. We've talked about doing something like that."

"Yeah, and we decided not to. Why do you have to get yourself locked into something permanent?" The thought of that almost gave him hives. He was happy renting where they were in Tiburon. "You never thought like that before."

"Things change sometimes. This just made sense at the time, and I fell in love with it."

"I know you did. Maybe that's what bothers me. It's so 'yours', not ours."

"Would you rather have bought something with me?" But she knew him better than that and he shook his head.

"That would just complicate our lives. You know that."

"You can't keep things simple all the time. And as those things go, I think we've done damn well. We're the most unencumbered people I know." And they had done it purposely. Nothing was permanent, written in stone. Their whole life could be unwound in a matter of hours, or so they thought, at least it was what they had told themselves for two years.

Tana went on, "Hell, I used to have an apartment in town. What's the big deal?" But it wasn't the house, it was her job, she had begun to suspect it weeks before. It bothered him, the fuss, the press, he had tolerated it before because she was only an assistant DA, but suddenly she was a judge . . . Your Honor . . . Judge Roberts, she had noticed the look on his face every time someone said the words to her. "You know, it really isn't fair of you to take it out on me, Jack. I can't help it. Something wonderful happened and now we have to learn to live with it. It could have happened to you too. The shoe could be on the other foot, you know."

"I think I'd have handled it differently."

"How?" She was instantly hurt by his words.

"Actually," he looked at her accusingly, the anger between them finally had words put to it, like a symphony with a chorale, but it was a relief to get it out. "I think I'd have turned it down. It's a goddamn pompous thing to do."

"Pompous? What an awful thing to say. Do you think I'm pompous for accepting the seat they offered me?"

"Depends on how you handle it." He answered cryptically.

"Well?"

They stopped at a light and he turned to look at her, and

then suddenly looked away. "Look . . . never mind . . . I just don't like the changes it's made for us. I don't like you living in town, I don't like your goddamn house, I don't like any of it."

"So you're going to punish me, is that it? Christ, I'm doing my best to handle it gracefully, give me a chance. Let me figure it out. It's a big change for me too, you know."

"You'd never know it to look at you. You look happy as can be."

"Well, I am happy." She was honest with him. "It's wonderful and flattering and interesting, and I'm having fun with my career. It's very exciting for me, but it's also scary and new, and I don't quite know how to handle it and I don't want it to hurt you. . . ."

"Never mind that. . . ."

"What do you mean, never mind? I love you, Jack. I don't want this to destroy us."

"Then it won't." He shrugged and drove on, but neither of them was convinced, and he remained impossible for the next few weeks. She made a point of spending the night in Tiburon whenever she could, and she cajoled him constantly, but he was angry at her, and the Christmas they spent at her house was grim. He made it clear that he hated everything about her house, and he left at eight o'clock the next day, claiming he had things to do. He made life difficult for her for the next few months, and in spite of it, she enjoyed her job. The only thing she didn't like were the long hours she kept. She stayed in her chambers until midnight sometimes, but she had so much to learn, so many points of law to read and refer to for each case. So much depended on her that she became blind to almost all else, so much so that she didn't see how unwell Harry looked, never realized how seldom he went to work anymore, and it was late April before Jack turned to her and screamed.

"What are you, blind? He's dying, for God's sake. He has been for the last six months, Tan. Don't you give a shit about anyone else anymore?" His words cut her to the quick and she gaped at him in horror.

"That's not true . . . he can't be. . . ." But suddenly the

pale face, the ghostly eyes, all of it suddenly made sense. But why hadn't he told her? Why? She looked up at Jack accusingly. "Why didn't you say something?"

"You wouldn't have heard. You're so fucking wrapped up in how important you are these days, you don't see anything that goes on." They were bitter accusations, angry words, and without saying a word she left Tiburon that night and drove home to her own house, called Harry on the phone, and before she could say anything, she began to cry.

"What's the matter, Tan?" He sounded tired, and she felt as though her heart were going to break.

"I can't . . . I . . . oh God, Harry. . . ." All the pressures of the past months suddenly began to pile up on her, Jack's anger, and what he had told her that night about Harry being ill. She couldn't believe he was dying, but when she saw him the next day for lunch, he looked at her quietly and told her it was true. She felt her breath catch as though on a sharp nail and she stared at him. "But that can't be true . . . that's not fair. . . ." She sat there and sobbed like a little child, unable to comfort him, desolate, in too much pain herself to help anyone, and he wheeled to where she sat and put his arms around her. There were tears in his eyes too, but he was strangely calm. He had known for almost a year, and they had told him that a long time ago. His wounds could cut his life short and they were. He was suffering from hydronephrosis, which was devouring him by degrees as he headed towards kidney failure. They had tried everything they could, but his body was just quietly giving up. She looked at him with terror in her eyes. "I can't live without you."

"Yes, you can." He was more worried about Averil and the kids. He knew Tana would survive. She had saved him. She would never give up. "I want you to do something for me. I want you to make sure Ave is all right. The kids are all set, and she has everything she'll need, but she's not like you, Tan . . . she's always been so dependent on me."

She stared at him. "Does your father know?"

He shook his head. "No one does, except Jack and Ave, and now you." He was angry that Jack had said something·

to her and especially in anger, but he wanted a promise from her now. "You promise you'll keep an eye on her?"

"Of course I will." It was hideous, he was talking as though he were planning to leave on a trip. She looked at him and twenty years of love raced before her eyes . . . the dance where they had met . . . the years at Harvard and BU . . . coming West . . . Vietnam . . . the hospital . . . law school . . . the apartment they had shared . . . the night his first child was born . . . it was incredible, impossible. His life wasn't over yet, it couldn't be. She needed him too much. But then she remembered the spate of bladder infections and she knew suddenly where all this would lead – he was dying. She began to cry again and he held on to her, and then she looked at him and sobbed. "Why . . . ? It's not fair."

"Damn little in life is." He smiled at her, a small, gray, wintry smile. He didn't care so much for himself as he did for his wife and kids. He had been worried sick about them for months, and he was trying to teach Averil to handle everything herself, to no avail. She was totally hysterical, and she refused to learn anything, as though that way she could keep it from happening, but nothing would. He was getting weaker by the day, and he knew it himself. He only came in to the office now once or twice a week; it was why he was never there when she went in to see Jack from time to time, and she talked to him about that now.

"He's beginning to hate me now." She looked so bleak that it frightened him. He had never seen her like that. These were difficult times for all of them. He still couldn't believe he was going to die, but he knew he would. It was like stuffing running out of a rag doll, he felt as though he were slowly disappearing until he would be no more one day. Only that. They would wake up and he would be gone. Quietly. Not with the squall and the pushes and the screams with which one comes into the world, but with a tear and a sigh and a breath of air as one passes on into the next life, if there even was such a thing. He didn't even know that anymore, and he wasn't sure he cared. He was too worried about the people he was leaving behind, his partner, his wife, his children, his friends. They all seemed to be resting on him and it was exhausting for him. But in some ways it also kept him alive, like right now with Tana. He felt he had something to share with her, before he went. Something important for her. He wanted her to change her life before it was too late. And he had said the same thing to Jack, but he didn't want to hear.

"He doesn't hate you, Tan. Look, the job is threatening to him. Besides, he's been upset about me for the past few months."

"He could have said something at least."

"I made him swear he wouldn't, you can't blame that on him. And as for the rest, you're an important woman now, Tan. Your job is more important than his. That's just the way things are. It's difficult for both of you, and he'll have to adjust to it."

"Tell him that."

"I have."

"He punishes me for what's happened. He hates my house, he's not the same man."

"Yes he is." Too much so for Harry's taste. He was still devoted to the same ridiculous things; staying unattached, a total lack of commitment or permanence. It was an empty life, and Harry had told him he was full of shit, but Jack only shrugged. He liked the way he lived, or at least he had until Tana's new job came along. That was giving him a major pain in the ass, and he made no bones about it to Harry. "Maybe he's jealous of you. That's not attractive, but it's possible, and he's human after all."

"So when will he grow up? Or do I have to resign?" It was a relief talking about normal things, as though the nightmare weren't happening, as though she could make it stop by talking about something else with him. Like the old days . . . they had been so sweet . . . tears filled her eyes as she thought of them. . . .

"Of course you don't have to resign. Just give him time." And then he looked at Tana, with something else on his mind. "I want to say something to you, Tan. Two things." He looked at her so intensely it was as though his whole body turned to flame, she could feel the strength of his words boring right into her soul. "I don't know from one day to the next what tomorrow will bring, if I'll be there . . . if . . . I have two things to say to you, and it's all I have to leave you, my friend. Listen well. The first is thank you for what you did for me. The last sixteen years of my life have been a gift from you, not from my doctor, or anyone else, but from you. You forced me to live again, to go on . . . if it weren't for you I'd never have met Averil, or have had the kids. . . ." There were tears in his eyes now, too, and they rolled slowly down his cheeks. Tana was grateful that they had met in her chambers for lunch. They had needed to be alone. "And that brings me to the second thing. You're cheating yourself, Tan. You don't know what you're missing, and you won't know till you're there. You're depriving yourself of marriage, commitment, real love . . . not borrowed, or rented, or temporary, or kind of. I know that fool's in love with you and you love him but he's devoted to 'hanging loose', to not making a mistake again and that's the biggest mistake of all. Get married, Tan . . . have kids . . . it's the only thing that makes sense in life . . . the only thing I care about . . . the only important thing I'm leaving behind . . . no matter who you are or what you do, until you have that and are that and give that, you are nothing and no one . . . you're only half alive. . . . Tana, don't cheat yourself . . . please. . . ." He was crying openly now. He had loved her so much for so long and he didn't want her to miss what he and Averil had shared. And as he spoke to her, her mind went instantly to the countless looks she had watched them share, the quiet joy, the laughter that never seemed to end . . . and would end so soon now, and deep in her heart she had always known that what he said was true, in some ways she had wanted it for herself, and in other ways she was scared . . . and the men in her life had always been wrong for that . . . Yael McBee . . . Drew Lands . . . and now Jack . . . and the people who didn't matter in between. There had never been anyone who might have come close. Maybe Harry's father would, but that was so long ago now. . . . "If the opportunity ever comes, grab it, Tan. Give up everything, if you have to. But if it's the right thing, you won't."

"What do you propose I do? Go out on the street and wear a sign? Marry me. Let's have kids." They laughed together, for a moment, just like old times.

"Yeah, asshole, why not?"

"I love you, Harry." The words sprung from her and she was crying again and he held her tight.

"I'll never really be gone, Tan. You know that. You and I had too much to ever lose that . . . just like Ave and I do in a different way. I'll be here, keeping an eye on things." They were crying openly and she didn't think she could live without him. And she could only imagine how Averil felt. It was the most painful time of their lives, and for the next three months, they watched him roll slowly downhill, and on a warm summer day, with the sun high in the sky, she got a call. It was from Jack. There were tears in his voice, and she felt her heart stop. She had seen Harry only the night before. She went to see him every day now, no matter what, at lunchtime or at night, or sometimes before her day began. She never knew how hectic things would get, but she wouldn't give that up. And he had held her hand and smiled just the night before. He could barely talk, but she had kissed his cheek, and suddenly thought of the hospital so long ago. She wanted to shake him back to life, to make him fight for what he had been, but he couldn't anymore, and it was easier to go.

"He just died." Jack's voice broke, and Tana began to cry. She wanted to see him just once more . . . to hear him laugh . . . see those eyes. . . . She couldn't speak for a minute, and then she nodded her head and took a breath to fight back the sobs.

"How's Ave?"

"She seems all right." Harrison had arrived the week before and he was staying with them. Tana looked at her watch.

"I'll go over there right now. I just called a recess for the afternoon anyway." She could feel him tense at her words, as though he felt she were showing off for him. But that was

307

what she did. She was a municipal court judge, and she had called a recess. "Where are you?"

"I'm at work. His father just called."

"I'm glad he was there. Are you going over now?"

"I can't for a little while." She nodded, realizing that if she had said that, he would have said something unpleasant to her about how important she thought she was. There was no winning with him now and Harry hadn't been able to soften him before he died, no matter how hard he tried. There had been so much he wanted to say, so much to share with those he loved. And it was over so soon. Tana drove over the Bay Bridge with tears streaming down her face, and then suddenly, it was as though she felt him next to her and she smiled. He was gone, but he was everywhere now. With her, with Ave, with his father, his kids. . . .

"Hi, kid." She smiled into the air as she drove, and the tears continued to flow and when she arrived at the house, he was already gone. They had taken him to prepare him for the services, and Harrison was sitting in the living room, looking stunned. He looked suddenly very old, and Tana realized he was almost seventy now. And with grief etched on his still handsome face, he looked even older than that. She said nothing at all, she just went to him, and they held each other tight, and Averil came out of the bedroom after that, wearing a simple black dress, her blonde hair pulled back and her wedding ring on her left hand. Harry had given her some beautiful things from time to time, but she wore nothing now — only her grief and her pride and their love, as she stood surrounded by the life and the home and the children they had shared. She looked oddly beautiful as she stood there, and in a strange way Tana envied her. She and Harry had shared something that few people ever had, for however long, and it had been worth everything to them. And suddenly, for the first time in her life, she felt a void. She was sorry that she hadn't married him a long time before, or someone else . . . gotten married . . . had kids . . . it left an aching hole in her that refused to be filled. All through the services, at the cemetery as they left him there, and afterwards, when she was alone again, she felt something she couldn't have explained to anyone, and when she tried to tell Jack, he shook his head and stared at her.

"Don't go crazy now, Tan, just because Harry died." She had told him that she suddenly felt her life was a waste because she had never married and had kids. "I've done both, and believe me it doesn't change a damn thing. Don't kid yourself, not everyone has what they did. In fact, I've never known anyone who did, except them. And if you got married looking for that, you'd be disappointed, because it wouldn't be there."

"How do you know that? It might." She was disappointed by what he said.

"Take my word for it."

"You can't make a judgment on that. You knocked up some twenty-one-year-old girl and got married lickety split because you had to. That's different from making an intelligent choice at our age."

"Are you trying to put pressure on me, Tan?" He suddenly looked angrily at her, and all the handsome blond good looks seemed suddenly drawn and tired. Losing Harry had been rough on him too. "Don't do that to me now. This isn't the time."

"I'm just telling you what I feel."

"You feel like shit because your best friend just died. But don't go getting all romantic about it, and the secret of life being marriage and kids. Believe me, it's not."

"How the hell do you know that? You can't decide for anyone but yourself. Don't try to evaluate things for me, goddammit, Jack." All her feelings suddenly came rushing out, "You're so fucking scared to give a damn about anyone, you squeak anytime someone comes too close. And you know what? I'm fucking sick of you punishing me all the time because I got made a judge last year!"

"Is that what you think I do?" It was a relief for both of them to scream a little bit, but there was truth in her words, and they hit home so hard he slammed out of her house, and she didn't see him for three weeks. It was the longest they'd been apart voluntarily since they'd met, but he didn't call her and she didn't call him. She heard nothing at all from him until his daughter arrived in town for her annual visit, and Tana invited her to stay with her in town. Barb was excited at the idea, and when she arrived at the little house on her own the following afternoon, Tana was stunned by how much she had changed. She had just turned fifteen, and she suddenly looked like a woman now, with long lean lines, and pretty little hips and big blue eyes with her flash of red hair.

"You look great, Barb."

"Thanks, so do you." Tana kept her for five days, and even took her to court with her, and it was only toward the end of the week that they finally talked about Jack, and how things had changed with them.

"He yells at me all the time now." Barbara had noticed it too, and she wasn't having a very good time with him. "My mom says he was always like that, but he never was when you were around, Tan."

"I think he's probably pretty nervous these days." She was making excuses for him for Barb's sake, so she didn't think it was her fault, but in truth it was a conglomerate of things. Tana, Harry, pressures in his work. Nothing seemed to be going right for him, and when Tana attempted to have dinner with him after Barbara went back to Detroit, it ended in more bickering again. They were arguing about what Averil should do with the house. He thought she should sell and move into town, and Tana disagreed. "That house means a lot to her; they've been there for years."

"She needs a change, Tan. You can't hang on to the past."

"Why the hell are you so desperately afraid to hang on to anything? It's almost as if you're afraid to give a damn." She had noticed that a lot about him of late. He always wanted to be free and unattached, never tied down. It was a wonder the relationship had lasted as long as it had, but it certainly wasn't in good shape now, and at the end of the summer, fate dealt them another blow. Just as she had been told, when she was offered her seat on the municipal court bench a year before, an opening had come up, and she was being kicked up into superior court. She almost didn't have the heart to tell Jack, but she didn't want him to hear it from someone else first. Gritting her teeth, she dialed him at home one night. She was in her cozy little house, reading some law books she had brought home, to check some remote statutes of the penal code, and she held her breath as he answered the phone.

"Hi, Tan, what's up?" He sounded more relaxed than he had in months, and she hated to spoil his good mood, which she knew her news would. And she was right. He sounded as though someone had punched him in the gut when she told him she was being made a superior court judge.

"That's nice. When?" He sounded as though she had just planted a cobra at his feet.

"In two weeks. Would you come to my induction, or would you rather not be there?"

"That's a hell of a thing to say. I gather you'd just as soon I not come." He was so sensitive, there was no talking to him.

"I didn't say that. But I know how uptight you get about my work."

"What makes you think that?"

"Oh please, Jack . . . let's not get into that now. . . ." She was tired after a long day, and everything seemed harder and sadder and more difficult now that Harry was gone. And with the relationship with Jack on the rocks, it wasn't the happiest time of her life, to say the least. "I hope you'll come."

"Does that mean I won't see you till then?"

"Of course not. You can see me whenever you want."

"How about tomorrow night?" It was almost as if he were testing her.

"Great. Your place or mine?" She laughed but he did not.

"Yours gives me claustrophobia. I'll pick you up outside City Hall at six."

"Yes, sir." She put a mock salute in her voice, but he didn't laugh, and when they met the next day, their mood was gray. They both missed Harry terribly and the only difference was that Tana talked about it, and Jack would not. He had taken another attorney into the partnership, and he seemed to like the man. He talked about that a lot, and about how successful the man had been, how much money they were going to make. It was obvious that he still had a chip on his shoulder over Tana's work, and by the next morning, it was a relief when he dropped her off at City Hall again. He was going to Pebble Beach that week end to play golf with a bunch of guys and he hadn't invited her, and she was relieved as she walked up the steps of City Hall with a sigh. He certainly didn't make her life easy these days, and now and then she thought of what Harry had said to her before he died. But it was hopeless thinking of anything permanent with Jack. He just wasn't that kind of man. And Tana didn't kid herself anymore. She wasn't that kind of girl anyway. It was probably why they had gotten along for as along as they had. Not that that seemed to apply anymore. The friction between them was almost more than she could bear, and she was actually grateful when she discovered that he was going to be in Chicago on a business trip when she was inducted into superior court.

It was a small, simple ceremony this time, presided over by the presiding judge of the superior court. There were half a dozen other judges there, her old friend the DA, who happily said, "I told you so" over her swift move up, and a handful of other people she cared about, and Averil was in Europe with Harrison and the kids. She had decided to winter in London that year, just to get away for a while, and she had put the children in school there. Harrison had talked her into it, and he looked happy when he left with his grandchildren in tow. There had been a heart-breaking moment alone with Tana just before that, when he actually put his face in his hands and cried, wondering if Harry had known how much he had loved him, and she insisted that he had. It helped assuage his sorrow and his guilt over the early years to take care of his daughter-in-law and his grandchildren now. But it wasn't the same without them at Tana's swearing-in and it was odd to look around and not see Jack.

The actual swearing-in was done by a judge of the court of appeals, a man Tana had met once or twice over the years. He had thick black hair, ferocious dark eyes, and a look which would have frightened anyone, as he towered over them all in his dark robes, but he also had quick laughter, a keen mind, and a surprising gentleness. He was particularly well known for some very controversial decisions he had made, which had been played up in the national press, and in particular the *New York Times*, and the *Washington Post*, as well as the *Chronicle*. Tana had read about him a lot, and wondered just how ferocious he was, but she was intrigued to see now that he was less lion and more lamb, or at least he was at her swearing-in. They chatted for a while about his superior court days, and she knew that he had also run the biggest law firm in town, before being made a judge. He had an interesting career behind him, though she suspected that he wasn't more than forty-eight or forty-nine. For a long time, he had been kind of "*Wunderkind*", and she liked him very much as he shook her hand, and congratulated her warmly again, before he left.

"I'm impressed." Her old friend, the DA, smiled at her. "That's the first time I've ever seen Russell Carver at a swearing-in. You're getting to be awfully important, my friend."

"He probably had to pay his parking tickets downstairs, and someone recruited him." They both laughed. Actually, he was a close friend of the presiding judge, and had volunteered his services for the swearing-in. He looked the part anyway, with his dark hair and serious face.

"You should have seen him when he was the presiding judge here, Tan. Shit, he threw one of our DA's into the can on contempt of court for three weeks and I couldn't get the poor bastard out."

Tana laughed, just imagining it. "I'm lucky that never happened to me, I guess."

"Didn't you ever have him as a judge?"

"Only twice. He's been on the court of appeals for a hell of a long time."

"I guess he has. He's not very old though, as I recall. Forty-nine, fifty, fifty-one . . . something like that. . . ."

"Who's that?" The presiding judge wandered over to them and shook Tana's hand again. It was a nice day for her, and she was suddenly glad that Jack wasn't there. It was so

313

much easier like this, and not having to hold her breath or apologize to him.

"We were talking about Justice Carver."

"Russ? He's forty-nine. He went to Stanford with me." The presiding judge smiled, "although I'll admit he was a few years behind." In fact, he had been a freshman when the presiding judge graduated from law school, but their families had been friends. "He's a hell of a nice guy, smart as hell."

"He has to be." Tana spoke admiringly. There was another leap to contemplate. The court of appeals. What a thought. Maybe in another decade or two. And in the meantime, she was going to enjoy this. Superior Court was going to be just her cup of tea. They were going to have her trying criminal cases in no time at all, since that was her area of expertise. "It was nice of him to do my swearing-in today." She smiled at everyone.

"He's a nice guy." Everyone said that about the man, and she sent him a little note, thanking him for taking the time to make her induction an even more special event, and the next day, he called and there was laughter in his voice.

"You're awfully polite. I haven't had a bread and butter letter like that in twenty years at least."

She laughed in embarrassment and thanked him for the call. "It was just a very nice thing to do. Like having the Pope around when you take religious vows."

"Oh my God . . . what a thought. Is that what you were doing last week? I take it all back. . . ." They both laughed and they chatted for a while. She invited him to stop into her court whenever he was around, and she felt a comfortable warmth at the confrerie she was a part of now, judges and justices, all working together. It was like having arrived at Mount Olympus at last, and it was a hell of a lot easier in some ways than prosecuting cases against rapists and murderers, building a case and arguing, although she had enjoyed that too. Here, she had to keep a clearer head, an objective outlook, and she had never studied so much law in her life. She was buried in a stack of books in her chambers two weeks later, when Justice Carver took her at her word and came by. "Is this what I condemned you to?" He stood in her doorway and smiled. Her clerk had long since gone home, and she was frowning in concentration as she pored over six open books at once, comparing statutes and precedents as he wandered in and she looked up with a smile.

"What a nice surprise." She stood up quickly and waved him toward a large, comfortable leather chair. "Please sit down." He did and she looked at him. He was good looking, in a quiet, virile, rather intellectual way. They weren't the same football team good looks as Jack's. They were much quieter, and much more powerful, just as he was in myriad ways. "Would you like a drink?" She kept a small bar well hidden for occasions such as this.

"No, thanks. I have too much homework to do tonight."

"You too? How do you ever get through it all?"

"I don't. Sometimes it makes you want to just sit there and cry, but you get through it eventually. What are you working on?" She described the case to him as briefly as she could and he nodded thoughtfully. "That should be an interesting one. It may even wind up in my lap eventually."

She laughed. "That's not much of a vote of confidence if you think they'll appeal my decision."

"No, no," he was quick to explain, "it's just that you're on new turf there and whatever you decide, if they don't like it, they may try to overturn it. Be careful you don't give them grounds." It was good advice and they chatted on for quite a while. He had dark, thoughtful eyes that gave him an almost sensual air, which didn't seem in keeping with his seriousness. There were a lot of contrasts about the man, and she was intrigued by him. He walked her out eventually, and helped her carry a stack of books to her car, and then he seemed to hesitate. "I couldn't talk you into a hamburger somewhere, could I?"

She smiled at him. She liked this man. She had never known anyone quite like him before. "You might, if you promise to get me home early enough to do some work." They chose Bill's Place on Clement. It was a simple, wholesome environment amidst the hamburgers and french fries and milkshakes and kids, and no one would have suspected who they were, how important their jobs, as they chatted on about cases they had suffered with years before, and the comparison of Stanford to Boalt, and eventually Tana laughed at him.

"All right, all right I concede. Your school is better than mine."

"I didn't say that." He laughed. "I said we had a better football team."

"Well, that's not my fault at least. I had nothing to do with that."

"I somehow didn't think you did." It was very relaxing being with him. They had common interests, common friends, and the time flew by. He took her home, and was about to drop her off when she invited him inside for a drink, and he was surprised by how pretty the little bijou house was, how well she'd decorated it. It was a real haven, that made one want to stretch out in front of the fire and stay for a while.

"I'm happy here." And she was, whenever she was alone. It was only when Jack was there, that it got so uncomfortable. But especially now, with him there, it suited her perfectly. Russ lit the fire for her, and she poured him a glass of red wine, and they chatted for a while, about their families, their lives. She discovered that he had lost his wife ten years before, and he had two daughters who were both married now.

"At least I'm not a grandfather yet." Russell Carver smiled at her. "Beth is going to architectural school at Yale, while her husband studies law, and Lee is a fashion designer in New York. She's actually pretty good, and I'm proud of them . . . but grandchildren," he almost groaned, and she smiled at him, "I'm not ready for that yet."

"Did you ever want to marry again?" She was curious about him. He was an interesting man.

"No. No one that important has come along, I guess." He looked around her house and then back at her. "You know how it is, you get comfortable with your own way of life. It's difficult to change all that for someone else."

She smiled. "I suppose. I've never really tried. Not very courageous of me, I suppose." Sometimes she regretted it now, and if Jack had twisted her arm before things began to fall apart. . . . She looked up at Russ and smiled. "Marriage used to scare the hell out of me."

"As well it should. It's a mighty delicate operation at best. But when it works, it's wonderful." His eyes glowed and it was easy to guess that he'd been happy with his wife. "I have nothing but good memories about that." And they both knew that that made it harder to marry again too. "And my girls are great. You'll have to meet them sometime."

"I'd like that very much." They chatted on for a few minutes, he finished his wine, and then he left. She went up to her den with the books he'd helped her bring home, and she worked late into the night and the next day she laughed when a court messenger appeared with an envelope in his decisive hand. He had written her a bread and butter letter much like the one she'd written him for her swearing-in and she called to laugh with him. It was a far easier conversation than the one she shared with Jack later that day. He was on the warpath again, and they were fighting about their weekend plans, so much so that eventually she got out of them, and sat peacefully in her house alone on Saturday, going through some old photographs when the doorbell rang. Russell Carver was standing there, looking at her apologetically, with a bunch of roses in his hands.

"This is a terribly rude thing to do, and I apologize in advance." He looked handsome in a tweed jacket and a turtleneck and she smiled at him delightedly.

"I never heard that bringing someone roses was rude before."

"That's to compensate for dropping by unannounced, which *is* rude, but I was thinking of you and I didn't have your number at home. I gather it's unlisted, so I took a chance. . . ." He smiled sheepishly and she waved him in.

"I had absolutely nothing to do, and I'm delighted you came by."

"I'm surprised I found you here. I was sure you'd be out."

She poured him a glass of wine, and they sat down on the couch.

"Actually, I had plans but I cancelled them." Things were impossible with Jack, and she wondered how to handle it. Sooner or later, they'd either have to work things out or give up, but she didn't want to face that now, and he was away anyway.

"I'm glad you did." Russ Carver smiled at her. "Would you like to go to Butterfield's with me?"

"The auction house?" She looked intrigued, and half an hour later they were wandering amidst antiques and Oriental works of art, chatting about sundry things. He had an easy way about him that was relaxing to her, and they shared similar views about almost everything. She even tried to explain her mother to him. "I think that's a big part of the reason why I never wanted to get married. I kept thinking of her sitting there waiting for him to call. . . ." She hated the memory, even now.

"Then all the more reason to marry him and have security."

"But I knew he was cheating on his wife by then. I never wanted to be either one of those women . . . my mother . . . or the wife he cheated on."

"That must have been difficult for you, Tana." He was sympathetic about so many things. And she told him about Harry that afternoon when they walked on Union Street. She told him about the friendship they had shared, the years at school, the time at the hospital, and how lonely it was without him now. Tears came to her eyes as she talked about him, but there was something gentle on her face too as she looked up at him. "He must have been a fine man." His voice touched her like a caress and she smiled at him.

"He was more than that. He was the best friend I'll ever have. He was remarkable . . . even as he died, he gave something to everyone, a piece of himself . . . some part of himself. . . ." She looked up at Russ again. "I wish you'd known him."

"So do I." He looked at her gently then. "Were you in love with him?"

She shook her head, and then she smiled, remembering. "He had a crush on me when we were kids. But Averil was perfect for him."

"And you, Tana?" Russell Carver looked searchingly at her. "Who was perfect for you? Who has there been? Who was the love of your life?" It was an odd question to ask, but he had the feeling that there had been someone. It was impossible that a girl like this should be unattached. There was a mystery there, and he couldn't find the answer to it.

"No one." She smiled at him. "Some hits, some misses . . . the wrong people mostly. I haven't had much time."

He nodded. He understood that too. "You pay a price for getting where you are today. It can be a very lonely place sometimes." He wondered if it was for her, but she looked content to him. He wondered who there was in her life now, and he asked her as much, in so many words.

"I've been seeing someone for the last few years, more than that actually, I guess. We lived together for a while. And we still see each other," she smiled wistfully and looked into Russ' dark eyes, "but things aren't what they used to be. 'The price you pay', as you put it. Things haven't been the same since I got appointed to the bench last year . . . and then Harry died . . . it's made a lot of dents in us."

"Is it a serious affair?" He looked both concerned and intrigued.

"It was for a long time, but it's limping badly now. I think we're still together out of loyalty."

"You're still together, then?" He watched her face carefully, and she nodded. She and Jack had never really called it quits. At least not yet, although neither of them knew what the future would bring.

"We are for now. It suited us both for a long time. We had the same philosophy. No marriage and no kids. And as long as we both agreed on that, it worked pretty well. . . ."

"And now?" The big dark eyes were probing hers and she looked at him, suddenly hungry for his touch, his hands, his lips. He was the most attractive man she'd ever seen, but she had to reproach herself. She still belonged to Jack . . . didn't she? She was no longer quite so sure.

"I don't know. Things have changed for me since Harry died. Some of what he said makes me wonder about my own life." She looked hard at Russ. "I mean is this it? Is this all there is? I go on from here, with my work . . . with or without Jack," Russ gathered who she meant, "and that's all? Maybe I want more of a future than that. I've never felt that way before, and suddenly I do. Or at least I wonder about it sometimes."

"I think you're on the right track." He sounded worldly and wise, and in some ways he reminded her of Harrison.

She smiled at him. "That's what Harry would say." And then she sighed. "Who knows, maybe it doesn't matter anyway. Suddenly it's all over, and then so what, who cares, you're gone. . . ."

"It matters all the more then, Tana. But I felt that way too after my wife died ten years ago. It's difficult to adjust to something like that, it forces the realization on us that we have to face our own mortality one day. It all counts, every year, every day, every relationship, if you're wasting it, or unhappy where you are, one day you wake up, and it's time to pay the check. So, in the meantime, you might as well be happy where you are." He waited a moment and then looked at her. "Are you?"

"Happy?" She hesitated for a long time and then looked at him. "In my work, I am."

"And the rest?"

"Not very, right now. It's a difficult time for us."

"Am I intruding, then?" He wanted to know everything, and sometimes it was difficult to answer him.

She shook her head and looked into the brown eyes she was coming to know so well. "No, you're not."

"You're still seeing your friend . . . the one you lived with for a while?" He smiled at her and he looked terribly sophisticated and grown up. She felt almost like a child with him.

"Yes, I still see him off and on."

"I wanted to know how things stand with you." She wanted to ask him why, but she didn't dare. Instead, he took her to his house, and showed her around. It took her breath away, from the moment they walked into the front hall. Nothing about him bespoke that kind of wealth. He was simple, easy, quietly well dressed, but when you saw where he lived, you understood who he was. It was a house on Broadway, in the last block before the Presidio, with small, carefully kept grounds, a marble entrance hall in inky green and sparkling white, tall marble columns, a Louis XV chest with a white marble top and a silver tray for calling cards, gilt mirrors, parquet floors, satin curtains sweeping the floor. The main floor was a series of exquisite reception rooms. The second floor was more comfortable, with a large master suite, a pretty wood panelled library, a cozy little den with a marble fireplace, and upstairs were the children's rooms he no longer used.

"It doesn't make much sense for me anymore, but I've been here for so long, I'd hate to move. . . ."

There was nothing she could do but laugh as she sat down and looked at him. "I think I'll burn my house down after this." But she was happy there too. This was just another life, another world. He had need of this and she did not. She remembered hearing now that he had considerable personal wealth, knew he had owned a profitable law firm a number of years ago. The man had done well in his life, and he had nothing to fear from her. She wanted nothing from him materially. He showed her proudly from room to room, the billiard room and the gym downstairs, the racks of guns he kept for duck hunting. He was a whole man, of many interests and pursuits. And as they went back upstairs, he turned to her and took her hand with a small, careful smile.

"I'm very taken with you, Tana. . . . I'd like to see more of you, but I don't want to complicate your life just now. Will you tell me when you're free?" She nodded, totally amazed by all that she had seen and heard. A little while later, he took her home, and she sat staring into the fire in her living room. He was like the kind of man one read about in books, or saw in magazines. And suddenly there he was, on the threshold of her life, telling her that he was "taken with her", bringing her roses, walking her through Butterfield's. She didn't know what to make of him, but one thing she knew, and that was that she was "very taken" with him too.

It made things difficult with Jack for the next few weeks. She attempted to spend several nights in Tiburon, almost out of guilt, and all she could think about was Russ, especially when they made love. It was beginning to make her as testy as Jack was with her, and by Thanksgiving she was a nervous wreck. Russ had gone East to see his daughter Lee, and he had invited her to go with him, but that would have been dishonest of her. She had to resolve the situation with Jack, but by the time the holidays came, she felt hysterical every time she thought of him. All she wanted to do was be with Russ, for their quiet talks, their long walks in the Presidio, their ventures into antique shops, art galleries, their long hours over lunch in tiny coffee shops and restaurants. He brought something into her life that had never been there before and which she longed for now, and whenever a problem arose, it was Russ she called, not Jack. Jack would only bark at her. He still had a need to punish her, and it was tiresome now. She wasn't feeling guilty enough to put up with it anymore.

"Why are you hanging on to him?" Russ asked her one day.

"I don't know." Tana stared miserably at Russ over lunch before court was recessed for the holidays.

"Maybe because in your mind he's attached to your friend." It was a new idea to her, but she thought it might be a possibility. "Do you love him, Tan?"

"It isn't that . . . it's that we've been together for so long."

"That's no excuse. From what you say, you're not happy with him."

"I know. That's the crazy part. Maybe it's just that it's been so safe."

"Why?" He pushed her hard sometimes, but it was good for her.

"Jack and I have always wanted the same things . . . no commitment, no marriage, no kids. . . ."

"Is that what you're afraid of now?"

She took a breath and stared at him. "Yes . . . I think I am. . . ."

"Tana," he reached out and took her hand. "Are you afraid of me?" Slowly, she shook her head, and then he said what she had both feared and wanted most. She had wanted it since they'd met, since she'd first looked into his eyes. "I want to marry you. Do you know that?" She shook her head, and then stopped and nodded it, and they both laughed, she with tears in her eyes.

"I don't know what to say."

"You don't have to say anything. I just wanted to make things clear for you. And now you have to clear up the other situation, for your own peace of mind, whatever you decide about us."

"Wouldn't your daughters object?"

"It's my life, not theirs, isn't it? Besides, they're lovely girls, there's no reason for them to object to my happiness." Tana nodded her head. She felt as though she were living a dream.

"Are you serious?"

"Never more so in my life." His eyes met hers and held. "I love you very much." He hadn't even kissed her yet, and she felt herself melting toward him where they sat. And as they left the restaurant, he gently pulled her toward him and kissed her lips, and she felt as though her heart would melt as he held her in his arms.

"I love you, Russ." The words were suddenly so easy for her. "I love you so much." She looked up at him and there were tears in her eyes and he smiled down at her.

"I love you too. Now go straighten out your life, like a good girl."

"It may take a little time." They walked slowly back toward City Hall. She had to go back to work.

"That's all right. How about two days?" They both laughed. "We could go to Mexico over the holidays."

She cringed. She had already promised Jack she would go skiing with him. But she had to do something now. "Give me till the first of the year and I promise I'll straighten everything out."

'Then maybe I'll go to Mexico alone." He frowned pensively and she glanced worriedly at him. "What are you worried about, little one?"

"That you'll fall in love with someone else."

"Then hurry up." He laughed at her, and kissed her again before she went back to court. And all afternoon she sat on the bench with a strange expression in her eyes, a small smile on her lips. She couldn't concentrate on anything, and when she saw Jack that night, she felt breathless every time she looked at him. He wanted to know if she had all her skiing gear. The condo was rented and they were going with friends, and then suddenly halfway through the evening, she stood up and looked at him.

"What's wrong, Tan?"

"Nothing . . . everything. . . ." She closed her eyes. "I have to go."

"Now?" He looked furious. "Back to town?"

"No." She sat down and started to cry. Where could she begin? What could she say? He had finally driven her away, with his resentment of her work and her success, his bitterness, his unwillingness to commit. She wanted something now that he didn't have to give, and she knew she was doing the right thing, but it was so difficult. She stared unhappily up at him, sure of what she was doing now. She could almost feel Russ sitting next to her, and Harry on the other side, cheering her on. "I can't." She looked at Jack and he stared at her.

"Can't what?" He was mystified. She wasn't making any sense and that was unusual for her.

"Can't go on like this."

"Why not?"

"Because it's no good for either of us. You've been pissed at me for the past year, and I've been miserable. . . ." She stood up and walked across the room, glancing at familiar things. This house had been part hers for two years, and now it looked like a stranger's house to her. "I want more than this, Jack."

"Oh, Christ." He sat down, looking furious. "Like what?"

"Like something permanent, like what Harry and Averil had."

"I told you, you'll never find something like that. That was them. And you're not like Averil, Tan."

"That's no excuse to give up. I still want someone for the rest of my life who's *mine*, who's willing to stand up in front of God and man and take me on for the rest of my life. . . ."

He looked at her, horrified. "You want me to marry you? I thought we agreed. . . ." He looked terrified but she shook her head and sat down again.

"Relax, we did, and that isn't what I want from you. I want out, Jack, I think it's time." He was silent for a long, long time, he knew it too, but it hurt anyway. And it spoiled all his plans for the holidays.

He looked up at her. "This is why I believe what I do. Because sooner or later it comes to an end. And it's easier like this. I pack my bag, you pack yours, we say goodbye, and we hurt for a while, but at least we never lied to each other, and we're not dragging along a flock of kids."

"I'm not even sure that would be so terrible. At least we'd know how much we'd cared." She looked sad, as though she had lost someone dear to her, and she had. She had cared about him for a long time.

"We cared a lot, Tan. And it was good." There were tears in his eyes and he came to her and sat down. "If I thought it was right, I'd marry you."

"It wouldn't be right for you." She looked at him.

"You'd never be happy married anyway, Tan."

"Why not?" She didn't want him to say that. Not now. Not with Russ standing in the wings, wanting to marry her. It was like putting a curse on her. "Why would you say a thing like that?"

"Because you're not the type. You're too strong." She was stronger than he was, she knew. But she had only come to understand that recently, mostly since she had known Russ. He was so different from Jack. So much stronger than anyone she had known before. "You don't need marriage anyway," he smiled bitterly, "you're married to the law. That's a full time love affair for you."

"Can't one have both?"

"Some can. You can't."

"Did I hurt you that much, Jack?" She looked woefully at him and he smiled and stood up, opened a bottle of wine, and handed her a glass, and somehow she felt as though she had never known this man. Everything was so bitter, so shallow. Nothing in him ran deep, and she wondered how she could have stayed with him for so long, but it had suited her. She hadn't wanted a depth during those years. She had wanted to be as free as he did. Only now she had grown up, and as much as the challenge Russ offered terrified her, she wanted it, wanted it more than anything she'd ever done before. She looked into Jack's eyes and smiled at him as he toasted her.

"To you, Tan. Good luck." She drank, and a moment later she set down her glass and looked at him.

"I'm going now."

"Yeah. Call me sometime." He turned his back to her, and she felt a knife of pain slice through her. She wanted to reach out to him, but it was too late. For both of them. She touched his back and whispered one word.

"Goodbye."

And then she drove home as fast as she could, took a bath and washed her hair, as though she were washing away the disappointments and the tears. She was thirty-eight years old and she was starting all over again, but in a way she never had before, with a man like no man she had ever known. She thought of calling him that night but her mind was still filled with Jack, and she was suddenly afraid to tell Russ that she was free. She didn't say anything to him until their lunch the day he left for Mexico, and then suddenly she looked at him and smiled mysteriously.

"What are you grinning at, Funny Face?"

"Just life, I guess."

"And that amuses you?"

"Sometimes. I . . . uh . . . er. . . ." He was laughing at her and she was blushing furiously.

"Oh shit. Don't make things so hard for me."

He took her hand in his and smiled at her. "What are you

trying to say?" He had never seen her so tongue-tied before.

She took a deep breath. "I straightened things out this week."

"With Jack?" He looked amazed as she nodded her head with a shy smile. "So soon?"

"I couldn't go on like that."

"Was he very upset?" Russ looked concerned.

She nodded, looking sad for a moment, "Yes, but he wouldn't admit it. He likes to keep everything easy and free." She sighed jaggedly, then, "He says I'd never be happy married to anyone."

"That's nice." Russ smiled and showed absolutely no concern. "When you move out, be sure to burn the house down. It's an old custom with some men. Believe me, it doesn't mean a thing. I'll take my own chances, thanks." Russ smiled ecstatically at her.

"Do you still want to marry me?" She couldn't believe what was happening to her, and for just a minute . . . just a minute . . . there was the temptation to run back to her old life, but that wasn't what she wanted anymore. She wanted this . . . and him . . . she wanted both marriage and a career, no matter how frightening it was to her. It was a chance she had to take. She was ready now. It had taken her a long, long time, but she had gotten there and she was proud of herself.

"What do you think? Of course I do." He reassured her at once and his eyes smiled at her.

"Are you sure?"

"Are you? That's more to the point."

"Maybe we should talk about this for a little while?" She was suddenly very nervous at the thought and he laughed at her.

"How long? Six months? A year? Ten years?"

"Maybe more like five. . . ." She was laughing too, and then suddenly she looked at him. "You don't want children, do you?" She hadn't gone that far. She was too old for that, but he only shook his head and grinned at her.

"You worry about everything, don't you? No, I don't want children. I'll be fifty years old next month and I already have two. And no, I will not have a vasectomy, thanks, but

I'll do anything else you want to guarantee that I won't knock you up. Okay? Want me to sign it in blood?"

"Yes." They were both laughing and he paid the check and they walked outside and he held her as no man had ever held her before, pulling her heart right through her soul, and she had never been happier. And then suddenly he looked at his watch, and hurried her to his car. "What are you doing?"

"We have a plane to catch."

"We do? But I can't . . . I'm not. . . ."

"Is your court recessed over the holidays?"

"Yes, but. . . ."

"Is your passport in order?"

"I . . . yes . . . I think it is. . . ."

"We'll check when I get you home . . . you're coming with me . . . we can plan the wedding there . . . I'll call the girls . . . what do you think about February . . . say in about six weeks? . . . Valentine's Day? . . . corny enough for you, Tan?" He was crazy and she was crazy about him. They caught the plane to Mexico that night, and spent a blissful week soaking up the sun, and making love at last. He had waited until she had broken things off with Jack for good. And when they returned he bought her an engagement ring, and they told all their friends. Jack called her when he read it in the papers, and what he said cut her to the quick.

"So that was what that was all about? Why didn't you tell me you were shacked up with somebody else? A justice, too. That must be a step up for you."

"That's a rotten thing to say . . . and I wasn't shacked up with him."

"Tell that to someone else. Come to think of it," he laughed bitterly, "tell it to the judge."

"You know, you've been so damn busy trying not to get involved with anyone all your life that you don't know your ass from a hole in the ground anymore."

"At least I know when I'm cheating on someone, Tan."

"I wasn't cheating on you."

"What were you doing then, fucking him at lunchtime, it doesn't count before six o'clock?" She had hung up on him,

328

sorry that it had to end that way. And she had written to Barbara, too, explaining that her marriage to Russ was precipitous, but he was a lovely man, and when she came out to see her father the following year, the door to Tana's home would be open to her as it had been before. She didn't want the girl to feel that she was pushing her away. And there were so many other things to do too. She wrote to Averil in London, and her mother almost had a heart attack when she called her.

"Are you sitting down?"

"Oh Tana, something's happened to you." Her mother sounded on the verge of tears. She was only sixty-one years old, but mentally she was twice that, and Arthur was getting senile now at seventy-four, which was hard on her.

"It's something nice, Mother. Something you've waited for, for a long, long time."

Jean stared blankly at the far wall, holding the phone. "I can't imagine what it is."

"I'm getting married in three weeks."

"You're *what*? To whom? That man you've been living with for all these years?" She had never thought much of him, but it was about time they took a decent position in the world, especially with Tana being a judge. But she was in for a shock.

"No. To someone else. A justice on the court of appeals. His name is Russell Carver, Mom." She went on to tell her the rest and Jean cried, and smiled and laughed and cried some more.

"Oh sweetheart . . . I've waited so long for this."

"So have I." Tana was laughing and crying too. "And it was worth waiting for, Mom. Wait till you see him. Will you come out for the wedding? We're getting married on February 14th."

"Valentine's Day? . . . oh, how sweet. . . ." It still embarrassed Tan but it seemed funny to both her and Russ. "I wouldn't miss it for the world. I don't think Arthur will be well enough to come, so I can't stay long." She had a thousand arrangements to make before she left, and she could hardly wait to get off the phone. Ann had just gotten married for the fifth time, and who gave a damn anymore? Tana was getting married! And to a justice on the court of appeals! And she said he was handsome too. Jean dithered around the house for the rest of the afternoon, in a total state, and she had to go into the city to Saks the following day. She needed a dress ... no ... maybe a suit ... she couldn't believe it had happened finally. And that night she whispered silent prayers.

Chapter 18

The wedding was absolutely beautiful. They had it at Russ' house, with a piano and two violins playing something delicate from Brahms as Tana came slowly down the stairs in a simple dress of off-white crêpe de chine. She wore her blonde hair long, covered by a wide-brimmed picture hat, with a faint hint of veil, and ivory satin shoes. There were roughly a hundred people there, and Jean stood in a corner and cried ecstatically for most of the day. She had bought a beautiful beige Givenchy suit, and she looked so proud it made Tana cry every time she looked at her.

"Happy, my love?" Russ looked at Tana in a way that made her heart fly. It seemed impossible that she could be lucky enough to find a man like him, and she had never dreamed of anything like what she shared with him. It was as though she had been born to be his, and she found herself thinking of Harry as she walked down the aisle. "Okay, asshole? Did I do good?" She smiled through her tears.

"You did *great*!" She knew that Harry would have been crazy about Russ, and it would have been mutual. And she felt Harry very much there with her. Harrison and Averil sent a telegram. Russ' daughters were there too. They were both slender, attractive, pleasant girls, with husbands that Tana liked. They were an easy group to love, and they did everything to welcome her. Lee was particularly warm in her reception of her new stepmother, and they were only twelve years apart in age.

"Thank God he had the sense to wait until we grew up before marrying again." Lee laughed. "For one thing, the house is a hell of a lot quieter now, and for another thing, you don't have to put up with us, behaving like turds. He's been single for so long, Beth and I are grateful as hell that you married him. I hate to think of him alone in this house."

She was a little bit zany, and wonderfully dressed in her own designs. She was clearly crazy about Russ, nuts about her own husband, and Beth doted on her entire family. It was the ideal group, and as Jean looked at them, she was suddenly grateful that Tana hadn't been foolish enough to fall for Billy, in the years when she was pushing that. How sensible Tana had been to wait for this extraordinary man to come along. And what a life. The house was the most beautiful place she'd ever seen. And Tana felt totally at ease with the butler and the maid he'd had for years. She floated from room to room, entertaining his friends, as people said "Your Honor" to her, and somebody else cited a funny poem about a justice and a judge.

It was a wonderful afternoon, and they went back to Mexico for their honeymoon, returning via La Jolla and Los Angeles. Tana had taken a month's leave from work, and when she returned she smiled to herself whenever she said her new name. Judge Carver ... Tana Carver ... Tana Roberts Carver. ... She had added his name to everything, none of this women's lib crap for her. She had waited thirty-eight years for him, almost thirty-nine, and resisted marriage for almost four decades, and if she had taken the plunge now, she was going to enjoy all the benefits. She came home every night, relaxed and happy to see him. So much so that he teased her about it one night.

"When are you going to start behaving like a real wife and nagging me a little bit?"

"I forgot, I guess." He smiled at her, and they talked about her house again. She had been thinking about renting it. It was so pretty that she didn't want to sell it, yet she knew she would never live there again. "Maybe I should just sell it after all."

"What if I rent it from you for Beth and John when they come home?"

"That would be wonderful." She smiled at him. "Let's see ... you can have it for two kisses and ... a trip to Mexico. ..." He laughed at her, and eventually they decided to keep the house and rent it out and Tana had never been happier in her life. It was one of those rare times when everything feels in total control, going just the way you want, when she ran full tilt into someone one day. She was hurrying from her courtroom to meet Russ for lunch, and suddenly found herself staring into Drew Lands' face. He looked as though someone had just struck oil on his front lawn when he saw who she was, and they stood chatting amiably for a minute or two. It was incredible to realize how much pain he had caused her once. It was even more amazing to realize that Julie and Elizabeth were eighteen and twenty-two. "Good lord, is it as long ago as that?"

"It must be, Tan." His voice was smooth, and suddenly she was annoyed by him. She could see from his eyes that he was making assumptions that were no longer appropriate, and hadn't been for a long, long time. "Eileen and I have been divorced for six years now." How dare he tell her that ... how dare he have gotten divorced after hurting Tan so much for her. . . .

"That's too bad." Her voice was cool, and she was losing interest in what he said. She didn't want to be late for Russ. She knew he was working on an important case.

"Gee . . . I wonder if . . . maybe we could see each other sometime. I'm living in San Francisco now. . . ."

She smiled at him. "We'd love to see you sometime. But my husband is just buried in a big case right now." She smiled almost evilly at him, waved her hand with a few garbled words, and was gone. And Russ could still see the victory in her eyes when he met her for lunch at the Hayes Street Grill. It was one of their favorite haunts, and she often met him there, kissing at a corner table, and necking happily over lunch, while people smiled at them.

"What are you looking so pleased about?" He knew her very well.

"Nothing. . . ." And then, she kept no secrets from him, she couldn't have anyway. "I just ran into Drew Lands for the first time in almost seven years. What a bastard he is. I guess he always was, the weak little shit."

"My, my, what did he do to deserve so many epithets?"

"He was the married man I told you about. . . ."

"Ah!" Russ looked amused at the fire in her eyes. He

knew he was in no danger of losing her to anyone, not because he was so sure of himself, but because he knew the kind of love they shared. It was one of those rare, rare things in life, and he was deeply grateful for it. He had never had a love like this before with anyone.

"And you know what? He finally divorced his wife."

"Predictably." Russ smiled. "And now he wanted to take you out again. Right?"

She laughed at him. "I told him we'd love to see him sometime, and then I skibbled off."

"You're a little witch. But I love you anyway. How was court today?"

"Not bad. I have an interesting case coming up, an industrial injury. It's going to be messy but it brings up some very intriguing points and technicalities. How's your monster case coming along?"

He smiled at her. "I'm finally getting it back into its cage. And," he looked at her strangely for a minute, "I had a call from Lee."

"How is she?"

"Fine." He looked at his wife, and she looked at him. There was something odd in the air.

"Russ, what's wrong?" She was worried about him. He looked strange.

"It's happened. They've finally done it to me. I'm going to be a grandfather." He looked at once delighted and distressed and Tana laughed at him.

"Oh no! How can she do a thing like that to you?!"

"That's exactly what I said to her!" And then he smiled at Tana again. "Can you imagine that?"

"With difficulty. We'll have to buy you a white wig so you look the part. When is she having it?"

"January. For my birthday, apparently. Or New Year's Eve, something like that."

As it turned out, the baby was born on New Year's Day, and Russ and Tana decided it would be a lark to fly to New York and visit her. He wanted to see this first grandchild of his, another girl, like his own two. And he reserved a suite for them at the Sherry Netherland, and off they went. Lee was happily ensconced at New York Hospital's Lying-in, in the best room they had, and the baby was sweet and pink, and Russell made all the appropriate noises and when they went back to the hotel, he made passionate love to his wife. "At least I'm not totally over the hill yet. How does it feel; to make love to a grandfather, my love?"

"Even better than it was before." But there was something odd in her eyes when she looked at him, and he saw it instantly. He grew very quiet and pulled her into his arms next to him, their naked flesh touching, and he loved to feel how velvety she was, but he was worried about her. Sometimes, when something mattered to her a lot, she burrowed deep inside herself and he could see her do it now.

"What's wrong, sweetheart?" He spoke in a whisper near her ear, and she turned toward him with a look of surprise.

"What makes you think something's wrong?"

"I know you better than that. You can't fool an old man like me. At least not one who loves you as much as I love you." She tried to deny it for a long time, and then much to his astonishment, she broke down and cried in his arms. There was something about seeing Lee and her baby that had filled her with the most awful pain . . . an emptiness . . . a void more terrible than any she had ever known. He sat looking at her, amazed at the emotions pouring out of her, and she was even more startled than he. She had never realized she felt that way before.

"Do you want a baby, Tan?"

"I don't know . . . I've never felt this way before . . . and I'm almost forty years old . . . I'm too old for that. . . ." But suddenly she wanted that more than anything, and she was suddenly haunted by Harry's words again.

"Why don't you think about it, and we'll talk again." And for the next month, the sight of Lee and her baby haunted her. And suddenly, after they went home, she began seeing pregnant women everywhere, and babies in strollers on every street corner; it was as though everyone had a baby except her . . . and there was an envy and a loneliness she couldn't even begin to describe. Russell saw it on her face, but he didn't mention it again until their anniversary, and then she was sharp with him, which was rare for her. It was almost as though it hurt too much to talk about.

"You said you were too old for that. And so am I."

"Not if it matters to you. It might seem a little foolish to me at first, but I could live with it. Other men have second families at my age, older in fact . . . a lot older," he smiled. And he himself had been surprised by how touched he was by Lee's baby in her arms, and then his own. He wouldn't have minded that at all. And Tana's child would have meant the world to him. But she got more and more sensitive about it, until finally he no longer mentioned it to her. In March, they went to Mexico again, and had a fabulous holiday. Tana barely got *tourista* that time, although she didn't feel well when she got back.

"I think you've been working too hard." She had had the flu on and off for almost three weeks and he was insisting on her going to see the doctor finally.

"I don't have time for that." But she was so tired and draggy and so frequently sick to her stomach that she finally went, and she got the shock of her life. It was what she had wanted so desperately, but now, suddenly it was there. And it terrified her. She didn't have time for that. She had an important job. She would look ridiculous . . . she had never wanted that. . . . Russ would be upset with her . . . she stewed so terribly that she didn't even go home until seven o'clock that night and Russ knew there was something terribly wrong the minute he laid eyes on her. But he let her unwind for a while, fixed her a drink, opened a bottle of Chateau Latour with their dinner, but she didn't drink a drop of it, and she was still tense when they went upstairs that night and there was an odd look in her eyes. He was actually getting very worried about her, and as soon as she sat down, he pulled a chair up next to her.

"All right, now tell me what happened to you today. You either lost your job or your best friend died."

She smiled sheepishly and visibly relaxed as he took her hand. "You know me too well."

336

"Then do me the favor of taking me into your confidence."

"I can't." She had already made up her mind. She wasn't keeping it. But Russ was not going to fool around. His voice rose ominously, the famous frown appeared, and her knees would have shaken if she didn't know him as well as she did. Instead she laughed at him. "You know, you're very scary when you look like that."

He laughed exasperatedly at her. "That's the whole point. Now talk to me, dammit. What the hell is going on with you?"

She stared at him for a long, long time, lowered her eyes, and then raised them to his again. "You're not going to believe this, sweetheart."

"You want a divorce."

"No, of course not." She smiled at him. Somehow he always made things less terrible. She had been hysterical all day, and now he had her laughing again.

"You're having an affair?"

"Wrong again."

"You were kicked off the bench."

"Worse than that. . . ." She was beginning to look serious again, because in her mind what had happened meant the same thing. How could she keep her job with that? And then suddenly there were tears in her eyes and she was looking at him. "I'm pregnant, Russ. . . ." For a moment everything around them stopped and then suddenly he swept her into his arms and he was laughing and smiling, and acting as though it were cause for celebration and not suicide.

"Oh, sweetheart . . . I'm so glad." He absolutely beamed at her and she stared at him.

"You are? I thought you didn't want any children." She was stunned. "We agreed. . . ."

"Never mind. Our baby is going to be so beautiful . . . a little girl that looks just like you. . . ." He had never looked happier and he held her close as she frowned unhappily. She had wanted this, but now that it had happened, she couldn't imagine it, except in the worst light.

"But it'll ruin everything. . . ." She was on the verge of tears again, and he was anxious to comfort her.

"Like what?"

"Like my job. How can I be a judge with a baby at my breast?"

He laughed at the image she had in mind. "Be practical. You work right up till the last day before it's born, and then you take six months off. We get a good nurse, and you go back to work."

"As easy as that?" She looked shocked.

"It can be as easy as you want, my love. But there's no reason why you can't have a career and a family. It may take a little juggling sometimes, but it can be done with a little resourcefulness." He smiled at her, and a long slow smile began to dawn in her eyes. There was the possibility that he was right about that, and if he was . . . if he was . . . it was what she had wanted more than anything, and she wanted both. For years she had thought she could only have one. . . . But she wanted more than just her work . . . she wanted Russ . . . she wanted his child . . . she wanted everything . . . and suddenly the void she had been feeling for months, that ache, the terrible emptiness, was gone again. . . . "I'm so proud of you, sweetheart." She looked at him, and the tears slowly overflowed as she smiled at him. "Everything is going to be just fine, you know . . . and you're going to look just wonderful."

"Ha!" She laughed at him. "I've already gained six pounds. . . ."

"Where?" Tickling and teasing her, he began to look for them, and Tana lay in his arms and laughed.

Chapter 19

The judge walked ponderously to the bench and sat down carefully, rapped the gavel smartly twice, and went on with the morning's calendar. Her bailiff brought her a cup of tea, at ten o'clock, and when she stood up at the noon recess, she could barely walk back to her chambers again. The baby was, by then, exactly nine days late. She had planned to stop working two weeks before, but she had everything so well organized at home that she had decided to work until the bitter end. Her husband picked her up right outside City Hall that night, opening the door smiling at her.

"How'd it go today?" The pride he felt showed easily in his eyes and she smiled back at him. It had been a beautiful time for them, even these extra days. She enjoyed the opportunity to spend these last days alone with him, although she had to admit that she was getting terribly uncomfortable. Her ankles looked like lamp posts by four o'clock in the afternoon, and she had trouble sitting for that long, but she didn't have anything else to do.

She sighed. "Well, the verdict is in. I think I might give it up at the end of this week, whether the baby shows up or not. What do you think?"

He smiled at her as he drove her home in the new Jaguar he had just bought. "I think that's a pretty good idea, Tan. You could sit around for a couple of days, you know."

"Fancy that."

But she never got time for that. Her water broke at eight o'clock that night, and she suddenly turned to Russ, terrified. She knew it was going to happen eventually, but suddenly it was *now*, and she had the overwhelming urge to run away, and there was no place to run. Her body would follow her everywhere. But Russ saw easily what she felt, and tried to comfort her.

"Everything's going to be just fine."

"How do you know that?" She snapped at him. "What if I need a Caesarean? Christ, I'm a hundred years old, for chrissake." Actually, she was forty years old plus four months. She suddenly looked at Russell and began to cry. She was terrified, and the contractions started almost as soon as her water broke.

"Do you want to lie down here for a while, Tan, or do you want to go to the hospital?"

"I want to stay here." He called the doctor for her, brought her a glass of ginger ale, flipped on the television across from their bed, and smiled to himself. It was going to be a big night for them, and he also hoped that everything would go well. He was confident that it would, and he was particularly excited. She had insisted on their doing Lamaze training together, and although he hadn't been present at the birth of his girls so many years before, he was going to be with Tana for the birth of their child. He had promised her, and he could hardly wait. She had had the amniocentesis five months before, but they had opted not to know the sex of the child. And Russ could feel a mounting feeling of excitement now for both of them. By midnight, Tana had had a short nap, and she was in control again. She smiled up at him, and he timed her pains, and at two o'clock he called the doctor again, and this time they were told to come in. He picked her bag up from the hall closet where it had sat for the last three weeks, helped her into the car, and out again at the hospital, and helped her to walk inside. She could hardly walk now, and the contractions took all her concentration and his help, just to get her through them, but they were nothing like the pains she felt once she went into transition three hours after that. She was writhing in pain on the bed in the labor room, and she was clutching at his arm, as he felt his own panic begin to rise. He hadn't expected it to be quite like this, she was in such agony, and by eight o'clock the baby still hadn't come. The sun was up, and she lay panting horribly, her hair damp, eyes wild, looking at him as though he could do something for her. And all he could do was breathe with her and hold her hand and tell her how proud he was of her, and then suddenly at nine o'clock everyone began to run around. They wheeled her into the delivery room, strapped her legs up, and she cried as the pains came now. It was the worst pain she had ever known in her entire life, and she felt as though she were drowning as she clutched at him, and the doctor urged her on, and Russell cried, and Tana knew she couldn't stand it anymore. She wanted to die . . . to die . . . to. . . .

"I can see the head . . . oh God . . . sweetheart . . . it's here. . . ." And suddenly a tiny red face popped out, as Russell cried, and Tana looked at him and gave another ferocious push which forced the baby from her womb, and the doctor held him in his hands as the baby began to wail. They cut the cord, tied it, and cleaned him rapidly, suctioned his nose, wrapped him in a warm blanket and handed him to Russ.

"Your son, Russ. . . ." The doctor smiled at them both. They had worked so hard and so long, and Tana looked at him victoriously now.

"You were wonderful, sweetheart." Her voice was hoarse and her face was gray, as he kissed her tenderly.

"*I* was wonderful?" He was deeply impressed by what he had just seen her do. It was the greatest miracle he had ever seen. And at forty years of age, she had it all now. She looked at him. Everything she had ever wanted . . . everything . . . her eyes filled with tears as she reached out to him, and Russ gently put the baby in her arms, as he had once put it in her womb.

"Oh, he's so beautiful. . . ."

"No." Russell smiled at her through his tears. "You are, Tan. You're the most beautiful woman in the world." And then he looked at his son. "But he's pretty cute too." Harrison Winslow Carver. They had long since agreed on that. He came into the world blessed in name, and life, and love.

They wheeled her back to her room that night, and she knew she would never want to do it again, but she was glad she had this once. Russell stayed with her until she drifted off to sleep, the baby asleep in the little bed they had left there for him, and Tana, all clean again, and so much in love with him. She opened her eyes once, drifting from the shot they'd given her for the pain afterwards. "I love you so much, Russ. . . ."

He nodded, smiling again, his heart forever hers after tonight. "Sshh . . . sleep now . . . I love you too. . . ."

Chapter 20

When baby Harry was six months old, Tana looked at her calendar with despair. She had to go back to work the following week. She had promised she would, and she knew it was almost time, but he was so sweet, and she loved spending the afternoons with him. They went on long walks, and she laughed when he smiled. They even dropped in on Russ at his office once in a while. It was a leisurely way of life she had never known, and she hated to give it up, but she was not yet ready to give up her career.

And once she was back on the bench, she was glad she hadn't given it up for good. It felt good to be back again. The cases, the verdicts, the juries, the decisions, the routine. It was incredible how fast the days flew by, and how anxious she was to come home at night, to Harry and Russ. Sometimes she would find Russ already at home with him, crawling around on the rug, and playing games with him. He delighted them both, and he was like the first child born on earth to them. Lee teased them about it when she came out to visit with Francesca, her little girl, and she was already expecting another one.

"And what about you, Tan?"

"Listen, at my age, Harry is enough of a miracle. Let's not push my luck, thanks." And even though the pregnancy had been a breeze, the delivery had been more painful than she thought. Though, with time, even that didn't seem quite as awful as it once had. And they were both so happy with the baby. "If I were your age, I might, Lee, and even then . . . you can't have everything, a career and ten kids." Not that it frightened Lee, though. She still had her job, and even now with the second one on the way, she was planning to work right till the end, and come back afterwards. She had just won the Coty Award and she wasn't giving that up. She

343

didn't see why she should. She could do both, so why not?

"How was your day, sweetheart?" She threw her brief-case on a chair and bent to kiss him as he scooped the baby into his arms, as she glanced at her watch. She was still nursing him three times a day. Morning, evening, and late at night, and she wondered when his last feeding was. She loved the closeness it gave her to the child, the silent moments in the nursery at three a.m. when only she and Harry were up. She had a sense of providing for his well-being which satisfied her too, and then there were other benefits as well. She'd been told that she was unlikely to get pregnant again as long as she was still nursing him. "Do you think it would matter if I did it till he's twelve?" she had asked Russ one day and he had laughed at her. They had such a good life, the two of them. It had been worth waiting for, no matter how long it took. At least she said that now. She had just turned forty-one, and he was fifty-two.

"You know, you look tired, Tan." Russell was looking carefully at her. "Maybe the nursing is too much for you, now that you're back at work." She fought the idea, but her body voted with him, as slowly, in the next few weeks, her milk dried up. It was as though her body didn't want to be nursing Harry anymore. And when she went to the doctor for a check-up, he weighed her, felt her, checked her breasts, and then said he wanted to do a blood test on her.

"Something wrong?" She glanced at her watch. She had to be back in court at two.

"I just want to check something out. I'll call you this afternoon." On the whole, he had found her all right, and she didn't have time to worry about it. She rushed back to City Hall, and when her clerk signalled her at five o'clock, she had forgotten that she was expecting the doctor's call.

"He said he had to speak to you."

"Thanks." She took the phone, scratching some notes as she listened to him, and suddenly she stopped. That couldn't be. He had to be wrong. She had been nursing until the week before . . . hadn't she . . . she sat down hard in a chair, thanked him, and hung up. Shit. She was pregnant again. And Harry was wonderful, but she didn't want another one.

She was too old for that . . . she had her career . . . this time, she had to get rid of it . . . it was impossible . . . she didn't know what to do. She had a choice of course, but what would she say to Russ? Tell him she had aborted his child? She couldn't do that. She spent a sleepless night that night, resisting him when he asked her what was bothering her. She couldn't tell him this time. It was all wrong . . . she was too old . . . her career meant too much to her . . . but Lee was going to continue her career after her second child . . . or was it meaningless? Should she resign from the bench? Would the children mean more to her in the end? She felt torn ten thousand ways and she looked like a nightmare when she woke up. Russ looked at her over breakfast and didn't say anything to her at first. And then, just before he left, he turned to her.

"You busy for lunch today, Tan?"

"No . . . not that I know of. . . ." But she didn't want to have lunch with him. She had to think. "There's some stuff I really should get off my desk." She avoided his eyes.

"You have to eat. I'll bring sandwiches."

"Fine." She felt like a traitor not telling him, and her heart felt like lead as she went to work. She had dozens of small matters in and out of her court, and at eleven o'clock she looked up to see a wild-eyed man, with a mane of frizzy gray hair springing out of his head like watchsprings gone wild. He had planted a bomb in front of a foreign consulate, and the matter had to be set for trial. She began to go through all of the motions, and then suddenly stared at his name and looked up with a grin. And for no reason anyone understood in court, she had to disqualify herself. The man's name was Yael McBee, the wild-eyed radical lover she'd had in her last year of law school at Boalt. The boy who had gone to jail for bombing the mayor's house. She saw from his records that he had been in prison twice since then. How odd life was. So long ago . . . it brought Harry instantly to mind . . . and the funny little house they'd shared . . . and Averil so young then . . . and the wild hippie commune she had visited with Yael. She looked across the court at him. He had grown old. He was forty-six years old now. A man.

And still fighting for his causes in his unruly ways. How far they'd come, all of them . . . this man with his wild ideas. His documents said that he was a terrorist. A terrorist. And she was a judge. An endless road . . . and Harry gone, and all their bright ideas a little dim, some of them forgotten, so many gone . . . Sharon . . . Harry . . . and new lives in their places . . . her son, little Harry, named after her friend, and now this new baby in her womb . . . it was amazing how life went on, how far they came, all of them. . . . She looked up and saw her husband, standing there, looking at her, and she smiled at him, and dismissed the matter of Yael McBee from her court, called a recess for lunch, and walked into her chambers with him.

"Who was that?" Russ looked amused. Her days were certainly livelier than his, and she began to laugh as she sat down.

"His name is Yael McBee, if that means anything to you. I knew him when I went to Boalt."

"A friend of yours?" Russ looked at her sardonically and she grinned.

"Believe it or not, he was."

"You've come a long way since then, my love."

"I was just thinking that." And then she remembered something else. She looked at him, hesitantly, wondering how he would react. "I've got something to tell you."

He smiled gently at her. "You're pregnant again."

She stared at him as he laughed. "How do you know? Did the doctor call you too?"

"No. I'm smarter than that. I figured it out last night, and I assumed you'd tell me eventually. Of course by now, you think your career is over, we'll have to give up the house, I'll lose my job, or we both will. . . ." She laughed and tears came to her eyes as he smiled at her. "Am I right?"

"Perfectly."

"And has it dawned on you that if you can be a judge with one child, you can be a judge with two? And a good judge at that."

"That just occurred to me as you walked in."

"My, my." He leaned over to kiss her, and they exchanged a look that belonged only to them. "What do you know . . . ?" He kissed her and her clerk walked in and hastily backed out again, smiling to herself as Tana silently thanked her lucky stars for the road she'd come, the man she'd found . . . the decisions she had made . . . from a career and no man, no child, to having it all, the man, the career, and her son. She had added each one, like wild-flowers to a bouquet, until she stood with full hands, full heart, having come full circle in the end.

WANDERLUST

Danielle Steel

At 21 Annabelle Driscoll was the acknowledged beauty,
but it was her sister Audrey – four years older – who had
the spine and spirit. She had talent as a photographer;
she had the restless urge of a born wanderer.

Inevitably it was Annabelle who was the first to marry,
leaving Audrey to wonder if life were passing her by. The
men she met in California were dull, worldly. Even in
New York, they failed to spark her. Only when she
boarded the *Orient Express* did she realise she was
beginning a journey that would take her farther than she
had ever dreamed possible. . . .

FINE THINGS

Danielle Steel

Living on the crest of a highly successful career, he was moving too fast to realise that he had everything – except what he wanted most . . .

Sent to San Francisco to open the smartest department store in California, Bernie Fine becomes aware of the hollowness of his personal life. Despite his success he grows increasingly disenchanted with his existence – until five-year-old Jane O'Reilly gets lost in the store.

Through Jane, Bernie meets her mother Liz, who finally offers him the possibility of love. But the rare happiness they find together is disrupted by tragedy and Bernie must face the terrible price we sometimes have to pay for loving . . .

KALEIDOSCOPE

Danielle Steel

THREE SISTERS, BONDED BY BLOOD, SEPARATED BY FATE ... COULD THEY EVER FIND EACH OTHER AGAIN?

When Sam Walker returned from the front lines of World War II, bringing with him his exquisite French bride, no one could have imagined that their fairy-tale love would end in such shattering tragedy ...

And, at the age of nine, Hilary, the eldest of the Walker children, clung desperately to her two sisters – five-year-old Alexandra and baby Magan. However, before the year was out, they too would be painfully wrenched from her tender arms. Cut off from every loving warmth, Hiliary swore she would one day track down the man who had destroyed her family, and find her beloved sisters again. But could they risk everything to confront a dark, forgotten past?

John Chapman – lawyer, prestigious private investigator – chosen to find the sisters, embarks on a labyrinthine trail which leads him to Paris, New York, Boston and Connecticut, knowing that, at some time in their lives, the three sisters must face each other and the final, most devastating secret of all ...

ZOYA

Danielle Steel

One woman's odyssey through a century of turmoil . . .

St Petersburg: one famous night of violence in the
October Revolution ends the lavish life of the Romanov
court forever – shattering the dreams of young Countess
Zoya Ossupov.

Paris: under the shadow of the Great War, émigrés
struggle for survival as taxi drivers, seamstresses and ballet
dancers. Zoya flees there in poverty . . . and leaves in
glory.

America: a glittering world of flappers, fast cars and furs
in the Roaring Twenties; a world of comfort and café
society that would come crashing down without warning.

Zoya – a true heroine of our time – emerges triumphant
from this panoramic web of history into the 80s to face
challenges and triumphs.

Other bestselling Warner titles available by mail:

☐ Crossings	Danielle Steel	£5.99
☐ Family Album	Danielle Steel	£5.99
☐ Fine Things	Danielle Steel	£5.99
☐ Going Home	Danielle Steel	£5.99
☐ Kaleidoscope	Danielle Steel	£5.99
☐ Once in a Lifetime	Danielle Steel	£5.99
☐ Remembrance	Danielle Steel	£5.99
☐ Season of Passion	Danielle Steel	£5.99
☐ Zoya	Danielle Steel	£5.99

The prices shown above are correct at time of going to press. However, the publishers reserve the right to increase prices on covers from those previously advertised without prior notice.

WARNER BOOKS

WARNER BOOKS
Cash Sales Department, P.O. Box 11, Falmouth, Cornwall, TR10 9EN
Tel: +44 (0) 1326 372400, Fax: +44 (0) 1326 374888
Email: books@barni.avel.co.uk.

POST AND PACKING:
Payments can be made as follows: cheque, postal order (payable to Warner Books) or by credit cards. Do not send cash or currency.

All U.K. Orders	**FREE OF CHARGE**
E.E.C. & Overseas	25% of order value

Name (Block Letters) _____

Address _____

_____

Post/zip code: _____

☐ Please keep me in touch with future Warner publications

☐ I enclose my remittance £_____

☐ I wish to pay by Visa/Access/Mastercard/Eurocard

Card Expiry Date

_____